BEST
EUROPEAN
FICTION
2018

Please see rights and permissions on page 324 for individual credits

Please see Acknowledgments on page 321 for additional information
on the support received for this volume.

www.dalkeyarchive.com
Victoria, TX / McLean, IL / Dublin

Dalkey Archive Press publications are, in part, made possible through the support of the University
of Houston-Victoria and its program in creative writing, publishing, and translation.

Cover design by Gail Doobinin
Printed on permanent/durable acid-free paper

BEST
EUROPEAN
FICTION
2018

EDITED BY
ALEX ANDRIESSE

 DALKEY ARCHIVE PRESS

Contents

PREFACE

LET'S SAY YOU'RE in Amsterdam. You arrive at the Centraal station, walk across the bridge, and soon find yourself in a neighborhood of familiar shops, eateries, and cafés, all of them endemic from Dublin to Berlin. Off in the distance, you catch sight of a Madame Tussauds and, in an evasive maneuver, turn right, toward the Grachtengordel, where the gray brownstones by the tea-colored canals put you in mind of a watery Brooklyn. A radio in an open window announces the ongoing influx of refugees; the spray paint on the walls debates the value of their lives. After some reflection, you decide you won't wait in line for a look at Anne Frank's annex and instead tramp down to the Rijksmuseum, where once in a while you get a moment alone with Vermeer's Delft, or Rembrandt's Jewish bride, before someone, or several someones, step up with glowing phones to obscure the view. Outside, you try to make light of the sight of your fellow travelers, come from every corner of the globe to take selfies on a stick designed for the purpose, as if there were such a thing as a *purpose*, or for that matter a *self* . . . By now, needless to say, you're having trouble subduing the sub-Bernhardian rant that began unspooling in your head the moment you stepped off the train, the rant about how dire, how moronic, how utterly despair-inducing it is to have to live the way we live today . . .

There really is nothing very special about the moment in which we live, except it's the moment in which we live, and to ignore it would be unwise, if not impossible. Setting too much store by the moment, however, seems equally unwise. The very concept of the present as somehow supremely significant strikes me as symptomatic of the disease of the times. "What's new is not that the world lacks meaning, or has little meaning, or less than it used to have," the anthropologist Marc Augé writes in his book *Non-Places: An Introduction to Supermodernity*; "it's that we seem to feel an explicit and intense daily need to give it meaning: to give meaning to the world, not just some village or lineage." *Non-Places*, first published in 1992, has proved to be prescient. More than ever, we exist in a world of places that are not places—tourist districts, international airports, chain hotels, refugee camps—where meaning is transient, and the only thing to do is pass through. As for the past, in these liminal, dehumanizing locations, it has been demolished, stashed out of sight, refurbished, or reduced to a set of signs. The Anne Frank House. The Jodenbuurt. The Windmill Capital of the World.

And yet the past is what's running the show. The past is the lit fuse leading to what John Saul, in his story "Armadillo" (England), calls today's "exploding Europe," a Europe where everything appears to be happening at once:

> Daniel or even Daniela scrabbles for transport, fighting the cold, soldiers with guns and no comprehensible English, one language after another, a struggle to get the necessary papers, hopeful papers, Daniel or Daniela secreting cash, yearning for food, sharing food, not sharing food, checking barbed-wire fencing in the dark, falling in mud, entering rivalries, enemies everywhere, acts of friendship turning up when totally unexpected, the extremely occasional miracle or no miracles at all, flu, no doctor, flesh wound, no doctor, cold, no heat, boats, lifejackets, snatches of television news with politicians in suits with warm houses to return to: The prime minister is to make a statement about the migrant situation later today. The content is already public. His use of terms has once again come under criticism. He will speak in Bradford. In Bratislava, Bucharest, Burghausen. But this is not this story.

This story, like all the others in *Best European Fiction 2018*, is not the anonymous one dictated by the press; it's the story of a Moldovan cleaning woman, a Czech grocery clerk, and a neglected cat which simultaneously manages to be an elegant meditation on storytelling, social station, and the question of the self. Ekaterina, the Moldovan woman, knows that she's only "a cleaner momentarily. She has *become* a cleaner. There will be a time again when she is not a cleaner." The trouble is that almost everyone around her is satisfied to take her, reductively, for what she seems to be.

Best European Fiction is not a themed anthology. Nevertheless, once these thirty stories were gathered together, certain patterns could be traced. Many characters, like Saul's Ekaterina, turned out to be facing down some disparity between their own consciousness and the delimiting world. In Maartje Wortel's "The Camp" (Netherlands), a well-meaning therapist tells the unwell narrator: "You want to be yourself . . . Maybe that's the problem." "The problem?" asks the narrator. "The thing that you want from me," explains the therapist. In György Spíró's "The Problem" (Hungary), two lovers lucky enough to want each other struggle to keep up with an increasingly complicated series of genital entanglements, which soon land them in a realm of the ridiculous reminiscent of Landolfi and Kafka. In Kalina Maleska's "A Different Kind of Weapon" (Macedonia), the protagonist must learn to adjust when not only her own sense of reality but the entire solar system is turned around.

A number of stories narrate more earthbound adjustments. The narrator of Ravshan Saleddin's "The State of Things" (Russia) recounts his efforts to accustom himself to the idea of losing his virginity, while at the same time caring for a ninety-year-old Frenchwoman whom he memorably describes as "the widow of the century I was born in." Nora Wagener's "You'd Have Larvae Too" (Luxembourg) lets us into the thoughts of a young woman coming to terms with the death of her long-estranged father, after years of telling everyone that he was already dead. Lídia Jorge's "The Age of Splendor" (Portugal) encompasses in a few pages an entire life, as an elderly woman thinks back from her hospital bed to an old-fashioned childhood of maids and goldfish ponds. In Eirikur Örn Norðdahl's *Evil* (Iceland), an unnamed narrator endeavors, over and over again, in a kind of mania, to contextualize, without mythologizing, the Shoah.

All sorts of threads connect these texts. There are several stories about, for example, unhappy children, dying fathers, absent friends, and dystopic amounts of bureaucratic paperwork. There are also two extraordinary stories of outright dystopia: Andrei Dichenko's "The Poet Execution Committee" (Belarus) and Davide Orecchio's "City of Pigs" (Italy). In Hugh Fulham-McQuillan's

"Winter Guests" (Ireland), the narrator contemplates "the pursuit of ultimate relaxation," while in Bruce Bégout's "Watching *My Best Fiend*" (France), the narrator brags of having reached "a certain refinement in the art of wasting time"—of "doing nothing with style." The choice to do nothing is, in a very different sense, at the heart of Thomas Morris's heartbreaking "Where We All Belong" (Wales). Yet, whatever these stories may have in common, they are each themselves, reflecting something other than the times and their trends. Taken together, they give a meaning to contemporary Europe quite apart from the noise on the news.

The present is a fiction, sometimes horrific, sometimes banal, but the life around us, as Elizabeth Hardwick wrote half a century ago, "is not a pageant of coldness and folly to which we have paid admission and from which we can withdraw as it becomes boring. You feel a transcendental joke links us all together; some sordid synthesis hangs out there in the heavy air." The stories in this anthology speak to the strangeness of that sordid synthesis, and assure us that, even as Europe's body politic convulses, its literary imagination is alive and well.

ALEX ANDRIESSE

BEST
EUROPEAN
FICTION
2018

THOMAS MORRIS

Where We All Belong

Q: TELL ME HOW it started.

A: When Mrs. Wood asked the bottom group to do something, like take out their books or sit on the carpet, they all counted to five—in their heads—before responding.

Q: And that just happened of its own accord? They each began to do that?

A: No, it was Ryan Small's idea. I think he wanted to exaggerate their perceived "slowness."

Q: A nice touch, I must admit. And then the group just—

A: Ryan told them they needed to act as one. I guess that was their strength: that they were a collective.

Q: How did the groups work?

A: We were all assigned groups, based on our ability, and each day we sat at the same tables, in the same groups. There were four groups in total, each one named after a branch of the *Mabinogion*. We had been grouped like this since our first week at school.

Q: Tell me about Ryan.

A: He was small and stout and he used to eat a packet of chocolate biscuits for breakfast. He always had a cough. On non-school-uniform day, he came into school with his own clothes under his uniform.

Q: So he could avoid paying the £1? The £1 charity donation that the teacher collected at registration?

A: Exactly. You could see his tracksuit bottoms tucking out under his school trousers. At break-time, he removed his uniform, and *voilà*— non-school-uniform for free. I don't think Mrs. Wood said anything to him.

Q: A smart move. But let's not get distracted by moving portraits of the dispossessed. Ryan's group—how many were in it?

A: Seven in total: four boys, three girls.

Q: So this merry band of seven were united; and the rumblings of collective dissent were sounding; there was a rift, a shaft of light where darkness had forever existed? What happened next?

A: The group did the five-second delay throughout the morning, and I think Mrs. Wood knew something was up. In the afternoon, when we came back from lunch, that's when it all kicked off.

Q: Had the group displayed displeasure before this day?

A: Oh, they were sick to bloody death. They were ten years old, and already half of their lives had been spent sitting in that bottom group—

Q: How else—

A: —dealing with teachers who asked the class to do one thing, and the bottom group another; teachers who couldn't subtly differentiate their lesson plans; teachers who asked the class to turn to page fifteen in the workbook, while handing the bottom group a separate sheet.

Q: But it's unfair to suggest the bottom group were neglected, no? Were they not, for example, regularly taken to the library for extra reading sessions?

A: They were, but each time they were taken out of the class, the class still went on. From our position at the top group, we'd look at the empty chairs and think: you can remove the bottom group and our class is still our class. It was unthinkable that our top group could be removed and that you'd still be able to say the same. Moreover, once the bottom group left the room, we eyed the third group with suspicion.

Q: Do you think these feelings were encouraged?

A: It's hard to say.

Q: When did you first become aware of the classes being grouped like this?

A: When I was six.

Q: And did you feel the system was unfair to those languishing at the bottom?

A: If I'm honest, no. I was six.

Q: Well, how *did* you feel then?

A: I came home bawling to my mother because I'd been relegated from the top group to the second group. A mistake had been made. A terrible mistake. I knew where I belonged, and I belonged with Andrew and Bethan and all the others in the top group who were being quietly ushered into the corner now, to be privy to some new concept in maths. As I said, I was only six.

Q: And you weren't at the top anymore. Seen another way, you were one step closer to the bottom?

A: I suppose.

Q: Another step closer to the kids who never listened; another step closer to the kids who chewed their Staedtler pencils until the yellow and black paint had all flaked off, and what was left was bare, sharp lead—an instrument fit for stabbing?

A: That's not what I'm saying.

Q: A thesis: everyone learns at different speeds, so we put the kids into the vehicles best suited to their needs. It's just common sense.

A: But it's the changes it makes in people—that's what I'm talking about. And then there's what's implied. When I was back in the top group and began going out with a girl from the third group, I knew the teacher disapproved. And I felt embarrassed. It was like one of those nineteenth-century novels about the impossibility of marrying outside of your class: *darling, do put these frightful ideas of your head!*

Q: Let's be clear: when we're talking about the bottom group, we're talking council flats and fathers with restraining orders, aren't we? If you glanced over the school yard, you'd see Ryan Small's three brothers, identical miniature versions, all with their uniform skew-whiff, all with their heads shaved the same way: a Russian-doll army of delinquents, each one worse than the last.

A: I never said Ryan's head was shaven.

Q: But wasn't it? And weren't shaven heads forbidden in the school?

A: It was, and they were. But that's beside the point.

Q: Be honest: did the system benefit you?

A: How do you mean?

Q: As a member of the top group, did you receive privileges that others didn't?

A: I would say I was rewarded for my good performance. My being in the top group was just a reflection of this performance, and any rewards I received were as a result of my hard work and good performance.

Q: You were the computer prefect, weren't you?

A: Yes, no one else knew how to work the CD-ROM drive. It was new technology.

Q: Did members of the bottom group make much use of it?

A: The educational games we had on CD-ROM were unsuited to their needs. Their games were stored on floppy disks.

Q: Explain to me how being in the top group positively influenced your sense of self.

A: I had confidence in my abilities, in my answers. I was regularly called out to give presentations in assembly. When the school inspector visited, I was asked to read him a story that I'd written. I was captain of my house.

Q: Tell me about the school inspector.

A: At the start of the year, Mrs. Wood told us an inspector was coming to the school in April. We weren't to worry, she said. He was coming to inspect her, not us. But the inspector quickly became a mythical figure, like Father Christmas or God. Mrs. Wood would say things like, "The inspector wouldn't be too impressed by this . . . " and we'd go back and redo our homework. You could tell she was anxious about his visit. The week before he arrived we rehearsed entire lessons, and then Mr. Richards—the headmaster—asked Ryan Small's parents to keep him at home.

Q: On the topic of important men: isn't it true that you got to meet Tony Blair, that you got to shake his squirly hand?

A: A few weeks after he won the general election, Tony Blair visited our town, and Mr. Richards took us all out to greet him at the shopping centre. We welcomed the Prime Minister with a song, and the kids from the top group spoke to the local press. But no, I never got to shake his squirly hand.

Q: Tell me, were there any school subjects in which you didn't excel?

A: I was terrible at art and I dreaded the homework. I once sat at the dinner table till two in the morning, attempting to draw a three-dimensional picture of a desktop computer. My mother stayed up with me all night, trying to help. In the end I got really upset. I said, "I can't do it, and I don't care anyway because art is stupid."

My mother said: "Remember this feeling, hold onto it. This is how some kids feel every day."

Q: In later years, did you not complain about a GCSE Geography class in which you felt your progress was being hindered because the teacher wanted to move at a pace *everyone* could handle?

A: I'm not proud of that.

Q: Were you ever jealous of the bottom group?

A: No.

Q: Cast your mind back. Year Four, when you were eight. Ryan Small again.

A: What about him?

Q: Did you not envy Ryan's chart on the wall? The chart made by his teaching assistant?

A: I don't remember it.

Q: The chart depicted a pizza, and beside it was a drawing of Michelangelo, the Teenage Mutant Ninja Turtle, skillfully rendered by the teaching assistant. Did you not envy the slice of pizza that was added to the chart—on the condition that Ryan behaved—at the end of each school day?

A: Look, I felt it was unfair that he was singled out for special treatment. I wanted a pizza chart—we all wanted a pizza chart—and part of me, the worst parts, felt that Ryan was being rewarded for doing the minimum of what could be expected of any of us: behaving well. But I was eight years old, and even then I knew I was being unreasonable.

Q: How noble. Didn't you and your friends exclude Ryan from football games on the yard?

A: It's important to note that Ryan was very violent and he was very dangerous, and he would often kick out. He may have been small, but he was wild—his legs flailing everywhere. Besides, he seemed content to play football by himself in the corner of the yard with a stone.

Q: Did you not sometimes go to the far end of the field, where there was a hole in the ground, and cover said hole with sticks and grass, and then ask Ryan to walk over it, so that Ryan would fall into the hole?

A: Ryan knew the hole was there. The whole thing was a performance, a performance he enjoyed participating in.

Q: You asked him to perform the role of the baddy getting caught in the trap?

A: He enjoyed it!

Q: Did you not attend Ryan's eighth birthday party, and the day after—in school on the carpet—tell everyone that his birthday cake had made you sick? Did you not, upon seeing him enter the fray, make "Ugh! Ugh!" noises in his direction?

A: He often mocked my stammer.

Q: Is it true that your father wouldn't let you attend the parties of children who lived on the estate?

A: That only happened once, and our car was at the garage, and it was raining, and Dad didn't want us walking to the estate because—

Q: Do you have any positive memories of Ryan?

A: The year of the Pizza Slices, our teacher—Mr. Williams—liked to mix up the groups. One afternoon he asked us to write limericks, and he sat Ryan beside me and told us to work together. I was initially anxious and a little aggrieved, but we made a good team. To this day, I remember the poem we wrote:

> *A spider playing tennis!*
> *But boy could he be a menace.*
> *He ruined the court*
> *And then he fought*
> *With his coach named Dennis.*

Ryan's drawing of a spider was also excellent.

Q: So Ryan was a talented draughtsman?

A: He was pretty good, yeah. He was better than me anyway.

Q: Tell me: what were you studying at the time of the incident?

A: Our theme for the term was "Where we all belong." We investigated the ideas of place and habitat. We picked up rocks, found woodlice, and made illustrative notes. We studied maps of Caerphilly, circled our homes, and memorised the counties of Wales. We coloured in atlases, and tried to see ourselves in a global context. We watched videos of Rosa Parks and learned all the words to "We Shall Overcome." At Easter, Mrs. Wood directed us in a moving production of the taking of Christ. She told us that every good child belonged with Jesus.

Q: How were you assessed during this year?

A: The big one was the SATS, which came in May. "These are exams, not tests," Mrs. Woods said each week when she distributed the mock papers. She'd stand at the front of the class with a stopwatch in her hand, while we scribbled furiously with pencils in ours. Each of us had been predicted a grade—a level—and some of us felt the pressure to achieve said grade. By February I was regularly bringing home a small mound of revision sheets.

Q: How else did you prepare for the SATS?

A: Mrs. Wood made us write a story and learn it off by heart so that we could write it out verbatim in the exam. Meanwhile, my group was continually made to re-record our oral assessment. There was always a valid-sounding reason: like the cassette had broken, or there'd been a lot of banging noises on the recording. On each occasion we just went back and did it again.

Q: Why?

A: Simply: we hadn't achieved our predicted grade, and we were being used as a benchmark. The exam board requested only a sample of the cassettes—if the board agreed with Mrs. Wood's grading of these samples, they would accept her grading for the rest of the class.

Q: A different interpretation: Mrs. Wood just wanted you to do well, to achieve the grades you all deserved.

A: Oh, of course, and I really do believe that. But also: our grades were perceived as a reflection of Mrs. Wood's performance and thus the school's in general. Had the top group not achieved the highest level, there would have been serious questions. At that time, head-teachers' salaries were determined by the school's position in the league tables.

Q: You're being sceptical, I know—but a few years later, when performance-related pay was introduced for all teachers, grades across the country did improve.

A: Making a kid stand on a chair doesn't make the kid any taller.

Q: Okay, let's agree to disagree. Was there ever any downtime? A school excursion, for example?

A: Yes, we went on a week's trip to Llangrannog—a Welsh-language activity centre in west Wales. Before we left, we had an assembly where Mrs. Wood explained that we would be joined at the centre by a special group of children from Belarus. She showed us slides on the overhead projector and told us about Chernobyl.
    "1986," she said, "the same year most of you were born."
    We looked at the photos in horror.

Q: You met these children?

A: They were at Llangrannog, but I didn't speak to any of them. I don't even know if they could speak English. We were mostly frightened of them, afraid of their bald and shaven heads, scared that we would catch their cancer. Bethan described seeing a faint glow emitting from one of their girls. The word "radiation" hung in the air all week, and my classmates ran around tagging each other: the schoolyard game of "germs on you" adapted, made toxic, nuclear. At breakfast, the Chernobyl kids sat at one end of the canteen, wearing old tracksuits, laughing and smiling. Mrs. Wood tried to encourage us to mix with them, but we didn't dare get close.

Q: Except Ryan Small?

A: Yes, the first day we arrived he went straight up to their boys and they invited him to play football with them out on the grass. Later, when we went for dinner, he was already sat on their side of the canteen. The rest of the week he went around with the Chernobyl kids and their guides: horse-riding, bike-riding, beach trails, the lot.

Q: What became of Ryan Small?

A: Last I heard, he stabbed someone.

Q: Is there a correlation between a pupil's wealth and their grouping?

A: There's a correlation, yes. Whether it's causal is open to debate.

Q: How do you mean?

A: At each morning assembly, the children eligible for free school meals were asked to stay behind to collect their dinner ticket. As the rest of us stood up to go back to class, it was pretty much always the children from the bottom groups who stayed behind. Believe me, no one wanted to be those free-meal kids. After my father left, we were really struggling and my mother signed me up for the scheme. I pleaded, please no, please Mum, please let me have sandwiches instead.

Q: Did she permit you that?

A: She did, and for that small mercy I am grateful every day.

Q: Okay, let's go back to the start here. What happened that afternoon?

A: Mrs. Wood asked us to read over our morning work. All the while she wrote the theme on the blackboard and drew a map of

Wales beneath it. Art was never her strong suit, and her version of Wales looked a bit off, a bit narrow.

Q: Okay, so all morning the stupid kids have been dissenting a bit, yes? Now you're all back from lunch, bellies have been filled, and the afternoon sun is high in the cloudless blue spring sky . . . Describe the atmosphere in the room.

A: Can we not call the kids "stupid," please?

Q: As you wish.

A: Okay, the bottom group were rustling, you could feel something stirring, there was an energy crackling.

Q: Then?

A: Mrs. Wood said she needed some red chalk, and that she was just going to pop to reception to get some. I suspect now that she didn't need chalk—I mean, she could have sent any one of us to get it. She probably just needed some time out. It had been a stressful year for her. My mother told me, sometime later, that Mrs. Wood's husband had been diagnosed with lung cancer.

Q: She left the class unsupervised?

A: There was another class next door, so it was safe to leave us for a few minutes.

Q: Okay.

A: When she was gone and at a safe distance, Ryan rose to his feet and moved towards the blackboard. And a few of us, myself included, started giggling.

Q: Why?

A: We were excited. We could sense a transgression at work, but we didn't know what was going to happen. Ryan was stood very close to the blackboard, his eyes right against it, studying the map. Then he tutted really loud, a proper tut of disapproval. There was class-wide laughter now, and Ryan folded his arms, imitating Mrs. Wood.

"No, no, no," he said, shaking his head at the blackboard. "Wales is *much* bigger than that."

Q: Was it a successful impression?

A: Seven out of ten.

Q: Pretty decent then.

A: We were all laughing and we watched as Ryan's fingers picked up the duster and rubbed out Mrs. Wood's effort at drawing the west coast of Wales. Then we watched in awe as he picked up a piece of white chalk and slowly—and generously—re-drew the map. When he was finished, Ryan took a step back to examine his work. The country was a little wider now and looked much more like the maps of Wales we'd seen in books.

Q: How did that make you feel?

A: We applauded—there was spontaneous applause and cheers and laughter! We were in shock and hysterics: we didn't know that you could do what he had done. Ryan bowed, and I remember feeling giddy. I felt on edge.

Q: Was your body firing with a fervour for rebellion? Were you overcome with an absolute swell of respect and admiration?

A: Maybe. Ryan had changed something, and it hadn't mattered to him that the thing he changed had been made by a teacher's hand. He had crossed a boundary, entered a holy realm, and when he sat back down, he was different for it. It was the closest I'd ever felt to him or his group.

Q: Did he do anything else?

A: Yes. Just before he sat, he crouched over the table and whispered something to the others.

Q: And then Mrs. Wood returned.

A: And then Mrs. Wood returned. We kept our heads bowed, afraid to lift our faces in case she saw the smirks. She asked us to put down our pens and face the board. She was standing in front of the map. She hadn't noticed that the map had been re-drawn in white chalk.

"Who can tell me which county borough we live in?" she said, and though we knew this starter question wasn't ours to answer, all the hands in my group shot up.

Mrs. Wood turned to the bottom group and smiled.

"Emma," she said, "come on now, you know the name of our county borough. What is it?"

Emma went to say something, but then she paused and looked at Ryan, who simply nodded.

"Emma?" Mrs. Wood said, but Emma just shook her head.

"Okay," Mrs. Wood said. "Michael, you can tell us, can't you?"

But Michael said nothing, and then he slowly folded his arms.

And then Daniel folded his arms.

And then Hayley folded her arms. And Kayley folded her arms. And Liam folded his arms, and then finally, Ryan Small folded his arms too. The whole class was hollowed quiet.

Mrs. Wood said: "What's happening here?"

Ryan put his index finger—dusted with chalk—to his lips, and the rest of the bottom group followed his lead.

Mrs. Wood shook her head. "I said what's going on?"

She asked the question several times, and no one gave an answer.

"Look," Mrs. Wood, said. "If you don't say something, I'm getting Mr. Richards right now."

Ryan removed the finger from his lips. Clearly and calmly, he said: "We're on strike."

Mrs. Wood looked at him. "Pardon?"

The room was quiet.

"A strike?" Mrs. Woods said. "What do you mean?"

Ryan returned his finger to its resting position on his lips, and he sat there, they all sat there, all seven of them, sat upright in their seats, looking straight ahead, their arms crossed, a finger on their lips, looking the picture of perfect discipline. Mrs. Wood went to the phone and called Mr Richards.

When she hung up, she turned to my group, as if we could offer an explanation, but we knew nothing and we said nothing. And though our collective silence felt conspiratorial, we were only quiet because we didn't know what would happen next. We thought the blackboard was as far as it would go.

Q: You had no idea about the strike?

A: None at all.

Q: Where did it come from?

A: I don't know.

Q: —

A: After the call, Mrs. Wood sat down in her chair. She looked strangely defeated; she looked so tired. The class sat in silence, and eventually the silence took on a sound of its own—I swear I could hear in it a soft beat, an elegiac rhythm. It was the same quality of stunned silence we had produced at the end of our Easter performance, when Andrew, dressed in white, stood with his arms splayed on a makeshift cross, as he was slowly and silently carried by two boys through the fire exit into the hall, and gently placed on the stage, his eyes opening and closing as Angharad played "The Last Post" on the bugle.

There came a sound then: Mr. Richards' feet climbing the steps, followed by the sight of his head growing larger with each ascent. Mrs. Wood went out to meet him. A moment later, Mr. Richards was standing in front of us. Quietly and calmly, he studied the bottom group. He was twice their size, and he looked from kid to kid, and you would swear that he was looking at seven pieces of shit. The group said nothing still. They just sat there, arms crossed, a finger resting on each of their lips.

Mrs. Wood whispered something behind her hand, and Mr. Richards nodded. He moved forward and crouched down chummily at Ryan's face.

"Look, Ryan," he said, and we all saw the bridges of saliva stretching from the roof of his mouth down to his tongue and teeth. "What's going on, eh?"

Ryan said nothing. He just sat there, looking past Mr Richards's face. Ryan was trying to hold it together, and I could feel the whole class willing him, giving him everything we had, to just hold on.

"Come on now, Ryan, tell me what's the matter. And what is it you mean by 'strike'? It doesn't make any sense."

Ryan didn't budge, and the others in the group tried to not look at him, tried not to stare as he sat there with his finger on his lips. But I did look and I did stare and I could see the change in him now; I could see it in his eyes and in the way he held his shoulders. He wasn't just holding things together—he was moving away, he was entering another place entirely.

"If you don't tell me what's wrong, we can't help," Mr Richards said. "Talk to me. And look at me when I'm talking to you."

Ryan continued to look past him, so Mr Richards placed a hand on Ryan's cheek and pushed it so that's Ryan head was facing his. He pulled Ryan's arm away, pulled it so that his finger was no longer resting on his lips.

I was afraid now; the whole class was afraid. But Ryan was already somewhere else, somewhere in his own mind, and travelling far away from our small class in our small school in our small town. Ryan was way above it all now: he was floating to somewhere bigger, calmer—floating off to a vast, open space where he was free to choose the place of his belonging.

"Come on now, last chance," Mr. Richards said. "Why are you on strike? I won't ask again after this."

And Ryan's eyes lit up with the biggest grin. "Good," he said.

There's some disagreement about what happened next, but in my memory Mr. Richards dragged Ryan out of his chair by his arms, dragged him across the lino—as Ryan screamed and shouted— then slammed his head against the door. Others will tell you it was an accident, that Mr. Richards was only trying to get Ryan out of the room, that the angle of the door in relation to Ryan's head was an unfortunate accident.

I just remember the thump, and the yelp, and the blood on the door—and then looking over to the bottom group, and seeing the six remaining kids slumped: their hands on their heads, their heads against the table.

Q: How long did the strike last?

A: Half an hour later, Mr. Richards returned for Liam, Ryan's best friend. Once he was removed, the rest of the group went back to work.

Q: And the rest of the class?

A: We went back to work.

Q: You did and said nothing.

A: We all went back to work.

JOHN SAUL

Armadillo

WHO IS THE woman standing before the house smoking a cigarette? That silver top with long sleeves, her black hair. She looks striking in the rain. She doesn't live there.

She stands easily, tapping on the cigarette. The smoke rises sinuously above the roof of the porch.

notes
{Moldavian name Ekaterina Mavrocordato

She could be a cleaner. Is she? She is too smartly dressed for cleaning. Did she change clothes to clean and now has changed back? What relation does she have to the couple in the house?

She moves to support her cigarette arm at the elbow. The position enhances the easy assurance of her stance. Beside her: the umbrella-stand, a sentinel at the door, in maybe brass, an animal with armadillo nose. From behind the umbrella-stand a ginger cat appears. It winds between her legs. At the neighbouring bungalow the louvres of a blind flick open.

Will she use a key to get back in? Or ring the bell?

The slow ribbon of smoke goes on rising.

Inventory
An *inventory* is a variation on Chekhov's well-known advice not to

place a loaded rifle on the stage if it isn't going to be fired. In terms of fiction, as opposed to the theatre, the first sentence has its rifles, its inventory. Things that can lead to other things. No matter if it has a loaded gun, or an armadillo umbrella-stand, the sentence sits there easily enough if these get used. If they don't get used, it squirms.

notes
{Ekaterina is determined; also aiding talented painter, ginger hair and beard
{see Milan Kundera
{she is obsessive as a poet

Ekaterina is tenacious, a fighter. She herself has said several times: everyone gets knocked down, it's how they get up that counts. And she will scrap it out even if it means scouring bedpans. Cleaning people's houses. Scrubbing floors. She will find poetry in drudgery, strength in obstacles. Think on the silver of women, said her grand-mother. She did say that: *argint*. Think on the maladies of men. Is painting a malady? Surely not. He goes calmly at his work, an admirer of early Mondrian. A malady will not be calm. Think on these matters. Spur him. Hoist, draw everything up, to your level.

She turns back to the door with a key. The silver shift has black notes snaking downwards.

Inventory
An example:
It is possible to walk across the whole of Europe.
It is only an example.

Her partner the artist has come across a print he would like to have. A shoreline with waves, probably the North Sea. It may aid his latest project.
   —This one? Is this the one?
   He's trembling. Staying silent.
   —We have more, the same. I'll get you one that isn't creased.

Shall I fold it? Would you like me to roll it up?

Still nothing. This happens, once in a while.

—Are you all right?

—I don't make decisions. Even little ones.

—But you do want this?

—Oh yes. I know what I want.

—Of course.

Fold or roll, Kat would have known what to do. His partner Kat. Her name at birth Ekaterina. She will have lain with her first black hair and eyes shut, beneath the hovering heads of her grandparents, in what was then Moldavia, as they blinked and blinked and eventually said: Ekaterina, her name will be Ekaterina. In this Smaragda and Dimitrie were one—the Moldavian grandparents, who gave her much. They gave their Romanian citizenships. They may have given her that easy way of standing, who can really know.

—There. Rolling's better. Is there anything more I can help with?

—I can't say. If there is or not. Would you wrap it?

—It is wrapped.

There can be no more unlikely partner for Ekaterina Mavrocordato. His ginger hair and his beard suggest the looks of a nervous animal. He is softness and hardness in one. He parallels her in one respect. He will stand resolutely still until he gets what he wants. Sit in rooms and refuse to move even when the caretaker / police / army ask him to, until he gets it. But that was long ago. Now he is happy to paint lone trees by ditches. He has been painting lone trees by ditches for over a year, à la Mondrian.

notes
{obsessive as a poet: use anaphora
{the unbearable lightness of being Milan Kundera
{look instead to Walter Abish

Inventory
It is possible to walk across the whole of Europe.
Since this is only an example, more avid readers need not detain themselves over it but move directly to the paragraph below. So,

there's the rifle. As a mixing of metaphors might have it: an exploding Europe. As this rifle is eyed and then picked up and moved and
locked away and taken out again and eventually fired—in other
words, the inventory is unravelled and the details emerge in their
thousands—Daniel or even Daniela scrabbles for transport, fighting the cold, soldiers with guns and no comprehensible English,
one language after another, a struggle to get the necessary papers,
hopeful papers, Daniel or Daniela secreting cash, yearning for food,
sharing food, not sharing food, checking barbed-wire fencing in the
dark, falling in mud, entering rivalries, enemies everywhere, acts
of friendship turning up when totally unexpected, the extremely
occasional miracle or no miracles at all, flu, no doctor, flesh wound,
no doctor, cold, no heat, boats, lifejackets, snatches of television
news with politicians in suits with warm houses to return to: The
prime minister is to make a statement about the migrant situation
later today. The content is already public. His use of terms has
once again come under criticism. He will speak in Bradford. In
Bratislava, Bucharest, Burghausen. But this is not this story.

As the key opens the door another woman—she lives there with
her husband—is going out. She wears a red coat. From top to bottom it is tightly buttoned. The two women go to her car despite
the downpour. The cat circles the umbrella-stand. A drip from a
gutter makes it raise its hackles, then a sudden splash down makes
it vamoose.

From the trunk the women lift a flat-pack the size of what, a
small radiator. Kat hurries back to the door to receive the square
of cardboard from her employer before the now-amplifying rain
might soak it. The woman returns smartly to her car and is about
to shut the door.

—Take anything you want from that pile of magazines Kat.

—The cat?

Confusion.

—I fed the cat.

—I thought so. She's out here somewhere.

Startling another woman in the next driveway—into dropping
a ball of garden twine—but not making Kat blink, or the cat blink,

she slams shut the door. At once she starts the car. The flustered neighbour hurries to tread on the twine to stop it unrolling. The car is red as well the coat. The front door too is red. The reds are close but the tones slightly different. All are sumptuous tones. She drives off up the hill. Ekaterina draws the evidence together in her mind: that woman identifies with what is sumptuous, thinks of herself as sumptuous. Or maybe not—is there not that very English phrase, *the benefit of the doubt*? She might have driven off to get a bag of peat, a new collar for the cat. No. Those jobs are for the husband. She's off to some spa day or other. Ekaterina is not mistaken. She has seen too much to be mistaken.

Inventory
Chekhov was silent as to how many rifles might lie around. There could be several. And if the public wanted a farce, why stop there? A cannon could stand centre-stage, the cannonball being rolled in to a great rumble from the wings—careful it doesn't roll out of control into the orchestra pit, stop it, stop it, mind your feet, watch out:
Kat spent years crossing Europe, never imagining it would lead her to seek revenge on a couple for their lifestyle of luxury and in the process make an orphan of their cat.

{anaphora: a literary and rhetorical device in which a word or group of words is repeated at the beginning of two or more successive clauses or sentences, adding emphasis and unity; not to be confused with *amphora*, an early container of a characteristic shape and size used for transport and storage, mostly of wine.
{an example of anaphora, Martin Luther King: Go back to Mississippi, go back to Alabama, go back to South Carolina, go back to Georgia, go back to Louisiana, go back to the slums and ghettos of our northern cities, knowing that somehow this situation can and will be changed.
{apart from a few dubious assertions on the Internet, announced in advance by paragraphs rife with misplaced apostrophes, there is no evidence of amphora used by Martin Luther King

In moving across Europe over many years, Kat has been a cleaner in many houses. In Austria, Germany, and the Netherlands. In Austria she discovered the house she cleaned lay across the way from a studio once occupied by the artist Gustav Klimt, which had led to an increase in house values in the street, whereupon she decided to double her previous prices. In Germany she identified Frankfurt as the dirtiest city with good money. This is what I'm paid, she'd say, because I'm good. But she has also waited in restaurants, hawked bibles, and ploughed earth in fields. She is a cleaner momentarily. She has *become* a cleaner. There will be a time again when she is not a cleaner. Thanks once more to the heritage of her Moldavian grandparents she can speak four languages, drive almost any type of tractor, and sharpen all kinds of knives.

Inventory
All sentences have an inventory. According to conventional thought, harmonious fiction will pay close attention to its inventories. Like the brass umbrella-stand outside: the plinth, the armadillo nose, those flaps of ears.

Ekaterina watches the car disappear around the corner at the top of the road. Magazines? A sop. That woman doesn't give, she takes. She takes and she keeps. Now she's gone I'll have another cigarette. Now she has gone I would like God to come up the road and make an evaluation of the situation. Is that Him? He waves. He walks through the rain in His robes. His body is so hidden from sight it can't be imagined. Why does He not dress in more modern wear? First, He says, put out your cigarette. Oh God, she says, I clean for her but I would like her to clean for me. I would like her to arrive with a sack full of cleaning products and go to it, on her knees. I would like Mirek to be beamed to Pridnestrovie with me for a holiday, so he could see where I grew up, the barn we played in, the pit we swam in, the church . . . Sh, Ekaterina. Where is Pridnestrovie? I mean, where the hell is Pridnestrovie? Oh God, *O* God, that's a little complicated. Well keep it simple Ekaterina. My time isn't infinite, or rather, my peoples' time isn't, you'll soon realise that one moment you're there, as you were, under the gaze of your doting grandparents, the next moment not, and that's people, they seem to run out of steam just like that, in the blink of an eye. Lord you're looking on the thin side yourself, I can bring you . . . What? Porridge. Porridge? No, well, not that, do you need any washing doing? As if I would, He said, as if I would. And who is Mirek?

{read Walter Abish for how to boldly work with sections
{Janet Frame for pinning words to the storyboards of life

He unrolled the print and taped it carefully on the back of the door.

—Given this scene is nothing much, Kat, a dreary scene, why do I want to keep looking at it?

—I can't even make it out. What are those in the distance, hills? It's a scene of what?

—A shore, in bad weather. Those silvery-white bits are waves.

—And not a soul in sight. Not even drowning.

—Don't touch it.

—I didn't. It's only a print.

—It's a picture of rain.

—You're studying rain, is that what you're saying?

—Is that a fair description? I can't decide.

{Inside the flat-pack is a desktop. Desktop in the original meaning of the words *desk*, *top*. A desktop is not what it was. Windows, apple, mouse. Amazon has lost its *The*, lost its giant hundred-and-fifty-mile-wide mouth, and, as if spraying down the scent of the philistine, has relinquished as tired old history the Spanish claims to have been discovered by the conquistador Vicente Yáñez Pinzón in March 1500. The mouse has likewise altered beyond recognition. It is no longer that prolific breeder known for causing damage to crops or being best kept in cages, under a palm it rocks and it rolls just a little, comes in sometimes garish colours with flashing lights and reacts only when clicked. No need to stand on a chair on account of it. But click the mouse to open a window. Or close one. There are more windows than there used to be. There are Windows that are no match for Apples, many say. Yet Apples have no taste, and it is pointless trying to bake them in silver foil with cloves and demerara sugar and serve them up with expensive ice cream. Again, Windows do not need men with cloths on extendible ladders to go and clean them, sweeping back their hair in the hope of gaining attention from some lonely housewives.

Ekaterina went to the doctor's on account of a shoulder pain.

—Miss Mav—

—McCord.

—Miss McCord, you may be performing more physical work than is good for you. Can you ease up?

—I'm not *that* active.

—So you say. I rather doubt it. If it isn't from activity I don't where it comes from, but you have the flattest stomach I've ever seen.

She dressed.

—These things are genetic, he said. Parents, grandparents. Postures.

—You just said they were related to activity.

—That too.

—Besides. I came about my shoulder.

She left. She wouldn't return.

Inventory

There is also the phenomenon of the reverse inventory. The rifle is not on the stage but someone brings it on and shoots. And leaves, as they say. Or the reverse inventory may take the form of what is called the backstory. This only emerges once the play is under way. A woman is standing before a house smoking a cigarette. In a silver top with long sleeves, her black hair. She looks striking in the rain. The smoke curls upwards. She doesn't live there. Where has she come from?

{anaphora. sumptuous. fishy. sop. peat. Mondrian. Ekaterina continues to heed the rules laid down by Smaragda and Dimitrie: if you must leave us, learn a new word every day, wherever you are, *mă înțelegi*, promise? Yes yes. Learn and use it. Yes yes. Words, said

Dimitrie, are the wheels of the world. Are money in the bank, Smaragda said, *argint*. Yes.

Yes.

—All those airs and graces, said Ekaterina. It's reached the point where the only reason I keep doing it is the money.

—Wasn't it always? Mirek asked.

—I could stab her.

—How? How would you stab her?

—Scissors. In the back.

—Not the front.

—That's for idiots. It has to be the back. In real life, the back.

The cat lost its collar. It was found in the neighbour's flowerbed: Millie, address, mobile number. It must have come off in a struggle, with a bird or a tomcat. Or it came off through being constantly rubbed against a fence, or even against the umbrella-stand. The neighbour, Marion, found it when stringing back up her trellis. She assumed it must have been rubbed away. Why didn't the owners look after it better? A good owner would have noticed it fraying long before it wore through. The trellis had come down in a gale.

—So how *was* the doctor's?

—It's nothing serious. I got the last appointment. Not the doctor I normally see.

—You don't normally go.

—He started talking. He was tired, he said, but loved his job. He said how much he liked Scotland and Blondie and wearing well-made boots. I went in as a patient and came out as a therapist. He had to go into the name thing. I told him in Austria I was Katrin. When I mentioned Moldavia he made a wild guess I'd flown in with Wizz Air.

—Wizz Air. There's no such thing.

—Wizz Air. It's Hungarian. He suspects I'm some illegal immigrant. As if I'd walked here, right across Europe. He was as bad as the woman I work for on the hill. I clean her house and she thinks *she's* doing *me* a favour. So. How was your work today?

—I've found a part-time job. The supermarket.

{research: what goes on when cats blink slowly

The job

If only Mirek had been born in Slovakia and not the Czech Republic. But at the supermarket they would still call him the Czech. We will put you on the Czech-out, they said, once you've got the hang of things. Your first job will be to Czech deliveries. Don't open every-thing, do a spot Czech now and then. You'll get paid straight into the bank. Do you have a Czech book? It doesn't matter, we can't just write a Czech. Anyway, you're here now. Czechs are reliable, we suppose, if on the old fashioned side.

—But you haven't really told me what the doctor said. Your shoulder.
 —It doesn't matter. I won't return.
 —What if it persists?
 —I won't go. He said I had the flattest stomach he'd ever seen.
 —I could say that too.
 —Oh you want to be a doctor, Mirek Zaturetsky?
 —You don't need me for that. Look in the mirror.
 —Mirror? My partner is my mirror.

Inventory

The magazines. Magazines suggest wealth. They may measure wealth. Be a coefficient of. The woman who employs Ekaterina is on a basic monthly salary of seven magazines, eight restaurant meals, wine unlimited, one Cartier or Hermès scarf, one pamper day, and a choice between one pair of Manolo Blahnik stilettos, a Zac Posen satchel bag or a sofa. It is reasonable to assume any of the latter will be red.

—I must rush Kat. Have a look in the basket in the hall, see if there's something you might like. And can you do the oven?
 Ekaterina watched her pat the armadillo.
 —Must rush.

Had she been a malicious person . . . once she'd gone she'd smoke another cigarette and hatch a plan to strangle it. No good crushing it. It was uncrushable. Armadillo, Mirek said, means little armoured one. Their shells are so impenetrable that bullets have been known to ricochet off them.

Had she been a malicious person she'd hang it by its stupid neck from the TV aerial, see it swing in the wind.

{Psychologists say people's characters are either malicious or not at all malicious. Few people's characters are in between. It's not clear why some are malicious and some not.

The job

We hear you worked at the post office once. So they still take Czechs, it's more than just a rumour? Oh and when you go, don't forget to Czech the locks, and Czech the doors.

God oh God, who is *Mirek*? He's a young man I met working for the post last Christmas. Oh God yes, you know all about that of course, Christmas. *O* God, O, sorry, *O*. Indeed Ekaterina, but we won't go into that now, you wanted me to come by and make an evaluation of the situation here. But all you tell me is what you wish for. O Lord, yes. I wish. I wish. Yes, but first stub out your cigarette, ah, and what do I have here between my legs, Millie the cat, with your fine new collar, isn't it a lovely red, and your new bell and your mobile number, splendid. Come to me when you're lost, I'll know who to call.

The job

There you are. I meant to ask, seeing as everyone likes a good mate, do you play chess?

The other woman, startled woman, neighbour Marion, almost trips over the cat scampering between her legs. She lets her husband know her feelings: she has become a film extra in a film in her own road. She tells him: once next door burns down, with its occupants locked in the bathroom, tied to the taps and gagged with duct tape, as she is sure sooner or later will happen, probably sooner, she will take the cat in. She has a theory. The cleaner has suffered so many indignities in so many years, all across Europe, only then to fall into the hands of that mean socialite next door, is socialite the word, with her airs and shoes and Wedgwood candlesticks and Chanel bottles and half-used jars of Crème de Mer moisturising cream, she left them standing beside the bin, and who knows what next, hooting her car horn in the night and yapping all morning on her mobile in the garden, grating and jarring, creating friction wherever she goes, suffering even, so much so that she, the cleaning lady who arrives for work and leaves so smart but inside puts on old grey pants and a scarf tied round her head, I've seen it Tony, seen her through the window dusting the piano, was bound to get vengeful.

—Marion, wife, it isn't like that at all. You've been watching too much Scandi noir, too much forensics and sleuthing in the dark. Where's the remote gone?

—My dreams are never wrong. It's going to happen. And when it does I'll be ready.

—Don't say it's down the side of the sofa, not again.

—All right, if it isn't her it be that partner of hers, I saw him once, up and down the road he went, after something, she'll send along her partner to set fire to the house and in the process orphan the cat, what's his name, Zarutsky?

—I don't know what the cat's name is but it isn't Zarutsky.

—Not the cat. The man, the idler she's got tucked in her back pocket. I'd send you in—send in the clowns, they used to say didn't they—but you're always so busy, what with the rugby and the darts and your interminable testing out your angles of recline, isn't that what you call them, in your stupid armchair.

—Here it is, I've got it.

Inventory
Ekaterina spent years . . . those, the mighty few—following the path of the rolling cannonball as it teeters at the edge of the orchestra pit—fear it will drop at any moment. Down it goes. The string section is decimated, the woodwind section horrified, the conductor's

baton has snapped in two. Some members of the orchestra think they are in World War Two, others, thinking this is the end of order and the opportunity to lunge for the partner of their choice, act as if they have arrived in ancient Rome.

—I chatted to the neighbour today. Marion. She asked how I was. So I asked her. She said she was psychic. She said she thought all kinds of things were going on and she felt like an extra, a film extra.

Ekaterina flicked her cigarette end through the window.

—Oh God, said Mirek, you could start—

—She was afraid for the cat. She said the people living next door—where I go—had arrived with a curse. I would be better off dropping them. If I was to drop them it would serve them right. On top of which, they had enemies. Many many, apparently. Who had spoken to her in the kitchen. Then again in the night, in the bathroom. She was told someone was plotting to come round in an evening and torch the place.

—Whose place?

—The neighbours'. Where I go. Torch it.

—With a cigarette end I imagine.

—Could be. She reckoned it could well be me doing it.

—She said that, to your face?

—I didn't have to get her to loosen up or anything. She was off as if she'd been a length of elastic and had been let go. Then she said if it wasn't me it would be you.

—Me doing what?

—Doing it.

—It. Me!

—No need to shout. It's just crazy stuff.

—Me! You're the one that goes there and gets wound up.

—You're winding yourself up, you crazy Czech.

—I'm the crazy one? You're the one with the family that went fishing through holes in the ice. You're the one ran with the aurochs. You're the one wants to put rugs on the wall.

—Anaphora.

—What?

—There's the doorbell. Mr. Simmonds?

32

—Are you all right Mrs. McCord? I heard shouting.

—No, it's nothing. I'm fine. Mirek come here so Mr. Simmonds can see you.

—Hello.

—Hello, you're shaking.

—It's nothing. It comes and goes.

—If anyone gets scared round here Mr. Simmonds it won't be me.

—So all's okay?

—It's okay. We were just being a bit crazy. Shooting off. This and that. Nothing serious. I have him under control. I'll tie him up if he gets worse. Sedate him.

—Okay. You know where I am.

—It's okay, really.

—Who was *that*?

—Our neighbour, Mr. Simmonds.

—I've never seen him before.

—That's because you don't get out enough. He works for the water company. Now that's enough about Marion.

—Maid Marion.

—She'll drive anyone crazy. Have me talking to myself.

—As if you didn't.

—I have the odd talk with God. That's all.

{An armadillo can walk six minutes underwater. Can cross a *large* body of water by inflating itself with air and increasing buoyancy. Its Achilles' heel—in one of best known of its twenty species, North American nine-banded armadillo: it tends to jump straight in the air when surprised. This leads to calamitous deaths on the road. A sensitive sculptor in metals, aware of the special character of the animal, of this weakness, will set the armadillo in a heavy concrete base. As has been done with the umbrella-stand, beside which Ekaterina stands.

Ekaterina will not touch the armadillo *that* woman pats. She impales the last of her cigarette to the snout to see what it looks like. Instead of allure, of something film-star about the umbrella-stand beside the house with the red door, she finds the English word: *gormless*. Whatever had she been expecting? Not this indignity, this *mârşăvie*. She takes back the cigarette and stamps on it, kicking it towards the bushes. She will give up smoking for good.

— *There* you are Kat.

—Extra work. At the people's home.

—How is the assassination coming along?

—No time for that. You don't think I would have done it and come home and get out a nail file. Cook a chicken and watch the seven o'clock news.

—Chicken. That sounds good.

—Like Marion says, *you* should go there and do it, Mirek. You've got the time. You take the key. Wear gloves. Ignore the armadillo guard dog, I know how you get diverted by such things. Make sure the cat's not in the house. If it is, get it out. Blink at it slowly, befriend it. Cats do that. Go straight into the living room, answering no questions. Say the husband asked you to call by immediately. You'd come as you are one of the few people who know how to handle scorpions. Tell her they like to hide in curtains. Pull the curtains shut. Then take the big square cushion from the sofa.

—Is it chicken with spices or herbs?

—And go at it. A lot easier than locking her in the bathroom and setting fire to the place.

—What about him?

—Never there.

—Well, to take the mature approach . . . Is there no room for you two to understand each other? What does she know about you? Does she realise you spent years crossing Europe—never imagining—it might lead you—

—To what?

—Have you tried telling her you have a doctorate in law? Studied Russian and Romanian?

—The mature approach. Mirek darling, is this really you?

—It's always me.

—Well we haven't really gone into backgrounds. It's all furniture and magazines, shoes and umbrella-stands. Her bit of charity on the side: me, in other words. If you ask me it's the decline of the west, in person. I should quit. Like I have smoking.

—Congratulations, Ms. Mavrocordato.

Marion is convinced she'll soon have Millie the cat. She should. It already comes round rubbing its neck on *her* drainpipes and flower pots. She comes across it at least once a day. She winks at it slowly. Her husband Tony smiles at it slowly, and it smiles back.

He says it does.

{It is strongly suspected the murder was done by Mirek with a palette knife in the observatory. He had a motive, a palette knife, and an opportunity. Miss Scarlet had none of these.

Nor did Professor Plum. Besides, he had been discovered already dead inside the rain barrel. Like Nelson in his vat of sherry. Was it sherry.

—I'm drawing up a family tree Mirek.

—I thought I was the drawer round here.

—You can't be. No such word, drawer.

—Well, there is a word. We have drawers in our cupboard.

—That may well be. But they can't draw trees. You can't take them out and leave them with a pencil and paper and expect them to get on with it.

—So you admit there are drawers.

—You said you were the drawer, singular.

—Do you want paper?

—I'll use the computer. The tree will go right back to Moldavia. The grandparents on both sides.

—Quite a tree. Do you need the mouse? It's in a drawer.

—Enough with the drawer. I just want to draw a tree. I don't need a mouse.

—It's very late to start a project. It's very dark out, dark and black.

—Have you been drinking?

—It steadies me.

—You've been drinking.

—You're right though, better without a mouse. It might run up your tree. Better put down a trap.

—You are all traps tonight, Mirek. This is a silly game. Where is your work from today? What have you done?

—I can't measure it by the day. Besides I was at my job. Replacing all that had found a way off the shelves. I said to them: it's a Sisyphus task. You're right, one said, it's a cissy job. But it's the last time I go there in a Czech shirt. Or take in porridge.

—There must be some nice English people.

—I'm sure. Those at work may be, somehow.

—The arseholes at the supermarket?

—The arseholes at the supermarket. They have an oblique way of being friendly. A slanty way.

—Slanty's not a word.

Ekaterina is told to drop everything and sit in the living room. Does she take sugar, of course not. Sit down, Ekaterina. I—we—that is, I—

—What?

—have decided, to move.

(Just when all was ready for the assassination to go ahead.)

—Michael and I, well, oh, this needn't concern you.

(They are separating.)

—Here is your pay. If you want a reference, of course I'll . . . Now I've put a few things in the basket which I really can't take with me. Cigarette? I've just started. The last of the Mohicans. I don't know what I'm saying, I don't know what a Mohican is. I don't know a Mohican from a Mohawk, do you? I don't know what I know, do you.

(The reference'd better be good.)

—I don't suppose this is so difficult for you. Not like it is for me of course, god no. It's not as if you'll want to scratch my eyes out, is it.

(.)

—Now it's all in the hands of, the hands of . . . Michael's hands.

It's in them, all in them. Well no it isn't just that, but that's no concern of yours, anyway the For Sale sign is due any moment and what I really mustn't forget is can you give me your keys. Thank you, thank you. Now go now. That's all, that's it. Oh have you seen Millie today, she should go to the vet. You don't want a cat do you? Maybe the vet should just top her.

Inventory
Bring down the curtain, sweep the stage, go to bed.

Having Czeched his till, straightened up the chocolates and biscuits, replaced the items on the shelves, swept the floor, Mirek has gone home and to bed. Ekaterina too has gone home to bed.

—In all the arguing Kat, for a moment I thought I'd lost you.

—You are a trial sometimes. I never want to hear again about the Mavrocordatos fishing through the ice. But I love you.

—Yes you love me.

—Silly.

—And I love you.

—*And*. Not but.

—Not but. It was you who said *But*. Now I rather wish I had. But I love you.

—You're just saying it, Mirek. Seeing how it sounds.

—How does it sound?

—Fishy. Do you know what I want? I want to feel free. Yes. I feel free. Stretch out in bed and be free. What about you?

—I don't know. I don't make decisions.

—But you're stubborn. You Czechs. Walk round softly and quietly and deep down—

—Look who's talking.

—Okay that's it, it's over. You Czechs are all the same.

—Over? What Czechs, all Czechs?

—I was just kidding.

—Is there any more to say?

—How did your work go today?

—The work work? It didn't. Tomorrow it will.

—I'll turn out the light.

—I'll paint you. Tomorrow. We'll start tomorrow.

—No sitting around, I've no time for sitting around.

—Standing. You could have a cigarette if you like.

—I've stopped, don't say you'd forgotten.

—I'd forgotten.

—There's a word for people like you.

—I know: perfect.

—That isn't it.

—Was I close?

—I'm asleep now. I'll tell you tomorrow. After you paint me.

—It could be my masterpiece.

—As long as you don't have me hang around in the rain.

—Would I ever? What an idea.

In the dark a wintry fog has come down. There is little light, partly as the local streetlighting has been curtailed. There is someone, hard to make out. But yes, she has a hat on like that sometimes, and there are the dark trousers she wears. It's definitely Marion, Marion with the umbrella-stand. She seems to be wrestling with it, hauling it off by its ears.

She's stopped. Why is she stopping? Her industry has gouged bright marks on her driveway. If they're bright in the dark, who knows how they'll look in the daytime. She scuffs her shoes at them. She takes a broom to them. She props the broom against the garage door and rings her own doorbell, presumably seeking help. She takes out her keys and looks at them, puts them away. She inspects her hands. When the door doesn't open she gets hold of the armadillo again, now by the neck, and drags it. She will have it stand by her door, and put canes in it, and long grasses, as if it had always been there.

AUDE SEIGNE

Walking Toward the Red Church

REGARDING A NOTEBOOK used during the
preparation and undertaking of a trip around Europe in 2005

Yellow, transparent, matte, spiraled. You chose this notebook
because you wanted something that would be able to withstand
the rain. On the first page, you drew fourteen different flags—all
of them more or less European—the fourteen flags that represented
your trip. You'd just finished the *bac*, your head was filled with an
enormous amount of knowledge that would be forgotten over the
next several weeks, and you'd learned the following expression,
attributed to de Gaulle: "Europe, from the Atlantic to the Urals."

It needed verification.

You went all the way to North Cape with V., you met up with
S. in Russia, in Ukraine, on a whim, J. came to join you. He would
later take his leave in Romania, and you would find yourself alone
again to make your way slowly back to Switzerland. You'd copied
out the symbology of the cardinal points in your notebook, telling
yourself that the progression of your itinerary—North-East-South-
West—had a certain logic to it:

North = look for obstacles to test one's resolve
East = find one's origins
South = look for calm
West = find what the future holds

You left without knowing when you'd be back. In the margin of
a page, you'd written:

Monday October 24th 8:15 > uni?
Beginning of classes: Thursday the 27th

The yellow notebook wasn't for writing, it was meant, rather, to help with planning. Inside, you'd copied out schedules for connections between the cities you were hoping to visit:

R5527 / Eger 7:15 > Füzesabony 7:32
D530 / Füzesabony 7:54 > Košice 10:04

You'd pasted notes inside from various forums found online— *Romania to Ukraine without passing through Moldova?*—and drawn up a table for foreign exchange rates, which you filled out during your visits to cybercafés. Under each destination, you put down suggestions for things to do and places to stay:

Just a quick stop in Plzeň? > beer
Olomouc: walk from the red church towards the other red church
General advice SWEDEN: mosquitoes! mygga repellant (mygga = Swedish for mosquito)

You also put down, throughout the duration of your trip, a list of criteria for an ideal youth hostel, a meticulous record of your spending, and a list of the rivers associated with the cities you'd passed through:

St. Petersburg ←→ Volga
Kiev ←→ Dnipro
Prague ←→ Vltava

You preferred a place by the window—tucked inside a square consisting of four seats—so that you could put your forehead against the glass, even though it wasn't particularly comfortable, even though you'd only do it for short stretches of time. The several-centimeter space between the headrest and the wall bothered you, and as a solution you often filled it in with various pieces of clothing. You'd feel the window's vibrations against your temple, the cold glass against your shoulder, the black rubber framing the pane against your arm. You dreamed of railways and highways, of grids. And in the spaces between all these overlapping networks, you dreamed of untouched lands, of cartographic holes that no one else had ever before seen. You could feel yourself moving along these lines, a tightrope walker in love with the void, perilously close to falling back into the real world. You were a daydreamer.

You developed surefire techniques to fall asleep without fear of being robbed: wrap the strap of your backpack around your ankle and lay out across two seats in the fetal position or on your back, your legs against the window. Once, during a twenty-five hour train ride from Trondheim to Narvik on which there wasn't a single seat left available, you grew so exhausted that you spread your mattress beneath two back-to-back pairs of seats and transformed the space into a dirty little cabin, where the state of being horizontal never-theless helped you drift off to sleep. You carried a second bag over your chest—smaller, equipped with a shoulder strap—which con-tained your first cell phone, your wallet, and this yellow notebook. Losing your phone would have been only a minor disappointment. The notebook, however, was another story.

You liked saying that you slept best on couchettes, soothed by the twin sound of the rails which, for you, was reminiscent of heartbeats. Truthfully, however, you were usually so eager to gaze out upon a new landscape, so excited by the coming arrival in a new city, that sleep rarely came easily. The morning after a night train—to Helsinki, to Simferopol, to Krakow—was marked by a distinctive, aching, ethereal form of fatigue.

On a train from Kiev to Simferopol, J's leg rubbed casually up and down against your own, and the light was so white, the sound of the tracks so soft, that it was as if time had come to a standstill.

One day in a hostel, you discovered—was this in Bulgaria or Slovenia?—a copy of the hefty *European Rail Timetable*, which con-tained the train schedules for the whole of Europe and could have saved you a great deal of space in your notebook. You spent a long time bent over it, amazed by the vast store of information beneath your eyes, hoping that someone would come up and ask the right question. To which you could proudly respond: "Keszthely to Balatonfüred? The next train leaves at 10:41. Change at Tapolca." But the book wasn't for sale, and anyway your monk-like ritual of transcription suited you just fine: find a cybercafé, go to the Deutsche Bahn website—the most comprehensive for European timetables—copy out the schedules in your yellow notebook, read your e-mails, write to friends following a well-thought-out rotation which guaranteed that no one could piece together the puzzle of your itinerary. This was also at the beginning of Europe's discovery of Sudoku. Your hometown newspaper published new quizzes daily, you'd visit their website to copy them out. They helped fill the hours when you grew tired of reading by the window, when you needed to push away questions regarding your life "afterwards."

In Romania, you developed a fondness for the local trains that traveled with their doors open, allowing air to circulate through the cars so as to provide relief from the stifling summer heat. The trains would sometimes stop in the middle of a field, and you could look outside and see people coming out from the tall grass, throwing bags on board and hoisting themselves up and into the train, which was far too high due to the absence of a platform. There was one such stop that lasted three hours. Your jeans stuck to the leather of your seat, sweat ran between your breasts. You were sharing a compartment with a Romanian family whose child pointed to you while asking questions of his parents. It made you laugh, it made them laugh, everyone laughed and sweated together. A conversation soon started up, it was a pocket dictionary for you, gestures and smiles for them, they were also confused by this prolonged stop.

You listened to "Moonlight Sonata" by Beethoven, to Raphaël who'd just released "Caravane". He sang, "It's good to be alive today on the same planet as you" and this "you" took on the face of N. while you were on a Swedish train, of I. on a Slovakian train, of P. on a Hungarian train, of J. a bit of everywhere, all the time, and with an overwhelming intensity. If a landscape could preserve some trace of one's thoughts, Europe in 2005 would have been covered with these names, with *that* name.

42

Today it seems that if you touched the notebook in a certain way, if you found the right combination of tenderness and pressure, the music you once listened to would come seeping out from it. Among Raphaël's songs, there was also "On the Road," like the book by Kerouac, the manuscript of which could have been unwound along its eponymous location. As for you, you unwound your thoughts along the rails, you watched your life rise up over the Russian forests, over the Ukrainian plains, over the Slovak mountains, you experienced a sensation of immensity and timelessness as never before. At the time, you weren't afraid of lofty words, of high-minded ideas, your emotions were complete and intact and you were blissfully ignorant of the destructive powers contained in nuance and analysis.

Ten years have gone by.
You rediscover your notebook.
You set off again by train towards the North.
You carry with you the yellow notebook.
For reading, or as a talisman.

T. stands on the platform in the freezing night air. You send him a kiss through the window, you hold back your tears. You'd been so excited to travel alone again, but now you wonder why you're forcing this upon yourself, wonder what person inside of you you're trying to seek out. You run your thumb along the edge of the notebook. At a first glance, it seems as if the words contained within were written by someone else.

On the night train to Hamburg, you wear a hooded fleece, a ridiculously comfortable piece of clothing given to you by your mother at Christmas. You reserved a seat by the window, the thick pullover cushions your arm against the rubber on the window frame while heat rises up from the floor and along the length of your body. You write an e-mail on your phone—it will be sent during the night with the next available Wi-Fi connection—you take out your computer, you try watching an American TV series filmed in Seoul, Nairobi, London, Berlin, and San Francisco. You can't get into it. You think about the trip you took ten years earlier. You remember how simple life was back then. Today you always have at least two chargers with you, it's extremely difficult to remain disconnected for more than a couple of days. You reconsider this idea, it's nothing but cheap romanticism. You tell yourself that the world's grid has simply condensed.

In the yellow notebook you find individual pieces of paper, slipped between the cover and the first page:

- a green Hungarian business card with, on the reverse side, fares scribbled out by a receptionist whose gentle movements you can clearly recall;
- a receipt from a cybercafé with, on the reverse side, a password;
- a pink ticket with Cyrillic writing on which the only word you understand is "Saint Petersburg," with, on the reverse side, the number of a certain Eugene, for the second time;
- two unused metro tickets from Prague, with, on the reverse side, nothing.

Certain sheets of paper were ripped out from notebooks similar to your own, which people like yourself had filled with schedules, contacts, memories. You wonder where these cousin notebooks are today. Or should one speak rather of grafting than of blood ties? And the several centimeters ripped out from the pages of your own notebook, are they still conserved in other notebooks? How many of your fellow travelers live in the texts and thoughts of other people?

At dawn, you see that compartment has filled up. Each seat is now occupied by a sleeper who's repeated the same ritual as you— try out every position, fill the space behind the seat with clothes, put on headphones, pull down your hood. You're all more or less the same age. Half of them later take out a notebook, in which thoughts get recorded between moments spent looking out the window. You smile for two reasons. First, because the immense pleasure of waking up on a train, something you haven't experienced in years, fills your heart with joy. Second, because this multitude of notebooks reminds that you're not so unique after all.

The anxiety of departure—felt by that strange girl inside you—has vanished. You now grasp the notebook with reassurance, thinking that it can do little more than offer practical information and spark a mild emotional reaction. However, you're surprised by:

- a page of contacts on which people you've forgotten wrote their names and the circumstances under which you met: a nun on the train from Oradea to Budapest, *A. (from Vienna with a cough), I., the weird guy from Finland;*
- a page on which someone tried to write your name, several times, in a child's handwriting peppered with stars. You think you can remember the boy who'd written out these lines, smiling at you as he did, and you feel a sharp sensation of nostalgia in your stomach;
- a full page titled "Guidelines to Lund" compiled by a certain Mårten;
- Eastern Europe's "Top Ten" according to Lonely Planet, which you copied up till number five;
- sentences useful for buying a train ticket in Russian. You'd placed the notebook on a ticket counter in front of an employee, who then wrote down her response inside. Your notebook thus contains the writing of a Ukrainian woman who worked at the Kiev train station's ticket office in 2005.

In Hamburg, you change trains and have a coffee—something you wouldn't have done before, when every cent counted. You find yourself caught up in the flow of morning commuters, suits and handbags, foldable scooters and tablets. Near Copenhagen, you cross the border and look out over the sea. Someone asks you in a mumble if you're reading the *MetroXpress* set in front of you, you signal that you're not, acting as if this was also your daily commute, when in fact you've already crossed an entire country. On the train to Stockholm you look out the window so as not to stare at an absurdly good-looking man on the other side of the corridor, who takes out exactly the same objects as yourself: a book, a Moleskine notebook, a travel guide, a thermos—it becomes a little ridiculous, this mimicry. The train passes through a tunnel and the two of you meet each other's eyes in the window's reflection. You both laugh and look away.

There's something in the notebook you'd completely forgotten about: a page filled with SMS's, copied out by hand a decade ago because your phone couldn't hold more than thirty. In this sentimental selection, you'd kept messages that today seem impossible for you to have received:

V: *"It's normal for you to be afraid. I'm going to miss you too"*
P: *"i am sure i can find a way to visit at some point"*
I: *"Feeling bad that I missed your message . . . But you had fun with those Polish guys . . . Damn . . . :-D*
Your sister: "miss u nerd"
J: *"2 bad we couldnt express ourselves btr"*

You think back on these relationships that no longer exist, or that have changed from what they once were. Today V. wouldn't say that she misses you, nor would J. say that a potential love story together had been thwarted because neither of you were able to express yourself. You know that I. works in Afghanistan and San Francisco, you know that P. got married. You wonder how many voices are trapped in this notebook, how many different lives you might have led if each one of these encounters had been taken to its natural ending. You wonder how you were able to put all these questions to the side, how you managed to come out so emotionally unscathed from all this. You'd been looking so straight ahead that you ignored the possibilities. You thought you could shut them away in this notebook, open it every now and then, brush against the ghosts that escaped from it and then order them back inside without being affected. It was simple. Now, you're not so sure. It was definitely you, whatever you might feel now, who went through all that. When you get off the train at Luleå, you feel that same old innocence—your backpack is still too heavy and you marvel at the snow falling down through the twilight as if it were your first time away from home. Taking a selfie in front of the Swedish railway company's vintage locomotive doesn't change how you feel in the slightest.

Sometimes, you dream about trains: Quimper to Moscow with friends, Tehran to Beijing via Delhi with T. Sometimes, you open the train app on your phone, just for the pleasure of knowing the schedule from Zurich to Belgrade. You read on the Internet that the body's cells regenerate at different speeds, depending on the organ. Those in the brain and in the heart are the slowest—they take more than ten years. And so only your brain, your heart, and this notebook made that trip ten years earlier, which is summed up on the final page:

16 books
44 rooms/campsites
282 hours spent on trains.

Your skin today, strictly speaking, never experienced those trains.

TRANSLATED FROM THE FRENCH BY JESSE ANDERSON

IZARA BATRES

Bureaucracy

Look, I'm probably too sensitive about this kind of thing . . . Or I find it hard to get used to it . . . Maybe it would be better to start from the beginning. Yes, that would be better . . .

It all started when I went to apply to change course at my faculty. The secretaries in there were pretty aloof. They spent the day talking on the telephone, and when you approached them, you were lucky if they didn't bite your head off. In the end, that's what usually happened.

I worked mornings and studied in the afternoons, so for me to make it to the faculty office took a great effort and meant taking time off work. I reckoned that the sooner I could resolve everything, the better. So I approached the only secretary who was momentarily free and said to her, "Excuse me, I'd like to change course." I remember she looked at me as if I'd murdered one of her children and snapped, "Honey, to do that I need your ID, a photocopy of your registration slip, a copy of your transcript, a copy of a bank slip, a copy of a payslip, a photocopy of the electoral register, a photocopy of your student card, proof of fee payment . . . " She carried on talking as though she were a machine gun and I tried to take a mental note of all the items she listed. She finished up by saying, "without all of those, I can't do a thing for you." And she picked up the telephone to make a call.

I tried to explain to her that I hadn't been told I'd need to bring even half of the documents she'd just listed, but the secretary sat looking at me for a few seconds, as if she didn't fully understand the reason for my presence.

"Look, sweetheart, I'm telling you," she said, "I am telling you that without those, I can't help you, do you understand me?"

"But . . . "

"Go on, you bring me them, okay?"

And she carried on with her phone conversation.

Two days later, I returned with all the required documents. I was proud of how quickly I had managed to get them—it had taken me two full, intensive afternoons, skipping classes—but there I was, and I had decided to get this business over with as quickly as possible. I approached the booth occupied by the same secretary, placed the mountain of perfectly ordered papers on the table, and looked her in the eye with total confidence and a satisfied smile, even allowing myself to drum my fingers on the wooden surface. She held my gaze with an aversion which, little by little, turned to hatred. I withdrew my hand. I decided that, if I was going to take this woman on, I would need all my wits about me. I remember that moment of my life perfectly, almost as though I were reliving it:

"Hi," I said, given that she hadn't greeted me. "Now I've brought everything you . . . "

"Good morning," she cut me off.

"Good morning," I repeated, and gulped. "I've brought everything now that you . . . "

"I can't hear you at all," she spat.

"Good morning," I said in a louder voice, wanting the nightmare to end. "I've brought everything I need and I'd like to change course . . . "

"ID, copy of registration slip, copy of bank slip, copy of transcript, copy of the faculty card, copy of family registration . . . "

"Yes, yes, yes, I already know, it's all here, here it is."

"We'll see, child, but what is it you're trying to do . . . " she asked while leafing through the papers, picking them up between finger and thumb and dropping them as though they disgusted her.

"Well, I . . . I want to change . . . I mean I want to add a subject . . . "

"But let's see, I'm telling you, with what you've brought here, you can't do a thing, you get me? Do you understand what I'm saying?"

"What? But I've brought the copy of my registration and the

bank slip and the photocopy of . . . ”

"But why on earth are you coming in here and dumping all this on my desk? Why on earth, what a nuisance!”

"But this is what you told me . . . ”

"But I'm not talking about what I may or may not have told you, I don't care about that, you get me? I don't care a bit, sweetie, not a bit, but what I'm telling you is that this is no use to me at all, do you understand what I'm saying?”

I stood staring at her, flabbergasted.

"Do you hear me? Do you understand?”

"But you see I brought everything and I had to ask to leave work to come here and . . . ”

"No, hon', I didn't ask you about your problems, 'cause down here, problems, we've got 'em all, love, and you're old enough aren't you, old enough at this stage to be able to get yourself organized and not come down here wasting our time . . . ”

"Look!” I insisted, "I also have the family registration, my residency card . . . ”

"It's like it goes in one ear and out the other with you . . . I'm telling you this is worthless, I can't do a thing with all this . . . ”

"But . . . ”

"And you come in here taking out papers that have nothing to do with anything, come in here with pointless documents! And as for these . . . invading my desk, you're messing up my space!”

"But . . . ”

"You pick these up, go home, and next week you come back in, and you bring what you're meant to bring . . . ”

"But, what are you saying? Everything's here!”

"No, excuse me, everything's not here, eh, sweetie, you come in here now and tell the professionals who've worked here our whole lives what's what, questioning us . . . ”

"What do you mean this isn't everything?” I asked, terrified.

She looked at me as if I were asking her which was my right hand.

"I'm telling you, because it seems you just don't get it,” she said, looking at me as though about to sentence me to a firing squad, "you're missing the receipt for the transfer of your transcript, honey."

"But you didn't tell me I needed . . . "

"Come on now, bring it here tomorrow, eh," she said, suppressing her irritation as she began tidying the papers on her desk.

"The thing is I have to try to get the time off work . . . and you didn't tell me!"

The murderous look once more.

"Sweetie, spare me your life story, okay? You understand what I'm saying? I don't need to hear about your troubles, 'cause down here, we've all got troubles. Or maybe you think I've got nothing else to do, maybe you think I come in here to scratch my ass. In case you didn't realize, this is your problem, maybe it's going to be mine too now . . . 'cause that's all I was missing, for your problem to be mine. Of course, it is . . . "

It was no use repeating that, in the endless list of requirements she'd given me, none of these documents had been mentioned. She started arranging things in her drawers, calmly, as she carried on complaining about her bad luck, and I walked out of there wanting to set myself on fire.

I decided to go to the bank to complete the paperwork necessary to move things along. When I arrived there, however, the woman behind the glass scowled at me.

"Excuse me, I'd like a certified fee payment," I said.

"To pay the fees we need the invoice from the faculty."

"Which invoice?"

"The payment invoice. What else?"

"The pink slip?"

"Yes, it's usually pink."

"They told me I'd be given that here . . . "

The woman looked at me as though she were dealing with someone who was mentally challenged and said:

"Okay, honey, but we don't give those out in here, you have to go to the department of education."

I went to the department of education, they gave me a form, they sent me to the administration, to the ministry of education, to the unions; I visited the Madrid courts, a police station, my old secondary school, a municipal dog shelter. When I finally got my secondary-school certificate, the transfer record document, and the form I needed, I once again asked permission from work to return to the faculty.

There I was told that the only person who could see me was the one who was dealing with my case ("my case"), so I had to tough it out once again with that woman hiding behind her dreary desk, reeking of nail polish and sucking the life out of me.

"Excuse me," I said to the secretary, "Now I have the . . . "

"Good morning . . . "

"Good morning . . . Now I have the . . . I have everything you asked me for."

I plopped down everything I'd brought on her desk, carefully, so she wouldn't accuse me of invading her space again. She looked at the pile of papers reluctantly, with a hint of disgust, as if they were the rags of a leprous beggar who'd sneaked into her house.

"Well, that's not what you need anymore, eh."

"What are you talking about, not what I need?"

"This isn't what you need, this is no good."

"What do you mean?"

"Because of the new law."

Her menacing look warned me she might smash my head through the screen of her computer if I asked her one more thing, so I decided to retreat. I waited in line for fifteen minutes so that another secretary could explain to me why these documents were no longer any good to me.

"Because they've amended Article 27 of the education law," the other secretary explained, in a professional manner and a robotic tone, "so now your transfer file's worthless, now you have to request a validation from the administration."

"A validation . . . ? And what do I have to do to get that?"

"Well, you need to go to the Ministry so they can give you the form, then pay some fees, request an appointment for the replacement . . . "

I went back to the Ministry, and from there to the bank, to the university, to the vice-chancellor's office, to the town hall, to the health center, and the Credit Agricole Bank of Portugal. At night I dreamed of a huge desk covered in papers and secretaries. They were all cutting and pasting, entering data into the computer, and more data. Lengthy codes of conduct, decrees, and by-laws were on display from the desk to the floor, and the space was filled with the shouting, complaints, and questions of the innumerable students crowded in front of the desks.

Suddenly, the face of the secretary in charge of "my case" could be made out. For the first time, she was looking at me in a pleasant way. She gestured warmly to me to come over, and then, in a very gentle voice she said: "the process will take no time at all; you needn't worry about a thing. Everything is settled now. Everything is settled . . . " I smiled from ear to ear, and she held out her hand to seal the deal, an unusually warm hand, and her smile was open and serene, a sure sign that the process had reached a satisfactory resolution. "Good luck, you can go now, everything will work out well. Everything will work out well . . . " She carried on smiling and kept repeating this phrase, but her friendly expression began to twist and transformed her face into a monstrous grimace, and then I could see she was trying to grab for the stapler without my noticing. Suddenly, she pounced on me shouting: "I'm telling you, honey!" and, just when she was on the verge of stapling my nose, I woke up sweating and screaming.

Some days later, when I finished the process of gathering the documents, I asked yet again for leave from work, where they were threatening to fire me, and I went back to the university once more.

"Good morning. Now I've definitely brought everything," I said to the secretary in a loud and determined voice.

She looked indifferently at the three folders full of papers.

"But the deadline's already passed now, eh?"

"What . . . "

"Of course, sweetie, the extension only goes up to the first fortnight of December . . . "

"*What*?!"

"I'm telling you, you won't get in at this stage. When they

changed the law, they changed the time-window too," she explained, calmly, looking at me as if she didn't know me at all. "Come back in March, next year, you might be in time then, eh . . . you'll have to go through the application process again, and then—that's it."

"*What?!*"

She looked at me as if I'd just woken her from a siesta by roaring at her and she was seriously peeved.

"What bullshit!" I shouted, utterly infuriated. I want to be told why, why nobody told me anything about windows. Why? *Why?!*"

"And I want to be told why too," she replied, placing the nail varnish in the drawer, "why I have to put up with you people. I've got the patience of a bloody saint, you wouldn't believe it."

"But this . . . "

"It's like this, sweetheart, you speak English? I'm asking you a question, do you speak English?"

"Yes."

"Then look, I think I'm speaking to you in very clear English, eh . . . I mean really clear: you're going to pick up these papers and bring them home, you get me, you understand what I'm saying to you? And you get up and walk out that door, because you're really starting to get on my nerves now.'

"But I want to change course! I want to enroll!"

"To drop out?! Why, I mean, don't get me wrong, it's not my problem, but why sign up to another course only to drop out?"

"But . . . but what do you mean I'm going to drop out?! But you . . . but . . . "

Faced with the impossibility of articulating my profound despair, I stood there staring at the useless stack of papers on the desk, as though hypnotized.

"And what do I do with all this?" I asked, on the brink of tears.

"Watch what I'm going to do with this."

She scooped up the papers and, with a rapid movement, put them in a plastic bag and threw them in the bin.

I didn't utter a single word, just stood there facing her, staring . . .

"Oh man, please . . . Mari can you believe what we have to deal with," she said to her co-worker, who shook her head sympathetically in reply, resigned and apathetic. "The things we have to deal with, I mean come on, what we have to put up with, you hear me? I must be talking Chinese or something . . . "

"But . . . " I asked. I couldn't say another thing. Neither my words nor my breath would come.

"Really, what we have to put up with . . . Hey, Mari, what was I going to say: tell me, how was the wedding . . . "

"But . . . "

I gave up, and, when I was able to move again, I walked away slowly, with very small steps.

After that, I decided to drop my studies, and I focused on sewing for a few years. Now I sell flowers. All kinds and colors of flowers. Red flowers, flowers with golden petals, flowers with violet blooms, huge flowers like shrubs and small ones like tiny parcels, green flowers, great bunches of flowers with leaves . . . The flowers are beautiful. They are *so* beautiful . . .

TRANSLATED FROM THE SPANISH BY URSULA MEANY SCOTT

XABIER MONTOIA

My Mother Calls Me a Pirate

MY MOTHER SAYS I'm a pirate and whenever she says it, she runs her hand down my cheek and smiles at me. But I know she's sad and she only does it to make me feel better. And to show her that I appreciate her caress, I smile back at her. But she can't fool me because I know all too well that she and the hospital people say what they say so I won't be scared. And I'm not scared. I like it: when I put the black patch over the place where my eye used to be and get up to pee, I look into the bathroom mirror and think I look quite dashing. I take my father's hat and put it on my head and I remember my mother's words and I can almost feel the buccaneers from the book Rafa loaned me by my side. Besides, I think I've seen enough of this world up to now, and I'll have to see worse later on, even with just the one eye. If it were up to me, I would never move from this bed and I would sleep forever and I would never again open the one friendless eye that I do have. And I'd do the same thing with my ears too: put a finger in each and push hard so that no words or shouts or sounds could get in. Especially my parents'. They're often loud, and even if I can't hear well enough to tell what they're saying, I can guess well enough what they're saying to each other. My father is stingy. I've heard my mother say it many times, and he scolds my mother that she spends the money he gives her too easily. He says he had to work hard for it and my mother lets the money fly through her fingers and she buys lots of things we don't need and if things keep on like that, if something bad happens at home, we'll be left without a cent. But that's not true because my mother's very careful in the stores, and the things that other boys eat we can have only once in a long while because they're too expensive and because she's hard pressed to make it to the end of the month. My dad asks her to account for that too, after the accident. Apparently that was my mother's fault and apparently he'd told her long ago that no good would come of us going to Aunt Manuela's house. "How many times have I told you your spinster sister is crazy as a loon?" He shouts the question at her. "It would be better to just put her in Santa Ageda." And then he adds that she spends her whole day drinking. "After writing love letters for years and years, Manuela Bilbao finally got married . . . to the bottle!" My father laughs and my mother is sad again, and sometimes she starts to cry, saying for God's sake have a little pity. And then I get sad too because I love Aunt Manuela. She may be a wino, but she never drinks except at lunch and dinner and even though she's quite peculiar, she is in her right mind. She does nothing but write letters and that, in my opinion, does no one any harm and besides, she always welcomes us and every time we show up at her place she always makes egg crème caramel for us or gives us candy. And besides, the day I had the accident I didn't even go to my aunt's house. To her street, yes, to Herreria Street. But I didn't go up to her apartment. I met up with Pablo and Joxean and we took out the pieces of plastic we had saved and, since it had snowed a lot for two days, we went to the corner where we turn to go to Santa Maria and slid down from there on the plastic. We had done the same thing a few times before and until then nothing had ever happened to anyone. But it had to happen to me. I don't know exactly what happened. I was going downhill and where I should have gone straight I suddenly turned and immediately stopped against a stone step and hit the edge of it. In such a bad way that I scraped my left eye and lost it right there. But I'll say it again: it was not my aunt's fault, it was mine, and as my mother says, surely it was the will of God. "Nice God, that God of yours!" My dad gets mad at her whenever he hears her say things like that, and says for her to leave him alone and not take the Lord's name in vain and she's a big liar. And that's not true either, because my mother doesn't tell lies, or at least not big ones, and when she does tell them, it's just a small one at the most and always, always for my sake, to protect me. And he blames her for that too, that I'm such a mama's boy. And then my mother tells him that I'm ill and she has to take care of me. And

when he hears that, my father gets even angrier and he stops arguing and leaves the house, slamming the front door with a fierce
thump. He goes to the bar where his friends are and those are the
worst fights, the ones that end with my father going out. When my
parents start fighting, I get frightened waiting for that thump
because I know that as soon as my father goes out, our poor mother
will start crying. Iñaki is sleeping, but I can't. After spending the
whole day in bed, I'm wider awake than an owl at night and the
sound of my mother's sobs reaches me from the kitchen. I would
call for her to come here but I keep quiet so I don't wake my brother.
He'd hit me if I woke him up. Iñaki is bigger than I am and stronger, and he hits me whenever he feels like it and I can't complain if
I don't want to get hit again. Thank God he spends most of his time
out of the house and that way I can take it easy. Too easy sometimes
because I feel lonely and I'm often bored, and since I've read all the
comics and books, I don't know what to do with myself. If my
mother doesn't go out, I call for her to keep me company for a
while. But often she has to make lunch and she doesn't pay much
attention to me and goes back to the kitchen again almost right
away. Some mornings she brings me the radio so I won't be bored
while she goes to the store, but seldom, because she knows my
father wouldn't like it and if he found out about it he'd get good
and angry. My father gets angry easily, for any reason. It takes very
little for something to get on his nerves and then he starts shouting.
My mother asks him for money and he starts swearing immediately
and he won't stop until he sees my mother's tears and he'll do the
same thing if he notices that someone has been messing with his
things. And that can happen easily because everything in the house
is his and earned by the sweat of his brow, according to what he
tells us every single day without end. "You all are living in my house
and while you live here you'll do what I say and if you don't like it,
you know where the door is." That's why my mother doesn't often
bring me the radio. Because she's afraid of my father and if he came
in and found the radio missing from the kitchen shelf, he would be
furious and would accuse her of always making him look ridiculous
in front of us. And besides, he doesn't even like music at all. At least
not the music I like. It's hippie music apparently and he hates

hippies so much but who on earth knows why. He only likes tangos and since he's such a bad singer, you can tell he's in a good mood if he sings. And then he starts going on and on about tangos. He loves Carlos Gardel above all others, and since he's happy every time he says that, my mother says, just in fun, that he loves him better than us. And she'll say it's just in fun but this is what I think: he does love that annoying Gardel better than he loves us and that's why I hate tangos so much. Because they're for people like my father. For bitter people. I, on the other hand, like happy music, the music that National Radio puts on before the news at half past two, precisely the kind that my father calls noise: hippie music or whatever you want to call it. Before I had the accident, the music I had to listen to with my ear glued to the radio and my eye on the clock so I could turn it off as soon as I heard my father come through the door. I'm a huge fan. Especially of black music: Otis Redding and Wilson Pickett and all those guys. My school friends like them best too and when we'd sing their songs and it was time for the brass instruments to play, we'd take our rulers and put them up to our mouths and play the trumpet on them. Hippie music. And to tell the truth, their music isn't the only thing my father talks about. There's no other topic in the air lately and tongues are wagging among my mother and the neighbors, and my aunt came over to our house too, and they won't talk about anything else. Apparently they have a place in Zaramaga and it seems that the bellies of the girls that go in there swell as fast as can be. Because apparently in that place they have lots of *orgies* and they smoke drugs besides. I've seen them in the newspaper and they look pretty grimy to me, these people with their long matted hair and beards. I like the part about the flowers, though. But maybe the ones from here aren't like that, because it's only Americans in the newspapers. They had plenty to write about them anyway. A thousand things to say about them and none of them good. The newspapers are pretty irritating, but after reading comic books so many times, I pick up the papers and read them almost from front to back. Especially the sports section and *Tarzan* of course, which could never be irritating, but I've read them so many times that now I have to read the rest of the paper and so that's why I know about the hippies here. Not as much as I'd like, unfortunately. I'd really like to know more. They could at least put in a picture. But it's all just words and more words and I have to resign myself to looking at foreigners. And I get bored again and I start calling for my mother again, and since she doesn't pay any attention to me, I get angry and then I keep calling my mother more and more angrily in the end. That's in the mornings, because in the afternoon my mother keeps me company. She sits on the side of the bed and sews and a little later, around five, my aunts come over and while the three of them sew, they chat and sometimes they swallow their words so I won't understand and finish their sentences with "well, you know!" But they're wrong, because even though it might not look like it, I understand everything they say and it makes me laugh to see the trouble they go to, the way they talk around things as if I were a little kid. For example, to say that the hippies get their girlfriends pregnant, they'll say that the girls go in thin and come out fat or something like that, thinking I won't understand, and I'm laughing my head off to myself about how stupid they are. And they do the same thing when they're talking about Aunt Manuela: half truths and trying to disguise things. I love those afternoon chats though. They entertain me and when they mention anything, even if it's the most trivial of trifles, I'm happy just listening to them. Sometimes I close my eyes and fall asleep to the sound of their voices. It's like a lullaby. But in the mornings I'm awake and I close my eyes and nothing happens. I hear the same sounds and the distant sounds of their radios and the neighbors'. And with my eyes closed it comes to me that I will never be able to get up from this bed and I will never be able to open my eyes again and that in addition to my left eye, I've lost the right as well. I'm all alone in the universe and everything is dark around me. But even with my eyes closed I can't close my ears. So some mornings I think I hear the sound of my mother crying in the kitchen, and it's a shock because my mother never cries in front of us, and it fills me with sadness. You can see it in the circles under her eyes. I notice things like that since I've been ill: she gets dark circles under her eyes and her eyes go very bright. One of these days I won't allow any such thing, and as soon as my father makes my mother cry the least little bit, I'll go right over to him and give him a good punch in the nose and that'll teach him to upset my mother. Because that man understands no other language. And one of these days I'll get up from this bed and then even with just my one eye I'll go to the hippies and I'll stay with them forever because I read somewhere that they like pirates too, and that's all I am: a lone and friendless pirate.

TRANSLATED FROM THE BASQUE BY KRISTIN ADDIS

MIHA MAZZINI

Avro Lancaster

"THE LORD IS watching you! We're not alone! He sees everything!" Nona pointed to the crucifix on the wall. Jesus seemed totally engrossed in the wound oozing blood down his ribs, but the boy still lowered his head, petrified. He closed his eyes and could still see the waxy body of Christ nailed to the charcoal-black wood. A few minutes later he heard his grandmother stiffly turn around and continue the unintelligible gurgle of her reading from the *Lives of the Saints.*

With Nona, being good entailed endless hours stuck in the corner between the bed and the balcony window. Carefully sliding along on his buttocks to the foot of the bed, he gazed at the cross, doubting the suffering Christ was paying him any attention whatsoever. He turned to the sky and at first thought that his eyes still held the afterimage of the cross that seemed to be floating before him, then realized that the object out there was something else, a metallic cross reflecting the sun. He pressed his cheek against the glass until it disappeared from his field of vision.

He'd once asked Nona about the things flying in the sky, but she merely waved her hand scornfully and snorted, "Argh! Contraptions, machines! Carry people! Human vanity!" She crossed herself twice as she always did whenever she became angry.

It took until a new cross came flying over. This one left a thick trail across the sky. There must be some kind of fire inside the cross, it was probably transporting people to Hell. Nona was right. He never dared question, but a small voice inside him often disputed with her, terrified, whispering, spilling out his doubts and taking flight before he had a chance to suppress it. It was particularly clamorous when his grandmother talked to spirits he couldn't see, or when she started predicting who would step through the door the next moment and never did. Nona would forget all about her prophecy, only to remember it when the person actually did turn up. "See, I told you! What did I just tell you?" Most often it was Mother's arrivals she'd predict, late in the evening when she was due back from work. In Nona's prophecies her other children were either dying or being injured in accidents, though they kept coming around to visit alive and intact.

Nona would often read from the *Lives of the Saints* to the boy, but she never liked answering questions about the world outside. She'd mention sin and wave her hand in front of her nose as if trying to get rid of a horrible smell. Whenever they went out for a walk, the boy would hurry across the block with his head down so that he would only hear the other kids' caustic remarks, without allowing them to exacerbate his shame by pulling faces at him as well. Once out of town, they'd walk alongside the railroad and occasionally a train full of people would ride past. The boy would wave until his hand felt numb.

Some of these trains were pulled along by engines that also had smoke coming out of them, but the people at the windows sat peacefully, slept, some even smiled. Was it possible that such a train could also fly like a bird? The boy shook his head. He'd have to ask Uncle Vinko, the only one of mother's brothers who ever talked to him, and who knew so much about everything.

*

When he played, he used his plastic truck to imitate the train as well as the metal crosses in the sky. Bees and flies were the only airborne things he ever had the chance to observe at close range, so he pressed the sides of his tongue against his palate and "Bzzzzzzz," the toy slowly flew past the bed, circled around, and then returned. He used his pencils to draw both crosses, the one in the sky and the one on the wall, placed the pages next to each other and compared them. The black one was easy to draw, but the one from the sky eluded depiction. He left Jesus out of the drawing and asked his forgiveness through prayer.

Some words stick and won't go away. Several times over the following days he heard himself say, "The black one is easy to draw."

Nona liked to explain the workings of the mind: we carry an angel on our right shoulder, a devil on the left, both of them constantly whisper things in our ear. But this voice was coming from inside him and he was unable to judge whom it belonged to.

He kept repeating the sentence—when Nona sent him to fetch potatoes from the cellar, when they sat in the kitchen peeling them, when he was playing with the broken rod of a lost wheelbarrow, when he was drawing or gazing out of the window as his grandmother fell asleep reading:

"The black one is easy to draw."

*

It took a number of days before he mustered the courage to slowly pull the chair up to the cabinet during grandmother's usual afternoon nap.

The following day he stepped up on the chair.

A day later, he pulled himself up onto the cabinet and had a close look at Jesus.

If he was sick, Mother went along to church with Nona on Sundays instead of him. She always looked annoyed. Didn't want any dealings with priests, she'd always say, before closing the door and leaving him alone, adding that they'd be back soon.

He needed to be alone, and the only way to achieve this was through sin. He hesitated and tormented himself, kept telling himself that both Nona and Mother were able to see into his thoughts. Pretending he wasn't feeling well, he could hardly believe it when they left. He had second thoughts and wondered whether it would be safest just to stay under the blankets, but he could already see his hand throwing back the bedclothes.

*

"Bzzzzzzz!"

How his black cross flew. He held it with his thumb and index finger, mounted a rather shabby-looking plastic figurine of a clown on it, and flew him off either to Hell or on a trip somewhere, depending on the day—he still couldn't decide about the purpose of the crosses in the sky. He flew low, never above the edge of the bed, and kept looking over at Nona. The first few days his heart plunged into his intestines every time Nona approached the cabinet, looked toward the crucifix on the wall, crossed herself, and muttered a greeting to the Lord. She'd often said she didn't see far-away things very well, but the boy couldn't imagine that there was anything in the crammed apartment that could be described as *far away*.

He was much less worried about Mother, he could not recall her ever looking over to the wall.

How his cross flew!

"Bzzzzzzz!"

Jesus did not strike him with a thunderbolt either. He continued to pore over his mortal wound and didn't appear to be bothered that he was now nailed to a cross that was merely drawn on the wall.

*

Uncle Vinko stepped over to the boy's corner and crouched.

"How are you, pal?" he asked, giving him a smile broad enough to show off his golden tooth. It was fashionable for men to smooth their hair with brilliantine, but after applying it Vinko would deliberately ruffle his, making it swirl above his pointy ears. As even the boy's mother would admit, with his moustache trimmed into a triangle and his tanned skin, Vinko looked like a movie star. He drove a truck and had seen the world. Only when he was around did Nona smile, and her eyes gleamed, though her mouth was always busy uttering warnings: "Sinner! Vinko, you're such a sinner!"

The boy forgot all about his secret and right away showed his uncle his new toy.

"Bzzzzzzz!"

"Oh, an airplane!" Vinko said.

The boy stared at him.

"What's up?" Vinko was surprised.

"There's lots of them . . . in the sky."

Vinko ruffled the boy's hair affectionately. "Pal," he laughed. "Lots? You ain't seen nothing! They'd fill the sky during the war. Cover the sun!"

The boy's jaw dropped and, as he always would in such cases, Uncle Vinko used his index finger to push it back up.

"You're not at the dentist, pal."

"Are there people inside? Like in a train?"

"Yes."

"Alive?"

"Yes, of course! What did you think?"

"They get in and . . . travel?"

"Yes, Paris, London . . . Stockholm for porn . . . " his uncle grinned and winked, though he knew the joke meant nothing to the boy.

"Uncle, have you ever flown?"

"Of course!"

The boy's jaw dropped again. All he managed to do was stretch out his hand, making sure it was a man that stood before him, not an angel.

*

How they flew! The plastic clown, Mickey Mouse's head, a rolled-up slice of bread, a bow-legged cowboy who lost his horse and now fitted most comfortably onto the airplane. They visited places the boy had often heard of: Jerusalem, Bethlehem, Canaan, Nineveh, Rehoboth-Ir, Calah, Sodom and Gomorrah, as well as those lesser-known places, mentioned by Uncle Vinko: Paris, London, Stockholm and Forporn.

Once, trying to avoid the Great Deluge, they made a hard landing on top of Mount Ararat and the plane shattered. All of a sudden, he was left holding two broken bits of wood, one of them split halfway down its length. He stood in the corner facing the wall and cried silently until he calmed down enough to push the remnants of the cross into the gap under the baseboard.

*

No longer did he want to gaze at the sky.

*

"Pal, I have something for you!" Uncle Vinko produced a crumpled plastic bag.

"Put your hand inside!" he said. "Close your eyes first!"

The boy obeyed, tried to feel the elongated metal object but couldn't hide his excitement, opened his eyes and, holding his breath, carefully peeled away the bag.

Mouth agape, he faltered.

"An Avro Lancaster bomber, pal!" his uncle winked at him.

The boy held the airplane as gently as a breeze.

"They'd fill the sky," Vinko went on to say, "but even spotting a single one while I was lying in that fucking ditch, looking up and there it appeared, out of the blue—you're too young to understand—I knew I wasn't alone. That we weren't just abandoned in that shit. That there were others up above who would help us. They were coming and would end this shitty war. Later, in the final days, they filled the sky! Wow, what a sight! I was already a tanker by then. How we rushed toward Paris! In the evenings the Lancasters would fly out against the Krauts, real murder machines! They'd return at dawn. Pal . . . " He picked up the brightly painted aircraft made of thin metal and held it by the fuselage. "They returned . . You wouldn't believe it . . . Sometimes they were missing half a wing, others had broken tails. Some had so many holes you could see right through them. But they still flew. How many of our lives they saved! And how many Krauts they killed! But that's how it goes, pal!"

He gazed into the distance, breathing deeply, then sniffed loudly and gave the bomber to the boy.

"Pal, just remember, memories are like the taxman, you can never get rid of them. Right, now for something more joyful! See this watch?"

He pulled up the sleeve on his nylon shirt and tapped the glass with his finger.

"Look what it says here!" he said and stopped mid-upcoming-narrative. "You can't read, can you?"

The boy shook his head, though he did think that the first letter was a *D*.

"This is a Cartier, the real thing, pal. When you get to wear one you can say you made it in life. So there we are, rolling into Paris with our tanks, and I see this shop . . . "

*

For the first few days he didn't even dare pick up the plane, let alone play with it. He gradually worked up the courage and started to examine it more closely, though he still didn't touch it: The colorful roundels on the wings and the sides, letters, tiny men that were simply painted onto the seats in the cockpit and in the back. And wonder of wonders, plastic propellers that actually rotated.

He didn't want his eyes to distract him from the actual contact, so he closed them tight when he first touched it. The body was made of two halves, the top and bottom of the fuselage, bound together with tiny hooks. He obsessively copied out the writing on the underbelly of the aircraft onto paper: Avro Lancaster B Mk.I.

*

Whenever Nona was dying, she always called for a priest to administer the last rites. On such occasions Mother would put on her coat and run over to the only neighbor with a phone.

That night, the priest said he had an urgent case elsewhere and that Nona had been given her absolution and final sacrament so many times that he was sure she could manage without him.

Mother lingered in the doorway and suggested she call a doctor but Nona refused. She didn't want other people interfering in matters that were strictly between her and God.

They all lay awake in their separate beds. The moon didn't appear that night. Sometime after midnight, workers at the nearby ironworks tapped the blast furnace—an event Nona accompanied with loud screaming about the advent of the Devil.

Nona's moans occasionally extended into a whining groan. Mother clenched her fists and gritted her teeth, more than once repeating her suggestion to call a doctor, but Nona only wanted a priest. "He said NO! NO!" Mother shouted, then realized how late it was and looked around, checking whether the neighbors were already pressing their ears to the walls.

"Light me a candle!" Nona cried out.

Mother obeyed. She held the candle in her hand for a while and then placed it on the cabinet, right in front of Jesus. They all watched the flame flicker until Nona had another spasm.

"Go bring the priest! Get the priest!"

"NO! He said NO!"

Mother ran into the kitchen and closed the door behind her. Nona started to cry. She called out Jesus's name, then gradually replaced it with that of the boy.

"Are you here?"

"I am," the boy said and lifted himself up.

"Good, good."

A new bout of groaning took away her words. She gasped for air before she could continue:

"Give me the cross, let me die with it!"

Obediently he jumped up, ran to the kitchen, grabbed a chair—Mother was sitting at the table with a coffee, holding her head—closed the door behind him, and climbed onto the cabinet.

Then he remembered that there was no cross.

"The cross! The cross!" Nona shouted.

He knew that Mother would soon storm into the room to grab the cross, throw it at Nona, and demand some peace and quiet.

He ran his fingers over the drawing and for a moment thought of just handing Nona Jesus. But the figurine alone without its mount seemed rather lost and powerless, Nona would instantly see the difference.

"The cross! The cross!"

He pulled at the baseboard and brought the sad remnants into the half-light. They sat mockingly in his hand. Nona continued to groan and demand, grabbing at her abdomen and chest.

The chair in the kitchen creaked—was mother getting up?

The boy's hands shook, his gaze drifted across the room lit by the flickering light.

A reflection on the metal.

*

Nona grabbed the object the boy had passed her with both hands and pressed it against her chest, burying it in the layers of shawls and cardigans. She held onto it with all her strength, begging Jesus, God, and Holy Mary to help her, not to let the Devil come for her, to redeem her and when her time was up, save her soul.

Slowly she calmed down, stopped groaning, and fell asleep. Mother came out of the kitchen, caressed the boy and said, "Go back to sleep, everything's all right!"

As soon as both Nona and Mother were breathing steadily, the boy carefully climbed out of bed, crept up to Nona and from her loose fingers retrieved the object she'd clung to in her fight for life.

*

There was not much left of the airplane. It had lost part of one of its front wings, the other was bent, the back wings had fallen off, the body was flattened, and the underbelly split. The plastic propellers had disappeared altogether.

Tears rolled down the boy's cheeks, though he did not so much have the sensation of crying as merely emptying his feelings.

Dawn was breaking. The apartment still stank of candles and the battle with Death, the prospect of day covered everything with a cloak of grayness. The boy stood next to the balcony window, holding the remnants of the airplane he'd never dared to fly.

Crying, he pressed the sides of his tongue against his palate and hummed.

"Bzzzzzzz!"

Quietly, so the sleeping women would not hear.

"Bzzzzzzz!"

He raised his hand above his head, held up the plane and took his first step.

Uncle Vinko was right, despite everything it did still fly!

"Bzzzzzzz!" it set out alongside the bed, past the footboard to the other side, into the darkness next to Nona, turned around, back toward the window and the faint light.

The boy knew that the airplane that had killed and saved so many was deciding what would happen to him. He summoned up his courage and jumped, feeling the soles of his feet leaving the ground and the airplane accepting him, the steady drone of its engines turning toward the morning and the world.

TRANSLATED FROM THE SLOVENIAN BY GREGOR TIMOTHY ČEH

GORAN PETROVIC

The Courtyard

A BALL THROUGH THE LEGS

OUR BUILDINGS WERE both divided and joined by an interior courtyard. Besides a lot of garages, there was a house in there, belonging to the sad tailor named Marko and his wife, Crazy Desa. Beyond that, there was another house, which before the war was a tavern and which was rented out at the beginning of the 1970s to a mysterious hawker of roasted pumpkin and sunflower seeds, Vebi Dalipi, along with his never-quite-enumerated family. Along one side of that house a row of rooms was added for guests; it was a long structure that, after the end of World War II, was transformed into modest apartments meant as temporary housing for the very poor. These folks had no running water, but there was a fountain for all to use. Even then these structures had been slated for destruction, but the people were never evicted. As soon as someone would move out of one of them, somebody new would move in . . .

All of that separated us, and it linked us. It was the same with the open space that was good for playing soccer; instead of goal posts we'd put out rocks or even our school satchels.

"Didn't you see the ball, buddy? It went through your legs. You gotta play defense! Get in position, and go out and face the other player. Don't be afraid!" Njule would shout all these things at me during games in the courtyard, but, unlike the others, he didn't make fun of my clumsiness.

AFRICA, ASIA, AND PORTUGAL

From the window in his apartment, on the ground floor of the building across the way, he could see our balcony. And from my balcony, I could see his window and watch Ljubiša (for that was his real name) as he beckoned me, with wide arm motions, to come with him to the fair held on the feast day of St. Peter. It had just set up at the Kvantaška market, where goods were sold wholesale.

We bummed around there, among the popping of air guns aimed at globes made of rags and the machines for spinning cotton candy, and we passed the wall of death, which wasn't working because, on the previous day, the motorcyclist on it had nearly bitten the dust. And when we pooled our money, we only had enough for part of this deluxe assortment of things on offer. So we played ten rounds of foosball. And we took one swing each at the big leather pear-shaped punching bag for measuring our strength (it didn't budge). But I absolutely, positively also wanted to go into that little tent that had its chubby owner standing in front, trying to lure visitors: "Come on in, people, a one-of-a-kind offer here. After a great tour, we're in your city—wild animals from all continents, Africa, Asia, and Portugal!" At first Njule tried to veto this, saying that the guy was just a smooth talker. He finally relented and I bought my ticket with the remnants of our common funds, promising to give him an honest report on everything afterwards.

"Admit it, buddy! Come on. Admit that there was nothing special to see!" With that, Njule descended upon me at the exit, but I kept quiet, despite our agreement; all there'd been inside were two snakes with pus in their eyes, a monkey that was out of its mind, and a few morose birds of a type I didn't recognize.

MYSTERIOUS CANYONS AND THE SECRET PLAN OF THE YUGOSLAV PEOPLE'S ARMY

We played Cowboys and Indians in the courtyard. The walkways between the garages, paved with panels of particle board and full of fast-growing nettles, were mysterious canyons and gorges through which bands of cowboys supposedly passed. And the Indians were up high, on the tops of the bluffs, on those uneven garage roofs that have since decayed to the point that they couldn't support a bird, much less two or three boys. From up there Njule ordered us to attack; he stood there with his arms crossed like Winnetou. Later he divvied up the booty into equal portions of marbles, counting out the shooters and the ducks, the aggies and steelies, the galaxies and wasps and cat's-eyes . . .

"Hey, buddy, do you see this treasure? It'll be a while before they even think about sneaking across our territory again!"

Actually we battled against the "officers," boys from the military apartment building next door, boys whose proud fathers and fatigued-looking mothers moved in and out, using the gigantic Tam trucks made in Maribor with olive-drab tarpaulins. They came and went frantically, as they were transferred around by the JNA, the Yugoslav People's Army, in accordance with its closely guarded secret plans. It was interesting to get a look at their furniture, and the most interesting thing of all was seeing their dress uniforms on hangers, along with Eiffel Towers constructed of matchsticks and built on nights when they had guard duty, and scores of framed commendations and certificates.

"Look at them, will you? My dad was in the war for real, not like these paper-pushers!" Njule would squint. He was right, because the man we called "Uncle" truly was one of the first Partisans. His real name was Božo Cuger and he was Ljubiša's father.

THE OLDEST MAN ON THE PLANET

We used to steal plums and walnuts from the large side-yard of the artist, Vladislav Maržik, an old Czech, a painter of delicate, sensitive watercolors and the first academically trained painter in our area. The half-deaf Maržik used to doze off in his garden, in his Adirondack chair, with his right hand absentmindedly cupping one of his hydrangeas, the way people often stroke a pet's fur; he'd have a cat or dog curled up near his feet. Maržik would nap like that, and we'd climb around in his tree.

"Hang on, buddy. A little more. Can't you see I haven't filled up all my pockets yet?" Njule was always the last one to climb back down the trunk of the tree.

Or we, leaning on the fence, would simply observe old Maržik as he, half-blind, even with two pairs of spectacles and a magnifying glass in his hand, was still trying to paint. His hand was shaking too much, but he wouldn't quit, as if his life depended on whether or not he produced one more watercolor.

"I don't wanna get as old as him. What good would it do? He can't hear properly, and he can't see right, either. My ma," Njule boasted, "says that Maržik is the oldest man on the planet. He's about two hundred years old!"

WHAT'S NEW IN THE WORLD?

And we read comic books. We were patrons of "Stajka's Library." That's what we called the best magazine stand in town, just there on the left, right after you come out of the passage. Stajka loved children and she would lend comic books to all of us, on the condition that we didn't crumple them up. And Zora, her younger colleague, she also liked children, but she was somewhat less likely to loan comics to us. Children adored Stajka. They loved Zora, too, but then again the grown-up customers of the male gender loved her even more. She was a bewitching brunette and was always decked out like an Italian actress. We were in the habit of checking out how much time they'd spend leaning against the counter at that stand, enjoying the exchange of pleasantries with Zora. The ordinary purchase of a newspaper, which a mere two meters farther on would end up in a trash can, could last fifteen minutes or even half an hour. That's the way that newsstand was. Stajka, the generous one. And gorgeous Zora.

"Hey buddy, let's roll! Stajka told me the delivery truck's been there and we should come see what's new in the world!" Njule rubbed his hands together as he passed this message along to me.

WE MADE SURE WE DID IT FOR HER

We used to run away from Crazy Desa, the wife of the sad tailor Marko; she was not very mobile and always wearing houseshoes, because her legs were terribly swollen. She was also known as a great enemy of dust.

Truth be told, we didn't run from her, because she wasn't capable of chasing us, but she loved to spray us with the hose while she was watering her garden in the interior of the courtyard. It was a strange combination of beds of onions, lettuce, and roses. Sometimes we withdrew to a safe distance and made faces at her, but sometimes, especially when it was hot, we deliberately did not retreat, instead allowing her to catch us with the streams of water she'd spray. We were wet, Crazy Desa was laughing sweetly, and Marko, the sad tailor, came out of the house with a cloth tape measure around his neck and dozens of needles pressed between his lips. He peered first at us and then at his exhilarated wife; he stared with that withered look of his that he had, God knows for what reasons. He gawked as if there were something he couldn't comprehend.

"I'm happy, 'cuz I could tell we were doing something for Desa's mood," Njule said, as we dried off in the summer sun.

AND THAT'S SEX!

We loved to crouch down next to the basement windows of the *Makedonac*, the nearby bakery where they made phyllo dough. We'd observe the whole family, busy at work around a special type of table that had no slab on top, so really they were positioned around a giant tin frame, over which the gauze-like dough was stretched. From underneath, several machines pumped out hot air. The giant phyllo would ripple up and then deflate, and then it would puff up like a triumphant flag devoid of any markings. But all that lasted only till the dough was sufficiently dry.

We loved to watch all the fluttering and how they made the cones of dried dough. Old Mr. Makedonac's niece, who was rather attractive, got flushed and agitated, both from the heat and from the work. With her shirt unbuttoned as far down as it could go, she'd pour the still somewhat soupy mass into ten funnel-shaped molds and gently pull the handle; this handle then moved a joint, and the joint moved a metal crossbar with a row of ten heated conical protrusions, and the hot conical protrusions slid straight into the molds; then you could hear something panting, and steam

75

appeared, and when the aromatic cloud dissipated, then ten cones were ready to hold ice cream, while the quite nice-looking niece of Old Man Makedonac wiped her flushed cheeks with a flour-coated arm . . .

And again: the sparse dough, funnel-shaped molds, the handle, the joint, conical bulges, insertion, panting, steam, finished cones, flour-covered arms, flushed cheeks . . .

"You see, buddy. That's sex!" Njule said.

THREE UNUSED QUEENS

In an alley between Njule's building and Maržik's courtyard, from which we could hear our parents when they called us, but where we were hidden from their sight, we would hunker down and exchange or "swap" photos. It was there that we played our first card games and then later, while having our first cigarettes, we tried out poker for small change.

Let's say I have three queens. I imagine myself to be the winner right away. Njule, however, confidently raises the stakes. I change my mind, and then throw down my cards and quit . . .

"Now look—if you'd paid to see what I have, you would've won! There was no pair, nothing, just five throwaway cards. I was bluffing, buddy!" Njule said as he counted his winnings.

TITO AND THE PARTY LEADERS ARE WORKING ON IT

In the fallout shelter of his building we made a thing we called "our bunker." We adorned the wall in one part of it with posters from the magazine *Jukebox*, and it was there, lounging around on easy chairs that people had thrown out, that we listened to our first rock and roll on a record player we'd mooched from Njule's brother. And it was really loud, despite the fact that we had lined the ceiling with egg cartons. But the neighbors didn't object. Njule's dad, a decorated veteran, arranged things with the building council.

"Oh, leave the kids alone. So what if they use the fallout

shelter?" That was his response once to a neighbor who wore a hair net and was extremely concerned about national security and the civil defense program.

"But, Comrade Božo, the enemy never sleeps!" said the self-important neighbor, shaking his extended finger in the air. Next to his window he had a bracket used to display the flag on holidays, and he thought he was in a position to inquire about all kinds of other government business.

"What are you doing calling me 'comrade,' when you've never caught a single whiff of gunpowder? We don't need the air-raid shelter for anything. You can see it's just sitting there empty. There won't be any more wars here, if Božo Cuger tells you so! And on our side, Tito and the party leaders—they are working to make sure there are no more wars anywhere in the whole entire world!" And with that, "Uncle" Božo pulled one of his suspenders away from his shirt and scratched his belly.

That ended the conversation, once and for all. There was no way of telling whether he was being serious or just horsing around.

WHY ARE YOU PULLING OUT THOSE BONES?

The neighbor with the hair net and the bracket for his flag didn't dare mouth off any more, because "Uncle" Božo was a recipient of a venerable medal given to the first participants in the war against the Axis. Later I came to realize just what a big deal that was at the time. But "Uncle" Božo Cuger never cared about his reputation, or any title or anything like that. He had, if I recall correctly, four children; my friend Ljubiša, that is, Njule, or rather Cugerificus, as people also referred to him, was the youngest of his progeny. "Uncle" Božo never wanted to exchange his two-bedroom first-floor apartment for anything larger, as his comrades were always trying to persuade him to do, and as he was entitled to do, given his service and his large family. It was only later that I understood just how great a man Cuger was in this regard. It wasn't just because of his larger-than-average belly. To put it simply: he didn't care much about the respect of the neighbor with the hairnet and the bracket for his flag, just as he didn't think much about the respect that other people accorded him, either. He lived his life, and he had but one passion: fishing.

I never visited his apartment without finding him personally, or one of his children, untangling or rewinding fishing line, or without seeing him oiling reels, or flicking rods to see how flexible they were, or without him sorting into little boxes the lead weights, floats, fly lures, or hooks.

"Come over here, little man, and give us a hand. Take this spool and wind it up." And "Uncle" Božo Cuger would give me my assignment, just like that.

I never went to their apartment without Njule's mother having "just then" finished frying small fish called picarels.

"Wife, bring us the food! OK, little hero, why are you pulling those out? Eat the heads and the bones, too . . . Look, this is how you grab it. Voilà! And the big fish, it swallows the little fish!"—"Uncle" Božo Cuger showed me how to eat picarels, and then he turned to Njule. "And now, Ljubiša, my son, point that fan in this direction. It's awfully hot."

THE CITY BEACH ISN'T THE REAL RIVERSIDE

One other thing: I also never went to their apartment without getting tangled up in at least one bicycle. Since he didn't have a garage, "Uncle" Božo kept bicycles, and eventually their Tomos mopeds, in the giant square foyer of their home. Sometimes there was one mode of conveyance there, sometimes as many as five, and that's not including sets of handlebars, rims, mud-guards and other spare parts. I actually never knew how big his fleet of vehicles was. But, unlike the parvenus around us, he never had a garage, and he never owned a car. Instead he had only bikes and Tomos mopeds. He probably favored them because of his fishing trips. For, only on a bike or a little motorcycle could you negotiate the trails along the Ibar River or the Morava, going through cornfields or stands of willows; an automobile would be of no use. Cars were only for "showing off," and with them you couldn't even get to the river.

The farthest you could go by car was the municipal beach, which "Uncle" Božo didn't consider a proper riverside at all.

"Screw all that baking in the sun, and jumping around and squealing," he used to say. "Water is water if you can look into it and keep your mouth shut. Come on now, Ljubiša, my son, turn that fan toward me. It's awfully hot."

CURTAINS THAT WERE NEVER WHOLE

Fishing tackle, means of transportation, one large fan and several smaller ones, because "Uncle" Božo was perpetually hot: all of that, plus a squirrel—those were the things people might find when they went to visit the apartment of Njule's parents.

As for that squirrel, a small furry critter, well, it's possible that you wouldn't have seen it right away. The drapes, however, the drapes that were never whole—you couldn't help but notice those. Never before and never since have I seen someone keep a squirrel in their apartment without a cage or something similar. Curtains with prominent threads were its favorite climbing surface. But since its little claws were sharp, the drapes were never undamaged. I don't know what Njule's mom said about all this. At any rate, she didn't seem like a woman who would get worked up over something like that to me. Anybody else would've gotten hysterical, but I never even saw her blink about it. The squirrel was forever scrambling up on stuff, and everything that it touched ended up with a scratch on it or a run in it. And when it finally got worn out, it was in the habit of leaping up on the table, stretching out its front paws, and staring for a long time right into the eyes of "Uncle" Božo Cuger.

"D'you see that, buddy? My pop could tame a lion!" Njule used to say.

REVEILLE

Njule's brother, whom people called Braco, played percussion. And he was one of the first rock musicians in the city. Even Njule took trumpet lessons for a while. From my balcony I could hear Braco getting new rhythms down, plus I could hear Njule blasting sounds out of his trumpet.

Sometimes, in the midday lull when people took their siestas, while everyone was dozing in the surrounding buildings and in the little houses in our courtyard, he'd stick the bell of his trumpet out the window and play "Reveille." It would resound in all directions and probably made everyone leap out of their beds, except for the old painter, the half-deaf man from Bohemia named Vladislav Maržik. So Njule's trumpet would blare and blare until I'd see his mother sneak up on him from behind, grab him by the ear, and yank him back into the middle of the room.

And once I even saw Njule's mother open that same window. At first it seemed like she was singing, because the first thing I noticed was that her mouth was all the way open. It took a moment but when her voice reached my ears, I realized that she was, in fact, wailing. This was the day on which her husband, "Uncle" Božo Cuger, had died. When I expressed my condolences, Njule nearly burst into tears. But he clenched his fists and changed the subject by responding:

"But hey, buddy, have you seen our squirrel? It took advantage of all the fuss to dash off somewhere . . . "

ONE OF THE FIRST SUCH CASES IN THE ENTIRE COUNTRY

But then, when we went off to middle school, we began to grow apart. As I recall, he went to a school for technical and vocational subjects, and I went to a classical high school. We had different social circles. We got together less and less frequently, and more and more often we just ran into each other. My departure for university made even chance encounters less common.

It's an open question whether, in all those years, I even saw him more than three or four times. It was always in the eatery called *Sloga* (which means "Harmony"), owned by the Srbija restaurant and hotel chain. We all called the place The Hoop, because it was right next to the big indoor-sports center. From another district of the smoke-filled restaurant a liter of white wine would simply appear, along with a siphon bottle of soda, and some of the famous chef's little sausages and mixed salads with peppers. We were all just poor students without a dime to our names, sipping on drinks we bought with vouchers that our moms had given us for hot meals. I believe Njule already had a job. He had money.

He had money, and he was generous. He treated us and paid with checks. Eventually it turned out that he hadn't been able to contain himself in his need to bring others joy: he was signing checks even when he'd already spent his pay. It was one of the first criminal cases anywhere in our country of someone writing bad checks. I don't know how much time he was sentenced to serve, and I don't know how he held up in prison; I never asked him. I just know he came back different, quiet, and I had the impression that Njule's shadow was now clearer than Njule himself. He said:

"It's a good thing, buddy, that you didn't see what it was like there."

THE ERA OF WATCH REPAIR HAS COME AND GONE

He got married. I'm not sure, but I don't think he had any kids. I began to write. Then I also got married. The wars started, and the demonstrations, and wars, and demonstrations . . . I published books, and word of them got around, at least in my city. When I'd meet Njule, he would always congratulate me on something. I don't know if he ever read anything of mine. But then again, I don't know if I have any right to think that way about him; it could be that he read more than I did. He and his wife had a watch-repair shop, inherited from his father-in-law. It was actually a kiosk on the street leading to the main bus station. Thus I'd always walk past it when I was going off to do readings. And if he saw me, he would come out to say hello. In the summer, when it was hot, he'd always be standing out in front of their little shop, watching the world coming and going. He didn't have all that much work to do. The era of fixing watches and clocks was over. If your alarm clock or wristwatch breaks down now, you throw it away and purchase a new one. He stood there like that, with his belly growing more and more prominent over the years. I got the feeling that he was always hot, just like his father, "Uncle" Božo Cuger.

He always used to say: "Hey, buddy, did you see this?"

I assume he meant something political, about the break-up of our country, but I never asked him exactly what he was alluding to. Maybe he was baffled by what we were doing to other people, or maybe he was perplexed by what others were doing to us. All I know is that he gave me these meaningful looks, quizzical ones . . . and that he would smile awkwardly . . . and that I was always in a hurry.

WRITING

Near the end of a telephone conversation with my sister, just as we were wrapping up our exchange of news, she added:

"Oh yeah, did you hear? Njule passed away. The funeral was yesterday, but I just saw the obituary today."

I hadn't known. In fact, for decades now I'd known very little about his life. And now I did not even find out about his death in time. For a moment I considered calling someone, to ask around about whether he suffered for long or whether the end came suddenly . . . But then I realized that such a thing would be terribly dishonest; I would be presenting myself as his close friend. Instead of doing that, I wrote a story about what I remember of him. And now I'm utterly convinced that this is odious work: you write about the deeds of someone's life, you write about someone's life, you write about life—as if you know anything.

You write and you write, little brother, like you've actually seen something.

TRANSLATED FROM THE SERBO-CROATIAN BY JOHN K. COX

RAVSHAN SALEDDIN

The State of Things

I LOOKED AFTER Esther, the widow of a mildly famous Soviet composer, for three months before she died. She always said she was
going to leave me her flat—she was probably worried I'd stop coming—but I knew she'd leave nothing because she had nothing of
her own except history. She was eighty-six or possibly ninety-three,
but I couldn't bring myself to call her Granny Esther, and I didn't
know her patronymic, if she even had one, and so like everyone
else, I called her Esther, as if trying to confuse time. I first saw her
in Ruza: she walked footpaths alone, limping a bit, in a dark blue
dress, smoking tobacco. Our neighbor Alevtina, my companion
on blueberry-picking forays, told me that Esther had once been a
famous Paris prostitute, brought to the Soviet Union by the composer, who, already mildly gray-haired and mildly famous by then,
had been there on tour. He bought her a flat in Sivtsev Vrazhek
and left his family. Alevtina knew everything about the residents of
Ruza: she'd taken a holiday there, subsidized by the Conservatoire,
year after year, just so as to know everything about everyone. Her
musicology must have all been gossiping of a similar kind—I hadn't
read any of it, but standing next to her, one bucket to share between
us, both of us wearing identical rain boots, I felt as if I were hugging a skeleton in her cupboard.

That summer I was looking for a compromise between the sym-
phonic poem "Phaeton's Kiss" and my rectum's virginity. A friend
of mine, Yaroslav, was desperately in love with me and said he'd
dedicate his new work to me. To facilitate the writing process, he
invited me as his muse to a composers' residence. I don't really
know why I accepted the invitation. I wanted to be a midwife at
music's birth. I liked Yaroslav, there even was something to being

friends with a queer, but when an overlong joke grows into a timid but serious declaration of love, a boy usually feels awkward, to a certain degree, and that awkwardness soon made me behave like a real girl next to him. Ruza was an unremarkable holiday camp with little cottages scattered around a pine forest. Each house had a musician, a stove, and a Petrof piano; a list as constant as the three dimensions. While Yaroslav was working, I chased my boredom around the square. I'd read, take photos or grab a rain boot and go blueberry picking on the hillside. Once the boot was half-full, I'd come back and ask the forester to chop some wood. We jokingly called him Mitka and played master-and-servant. I'd put the kettle on while Yaroslav spread some diagrams on the floor and tried to teach me composition. I wrote a piece called "The Bug Waltz" but never showed it to him.

A few times Yaroslav tried to kiss me. I responded awkwardly, but in such a way that it wasn't clear whether I was kissing him back or turning away. In actual fact I was contemplating, weighing all the pros and cons. His red beard and lips were so unusual to kiss they felt rather unpleasant. A huge man, he looked like Brahms. I dreamed of a young girl with tender lips and hands. I wanted to walk with her in that forest outside, to go to the lake and hum the newly composed "The Bug Waltz." That was a con. "Phaeton's Kiss" and all the classical music in the world were a pro, along with a possible experience of a kind I might never have again. We'd go to a cafeteria in the main building, where Olesya, a plump Ukrainian girl, served us dinner. I dreamed of a behind-the-sheds fling with this pretty lass from a nearby village, I dreamed of Yaroslav finally catching us and realizing that I didn't love him. But Olesya mostly joked with Yaroslav, not with me. He attracted everyone's atten-tion, he called her Olesykins, he was the king. I remained silent and ate soup, including when he introduced me to some composer or another. We were a couple, there was no doubt about that, and no one could guess I was a man guarding my ass like a chained dog. Shuddering, I waited for darkness. In the evening he'd switch on an acrobat lamp above the piano keyboard and I'd phone home to tell Mom what a good holiday we were having. Yaroslav would start playing, he'd give funny impersonations of opera singers, who were all queens, according to him, every single one of them. Those who take opera seriously have simply never been backstage. Those who roll their eyes at the word "Mozart" would go mad at betrayal. Then Yaroslav would plunk the keys, which sounded like the left-hand part of a Haydn sonatina, to prove the origins of minimalism. In those moments I adored the man, the lightness of his talent, his foreseeable future. We'd turn off the light and lie down on our separate beds; I already knew that imminent developments were inevitable. Yaroslav was so shy that I'd say, to hell with you, you can lie with me, but we'll just sleep—and I knew I was giving in. Then he'd lie down next to me, and I'd think that it might, perhaps, be easier to take his penis into my hand, and then into my mouth, and it would be all over. But I couldn't pluck up the courage to reach out my hand, so I pretended to be asleep. Yaroslav tried to wake me up, but he was afraid of touching me, so I woke up in the morning, feeling relieved.

In the morning I went to take some photos with my camera. I'd got Esther burnt into my brain. Not Esther herself, but a prostitute who survived everyone who'd ever felt anything toward her. I couldn't find her for a long time as I walked among the pines. On reaching the lake, I started back. She stood by a two-story house, with laundry ropes twining around it; she threw her head back and seemed to be listening rather than looking. The courtyard had been taken over by naked children running around in circles. I came over and asked her permission to take a picture of her. She said it would be better to take pictures of the children. I took a few snaps of the children and then asked if I could now take a picture of her. Esther looked into the camera with the same heartfelt gaze as when she looked me in the face, and I asked her to light up in the frame.

She managed to keep a sound mind at her age, even though her speech was somewhat slow, as it can be at the onset of MS; however, it might have been the result of her struggle with her non-native Russian, which had become the language of her old age. I hesitated to ask her about Paris: I thought that she must have let many, many creators of the twentieth century there go crazy over her, but she was reluctant to talk about them, or didn't even know who I meant. I'd find her in the morning, and we'd walk till lunchtime. She was my Olesykins behind the sheds, my holiday fling. In her cottage, Petrof never woke up.

Meanwhile, Yaroslav wanted more, he said he could never go to sleep next to any of his lovers, whereas it was really nice just to sleep in the same bed with me. It was painful to hear that; I'd get annoyed and moody over petty things. One evening I was reading on the sofa, and he brought me a blanket. Then he asked if he could put his head in my lap. I sighed as usual, to show that I didn't like it, and asked if I had a choice. Still, he put his head there, and then I heard him cry. Those were not tears but hailstones freezing in his red eyes; blowing his nose with a hanky, he said, you don't love me, but why don't you love me, I'm very lonely, he said, and all because of this bloody music, for which you have to pay like this. I hugged his giant head and all I could utter was a repeated, "Why, Yaroslav, come on now, stop it, please please stop it."

The next day we paid Mitka to let us in the bathhouse, so we could have a wash. Yaroslav refused to go in the steam room and started doing his laundry, while I kept cranking up the heat, shouting that a real macho is supposed to like the steam bath. Then I ran out and stood under the shower. Yaroslav looked me up and down without hesitation, and I pretended not to notice. He resumed the interrupted conversation we'd begun outside, about Louis XIV and court entertainment, and the phrase "After me, the flood" rhymed in a strange way with the jet of water over my head. Then he said he had a circumcised penis, like a proper Jew, and that's way more convenient, both in terms of sex and hygiene. I went yeah, knowing that he wanted to make me look, and went on washing without looking. Then I opened my eyes and saw Yaroslav, who was staring at me and lightly, with two fingers, wanking his penis, small but sharp, raised at an angle, circumcised and hygienic. I went ballistic, leapt over to him and punched him near the solar plexus, right above his rounded stomach. It was clumsy and not quite a fist blow, more a push than a punch, but Yaroslav sat down on the bench, letting go of his penis, which was dangling this way and that. I took aim and, after a second, hit him again, with my foot, somewhere around the ear, and judging by the pain in my foot, it was a hard kick. Slipping on the floor, my head soapy, I ran to the cottage and started throwing my wet things into my rucksack.

Yaroslav came running very soon after, wet and hastily dressed. He cried and apologized to me, saying he meant no offense, he wouldn't touch me again, ever, just so long as I stay, it's just he loves me so much, and he sometimes wants my body so badly. I rushed around the room, doubly angry because my foot hurt while his ear hadn't even gone red; I carried on packing, not saying a word. I felt strong for the first time in days, and I knew that the situation was in my hands, but strangely enough, I really didn't want to remain in that state. Walking out the door, I said to him, "I can see now that you loved my ass, not me," or something like that, amazed at my own stupidity, which led me to downgrade my revenge, achieved with such effort, and to reduce violence to nothing. I didn't pop by Esther's—I wanted to get out of the place quickly. Not so much because of what had happened as because I worried I might make up with Yaroslav again and this whole business would continue. On the bus to Moscow, I thought of the strange-looking erected Jewish penis, of the whole absurdity of our queer bathhouse fight, and I imagined hailstones growing out of Yaroslav's tired red eyes.

Two weeks later, when the season in Ruza should, by my reckoning, have ended, I decided to visit Esther. Alevtina might perhaps be able to help me with the address, but all I knew about her was that she was a musicologist and taught at the Conservatoire. The security at the entrance wouldn't let me in, they demanded that I give them at least the teacher's surname or full name. Finally a little old man passing by, a professorial type, said he knew Alevtina and would ask her if she could come downstairs. Alevtina appeared without a bucket or rain boots, but we hugged each other like close friends. Straight away she began telling me how gloomy Yaroslav had been after my departure, how the girls in the cafeteria had asked him where his other half was. I tried to change the subject and asked her about Esther. Alevtina said she'd be sure to find out, especially seeing that Esther lived alone and would be happy to have a friend. I wrote down my phone number on a piece of paper, we stood on the stairs for a little longer, and then she went to work, this strange woman without a bucket or rain boots, who knew about every Moscow musician's private life.

The next evening, the dutiful Alevtina called me at home and told me the address. I was working till late the following few days, and then on Saturday morning I went to Sivtsev Vrazhek. Esther lived in a gray building that used to house party officials, with a clean and spacious lobby, and when she saw me at the door she smiled for the first time since we'd met. The flat was chock-a-block with books and sheet music. Books on the shelves behind the glass, on the table, under the bed. For some reason there were also books in a broken spare basin in the bathroom. We drank tea, and I noticed a record player and suggested that we listen to some of her husband's works. She considered it for a while, as if she'd never heard of her husband ever composing anything, and then she waved her hand, as if waving off a fly. There was a photo on one of the walls, in which she sat next to Gorbachev. Esther was about twenty years younger in it, and you could divine traces of her beauty, not long gone. When I asked what she was doing with Gorbachev there, Esther was surprised: how did I know this man?

I began coming over, first twice, then three times a week, to bring food and cook something. I made porridge, sausages, and simple soups, and fed her and two smoky cats, the only source of living movement in a flat devoid of any news or events. I brought kiwi fruit: Esther liked to sit in the armchair, peel the skin with a small knife, taking a long time, bite off some jellied flesh, and slowly chew. I'd probably never look after my own grandmother the way I looked after this old lady, who wasn't my kin. Sometimes, at night, I had a dream: I lie down on her bed next to her, and then she puts me on top of her. In the morning, coming in to cook sausages, I couldn't look her in the eye. Not because she was ninety, but because she was the widow of the century I was born in.

Yaroslav called several times, but on hearing his voice, I put the phone down straight away, and soon he stopped calling altogether. In September Esther forgot how to use a fork, and I called Mom to say I was moving to her place. A desperate tremor had taken over her hands, and I had to spoon-feed her. All I brought with me was a single bag with shirts, underwear, and a toothbrush. A relative of the mildly famous composer came round a few times, but she spoke to Esther as if to a half-deaf madwoman. Esther did her best to play along. The relative circles around the flat like a vulture, she said, but the flat will be yours. The relative tried to force some money on me for the care, but I didn't take it. Then she put five thousand on the chest of drawers, and the note stayed there, collecting dust. By mid-September Esther, although still breathing, could no longer chew the pieces of kiwi fruit I put into her mouth. They stayed there, slowly melting. I ran out of money, so I had to take that five thousand from the chest. I thought I'd put it back on the same spot as soon as I had a chance. I never had the chance, and a clean rectangular trace remained where the note had been. In those days, when leaving for work, I knew that when I came back Esther would most likely be no more, but she always opened her eyes—that was her greeting. I'd long forgotten waltzes, but sometimes I'd find a simple piece among the sheet music on the shelves and play a polonaise for my dying old lady. Haydn, too. I was a lousy player, but it was all the same to Esther. Perhaps it was that very "all the same," from a former prostitute (if they can ever be former, of course), in reference to his talent, that once brought about the mildly famous composer's death.

However much I'd prepared myself for Esther's death, it took me unawares. Everything happened just the way I'd imagined: she died alone. One Sunday I went to buy a pair of plimsolls, and when I got back I found her there. She sat in her green armchair with her head dropped, as if asleep, but there was such an airless silence concentrated around her, as if the windows in the flat had never been opened. I came over to her, touched her hand and wept at the suddenness of it: I was, perhaps, the second man ever, after her composer, to weep for her. Then I called the relative and told her everything, packed my bag, and sat down "for the road." Buttons, pieces of twine, a dressing gown, belladonna boxes; her things had stopped existing and gone into the same funnel as their owner. The entire flat had died with Esther, both the piano and the piled-up books. I suddenly saw it so clearly I wanted to leave at once. I kissed Esther on the cheek and left. Perhaps we belong to things, and they really don't want to lose us, so bravely do they rush after us.

A couple of days later, I remembered the cats locked in the flat and thought I should return to decide their fate. The door had been replaced with a metal one, and no one answered the buzzer. I wouldn't, of course, have said no to the flat had such an opportunity presented itself, but I didn't really have any claims to it, so someone deliberately changing the door to make sure I couldn't get in hurt twice as badly. I looked in the lobby and in the courtyard: there was no trace of the cats; someone must have found a place for them. The past had shut itself off from me with a steel door, leaving on the other side the cats, Esther, Ruza, and all the mildly famous composers of my youth.

TRANSLATED FROM THE RUSSIAN BY ANNA ASLANYAN

LÍDIA JORGE

The Age of Splendor

LISTEN TO THE silence of the house in the early morning. The passageway is still dark, and the door at the far end is closed, but the voices behind it have already laughed and talked and fallen silent. The room, though, is still locked.

Now the outdoor maid, coming in through the garden, is walking across the kitchen to fetch the bag in which she'll put the bread she's going to buy in the village. She's gone. Meanwhile, the indoor maid has heated the water and placed the jugs outside the bathroom. The jugs are made of metal. Then, at last, the door at the end of the passageway opens, my mother comes out and goes back in, and only then is it my father's turn to walk down the passageway. I stay in bed. When the indoor maid comes to find me, I have my eyes tight shut, but she knows very well I'm not sleeping. Then, wrapped in a shawl, in the maid's arms, I go to watch my father eat his breakfast. This was the age of grand houses for just three people, the age of maids, the age before running water, the age of a single lamp hanging from the ceiling, the age of private gardens with ponds and goldfish, the age of teachers of Latin like my father.

Notice, too, how beautiful the house is. My mother is lovely as well, she has long waist-length hair and a slender waist, so slender that many people said it didn't seem possible that she'd had a child, given birth to a daughter. When she leaves the house, she wears a hat with a floppy brim, and through the veil decorating the brim at the front, she smiles at anyone who passes. But I love my father. He has a smooth neck, a gray hat, broad shoulders and dark suits— vast, immense. Vestments. My father's suits are vestments that I watch being cleaned and pressed every afternoon. It's the indoor maid who irons them. She also irons his socks and handkerchiefs— large white handkerchiefs, because my father suffers from chronic rhinitis. The indoor maid irons the handkerchiefs with almost religious devotion. The suits, once ready, go straight onto a hanger or onto a wooden valet, and the handkerchiefs are placed in a pile. To iron them, she uses a big, heavy starching iron, with a little chimney on it, rather like the one on a kiln. Inside, there are red-hot coals that you have to blow on to keep them alight, and when that metallic monster presses down on the white cloth protecting the suits, the steam and the hiss create a fantastic whooshing sound in the laundry, not that I'm afraid. I like to watch. It's as if a train engine were passing over father's clothes, but the outdoor maid is always terrified I'll get too close to the iron. There's a kind of general panic that I might be in danger, that I might burn myself. Be careful with the starching iron, be careful with the noise that troubles the silence in the house.

Listen then to the silence in the house in the late afternoon, when father returns, bringing with him, inside his briefcase, the exercises of *rosa pulchra est, rosae pulchrae sunt.*

Mother left for town with the outdoor maid, and I stayed at home with the indoor maid, and then off I went into the garden on my tricycle so as not to disturb my father. There are the two beech trees, the five poplars, the Judas tree and, in their shade, a few leggy rose trees and some box hedges trimmed into the shape of birds. And all of this is arranged around a pond where the lily pads float, and where, in the water below, a shoal of goldfish swims. I race round and round the pond that we call a lake. In the middle of the lake is a stone mermaid holding a conch shell, from which flows a constant stream of water. As it pours over the mermaid's hair, the water makes no noise. I make as much noise as I possibly can, shouting: *Wheee!* And the trees listen to me as I pass. The indoor maid goes: *Sh!* We're near the window behind which my father sits reading page after page. When he reads out loud, he says words that make no sense—*Sub tegmine fagi silvestrem tenui musam* . . . And other such enigmas. This mystery is the stuff of his unending study. Looking through the window, I can see him hunched over his desk, concentrating, solemn and dignified in his suit, as if he were in the classroom; he looks so well-turned-out, my father. As I ride back and forth on my tricycle, he smiles at me from time to time, and blows his nose on one of those white handkerchiefs, but he says nothing. *Wheee!* I cry, as I race round the fish, pedalling furiously. This was the age when people studied *Sub tegmine fagi,* when teachers kept their jackets on, when mothers would accompany fathers to catch the bus, followed by their daughter, followed by the indoor maids and the outdoor maids. The latter would each hold one of the daughter's hands. The daughter would follow behind her mother and father, swinging back and forth, arms spread wide, supported by the two maids. Before father got on the bus, mother would say: "Be careful with your rhinitis, Eduardo. Have you got your hankies with you?" Yes, he had his hankies with him. Father would get on the bus. He was a Latin teacher, but, to me, he was a great man surrounded by handkerchiefs. I loved my father.

Listen, then, to the silence of the laundry room in our house, where his handkerchiefs were kept.

*

They're still waiting to be ironed, and are big, vast and ugly. They're white and smooth as sheets his handkerchiefs. Not like mother's. Hers are small and edged with lace, and decorated with flowers and colorful dolls, figurines in skirts with tiny pleats that I've watched being embroidered. You have to wind threads around pins that you then remove to create a raised effect that you can feel when you run your fingers over it. Feats achieved by delicate hands. Mother's handkerchiefs are full of such feats. It makes you think. They're full of flowers and lace, and mother doesn't have rhinitis, and father, who does have rhinitis, has no embroidery on his handkerchiefs at all. They're as big as the bits of faded fabric the maids use as table cloths downstairs. Mother has long hair, which she weaves into a plait, a plait that she wears caught up at the back, where the brim of her hat rests, and sometimes the plait comes undone, mother is

* Treichville: a working-class neighborhood in Abidjan.

always so pretty, though, that she deserves those handkerchiefs, but I love my father, and he has chronic rhinitis and no embroidered handkerchiefs. I don't find this injustice painful, but I can sense it and feel it, real and palpable, I can see it there before me, and I want to undo that injustice. I need to hold in my hands one of my father's handkerchiefs. Should I just take one, without saying anything, or ask the indoor maid? The indoor maid is as startled as if I were about to commit a crime—"What an idea, Miss Marina, what madness! Whatever do you intend to do with one of your father's handkerchiefs?"

*

No, I can't use one of father's handkerchiefs. Nor a square of white cloth of the same size either. In the age of no running water, the age of hats, gloves and maids, a piece of cloth is valuable— "Here, have this, if you like . . . " And the indoor maid gives me a small piece of white cloth, a square of cloth slightly bigger than the palm of her hand, and, what's more, irregular, a scalene trapezoid that you couldn't make regular even with a pair of scissors—an object forbidden to me. It doesn't matter, it will do. Now all I want are some needles and thread. That's all.

The indoor maid also doesn't understand why I would want a length of red cotton threaded through a needle. And a knot, because I need a knot at the end of the thread. While the great starching iron glows and steams over father's shirts, I stick the needle into the surface of that trapezium, give it a tug, then draw it back creating a red line in the middle of the cloth, then I stick the needle in again and pull. Two lines. A star. Another star. Another needle, this time threaded with green. A green star, one line crossing another, and suddenly it's a sun. A green sun on the cloth, surrounded by stars. The kitchen maid is annoyed at having to stop her work to help me. She threads a needle with yellow cotton, always with a knot at one end, as requested, and a flower appears in the middle of the cloth. Then a fish, then two fish. I overlay lines upon lines. Suddenly, in the middle of the cloth a mermaid appears. So lovely. The lilac-colored thread is excellent for embroidering fish, and there's still enough left for the mermaid's tail. Isn't it pretty? The indoor maid thinks it's just a nuisance, having to keep threading needles, because she doesn't know I'm embroidering the handkerchief for my father. I swear that justice will be done. Eduardo Pestana, my father, the teacher with chronic rhinitis, will use that lovely handkerchief embroidered by his daughter. It's finished. The next day, I hand over the cloth covered with dozens of crisscrossed lines and ask the kitchen maid to iron it.

With all the skill of a blacksmith, she lifts that blazing, steaming instrument, places a white cloth between the base of the iron and my work, pressing down hard on that mass of crisscrossed lines. She presses down again and again. It's done. She hands me the flattened object, holding it by one corner. I take it. I hold all my wealth between my fingers. I'm going to put it away somewhere. I've already found a place. There's a drawer in the chest in my room, which I can open and close. I pull it out, and beneath the clothes, I put the embroidered handkerchief that I'm going to give to my father. Stars, sun, moon, flowers, waterlilies, pond water, goldfish, even food for the fish, which are embroidered in blue on the cloth, and the stone mermaid, who is black, because there are black lines too, an indestructible tangle of lines, all put away for when the right moment arrives. Tomorrow? The day after tomorrow? I have to be careful, because beyond the day after tomorrow the future no longer makes sense. I don't understand this business about "when you grow up." I only know that I'm closing the drawer, then the bedroom door, and that my present is there. Watch out. My name is Marina Pestana, I'm five years old, and I've made a handkerchief to give to my father.

Then time began to pass, and the important moment never came.

Father left in the morning, well provided with beautifully ironed handkerchiefs, and returned in the afternoon with his pockets full of crumpled handkerchiefs, which he would leave in the laundry room, where they would be washed, hung out to dry, ironed, then put back in his pockets, and so on for a long time, *per nunc et semper, per omnia saecula saeculorum, amen, Dr. Pestana*. With not a pause, not a gap. With no going back to yesterday and no calendar for the next day. And meanwhile, one morning, something unexpected happened. It was half past eight, the clock in the living room had chimed loudly. When we were nearly at the bus stop, father, as was his custom, felt his pockets, patting both sides of his jacket, and there were no handkerchiefs—"Where are my handkerchiefs? I forgot to bring them!" Mother, her hair in a very long plait and looking very elegant, very pretty, shouted at the indoor maid: "You didn't leave the master's handkerchiefs next to his suit. Go and fetch them now!" The maid broke into a run and headed back to the house. I let go of the outdoor maid's hand and managed to run even faster than the indoor maid. Besides, she didn't know what she had done with the handkerchiefs, but I knew where mine was, where I had stowed it away days or possibly weeks ago, in the chest of drawers in my bedroom. I opened the drawer, took out the embroidered handkerchief and ran, almost flew, back to my father. I made it. I stopped right next to him, panting, and held up the handkerchief, murmuring a few words, but my arm only reached his jacket pocket, and however hard I gazed up at him, my father's eyes were fixed on the bend in the road, which is where the bus would appear, while the indoor maid handed him three handkerchiefs. Then my father ran to the bus stop, and we watched him leave. That's how it ended. There I was, holding the embroidered handkerchief and no one even noticed. How was that possible?

My handkerchief had stars, sun, moon, fish, and flowers, and no one noticed. My father hadn't even heard what I said. I should have said *Wheee*, but no, I had spoken so very very softly, and I was so small while he was so tall that, instead of accepting my handkerchief and putting it in his pocket, Dr. Eduardo Pestana, Latin teacher, had merely patted me on the head in his haste to leave. Now what could I do with that handkerchief? It was the age of long nights spent reading, the age of live-in, full-time maids, the age of hot water in jugs and pitchers, the long-ago age when a few electric lamps swayed on the walls, and the rest of the house was lit with oil lamps. The age of coal-fired irons, the age of big hats. The age when the indoor maid would weep because she hadn't left the master's handkerchiefs next to his suit as she should have done, and she would go on and on about it to the outdoor maid while we were walking across the garden back to the house. What more is there to say? I would return to my room, to the chest of drawers, where I would put my handkerchief back in the drawer, and time would pass until the handkerchief ceased to have any significance, until it disappeared in subsequent changes of furniture and houses. *Finis finium* for that handkerchief. And one evening, many years later, when I was already a grown woman and father was a man on the downward path of life, I would tell him what had happened to a certain piece of cloth the size of a hand and crisscrossed with threads. And we would both laugh, safe in the distance of time.

But that isn't what happened. No, on the contrary.

On that morning, mother went back to her room, and, out in the garden, the maids continued to discuss their mistakes, their punishments and their rewards, and I could run over to the trees that I loved, to the straggly rosebushes reaching out for the light, to the waterlilies and, especially, the fish. Of all those creatures, the ones I loved most were the fish. Listen, then, to the silence of the fish, listen to them listening to me and how, at the slightest movement of my hat, they come to the edge of the pond. The pond is filled almost to the brim with water, and the fish shelter beneath leaves that serve them as parasols and umbrellas; they, the fish in the lake, come and go, they listen to me and love me, I have something to give them. I lean over to meet their smooth bodies, their red shapes slipping noiselessly through the green water. I lean further over, I slip into the water, I reach out my arms to them, I'm drowning, it's both very hard and very easy, their silence, my silence, I can see them coming closer, even though I can't open my fist in the water to set the handkerchief free. On the contrary, the more I want to give the handkerchief to the fish, its only rightful recipients, the more tightly I grip it between my fingers, and everything is dark. Water-green, slime-green, dark-green, mute-green. A long time in the kingdom of slime-green water. A long, long time, and it's so easy. It's very restful to sleep in that slime-green kingdom, and I myself am entirely made of water and greenness. Complete, absolute rest. Until I feel my watery body sitting on someone's lap, the silence shattered, screams crossing the garden, the outdoor maid, the daughter of a fisherman, has her mouth on my mouth and I breathe again, and painlessly, without even a suspicion that pain exists, I exist. Taken by surprise, out of the water, my mother screaming, the maids screaming, me being carried back to the house, I exist. How long has Marina spent among the slime and the water? Then the doctor came, he came at midday, he came at lunchtime, he came in the afternoon, then father came, along with his shock, father screaming too, because they hadn't called him at once, angry with my mother, with the maids, with the light streaming in from outside, with the doctor, with the room, and then father came closer and took off his hat, I was lying on my parents' bed, in the room at the end of the corridor, where I rarely entered, and where the laughter in the morning came from, and suddenly, in the midst of all this, there I was, surprised, incredulous, guilty, silent, me, at the center of an inextricable knot. And lying on a towel, on display, was my trapezium of cloth strewn with lines.

"What's this?" asked my father, looking at the piece of cloth covered in crisscrossing lines as if it were some witch's charm. Holding it up, he said: "This is what she had in her hand, but why?"

The outdoor maid pressed her hands to her chest, swearing that she knew nothing about it and had never seen the thing, and couldn't understand why the master's daughter had been found in the lake with that scrap of cloth in her hand. She swore she knew nothing.

"I know what it is, sir,' said the indoor maid.

My father continued to wait, still clutching the piece of cloth.

"It was a handkerchief she embroidered for you, sir."

"For me? But why?"

My father put the handkerchief back down on the towel and stared at it. Mother, the maids, and their guilt-ridden tears, all stared at that witch's charm. Father was examining it now as if it were an object of scientific interest. An object of human science which he— an expert in the matter, a teacher who could read Horace and Virgil as if they were his catechism, and Comenius's *Didactica Magna* as if it were a diary—was having difficulty in understanding. Until he took off his tie, took off his jacket and picked me up and held me to him, and there was nothing between us but the fabric of his shirt. The maids left, mother left, and I stayed there with my father, my head on his shoulder, the witch's charm lying on the towel at the foot of the bed. It was the hour of splendor. Stars, fish, flowers, the sun, the moon, the slime from the green pond. Listen to the silence of the pond. Listen to the silence of the house. Close your eyes to that dazzling splendor, because now time has passed.

Yes, now, decades upon decades have passed.

There are no longer huge houses for just three people, all the houses have running water, gardens are no longer private, there are no maids, no coal-fired irons, no teachers of Latin. The big houses in the towns were turned into solemn mansions with a communal function. In some, above the doors, you can read the word SILENCE written in blue light. Silence, please. Listen, listen to the silence of this other house. Listen to the silence of this mansion, interrupted just now by the faint sound of shifting furniture. The girl in white comes in, pushing a trolley full of things that rattle: liquids, scissors, needles, glass bottles. Listen to her as she picks up the bottles. Listen to the girl's silence. She breaks the silence and asks: "So the big day has finally arrived. How do you feel? Are you afraid, Dr. Marina?" Listen to the words of the girl in white. "You're going to be the first, everyone's waiting for you. Off we go. And don't be afraid."

Me, afraid? Afraid of what?

My name is written on the bars of the white bed. I'm still the same person, I'm still Marina Pestana. Listen, then, to the silence of the corridor I'm being wheeled along. The splendor comes to meet me halfway down and carries me with it as I lie on the bed. I'm going to be the first one this morning, and whatever happens, bathed as I am in the light calling to me, I'm not afraid of anything. On my chest, stars, sun, moon, flowers, the water in the pond, the goldfish, and my silent mouth, knowing everything.

TRANSLATED FROM THE PORTUGUESE BY MARGARET JULL COSTA

JULIA FIEDORCZUK

The Midden

THE WRITING FIRST appeared by the river; late that summer, some-one had scrawled with a stick in the dirt: WEEP WITH ME. That's all. In the beginning, the first few nights, Stefanida from the ram-shackle cottage was the only one who went. How did she know to go in the night? She read, as they say sometimes, between the lines. And how did she know where to go? That at least was completely clear: to the midden.

So that first evening, she dug out a Turkish jersey dress from the wardrobe; she'd bought it for a song twenty years back from a friend. She went out front. Narrowed her eyes. The orange sun hung low in a cloudless sky. Stefanida had not ventured outside her own orchard for quite some time. The orchard descended to the river; there were old apple trees and plum trees and, at the end near the water, tall thistles and wild rose bushes. These last few years it had been world enough for her, nothing beyond stirred her curios-ity, she made no more plans. Until the moment when she read that scrawled plea among the bushes and understood that her work was not yet done, that there was still this one last task ahead.

The orange sun seemed bigger and brighter than usual to Stefanida. She squinted at it for a moment as though at someone she once knew well, uncertain now if they were still friends. The gate resisted. It was so rarely opened that the hinges were grown completely stiff, like unpracticed joints. Leaning over, as though bowing slightly, in a gray dress blocked in black and brown, a blan-ket rolled under her arm, Stefanida took the road leading to the forest. She was surprised as she went at how much traffic there was. People and vehicles. And the people were surprised by her. They paused in front of their houses, followed her with their eyes and sensed that this outing of hers meant something, but whether something good or bad—they didn't know.

The sun was reddening and about to rest on the horizon when Stefanida reached the forest. She would have found the midden with her eyes closed, she didn't need the light. The last rays filtering red through the branches of the pines did, in fact, highlight a heap of rubbish strewn at the road's junction. Like a burial mound, thought Stefanida, and turned her gaze inward. Of all creatures, only humans produced waste of this kind: the world and themselves faked in plastic. Not much angered her now, but this did. The sunset was very beautiful and quiet—every step was amplified in these surroundings. She was careful not to tread too heavily. She left the footpath and moved slowly between the trees. A chance to share the life of the crippled forest through eyes gazing inward-out imparted new strength to old bones.

The midden was part of the old forest, where the trees grew dense and various: pines, oaks, beeches. The moon rose and it grew lighter again. Stefanida stopped. A big moss-covered tree-trunk lay across her path. The forest had changed, but not so much that it confused her: she remembered this fallen trunk from years back. It still harbored life, life coming from without, through its neighbors, for trees can keep the dead for decades at their side. She walked around the log. A little further and she found herself in a clearing. They called it a midden because something had been hidden there for a long time. It had always been called that. Stefanida found a flat spot, spread out the blanket, knelt, and waited for the tears to flow down her lined face.

It wasn't a problem, this waiting among the ancient trees, because time for trees is different, slower: let go the grip on human time, on your own self, that is, and you can feel it. Stefanida relinquished her own time and then the tears came. She cried kneeling, without sobbing, almost without moving. People had all kinds of ideas about what was in the midden, in the earth, buried; maybe something from the war, maybe something even older. When the tears ceased, Stefanida sat back on the blanket. She raised her head; the sky was clear and full of stars. It got cold, then colder still. The stars moved quietly across the sky. Her legs grew numb, but Stefanida was accustomed to vexations. She sat like that till daybreak. When the first pink light spilt into the clearing, Stefanida got up, waited to regain the feeling in her legs, and very slowly returned to her ramshackle cottage, just as the village was beginning to stir.

In the days that followed, the writing appeared in new places, scraped into the earth or arranged in sticks and pinecones. Stefanida would go to bed in the morning, get up in the afternoon, and fill her days in the usual way; she'd read, make plum jam, arrange cuttings from yellowed newspapers in an old stamp album. Before the sun set, she would pull on the Turkish dress and set off. People came out of their houses; the whole of Głody watched Stefanida march past. And then she'd plunge into the forest, pass the mounds of plastic, advance between the trees, and, as night began, she'd reach the midden. She would spread out her blanket and cry. And when she had no more tears, she sat peacefully, hoots and rustles all around. Before dawn, dew and cobwebs would settle on the grass. Stefanida would get up, fold the blanket, and slowly return home.

On the sixth night, a Friday, she was joined by Franciszek the artist. When Stefanida reached the place, he was already there, waiting for her, sitting directly on the moss. It wasn't really a surprise. They didn't speak. Stefanida spread her blanket and knelt down. The tears flowed. At first, they cried separately, but soon they each relinquished their own time and then they cried as one. In their own separate time, Stefanida and Franciszek hadn't seen each other for ten years, hadn't spoken for fifty. Long ago, according to his own, separate time, Franciszek the artist had offered Stefanida his heart, his soul, his body, and his art. Stefanida, set within her time, had accepted these gifts. This was soon after the war. Then Franciszek left Głody in search of a better life. For him and for her. Six years later he returned, but she was married already with two small children. Franciszek never married; he arranged and rearranged his time on large blotchy canvases which he managed to sell occasionally to wealthy marketeers. Now, when Stefanida's husband was no more than a handful of dust and both her daughters had departed for different European cities, Stefanida and Franciszek could sit once more opposite each other in the deepening night, under the piercing (there was a new moon) stars, to wait for dawn.

At dawn, Stefanida helped Franciszek to his feet. Together, they returned to the village as though they were returning from a walk stretching half a century. The morning was like crystal, a few yellow leaves here and there on the trees the sole reminder that autumn was approaching. That day, the writing appeared in front of the shop, arranged in bottle tops.

At the start of the second week, the Bujno couple joined them. They followed Stefanida and Franciszek right from the village, but they said nothing; it was not until they reached the place that Mrs. Bujno said, very quietly, "Good evening." Her name was Krystyna and, until quite recently, she'd been a great beauty. Tadzio Bujno had courted her for a long time. Finally, he succeeded, and their parents had thrown them a riotous wedding. But then it transpired that the beautiful Krystyna could not carry a child to term. Each time she fell pregnant, she would lose the baby. Year after year, it was the same: hope, joy, pain, fear, the hospital, and mourning. The doctors were clueless. Krystyna would not give in. She went to the herbalist. She went to the priest. And finally, she succeeded. After nine months spent in bed under the ceaseless care of her husband and mother, she gave birth to the long-prayed-for daughter. They named her Beata. There was no child more indulged in the whole village. Nor a greater grief a month later when, without warning, the child's heart ceased to beat. Beata's life ended. And Krystyna's life ended, except that her heart continued to beat.

When Krystyna knelt on the moss, all four of them wept with grief for little Beata. They cried a long time, until the grief joined something bigger, foresty and underground, and though it grew no smaller as a result, but actually larger, it became bearable. It was an exceptionally beautiful and quiet night. The beating of wings could be heard in that silence, the murmur of falling leaves, the crack of breaking twigs, and a humming from inside the trees. Toward morning there was a frost. They had to share the blankets to endure the cold, but no one wanted to disturb the vigil. The sun, when it rose, was red as fire. "The second summer after the war," said Francis, when they were returning through the village, "I went to the midden once, when gangs were still shooting at each other in the forests." Stefanida was silent. "I saw," he continued with an effort, "I saw them drag a man into the center of that clearing. There were three of them, and him. It must've been a Sunday. I dropped to the ground; luckily I was hidden by bushes. He must've been very weak then, the man. I only saw him from the back, face-less. The others were quarreling over something. All of a sudden, one of them says to the other: shoot him. And he did, right then. I thought they'd dig a pit. But they didn't dig. They rolled him up in some rag and carried him off. To the river probably . . . " "Do you know who it was?" asked Stefanida. Her voice trembled a little. "Do you know who killed him?" "Not one of ours, for sure," he replied immediately. "I saw the one who gave the order later, in Hajnowka. At the lumber mill. Just the once." "How lucky we've been," said Stefanida, her hand already on the gate, "so much of our life in peace. We've been so lucky."

Krysia Bujno was the first to think of bringing tea in a thermos. They were already five by then: Ewa the history student had joined them—a strange, quiet girl. It wasn't entirely clear why. She'd been waiting for a bus when she saw a word scratched with something sharp next to the timetable: WEEP. She went off to her lectures, but couldn't concentrate. So when she got home, she left her things, dressed warm and told her mother she was going. At first, her mother was against it, but the following day, a Friday again, she came too. Luckily, it wasn't raining. That autumn, it hardly rained at night at all, and only the mornings brought a thick gathering of mist, dipping the tree trunks in milk. It would have been easy to lose the way, easier than at night, were it not for the old people who had the forest in their blood. For now they went into the forest, but it was the forest that had gone into them first, through and through. Other people began bringing thermos flasks too. Only one rule was observed: silence reigned from the first tear until first light; not a human word was spoken.

The days grew shorter quickly then; sunset came too soon, so they'd set off around eight in the evening. An hour later, they'd reach the place and sit, keeping vigil through the night, the trees scattering dry leaves on their heads. In the end, all the old people of the village were coming, that is, all those who remembered houses burning, hiding among the cows, the joy of sleeping under an open sky, and the fear, and who remembered these particular trees, even as each one remembered a slightly different war, a slightly different death. And mortal enemies suspended their disputes, since it's difficult to quarrel without words. The young tagged along out of curiosity and sometimes they'd stay. Once, the priest came, knelt down on the blanket, and began: "Let us pray," but they hissed him down and he cut it out.

Stefanida would get up just before dawn, go out of her ramshackle cottage, and look at the sun. There was little left to do in the garden, just some wild roses to gather. She went down to the river, where she'd found the first writing. It was long gone; the rest all disappeared. She never speculated about who had done it. She picked the red fruit, full of hairy seeds, and back inside she peeled them, strained their juice. By the lamp's faint light she assembled newspaper cuttings and photographs into the stories of the dead. This way, that way. This way, that way. Such was the right of the living, to take these stories for themselves. To the dead, it made no difference.

One morning, when he was in the middle of another tale, Stefanida invited Franciszek for afternoon coffee. When she woke up, she hunted through the cottage but she could find no coffee or tea. But there was money. She hadn't spent her pension in a long time and her daughters sent a little now and then. So, for the first time in an age, Stefanida headed for the shop. "Excuse me for asking," said the assistant when Stefanida had paid and was about to leave. "Excuse me for asking," she repeated, "but aren't you afraid?" "What should I be afraid of?" Stefanida met the question with a question. "Well, the radioactive stuff. What's buried where you pray." "I don't pray," Stefanida answered decisively. "What the Reds buried there," the store assistant specified. "A midden must have something buried in it." "I don't pray," answered Stefanida, and she left.

Franciszek turned up with half a liter of quince brandy. Stefanida considered the bottle and understood that the time of communal weeping would soon draw to a close. "I remember your parents dying," she said, "one after the other." "Apart from those six years," Franciszek answered, with a moment's pause, "I've spent my whole life in the same house." They were sitting at a small table with a blue and white checked cloth, the brandy glasses glowing yellow next to a heavy crystal ashtray. The room darkened in the half-light, outside it was drizzling. "Your father," Franciszek was hesitant. "Did you find anything out?" "Nothing," she replied. "Nothing significant. He went out that summer night and never came back." They downed a glass.

Stefanida sensed a hard night ahead; she felt her strength fading and the weather deteriorating. They dressed before eight, gathered the blankets, sleeping bags, thermos and brandy, and went out. Fortunately, the drizzle had stopped, the clouds had dispersed, and the clearing was cast in bright moonlight. The almost-bare branches surrounding the midden stood out in a stark black mesh. A wind whipped up, and the forest and the people sighed. Stefanida was freezing, but she was used to all kinds of vexations. Besides, when a person really relinquishes their grip on time, that is, on themselves, then benumbed legs or cold weather don't pose much of a problem, particularly among old trees, when one is listening to their slow, slow talk. The impossibility of repeating any of that conversation later was another matter. Toward morning, she must have dropped off, probably because of the brandy, because in the end the time slipped quickly by. At dawn, Franciszek helped her stand. Everyone was completely frozen. Only Krysia didn't complain. Krysia shone with a strong warm light; she glowed.

That afternoon, a journalist hammered on the door of the old ramshackle house and asked for an interview for some women's magazine. She was nice and bizarrely dressed, so Stefanida let her in and brewed some coffee. The journalist took a few pictures and then got down to her questions. "This place where you pray . . . " "I don't pray," protested Stefanida with irritation. "So how would you describe what you do there?" "I sit," the old woman retorted simply. "And it's not just me. Anyone who wants can come. Anyone who needs to cry can cry." "Why there exactly?" the journalist probed. Stefanida shrugged. "Is there something special about it? A chakram? An old cemetery?" Stefanida's eyes widened. She'd remembered that on the other side of the Bug, next to the Orthodox cemetery, there was a little hill that they said had energy.

She told the journalist about it and she made a note to check it out. "Maybe you know where the term "midden" came from?" "A midden means something's buried," Stefanida recited like a schoolgirl. "Precisely," the journalist pounced, "but what is it that's buried?" She looked deep into the old woman's eyes. "Time," thought Stefanida without any hesitation, but she bit her tongue and answered instead: "Apparently, something toxic." The journalist frowned. "Weedkillers? Fertilizer? Has anyone checked?" Stefanida spread her hands. "What do you get out of this?" the visitor asked finally, after a long moment's silence. "It's such an enormous effort night after night for . . . how long now? They tell me it's five weeks." Stefanida smiled. "It's all one and the same night, every time," she replied. "And I don't get anything out of it, no. But the trees there are really exceptionally beautiful. Would you be wanting to sit with us?"

It was the second-to-last afternoon of October: low, leaden clouds slid across the sky, driven sharply by the wind. The wind whistled through the gaps in the ramshackle cottage; the wind pierced to the bone. Stefanida went outside but there was no sun; a few drops of red dribbled through just moments before sunset. The journalist sat in her car, her phone in her hand, and wondered what to do. She hadn't managed an interview. The old bat didn't seem to have a clue. But despite everything, it was worth following up. She decided she'd go with them for a bit; she could always bail. She had GPS on her phone. And she wasn't afraid of the dark. She moved to the back seat to close her tired eyes, albeit briefly.

She woke to the two old people knocking at the window. Unbelievable! Stefanida looked inflated, in all her layers. The old guy was no better, in a hat with earflaps like he was setting off for Siberia. They were merry as children. A proper madhouse. She scrambled out of her car. The man handed her a blanket and some old cast-offs. She took them out of politeness. They moved off, at the old-timers' slow pace, across the village. Here and there, someone would join them. After interminable wandering, they finally entered the forest. It was immediately pitch-black. The journalist glanced at her phone, the signal was weak but still there. When the screen went, she could see nothing, only the outline of the old lady's shoulders, all wrapped up. She had no choice but to follow Stefanida, step by step, keeping to her pace. Suddenly, they had to skirt a fallen tree trunk. It got a little lighter and the journalist looked up at the sky. The crowns of the leafless trees marked the edges of the clearing where, as she understood it, the show was going to happen. Nice, but what the . . . ? She was mad at herself for getting mixed up in this. Thankfully, everyone sat down and began passing round mugs of hot tea. But then these people—and there were over a dozen—quickly fell absolutely still. A few moments later, she realized that, yes, they were crying. Some of them were actually crying. Not loudly, but in this silence you could hear every sniff, even the falling of the tears. Good grief, something in her began to soften. She didn't join in with the weepers, but she did feel a strange momentary extinguishing of her thoughts, and in this newborn peace a space emerged for—whatever. For cold and hunger, if you like. The night drew on interminably. She'd never been so uncomfortable. But the more her legs ached, the longer the time stretched out, the more certain she was that she would endure it. And she endured. At daybreak, Stefanida was the first to move. Still sitting, she said, in an official sort of way, that she would like to thank everyone very much, this would be the last time. And she was inviting everyone to her place, to her ramshackle cottage, that evening, for a bonfire.

*

At Stefanida's, the journalist went to bed. She didn't even call anyone. Her phone was completely dead and she didn't have the energy to give it a thought. Stefanida showed the girl to the bedroom and tucked her in like her own daughter. She herself lay down on the divan in the kitchen. The girl slept like a log until late afternoon. The first sounds to reach her as she came back to consciousness were the hushed voices of the two old people and the clinking of bottles. She scrambled out of bed and peeked into the kitchen. Stefanida and Franciszek were preparing for the party. There was vodka and a variety of liqueurs, beer, bread and sausage, and at least six types of jam. Stefanida explained the bathroom to her. The old cottage had running water, but its temperature depended on the whims of the old stove. There were no mirrors. Not one.

At six o'clock, the guests began to arrive. Stefanida lit the bonfire. The table covered in the blue and white checked cloth was taken outside and the food arranged on it. Bottles were passed around. People kept arriving. In the end half the village must have got together, including the priest. Not a word was said about the midden, its poisonous secret, or who had learned what from the trees. Later in the evening the first squabble erupted, it almost ended in a fight. They managed to separate the adversaries but failed to make peace. The journalist charged her phone and replied to her texts and emails by the light of the bonfire. She wondered if she'd get an article out of it. Someone got drunk and began to sing, someone fell asleep, others got caught up in conversation. Stefanida disappeared into the shadows of the house. When she returned a moment later, she was carrying a fat old album beneath her arm. Only Franciszek noticed her adding it to the bonfire, like any other piece of wood. He filled up the glasses. They took small sips and looked at the stars, but the sky was clouded over. Midnight struck, All Souls' Day had begun. In this final—for these two—year of separate time.

TRANSLATED FROM THE POLISH BY ANNA ZARANKO

MAARTJE WORTEL

The Camp

ACTUALLY I'VE BEEN not quite well for a while now. Unwell even. At first I was secretive about it, but soon I was telling anyone who would listen that I was finding everything pretty difficult, including simply carrying on. Someone recommended therapy.

"What kind of therapy?" I asked. I didn't dare add that I'd already tried almost everything, that not only I but also my last therapist had given up hope.

The last one: she was a kind woman, perhaps a little too kind for a therapist. During the first visit she said, "I'm not a therapist but an analyst specializing in treatment. I'm going to treat you." She asked, "How would you like to be treated?"

I looked at the posters on the wall. They were exhibition posters from the William Henry Singer Museum in Laren. The kind woman, judging from the posters, must have been treating patients for years, but the years had been kind on her appearance. She was perhaps even attractive. Her hair was disheveled, yet arranged in an elegant updo. She was wearing a loose, pink jacket over a slightly see-through white blouse, and it seemed like she was not wearing a bra. Not that she needed one.

I don't want to give the impression that I was distracted at this point, that I paused for a long time before answering her question. I took all this in within a single second, understanding where I was and who was standing opposite me, and I almost immediately gave my new analyst a louder response than I intended: "As myself."

The lovely woman put her pale transparent hands—almost as transparent as her blouse—in her lap. The gesture came across as rather unnatural, as if she were a newscaster from back in the days when newscasters used to sit behind desks, and as if she now had to read the world's worst news to millions of viewers. Her eyes took on a certain glow, actually quite beautiful, as if the sun was shining inside them, but also demented, as if this sun within was also hell.

"That's a new one," she said. "No one has ever said that to me."

"Oh," I said. The analyst was still giving me that strange look, so I quickly added, as if it were my task to put her at ease, "These things happen." And I thought, even while uttering these words, that perhaps the fact that no client has ever given her this response might matter to her, and I asked myself whether I had done something wrong, whether I had scuttled the therapy with my very first answer.

The analyst cleared her throat. She had gathered herself and was speaking in a clear, powerful voice: "As yourself. Good. Then we'll start with that."

In my mind's eye I could see us both rolling up our sleeves and getting to work on a task that would require substantial effort but that we would nevertheless follow through to the end.

For a few months I spoke to the kind analyst every Friday morning. For the most part, I would be doing just fine at the beginning of the week. Not wonderful, but okay—more or less the same as the majority of the world's population usually feels. But on Fridays, walking out of the analyst's office, shutting the door behind me, heading into the fresh air, back into my everyday life, I was bone-tired, as if the analyst had taken something away from me. It was as if I had left a piece of my heart behind with her. That's literally how it felt: a piece of my heart still lying in the room with the Singer Museum posters, on top of her large shiny desk, an object that she would use to confront her other clients (she didn't like to call us "patients").

"What is this?"

"Meat, I think. At least that's what it looks like."

"Almost."

"I don't know."

"Have a good look."

"No idea."

"Look closer."

"A piece of a heart?"

"Exactly. And what do you make of it?"

"That someone must be dead now?"

"You think about death when seeing a heart . . . Very interesting."

"Well, someone is walking around with a hole in their heart—that was my first thought. No one can live without an entire heart, hence my thought about death."

"Your first thought was right. Why didn't you say it aloud? Someone is walking around missing a piece of heart. That's it. So what do you think it means?"

Time and time again I would be amazed at how my body could continue to function normally. Without a working heart. Empty. And yet just keep going. Until I thought: when everything has been taken away, I'll eventually collapse at the tram stop, or in the supermarket. Or worse: at home.

One day, after a few months of treatment, I thought that I should share my feelings with the analyst, that they properly belonged to the therapeutic conversation, and so I told her that I had a strong impression that she had taken something away from me. Of course, I was supposed to be revealing what I felt and thought and experienced and saw and faced for months already, but it turned out that we mainly talked about my childhood. And the child from my youth was a different person from who I was now; it was as if I'd outgrown myself.

I was sitting opposite the analyst again. She was wearing a long skirt, covering her knees, with a light blue blouse. I told her that I found her a very lovely woman. She smiled and responded that she found me a very lovely woman too. We thanked each other. We looked at each other for a few seconds without saying a word—it was a look of understanding. She held her hands just like she did during our first meeting, at my intake interview. I looked at how she pressed her palms against each other. Small white hands that also occasionally had sought out other hands to hold.

I thought I saw her blush. And because she was blushing, I began to blush too, the red creeping over my entire face.

"When I am in love, I leave myself behind in the object of my affections, after we part company. As if I've given away my place. And this is how I feel now. Every time. When I leave here. From this practice. But then differently."

"When you leave here it feels as if you're leaving yourself behind?" asked the analyst.

"Yes," I said.

"As if you've given yourself away?"

"Yes."

She cleared her throat and cast her gaze on one of the posters hanging behind me on the wall, or maybe she was looking into the distance, at nothing in particular, after which she turned her bright eyes back to my eyes.

"Okay, Liseth. This brings us to the following question, and I have to ask it, do you understand?"

I didn't know what question she wanted to ask, and so I said that I understood.

"Okay," she said again. "Are you in love with me?"

I hadn't anticipated this question. I'm always thinking about entirely different things whenever it comes down to ineluctable questions.

"No," I said.

"Are you certain?"

"Yes."

"For the record, it's an entirely normal phenomenon. People fall in love. Men with women. Women with men. Men with men. Women with women. Clients with analysts. These things are run of the mill."

There are plenty of things that are run of the mill that don't particularly concern me.

I repeated: "No, that's not it. I just don't want to leave so much of myself behind any more."

"You want to be yourself."

I nodded.

"You said that when you came in the door," she said. "The first time. Maybe that's the problem."

"The problem?" I asked.

"That you want that from me."

"I want nothing from you," I said.

"But you do. Are you a hundred percent sure that you aren't in love with me?" asked the analyst.

"No. I mean, yes."

The analyst doesn't respond. She just waits me out.

"I did once dream about you," I said.

"Dreams mean nothing to me."

"Don't you want to know what I dreamt?"

"No. For me it's all about the facts."

"I was never in love with you."

"But it still feels like I take something away from you? You experience the same thing with me that you experience with someone you are in love with?"

"I think so. But that's because of me. I begin to think that I should give you something. Which I then do. And then I begin to have doubts. I want to come back and reclaim it. But I can't. That's why I don't think that it's working."

"That what is working?"

"This. It's not working. Not in this way," I said. "The talking doesn't help. I've already tried so many therapists, but it never really works out for me. I'm never any better."

"Are you tempted to give up hope?" she then asked.

I nodded. And for a moment I truly did give up hope. But giving up is not something to be sustained.

So basically we are back at the beginning now. I've already mentioned that someone recommended a specific brand of therapy for me.

"What kind of therapy," I asked.

The giver of advice, a man, knew another man who had derived a lot of benefit from a lumberjack camp for men. "You don't have to talk all the time. You'd be in nature. You'd chop wood. You'd make fires. You'd be among men. And if you wanted to, you could scream at the trees. If you don't want to, you don't have to. You don't have to do anything. You go there after signing up and checking 'one week' on the application."

"I'm a woman," I said.

"That doesn't necessarily pose a problem," said the tip-giver whom I'd met at a party where I didn't know anyone else.

So I called up the organizer of the lumberjack camp. I told him my name is Liseth.

"Liseth?" asked the organizer.

I heard him repeat my name and for a moment it was as if I had never gotten this close to the truth. I mean: I called the man. I said my name. The man repeated my name. And I returned to myself. It was my turn again.

"Yes," I said.

"And you are calling for . . . ?"

"I'm calling for myself."

I won't repeat the whole conversation from A to Z, but it comes down to the organizer seeing the fact that I was not a man as an insurmountable obstacle at first, but after a while he said: "Maybe the line is not so easy to draw. If you have no problem peeing in nature, you can sign up for our camp."

"No problem at all," I said. "With the peeing thing."

The camp began on a Friday afternoon at five o'clock. Beforehand, participants were sent a roadmap in a large brown envelope, the top of which was sealed with a startling amount of tape. There was also an Opinel folding knife in the envelope. It all connoted a semi-dangerous quest, as if that's what life was in the final analysis.

I used to strip down branches with my father's Opinel until the point was sharpened and I had my own weapon. At night I would take the sharpened stick to bed with me, not only to protect myself against intruders, but also to stroke the soft wood having debarked the shaft. The stick felt smooth and soft, even though I could have used it to kill someone.

I was once dropped off with a group of primary-school children at a forest near Lage Vuursche. I remember thinking that this must be a fake drop-off, that they wouldn't leave a bus full of disoriented sleepy schoolchildren alone in a deserted forest with nothing more than a "figure it out." Apparently that wasn't a problem back in the day—after an hour of loafing about, shouting, cracking dumb jokes, playing with flashlights and pulling funny faces we realized that we would actually have to find our own way home. We weren't scared. We just started to walk. I remember feeling truly grown-up for the first time as I wandered down my street at sunrise and saw my house.

We would often play charades at home in order to stave of boredom during long winter nights. We didn't play in teams or for points; our family wasn't big on competition. We took turns acting things out and everyone was allowed to guess what it was. It was my turn to act out a profession. I got up from the leather pouf, had it in my head that I would be a lumberjack, and as I was walking to my spot an axe emerged from my hand, a trucker's cap appeared on my head, my muscles began to grow, straining against my blouse, and I became a man. I was in the woods and began chopping wood.

"A lumberjack!" my mother, father and brother cried out at once.

For a second I glowed from pride at the fact that they could so quickly tell that I had become a lumberjack. At the same time I felt caught out—it wasn't ideal for the correct answer to be guessed immediately, ending the game.

So I said: "No, I'm not a lumberjack." No one believed me, but I confidently maintained that 'lumberjack' was not the answer they were looking for.

They kept guessing for about ten minutes while I chopped down one tree after another, cleaving wood, producing kindling to last me all winter.

My brother kept sighing impatiently and after a while said: "But you really are a lumberjack. Either that or you're an idiot swinging her arms through the air and imitating a lumberjack. I can't imagine you as anything else."

I knew that I had to give up then.

Unwilling to accept my losses, I said: "Yes, but I'm not only a lumberjack."

"Not only?" my father asked.

"No."

"What kind of lumberjack are you then?"

I couldn't express what I meant. I knew it, but knowledge didn't translate into words.

There were already a few men present when I parked my car in front of a lone house surrounded by fir trees. The ground was wet (earth, needles, moss, insects, something alive) and bouncy under my feet. The air I breathed entered deep into my lungs, awakening me.

The men stood in front of the house drinking tea out of large mugs. It looked cute, the men with their cups of tea, having a chat in the middle of a forest. Somehow I expected bottles of beer, which of course says more about my ideas about men than it does about the camp. However, alcohol was forbidden this week. The pamphlet stated it was best to avoid easy ways to make the issue that brought you to the camp more difficult.

I noticed the men looking at me. They didn't know how to approach me: as a woman participating in a camp for men, or simply as one of them.

The camp conductor said: "This is Liseth."

I recognized his voice from the telephone.

"This week she is one of us."

All the participants seemed to accept this without difficulty, though I myself had some qualms over the qualifying "this week," qualms I kept to myself.

We had all paid a pretty penny for this week in the forest. We had paid a lot for a week in which nothing would be expected from us. For the most part the week consisted in a scenario wherein you could speak when you actually had something meaningful to say, which meant that most participants said nothing. We spent the days walking through the forest, in search of wood that we would use to make two fires at night. One fire to keep us warm, another fire for sausage and hamburgers. When the meat was on the grill, the usual weak jokes were told about my femininity. Jokes along the lines of: "Best leave the meat to us," and "Here's a nice sausage for you." But for the most part the sexism was manageable.

"Sexism is in your head," said one of the men.

"Everything is in your head," said another.

"I'm adapting to fit in with you this week," I said, "not the other way around. Surely that's not just in my head?"

"It's a camp for men," said the conductor. "That's the way it is. You knew what you were getting into."

"Yes," I said softly. But I was grateful for all the radical women who had come before me over the centuries.

We were each assigned a tree in the forest to shout at. We were arranged in a sort of circle, not too far from each other. The conductor would tap a tree and then point at one of the participants, like the gym teacher used to pair up kids so as to avoid bullying.

The idea was not to physically attack the tree. We had to tackle it with words. The men began, without exception, by shouting. If one of them shouted louder, another would in turn outdo him. If someone happened to be hiking through the woods right then, they would have thought they'd stumbled on a brutal massacre and would have called the emergency number just in case. The police would have come out to find a group of men shouting at trees, apparently without reason (though we knew better).

"Quiet now," the conductor called out. "Listen to the tranquility. Take a moment to just listen."

We each stood in front of our own tree, listening to nature, to our own breathing, to someone coughing. A couple of men were out of breath from all the shouting; they had really given it their all.

"And go!" prompted the conductor.

Everyone began to scream at his tree anew. I myself did nothing. I looked at the tree trunk, at the ants crawling off and onto it, and I listened to the screaming participants, to their echoes spreading through the forest. Those dark voices had enormous reach, but the men were shouting nothing in particular, one shouting out names, presumably of family members, most of them simply shouting: "Aaaaaah, aaaaah, aaaaargh!" until red in the face. This empty shouting rendered me silent though. It sounded beautiful. It sounded like something was being released, almost like a secret.

"Don't you want to?"

It was the conductor's voice.

"No," I said.

"It might seem scary, but . . . "

"I don't find it scary. This is what I want. To stand here next to the tree. Listening to the others. Listening to the echo. How everything always returns to you. Is that okay?"

"Yes, of course," said the conductor. "Very well."

Actually I was hoping that he would tell me no. No, that is not okay. Also you can let things go. You have to shout. You too.

But the conductor knew how nature operated. He was a follower of *The Circle of Life*, whereby each thing always contributed to the next.

For the final night of the week, a new activity was added: *Sitting in the dark.*

For my sixteenth birthday I went to a camp at Texel. There was a young guy with whom I didn't dare to dance. And he had no desire to dance. He asked whether we'd go sit in the cloakroom. We sat there between the coats in the dark and drank Coke. The coats smelled of the sea.

"We're sitting by the sea," he said.

"The North Sea?"

"Whichever sea you want," said the guy.

I wanted the North Sea.

Since then I haven't divided people up into categories such as good-looking or ugly, sympathetic or unsympathetic, instead thinking: Is this someone whom I'd like to sit next to, in the dark, by the sea?

My neighbor is a Jewish woman who survived the war. She said: "If you want to sit in the dark with someone, it means that person is good. The rest of the people are bad." She said: "I know instantly when I first see someone. Traitor or not. Yes or no."

"But sometimes you also want to know more about someone who's bad," I said.

"Yes," said my neighbor.

"And sometimes it seems that a bad person can still become good."

"Yes," she repeated. "You think those things when you're young."

She didn't blame the war but my youth.

Shortly after the Liberation my neighbor was sitting in a tram in Amsterdam. It was hot and crowded. She had taken off her sweater; the number on her arm became visible. "Hey!" a blonde woman shouted across the tram. "Look at that woman—she's gotten a number tattooed on her arm."

"It's my telephone number," my neighbor quickly said.

When she got home she felt ashamed of her response. Why not just tell the truth? Why don't people just tell the truth? She decided to dial the number on her arm. It was the number of the Amsterdam library.

In the new Amsterdam library building I once ran into a man at the magazine table who asked for my telephone number. I gave it to him; I thought that we could perhaps talk to each other. Talk we did not. He has spent years invading my life by sending vulgar text messages. Mostly in the middle of the night. It was at night that he thought about me and at night that he disturbed my rhythm, my thoughts, my mood and my dreams, until I finally got a new number.

There are things that happen at night different from those going on by day. Things you cannot learn about during the day. That is what the night is for.

I had applied to *Sitting in the dark* with just one other man. We could choose whether we wanted to sit in a dark room, or outside, next to the house. I wanted to be outside. It was less dark there and I didn't know whether I could trust the other participant. We sat with our backs to the wall of the rear of the house.

"You still have to look at me every time you say something," the man said. "Because I'm really quite deaf."

All this time I hadn't noticed his deafness.

"I wasn't always this deaf. Because all the sounds are stored in my brain, I can hear sounds. People think that it's silent in your head when you're deaf. But it's never silent."

I nodded, asking myself whether he heard a sound to go with it.

"What are you hearing now?" I asked.

"I hear you talking," he said, pointing to my lips.

"You mostly *see* me talking," I said.

"That is the same," said the man.

He told me that most people looked into each other's eyes while they were speaking. Not him. He had to look at lips, at the movement of the mouth in order to understand and comprehend people.

"While the eyes . . . "

"Seem to say so much," said the man.

I was shocked. Shocked that he could follow me and also shocked that he finished my sentence.

"I know whether I find someone attractive by looking at the eyes. Don't you miss that?"

"You mean to ask whether I still find people attractive?"

I saw him still looking at my mouth.

"I don't enjoy looking at eyes. And I don't appreciate it when people look at my eyes."

"That's how I feel about my mouth. I find mouths dirty," I said.

"We could also look into the dark," said the man. "Just sit here, in the dark."

"OK," I said.

I thought about the analyst, the lovely woman. How I left my heart behind with her. I could now say to this man whatever I wanted, as if he were a tree. He said nothing. We just sat there. The silence contributed to something else; it was outside us and simultaneously present within us. An echo of something that couldn't be heard.

"Did you know," I said after a while. Then louder: "I am not simply a lumberjack." I stood up, the man looked up, and I began to scream as loud as I could, like the others had screamed. I screamed at the man, at the animals, at the night, at myself.

"I am not simply a lumberjack! I am not simply a lumberjack! I'm not!" I shouted for at least ten minutes, until the other men who were sitting inside the house had come out and toward me, silently looking on until they got it that I was not a lumberjack, not simply that. I was myself, singular and demented.

TRANSLATED FROM THE DUTCH BY JAN STEYN

KALINA MALESKA

A Different Kind of Weapon

FOR THEIR FINAL exam, Sylvia Pepenovska and her group of twenty fellow classmates from Skopje University's Law Faculty were required to participate in a mock trial in which each student would have his or her own role: prosecutor, defense lawyer, or judge. Heeding their professor's suggestion, they also decided to form a jury, even though trial by jury was not the norm in Macedonia. The simulated trial involved a group of former employees bringing legal proceedings against the employer that had decided to dismiss them.

Sylvia Pepenovska had been hard of hearing from birth and wore a hearing aid. When she was very young, she realized that she was different. Many children at both primary and secondary school shunned her because of her disability. As a result, Sylvia withdrew into her own private world. Observing her suffering, her mother often told her about others who had difficulty hearing. In that way, Sylvia Pepenovska became familiar with the life of Annie Jump Cannon, and through her also with the life of Cecilia Payne. Annie Jump Cannon was a twentieth-century astronomer who worked classifying stars at the Harvard College Observatory. Her extensive efforts led her to classify more stars than any other scientist. Like Sylvia Pepenovska, Annie Jump Cannon was almost completely deaf; in those days there were no hearing aids such as Sylvia wore. Sylvia Pepenovska felt close to Annie Jump Cannon, and never missed an opportunity to read something about her life and work. That's how she also found out about Cannon's colleague at Harvard—Cecilia Payne—whose doctoral dissertation in astronomy, concisely titled "Stellar Atmospheres," was lauded by several twentieth-century astronomers as the most brilliant thesis ever written in the field of astronomy.

At her final undergraduate exam, Sylvia Pepenovska, who was the defense lawyer for the dismissed workers, had one thing on her mind: Cecilia Payne's thesis "Stellar Atmospheres." The structure of its arguments, based on long-term, thorough observations, were for Sylvia an example of how to proceed in an exam, present arguments in a courtroom, and even engage in everyday conversation. At times, her insistence on argument annoyed her more relaxed and easygoing peers. But it was undoubtedly of immense help in this mock trial. Every statement put forward by the company's defense lawyers, Sylvia Pepenovska responded to with counterarguments; every witness statement, she responded to with incisive interrogation. When she imagined Cecilia Payne observing the absorption lines in stellar spectra, Sylvia immediately analyzed the information in the witness statements and revealed the inconsistencies in them. When she thought about Cecilia Payne's great struggle to uncover the origin of certain unexpected facts about the spectral lines of stars, and when she considered the methods with which, in the end, Payne succeeded in logically explaining all those facts, Sylvia Pepenovska immediately applied a new analytical method in order to reveal the illegal operations of the company that fired its workers.

During the mock trial, Sylvia Pepenovska managed to expose the fact that, for its own financial benefit, the company had undermined all efforts by several of its scientific staff to come up with alternative forms of energy. She also revealed precisely which managers were involved in the efforts to sabotage the workers. After finishing her research and analysis, and despite the accepted belief of the time that the stars had the same or a very similar composition as the earth, Cecilia Payne concluded that helium and particularly hydrogen were far more abundant in stars than on the earth. After concluding all her investigations and enquiries, Sylvia Pepenovska determined the exact reasons why the company illegally fired several of its workers. She managed to gather so much evidence that some of the students who were acting in the role of the company's management team got angry with each other and began to quarrel, accusing one another of having passed on all the details to Sylvia. But that wasn't true—each one of them adamantly denied having said anything, and Sylvia explained how she reached her conclusions—what she had drawn on from the labor law, what she had learned from the testimonies, what the evidence had revealed.

The professor and all those present were impressed, as were several of the journalists—former students from the university, invited to attend by the professor, who wanted to involve them in some interesting university events. They immediately agreed that Sylvia Pepenovska should be a guest on a TV show. Sylvia was worried that the speakers and microphones might interfere with her hearing aid. The journalists promised to look into this. Once they established there shouldn't be any problems, they arranged for Sylvia Pepenovska to appear on a science-based quiz show that included an interview between the host and the two guests answering the quiz questions. It was Friday. Her appearance on the TV show was scheduled for the next Friday evening.

*

On the next Friday morning, Sylvia Pepenovska woke up early, excited about her appearance on the evening show. That day she had an errand to run—to obtain a financial document from a certain establishment—and she wanted to do it as soon as possible so that she could then be free, and could mentally prepare herself for her first appearance on TV.

She entered the establishment in the center of Skopje and inquired about obtaining the necessary document. The clerk sent her off to get a form on which, among other things, she was required to list information that was contained in the financial document itself. Sylvia turned around to ask the clerk whether to leave those fields blank, because she was yet to obtain the document, but the clerk had already disappeared. She filled out the other fields and, when it came to her turn at another counter, she handed the form to the female clerk working there. The clerk handed it back to Sylvia, explaining that she also had to fill out the empty fields.

"But I still haven't obtained the document," Sylvia said. "That's why I'm submitting the form."

"You can't obtain the document you want if you don't fill out these fields," the clerk replied.

"How can I fill them out when they require information from

the document that I don't have?" Sylvia asked.

"Well, get the document, fill out the empty fields, and come back," the clerk said patiently.

Sylvia wasn't sure she'd heard correctly. She adjusted her hearing aid and asked the clerk to repeat what she'd said. The clerk did as she asked.

"But if I already had the document, I wouldn't need to obtain it; that's why I'm here—to obtain the document because I don't have it. And how can I obtain it if you won't accept my form?" Sylvia asked.

"Go back to where you got the form," the clerk said, waving her away.

Sylvia went back, thinking she had the wrong form, and asked for another. The clerk told her she had the right form and Sylvia explained why they'd sent her back.

"Well, obtain the document, and then you'll be able to fill out the empty fields," the clerk suggested.

"But in order to obtain the document, I have to fill out the form, and in order to fill out the form I should already have the document." Sylvia was bewildered.

At that moment, Sylvia Pepenovska thought of Cecilia Payne, who'd completed her studies at Cambridge but who hadn't received her degree. The reason: she was a woman. At Cambridge in the first half of the twentieth century, they didn't award university degrees to women. In order to continue her studies, Cecilia Payne had decided to go on a very long and uncertain journey to the U.S.A., to Harvard, where she completed her celebrated dissertation. Sylvia thought to herself, if Cecilia Payne had fought against all the obstacles that society placed in the way of women and managed to write a brilliant thesis, then I too can wrestle a mindless bureaucracy and get a simple financial document. But no matter how many arguments she put forward to the employees at the establishment, she failed to convince any of them. When Cecilia Payne gave her thesis to a famous astronomer to read, he convinced her not to release it to the public because her conclusion—that the dominant element in the composition of the sun is hydrogen—was wrong. He was convinced that Payne wasn't right because her findings were at odds with the accepted belief of the time that the stars have the same composition as the earth. Cecilia Payne respected her colleague and heeded his advice, disappointed at the same time with her own methodology. Four years later, that very scientist came to the same conclusions as Payne, and, although at the beginning of his work he briefly acknowledged her contribution, nevertheless, he received greater recognition for the discovery. Sylvia Pepenovska was convinced by her own logic, but, just like Cecilia Payne, she became disappointed with her own methodology. To achieve the result she wanted, she saw that a different approach was required, but she didn't know which. She tried to imagine what Cecilia Payne would have done. But none of Cecilia Payne's arguments had managed to convince the scientists of her time she was right. That discouragement—the realization that nothing would succeed—depressed Sylvia Pepenovska even more. In actual fact, several decades later, Cecilia Payne's doctoral dissertation did receive acclaim, but for Sylvia Pepenovska this recognition was too little too late.

She turned toward the plate-glass exit of the establishment. It was strangely lit up. Because she lived nearby, Sylvia occasionally came here to deal with administrative matters, and it was normally quite dark here in the early morning. Where did this light come from? Sylvia wondered. When she went outside, there was something unusual, but she wasn't quite sure what it was. She headed off home. The sun, which was low down on the horizon, was shining directly in her eyes and she was forced to put on her sunglasses. She thought it strange that the sun was still so low—yet surely it was around nine in the morning. She immediately stopped. She turned around. She looked at the buildings and turned back again. She thought that she was probably dreaming. The sun was in the west—therefore it must be late in the afternoon, but where had she spent the whole day? She couldn't remember. She was certain that she'd gone to the establishment early in the morning. Surely it hadn't taken her more than half an hour, and now it appears that she had remained inside for more than ten hours. She knew that just wasn't possible. I must be dreaming, she thought again—in dreams we don't know how we end up in a certain place, and time doesn't go by in the same way as when we're awake. However, Sylvia

Pepenovska wasn't dreaming and she knew it quite well. She was quite sure that it was afternoon, and she no longer wondered where she'd spent the day. Instead, a feeling of dread about appearing on the TV show began to come over her. The clock at home said 9:12. It couldn't be 9:12 p.m. because it would have been dark. That meant it must be 9:12 a.m. She looked through the window again. The sun was still in the west, only a little higher up in the sky. She called her friend, Ana, and asked her whether she could reliably tell her what the correct time was. Ana replied: 9:15.

"In the evening?" Sylvia asked.

"No, man, what do you mean evening, what's up with you? It's morning," Ana said.

"Well then how come the sun's in the west?" Sylvia asked.

"Well, where else should it be?" Ana said.

Sylvia Pepenovska went to bed. She forced herself not to think of which side the sun was on, but rather to think about the role that hydrogen and helium play in it. Sylvia Pepenovska fell asleep and woke up that same day around four in the afternoon. The entire incident from the morning had woven its way into her dream, so that she laughed to herself when she remembered that she'd thought she'd actually been to the establishment. Today she'd failed to obtain the document, but she would go on Monday. She didn't even think to look out the window to reassure herself that she wasn't still dreaming. She was too nervous about that night's appearance on TV. She began to go over everything she thought she might be asked on the quiz show, based on the type of questions she'd seen on previous episodes of the program. She only had two hours, because the show began at 7:00 p.m. and she had to be at the TV studio at least half an hour before that.

At 6:00 p.m., Sylvia Pepenovska got ready and went out. She headed toward the TV studio, which was located east of her apartment. The sun, low on the horizon, shone in her eyes and got under her skin. Sylvia stopped and looked around—but she was going in the right direction. She went into the local bakery where she often bought croissants and asked the shopgirl:

"Is it afternoon, or have I slept right through the whole night and woken up in the morning?"

"It's afternoon," the girl said.

"Then why's the sun in the east?" Sylvia asked.

"Well, where should it be?" the girl said.

Sylvia Pepenovska felt trapped within her never-ending dream. She didn't even know how to force herself to wake up. She looked around her and found that all the buildings were where they were supposed to be. Sylvia Pepenovska knew for sure she wasn't dreaming: in the morning, the sun had risen in the west, and now, in the evening, it was setting in the east.

She headed toward the TV studio, but she couldn't shake a certain feeling of dread. When she was passing through Women's Park, everything seemed a little odd, as though something weren't in its rightful place. She paused to take a good look around. She realized what had changed: a monument, which for years had faced the Parliament, was now facing the shopping mall. Sylvia looked at it intently, but the more she looked the more uncertain she became that it had once faced the Parliament. Then she closed her eyes and tried to remember the monument the way she knew it. She saw it clearly in her mind's eye, facing the Parliament. She even recalled a few recent incidents that had occurred very near it. There wasn't a shadow of doubt that the monument had faced the Parliament. She opened her eyes: the monument was facing the shopping mall.

In a daze, Sylvia Pepenovska continued on toward the TV studio. As always, there would be two contestants on the program. On this occasion, the other guest was also a recent graduate, known for his Facebook attacks on innumerable public figures. Aside from the warm-up chat in which the host asked Sylvia about the mock trial, the main thing was, of course, the competition itself: answering questions. The other contestant had a sheet of paper in his hands, which he read from whenever he had to answer a question.

"Come on, come on," the host encouraged Sylvia, "you'll only win if you know more answers than your opponent."

"How can I win when he has the answers?" Sylvia was amazed.

"Why didn't you organize things for yourself so that you'd have the answers too? Resourcefulness—that's what's needed," said the host, at which the entire studio audience stood up and applauded.

Sylvia Pepenovska wondered what arguments Cecilia Payne

would use, in order to draw on them and demonstrate that "to organize things for yourself" is contrary to observation, experiment, and deduction, contrary to everything she could remember from "Stellar Atmospheres" and her degree in law. In vain, Sylvia sought after arguments. But logical argument was of no help here—this battle required a different kind of weapon, one she didn't possess.

*

Ten years later, Sylvia Pepenovska was returning home from work around 6:30 p.m. Her apartment was located east of the building she worked in. On the way home, she went into a shop to buy a few things she needed. A short while after she'd left the shop, she remembered that she'd forgotten to pick up some honey. She was of two minds whether to go back. But she just didn't feel like it, and continued on home. The sun was setting in the east. Its rays shone directly in her eyes and Sylvia put on her sunglasses. She was annoyed about the honey. She didn't like to leave things to the next day. When she entered Women's Park, her gaze fell on a monument facing the shopping mall. A sudden thought flashed through her mind. It was just a vague feeling that something was off, that something wasn't quite right. But she didn't know what. She looked again at the monument. A few rays glinted off it from the sun, setting in the east. A memory buried deep in her mind struggled to come to the surface. A flutter in her stomach seemed to remind her that something was not as it should be. But in no way could she remember what it was. Within a few seconds, though, she was able to forget the unpleasant thought. Then she remembered another shop on the way home where she could buy some honey, and calmly went on her way.

TRANSLATED FROM THE MACEDONIAN BY PAUL FILEV

NORA WAGENER

You'd Have Larvae Too

OCTOBER 24

Around noon, I got a call from St. Eberhard Hospital, some 300 kilometers away. When I picked up, an inhuman-sounding voice told me my father was dying. There must have been some sort of mistake, I replied. I don't have a father. Then I hung up. This conversation had become more and more frequent before I finally admitted to being the Loser's daughter.

October 25

Three years ago I'd have just gotten in the car, looked in on him briefly, and then gone on with my day—in and out without a single world. Three years ago I didn't have this ring on my finger: I'll always try to be honest with you. Luckily, the topic didn't ever come up again. And just how am I supposed to break it to Matthias that my parents are still half alive? When we met, I told him they were dead, both of them, and that my father had been the first to go.

You're crazy, he'll tell me. Forget having a screw loose—you don't even have any screws left! You're a monster! Which shows me just how convenient my being an orphan was, even if he'd never admit to it. Whenever I did something strange, he always had an easy explanation: She lost her parents at such a young age. That's why she's like this. But not to worry—he was never short of explanations. If he'd ever met them, he could have said, She's like that because of her parents.

October 26

As I walk through the doors of St. Eberhard, I feel briefly as though I've been lured into a trap. It's inconceivable to me that here, in such a shiny, state-of-the-art facility, doctors must capitulate to sickness. End-stage liver cancer. The doctors didn't even know how much he could understand anymore—he hadn't said a single word since his arrival. A shock ran through my heart. That he would even have the capacity to speak in his current condition, to say something to me at the end of his silent existence—that hadn't occurred to me for a second.

The nurse leads me down a truly odd-smelling hallway. It can't be much farther, I think to myself. Try not to breathe through your nose. She stops in front of number 52 and gives a solemn nod in my direction. I nod back, welded to the spot at her side. After a moment, she opens the door for me, her friendly gestures forcing me to enter the room . . . Then the door will shut, and then I'll be left alone with my father.

He's gotten smaller . . . either that or the machines surrounding him are far too big. I sit down on the empty bed beside his, not knowing at all how I should act. I lie down on the bed and look at him from the side. His skin is the color of chalk. "You don't look good," I say.

October 27

Yesterday I called Matthias and told him that I'll be staying. After a long night in the hotel, I arrive back at the hospital at eight in the morning. They're stricter about visitation in the west wing. The west wing is where they keep the dying people.

A nurse is in his room switching out one of the transparent medication bags his life is hanging from. She turns around and tells me I have to wait a minute. I step back into the odorous hall. When the nurse comes out, I ask her cautiously,

"What did you give him?"

"Something for the pain."

Of course.

"Do you know how long it will be?"

"It will probably be pretty quick," she replies, sorrowfully lowering her gaze. "Your father never got treatment. He just called us when he needed an ambulance. And when our people got there, he'd already lost consciousness."

I wanted to sit quietly beside him and wait for Death to show his face. Instead, I fill the room with noise, scratching myself, coughing, adjusting the chair. But after a couple more times through, my repertoire of irritating sounds loses its hold on me. I go over to the closet and take stock of his belongings. Nothing that awakens unwanted memories. Some clothes, a comb, a set of dentures, a thick book. That must have been left by a former occupant. For one thing, Stephen King and my father don't exactly mix. And besides, who would have thought to pack reading material? I pick up the book and walk with it through the room, commenting: here is the window, here is the TV, here is the empty bed, and there lies my father.

I hold the book under his nose and then lift it up until it's level with my shoulders. How many years has this man humiliated and demeaned those around him? If I were to let the book go, it would crash down onto his old, sick chest, forcing his last breath out of him.

It looks like I made the Loser cough, I notice with surprise. I lower the book. Don't worry—I'm not going to kill you. You seem to be managing that just fine on your own.

October 28
On my third day at the hospital, I finally make a concerted effort to communicate with my father:

"Sometimes, when my husband isn't there—I'm married—and when it's really quiet, I can still hear the heavy beat of your shoes coming up to my room. Even though I'm an adult now, this childhood sound hasn't faded. Can you even hear me? Please stop pretending that you're asleep, dear Father. Your footsteps in my house. When you're finally in your grave, I hope the devil takes you. I hope Mother takes you! I always thought she'd outlive you—I still can't believe she didn't. But either way, you'd have never met your grandchild. Third month. What else do you own, aside from this comb and these dentures? I hope you didn't drink everything else away. In a couple years I'll have assembled half a soccer team around me. And none of my players will be benched—I'll tell you that right now. None of them will feel those rough fingers digging into their necks, banishing them from the field. And my coatrack will be filled with bright raincoats, and the dresser covered with hats. Under every washbasin there will be a stool. I will have a child with red cheeks—red from playing. It will be a happy child. All my children will be happy. And the more children I have, the fainter your footsteps will become."

At some point while I was talking, my finger must have drifted toward his thumb. It feels like he's pressing back, but they told me he's too weak to move. I let him go and get up for some coffee. I drink a lot of coffee as the day goes on.

October 29

Over time, I've gotten to know the nurses' rhythm. In between their visits, I lay a thin cloth over my father's face. It's not easy, after so many years, to be in the same room with him for this long.

I've moved my chair to up next to the window and haven't budged from it. I want to be able to hear if he's still breathing. When it gets dark, I can see the cloth rising and falling in the window reflection. Let us pray he never rises from the dead.

I will stand at his open grave, next to the other mourners, mumbling through their beards, next to pimple-faced altar boys, and I will throw on clumps of dirt. The priest will read from the Gospel of Matthew, imploring God above to deliver us from evil. But I will go up to him and say that we can never be delivered from evil. Evil can grow weaker, but we'll never be free of it. Don't you know that?

I wish he still had a little strength left so that I could wrap my fingers around his throat and pretend to strangle him while he pretended to defend himself. He's become unbelievably small. I could never do anything to him now. But I won't leave here until he's departed this world. I'll check his pulse every hour, and if I have to, I'll pinch his IV tubes. He deserves death, and death is what he'll get. He's worked for it—shouting, lashing out. Always forgetting what's important. Always remembering what's not.

October 30

All quiet in the west wing. My dying father is still dying. I call Matthias and ask him to tell me everything that's happened since I left—every tiny detail, every banality. Somewhere out there is our life. When he has nothing left to report, he asks me if I want to talk about it. "Read me something," I answer wearily. "I want to hear your voice for a few more minutes."

My father opened his eyes for the first time since I got here. His gaze is rigid, frozen—he probably can't see anything. He might not be fully conscious. "It's me," I say, sitting down on the bed next to him and laying my hands in my lap like old Auntie Whoever. "What have you even been doing these last years? Watching TV? Isn't really worth it anymore, is it?" I can hear the decay gurgling in his lungs. Drool drips onto his pillow. He's on the right track, and he'll be there soon.

His roommate barely left anything behind. The night table next to the bed is empty. A sachet of lavender is still hanging in the closet. The dried buds look like larvae. If Mother were still alive, you'd have some too. I hang the larvae in my father's closet. I turn to the dentures and the comb and say, "I should actually be grateful to you. Ever since I was young, it's been easy to say goodbye. In a couple of days you'll be under the ground. And I'll stand above you and shake hands."

October 31

Twenty minutes ago, Death kissed my father.

He doesn't look good. Just like before, his skin is the color of chalk. I lay the white cloth over his face. It doesn't move. I take it off again, touching him where Death touched him. His mouth hangs slightly open.

That evening, I call our house. When Matthias picks up, I try to tell him exactly what the nurse said, just like I tried earlier. I get through two, maybe three words before it's gone—my voice has failed me. In this moment, I must admit my defeat, and in this moment, I feel even more powerless than before.

TRANSLATED FROM THE GERMAN BY JEFFREY D. CASTLE

ALVYDAS ŠLEPIKAS

The Fishermen

YES, THERE'S NOTHING astounding here. In this town. Everyone who doesn't end up here by accident says it's nice. They're probably right. Huge old trees grow on both sides of the main street, the scabrous roots of which curl across the earth's surface and plow up the asphalt of the street, while sad old women look through their old windows that have seen fires and wars, and in the evenings buckets clang and cows moo. There's a beautiful Renaissance church in the center of town, and a bit further on—a grocery store, a school which has fewer and fewer students each year, an office building with a fluttering Lithuanian flag, and a culture house that's been quiet and empty for some time now. Still further from the center, on the rather wide bank of a pond choked with sludge, is a public sauna, where almost all the inhabitants of the town gather on the weekends—women on Friday and men on Saturday. If you, not having anything to do, should wander the empty streets of town and finally find yourself there, you would, no doubt, see two people sitting motionless on the shore of the reservoir not far from the public sauna, fishing. Every once in a while, they exchange a word or two, praise each other when one catches a bigger fish, of which there aren't many—just little yellow pond carp, which are fearless and not choosy about bait. The older man, past sixty, hardly catches anything, he observes the younger man, the forty-year-old, he removes the fish the other one has caught, then puts the bait on the hook—all with the greatest of love. The younger man, having landed a fish, watches the old man remove it, and lets it slip into the bucket. Sometimes, after some brief quarrel over something, they trade a few words, like when the old man sometimes scales the back of a carp that's still alive, seasons it with salt, and eats the meatiest part of the fish with relish, before throwing what's left off to the side, where generally there's some clever purring creature in attendance. Most of the time, they sit in silence, their faces radiating tranquility; they put their fishing rods down and watch the bobbers, the water of the reservoir, the water striders buzzing about on the surface of the pond—life goes on. Looking at these two silent men, it might appear to you that they've come to understand something very important, essential, eternal, something they'll never lose. It's doubtful whether you'd have the courage to strike up a conversation with them and disturb the tranquil atmosphere that surrounds them. Perhaps the people that gather in the public sauna or the people hurrying by feel this—only one or two greet them with a nod of the head, while many go past as if they were inanimate objects, trees or tree stumps. These two silent people have first names, and a shared last name, but in the town they haven't called them these for ages, just the fishermen.

If you'd drum up the courage to strike up a conversation with one of the townspeople and ask about those strange men fishing near the public sauna, you'd probably be surprised to learn that no one likes them. Someone would joke, someone would say that they are horrible, godless creatures who don't even go to confession at Christmas, others would growl that they're simply idiots, and yet others would become obviously flustered and clearly annoyed by your question. Nevertheless, they'd all tell you more or less the same story.

The Motūzas family lived on the outskirts of town, beyond the church and the student dormitory. Their old, unpainted wooden house was squeezed between the houses of Augustinas the organ player and the milkmaid Marilė, the town's only Pole. Old Marilė and the other older inhabitants of the town still remembered Mrs. Elena very well, she was the wife of the cripple Motūzas, the mother of Algis Motūzas—a good-hearted pious woman, however downtrodden and without any say in life. She would often appear in town with a dark, flowered scarf wrapped around her head, it almost covered her face—everyone knew that Mrs. Elena was hiding bruises and beatings. Her husband, who was not yet lame at that time, would beat her almost every day, brutally and mercilessly, and Algis, still a child then, would hide from his father almost every day in the doghouse of the incredibly angry sheepdog, Dikas, or in the barn, or at the neighbors. And then one day hunting for mushrooms with his grandson Kęstas in the pine forest near the town, Štencelis, the resident intellectual, found Mrs. Elena swinging from the branch of a pine tree. Afterward Kęstas told the town boys about Mrs. Motūzas's blue tongue, the froth, and her bulging eyes. No one blamed Mrs. Elena, everyone felt sorry for her. Even the gray-haired parish priest who was loved by everyone, though he did not bless the grave site, put on civilian clothes, stood in the cemetery a bit apart from everyone, watched the coffin of the suicide being lowered into the ground, and said prayers. Disbanding home after the funeral, the townspeople opined that now something had to change in that lecher and wife-beater Motūzas's life; after all, even such a horrible person as him has to have a conscience that wouldn't let him sleep at night. They were all wrong—nothing changed in that man's life, if anything he began indulging his lusts even more openly, taking loose women home and fornicating with them in plain view of his young son. Just a week or two after his wife's death, Lord have mercy on her, Motūzas had a fight with the Žegunis brothers and, being rather drunk, waved a long German knife at them. However, the brothers were also no slouches: the middle brother, Vladas, grabbing a crowbar to defend himself, beat his opponent in such a way that not only were a few of his ribs broken, but his leg was shattered. Motūzas returned from the hospital crippled, and people said, see, "God has punished him." The old man got himself a heavy oak cane, but he didn't change his way of life, though he did calm down somewhat. When suddenly the Žegunises' hay and animal barns went up in flames like a box of matches, though there was no evidence, no one doubted whose work it was. Motūžas continued to be an angry, insatiable stallion who defiled women, the bogeyman for all of the town's children—a person who never smiled.

Algis was afraid of his father, too. The boy grew up ill-tempered and irritable, he was friendless, and would only go visit with old

Marilė. She would treat him to pears and garden berries, taught him to say hello and thank you in Polish, and during feast days gave him colored *abrozdėliai*, or holy cards with pictures of patron saints, which he would throw away once he got home. Though Algis was a decent student, no one liked him—neither the teachers, to whom he was rude, nor the pupils, whom he'd beat and whose kopecks he'd take. In general he was almost always quiet, taciturn like his old man, he lived with his father as if he were a stranger, and the only thing that linked them was fear. After finishing school, he studied at a technical college, then began working as an electrician, later went to the army and returned a grown-up handsome man, with more than a few women and girls who gazed after him, however Algis didn't dare bring any of them home, and he'd rarely go out with anyone. Though lame, Motūzas remained the same as before, and it seemed that time was powerless against that man.

After Gintas, the director of the town's culture house, in a rather tipsy state, struck a student from Vilnius in a Voschodu car he'd borrowed and, found guilty, went to jail, the culture house was empty for a time. However, once a few months had gone by a new female director was put in charge. She was a newcomer with a funny last name, Kriaušytė, which means "pear" in Lithuanian. And that was how she looked—like a sweet pear with rounded cheeks. She was young, quiet, spoke sometimes using Samogitian dialect words, and as a result she seemed strange to many. Kriaušytė settled in the attic above the District Executive Committee (now the administrative office for the head of the district). Creaking wooden steps rose up to it and, after she'd settled there, the steps began to creak more and more. The boys of the town sensed treasure and tried to pop by regardless of the occasion. Fall passed, and then it was halfway through winter, the director was no longer a total stranger to the people of the town, and perhaps because of the fact that she didn't show overwhelming hospitality, or perhaps for other reasons, the guests in the attic grew fewer, it was cold and sad there. Winter came to end, the spring ice was cracking, and here and there the townspeople began to whisper that something had happened to lame Motūzas. The old man had calmed down, drank less, wasn't bringing loose women home anymore, just occasionally the iron tip of his oak cane would click down the main street. People wondered and waited. One day, the District Executive Committee's janitor, Žemaitytė, astonished, told her neighbor that she had seen old Motūzas for the umpteenth time, clambering up the wooden stairs to the culture house director's place. This rumor soon spread, and it wasn't just women curious about everything who talked about it, but the men as well. They laughed and discussed lame Motūzas's love while drinking wine or beer. However, it soon became clear that it wouldn't be enough to call the feeling that had overcome the old lecher falling in love: it was true passion, obsession. Motūzas began to dress up—he bought an expensive new raincoat, patent leather shoes, and not only a top hat, but also a brightly colored tie, he began to walk with perfect posture and monumental pride, he shaved off his mustache, and some thought that he even dyed his hair. Kriaušytė would pass people with her eyes lowered guiltily, greeting them in a barely audible manner, a golden chain sparkling on her tender neck, with huge earrings, also of gold, dangling on her ears, and old Marilė swore that she'd once seen precisely those earrings in Mrs. Elena's jewelry box. Lame Motūzas brought and gave everything he could to his beloved: shoes, clothes, a television, furniture. He bought a splendid new Zaporozhets and began driving Kriaušytė into town. To accomplish all of this he not only sold his piglets, but the very pig he used for breeding, took everything he'd saved in his savings account, and finally butchered a calf and put on a feast—they basked in the revelry for almost a week. The old man began to be short of money, and he started demanding funds from his son Algis, who looked at his father's flights of fancy and clenched his teeth in silence, because the only person in the world that he feared was his father. The townspeople, seeing lame Motūzas's folly, laughed and waited to see how everything would turn out, and those few friends with whom Algis spoke called him a fool and chewed him out. Once, while drinking beer, Prancius Dainius, who'd done a stint in the clink for social parasitism, and because he wore glasses, was called the Professor, said to Algis:

"Don't be a wimp. Go over to that whore and talk to her. How long are you going to watch your old man throwing your money to the wind?"

Finally, once when his father had gone off somewhere, Algis gathered his courage, climbed the creaking stairs and knocked. When Kriaušytė opened the door and saw Algis, she looked somewhat ashamed, lowered her eyes, but invited him inside. Algis stepped over the threshold into the room, where the light burned brightly, and stopped. They stood across from each other in silence. Algis's chest was flooded by a strange warmth, while his legs shook like the legs of an old nag after carrying a load of manure.

Now that he knew the way, Algis began to visit the director's attic more and more often, keeping it secret from his father, and it seemed as if life began to open up for him. He didn't want to think about what would happen when his father found out about these visits, but he understood he would find out. And then old man Motūzas returned from the city earlier than he'd promised, climbed the creaking stairs, and was holding a new flower-print dress in his hands. After climbing up he tried to open the door, but it was locked, so he pulled out the key and tried to open it, however there was another key in the keyhole on the other side. The old man began to knock, but no one answered, then with a bad feeling, he grabbed the door handle with that bestial force he had more of than brains, and broke through the cardboard door of the attic. Once he had broken through the door, the old man saw his son Algis standing on the other side of the threshold, and Kriaušytė behind his back, cowering and instinctively covering her white breasts that had never seen the sun. Algis looked his father in the eye and, clenching his fists, was ready to fight him. He was prepared to kill him, if he had to. For the first time he did not fear his father. The old man, unsettled by the surprise, took a backward step, and Algis moved toward him, but suddenly his father, snarling or moaning strangely, waved his heavy oak cane, struck his son, who fell as he turned, awkwardly. The stairs were old and steep. Algis rolled down them and hit his head on the iron shaft of the television antenna. Blood spurted out, his legs were twisted in a horrible way, and a terrible sound like the howling of dying animals erupted from somewhere in Algis's chest. Having lost his strength, the old man sat down on the stairs and looked at the blood gushing from his son's ear. Kriaušytė, barely covered by her robe, rumbled down the stairs, jumped over the prone man and ran toward the town, shrieking. The ambulance arrived. The doctor, having seen the stairs, said:

"What a terribly steep staircase. He slipped?"

"He slipped," old man Motūzas announced, and his tongue twisted around in his mouth like a piece of ice.

After this, old man Motūzas forgot Kriaušytė, as if he'd forgotten his entire earlier life—he sat at the hospital day and night. When Algis regained consciousness and began to eat, he brought his son juice and jam. And he cried. His son looked at his father crying for the first time and tried to smile.

He took his son to the bus when he was discharged from the hospital—Algis had broken his back, and now had lost the use of one arm, and he dragged his left leg, and the left side of his face was paralyzed too.

Kriaušytė didn't visit Algis even once while he was in the hospital, and she left before he returned home. Afterward there was talk that she'd got married; however, no one knew where and to whom. Algis began receiving disability payments, and the old man his pension. And now, if you'd happen to find yourself in this quiet town and go near the pond, where the public sauna is, you would certainly see two men whose last names the town's inhabitants are beginning to forget. Almost everyone now simply calls them the Fishermen.

TRANSLATED FROM THE LITHUANIAN BY JAYDE WILL

DAVIDE ORECCHIO

City of Pigs

SUPERMEAT THAT'S REDDER *than red. Bloodier than a slit vein. Tenderer than a mouthful of petals. More nutritious than three whole meals. Humans eat it. Pigs find it revolting ← its sponginess, its smell. Pigs refuse PanCarnis. SuperMeat.*

*

On the marble of the masters, on the plasterboard of the servants. In the conurbation of the forebears and the conurbation of the offspring. In the wake of the fathers, in the mold of the sons. A pig awakes, regains consciousness, blinks bleary eyes, finds himself in an urban park that opens, beyond a roundabout, onto the asphalt, and he's back in the city, he knows the diorama and the ramps of the cloverleaf.

He opens the door of the MightyJet and steps onto the grass, domesticated grass, typical of the microlife of the macrocity—*what a disaster, or maybe a stroke of luck, I can go home, rest a little, get my thoughts in order, but how do I find home, where am I?*—thinks Felix and catches sight of a building on the other side of the hedge, of the street, that he wants to get to.

He finds the gate, leaves the park, hastens ahead on the WildBunch but finds no one. The city has phony intermediate zones between industry and services, intervals that if they were a human you would struggle to find character, and if they were a book, you'd say they had no character at all. The building that drew Felix's attention has no character → warehouse that's been locked and sealed for who knows how long, windows closed tight with shutters shedding woodmeal. There's nothing. No one. No work, no voice, no production.

He continues along the WildBunch between dozens of similar buildings. *Sooner or later I'll come across something or someone, but maybe it's better if I don't.* He's losing heart, weak from hunger, dejected as his energies abandon him, discouraged by the way everything and every creature disintegrates and dissipates, now he heads down a narrow street and feels the darkness of empty rooms reflected on the front windows, no life and no death either, the gutters are dry, full of spiderwebs and home to mice and cockroaches.

Past sewers past manholes past drains, Felix continues, very unhappy. His snout is leaking fat, the sweat of his exertions soiling him. Gates of lead, gates of aluminium. Reinforced concrete, plaster. Not even a BigWagon going by. No mettle, no curiosity, no logic to his movements, he doesn't know where he's headed, but he keeps going. The empty house is him, the empty street, him, he's the protagonist of a walk through the rubbish of the neighborhood where, among the trash bins, he finds himself in the rout, the dream, the lost souls.

He sees himself in the rat's tail. Sees himself in the sludge. In the ash heap in the corner. In the locks smeared with grime. In the flint and gravel soup. A blotch of dried urine dismays him. Every ugly thing announces his decline. He meets broken glass and loses bone and muscle power, because of his past inertia, because it was enough just to crawl? An old man breaks a femur and just sits down, accepting the bed sores as a kind of life. The blind man thinks hearing is enough, and clings to it. The pig has nothing but the journey, the journey's necrosis, the journey's torment, the burden of gangrenous journeying. Felix moves on, skimming by, out of focus; he doesn't know where he's headed.

He's losing the will to go on. Now he sees that down there, three intersections ahead, two NormoLimbed are instructing pigs, he's ambushed by enterprise. He stares at them the way you stare at fog, at your own sleep. But he doesn't approach them. He wants help but doesn't ask for it. He trains his bleary eyes on his hooves, takes an even narrower street, finds an alleyway in which to stumble. It's dark, cramped, filthy. The wind pours in, lifting up discarded paper, plastic wrap, feathers, hair, bringing them back to life, then sucking them in so they lie, cradled, on the ground. Soon the wind will return to start up the circus again.

Think of it as bowels whose job is not to let flow but to retain, and in this gulag under the stars, driven left and right by the high walls of colorless tower blocks, install a pig moving through the chute. You could liken it to a death rattle, this chute; shift your eyes away so as not to see the hooves humiliated by what they trample. But what's trampled is really there, however, its stink and the stuff that sticks to you and contaminates you, as well as the ashes, particulate, dried shit, parched dust of the ages, walls that grow and loom, vomit of stray animals, feathers of dried-up birds, every stain revealing its organic origin, the task of advancing and being only a further type of being, the determination to breathe a type of being that nobody cares about except you (solitude, a feeble type of being), appetite and nausea, appraisal and revulsion, weakness and inertia → it's all there together in the pig, until there appears a slit in the wall at the end of the alleyway's narrow berth: a cleft in this cul-de-sac.

An opening. Felix approaches and studies it. It's free and offers a way through if you crouch on your knees. Investigating the thing Felix wakes up a bit, becomes curious, wonders: *what is this hole? should I maybe go in?* Waves of heat and the sound of air being expelled by a machine emerge from the opening. It's dark inside but he can just see a tube that might be connected to something circulating air. Nearby, on the floor, the seal someone's ripped off. Felix sees discarded food cartons, empty tin cans, beans, rucola leaves, dried-out bread, bottles, a pack of sugar, jars of coffee, bones resting on polystyrene tubs smeared with blood. Leftovers scattered on the floor below a red wall, as if digested and evacuated. They look like the remains of a meal, and he hunkers down, puts his head in the tube, then a front hoof, then a knee, the other hoof, the other knee, and he's in.

Now he's crawling through the dark tunnel. Drops of water, steam disintegrating, fall on him. He slips through the wet walls. Hits a shoulder. Pants. Gets up. The air is whirling, the cavern humming. He skins his knees a bit, his hooves, his forelegs, sneezes into the damp, bores through the heat. He's moving backward through this gut from the exit toward the entrance. Now there's light. Something light. He can see that the other end is near. There's light but it's still dark: one defines the other and vice versa. However, the light is growing and the darkness receding.

The tube is not long. He's already through. Felix is facing a plastic grate. He eyes the window slits. There's a flash and then more light, a light source, in a clean white space surrounded by white shelves loaded with goods that Felix doesn't recognize from a distance. It must be food. This must be a bazaar. Of the NormoLimbed. It's the strategy. The food depositories appear in zones of desolation, it wards off danger and attacks, the food protected by automatic conveyor belts ← robots distribute the merchandise toward Mushrooms, toward Orchids. Pigs don't visit the bazaar, PanCarnis doesn't interest pigs, pigs are forbidden to enter the bazaar but Felix, undone by coincidences, puzzled by enigmas, discouraged by adversities, convinced he's been shipwrecked, wants to check, wants to know, decides to go in, knocks off the grate (which announces that Felix is entering), swings his body round, grabs at the wall, lowers his hooves and rests on the highest shelf, then the next highest, then the third down meanwhile clutching at the bottom shelf, in short descends to the floor and immediately runs to a corner to hide where the robots can't see him.

In the aisle of the victuals. It's all white. The boxes too. It's a long white gondola stacked with shelves full of foodstuffs packaged in white. Felix rests a shoulder on the shelves. He's hungry, but what to eat? He sees no grass and acorns among the merchandise, among the edibles, the beverages, prepared foods, baked goods, labels, marzipan, delicacies, dainties and every kind of indulgence, canned foods, powdered foods, packaged, frozen, precooked, macrobiotic, vitamins, proteins. No grass and acorns. He guesses there's an assortment of pseudomeat, pseudofish, pseudomolluscs → simulacra to meet the NormoLimbers' polyfagic desire to ingest creatures that fly, graze, swim. He imagines the surfeit, the glut, the nausea, and feels breathless. He's hungry. But he sees no grass and acorns. Even the most innocuous bread might be some filthy swill.

He doesn't know what he's looking for, or what he's come to ascertain. In this wan white space. A mechanical hoist starts up and frightens Felix. He's fearful of the consumption and the abundance he senses in these goods. The bazaars of the WideNostrils are not this opulent. All this squandering upsets him too. What's in those packets, he asks himself again. What processed edibles? What forms—once of life, now of feed? Showcases dozens of meters long, many meters high, in the white. Strong white light that gives him headache. No window. Merchandise that's deceased, containing refined ex-pseudocreatures as inert products, maybe nutritious maybe harmful. A cemetery of disguises. A shell game of packaging and the multiplication of packages, white.

Felix understands the secrets of these places, but they repel him, they're not made for him. He sees no grass, no acorns. He doesn't know what PanCarnis is. He's never wanted to know, but now he must learn, and he thinks he's seen where to go, far away, shaped like a conveyor belt, at a point where the aisle ends. On the other side to the right there's nothing as far as he can see, as far as where his vision expires short of the fog of shelves under the obstinate light. White. And so he moves to the left, without confidence, without courage, without making a sound.

A mountain range of immobile products—apart from the air conditioning, which riffles box tops and shifts plastic wrap—presides above Felix as he clambers forward cautious as a turtle, and it seems he'll never arrive. Left hoof, right knee, right hoof, left knee. He neither stands nor stops nor retreats, like a turtle → the place is empty. The robots pay no attention. What's he afraid of? ← in this system he barely understands. Fear and stubbornness: the mixture that makes him move forward even though hunkered down, but without stopping, like a turtle. More noise. Forklifts, things shifting about heard but not seen, deliveries going out on drones, maybe a laugh or a recorded voice, frighten him and make him stay down.

And still he moves forward, hoof and knee, hoof and knee until he arrives at the moving belt, a belt of meat. Loaded with rolls, slices and slips. There's a cutting board. A meat grinder. Chicken shears. A cleaver. Thighs of pseudoveal and pseudoturkey. Quarters of synthetic beef in the background. Steaks, cutlets, loins, rumps and rounds. Also filet, if anyone wants it, and ground meat.

Felix lifts his snout and senses that it is all the same, this meat; the form may change but the substance no, substance that is nearer to orange than to red, shiny, and phosphorescent, laid out in slices on the majolica tub. *Maybe it's not even meat*, thinks Felix. But it is. What it's not, is pseudomeat. It's meat, SuperMeat, PanCarnis, and he can see that. The category expands to reveal the subspecies: "Chicken-flavored PanCarnis," "Lamb-flavored PanCarnis," and "Tuna-flavored PanCarnis." Chameleon-meat. That assumes the desired form. As desired. Like a prostitute. It's the seasonings, the genetic engineering. Meat that risks being nothing in order to be everything. *What strange habits these humans have*, thinks Felix, *they eat things that taste like other things, they don't demand the real one,* but it seems he's wrong because the list of products continues on the display until it arrives at Natural PanCarnis, "the original flavor of PanCarnis, from city pigs," either "fresh, five years old" or "cured, salame."

"From city pigs."

No grass and acorns here.

"Fresh, five years old."

"Cured, salame."

Loin, ribs, belly, shoulder, neck, blade, hock, jowl, bacon, leg, foot, head; pork chops, butt, cottage roll, spare ribs, fresh picnic shoulder, smoked picnic shoulder, fresh ham roast, pork blood sausage, lard. So many pork products → in the city, on the marble of the masters and the plasterboard of the servants, in the conurbation of the forebears and that of the offspring. In the wake of the fathers, in the mold of the sons ← pork meat is sold, pork is bought, pork is eaten, and the pig falls to the floor in the bazaar, his shoulders against the floor of the world, his eyes wide open on the world, his mouth wide open to the world entering Felix's new life, Felix, pig without memory, without knowledge, the pig that today sees → a hologram over the belt and the PanCarnis, like a twentieth-century advertisement, shows a woman inside her house in a mushroom in the city center, in her feeding zone, cutting a slice of salame not very different from the one in the peasant's hut in the woods, and offering it to her son, who puts it in his mouth, tastes it, chews it, and says "good!" with his eyes.

"The original flavor of PanCarnis, from city pigs."

The NormoLimbers say good with their eyes while, on the floor of the world, crouched against the shelves like someone playing hide and seek, belly on the floor, brow on his foreleg, Felix screams, *No! What is this?* he moans, *What's happening?* The hologram continues. Prosciutto from the mother's hands into the child's mouth. Delicacies. Happy faces. The NormoLimber's good manners. The clichés. The flavor of meat. A new flavor. Mortality. Barbarity. Power. Window-dressing. Hypocrisy. The price of meat. *I don't want to watch. I don't want to know.* Astro Eclipse™ white light. The dazzling color orange. The truth. Human taste, human gluttony. The condiment, the preserve. Peppercorns between the teeth, dregs of skin. Fat. Salt, thirst.

He hears himself weeping. Hears a lament. From below. A grunting lament. Tears fed by a lament, growing by spontaneous generation. They swell. They stoke. Now a robot comes to life. Comes forward from the moving belt, staying in the middle of the aisle. Looking down. Where the lament grows louder. The tears explode. Desolate, and hearing himself aggrieves him. Shrill, explosive weeping. He listens, hears nothing else to listen to and so he weeps. Brow on foreleg so as not to see. Belly on the floor. Cold knees. Snot blocking his breath. Moans gushing from his throat, needing to breathe but choking.

The robot bends over, sees the pig. Teeth, dust, claws. The truth. The desolation. The derelict under the shelf. Life, a journey from the past that ends up in this cul-de-sac. The tears have only tears. Eat tears, drink tears, breathe tears. Tears that refuse. Tears in revolt, without the strength or the violence. Tears that hunker down and don't want to be seen, but inside the body (nature) the individual reacts, escapes and screams by weeping. With every sob, every convulsion, he evades a feeble tamer. It was pointless to cower. Useless to weep between the wall and the shelf. Superfluous to hide his eyes under his foreleg. By now the tears were public. The pig's lament in the bazaar of the humans, between cuts of meat and robots. Tears on stage.

The robot is studying him: a crouching pig weeping in the bazaar, where he shouldn't be ← the order comes through to take him away. The weeping, following the order, rises to a shriek. Now there's a drumming from the gondola aisle. Footsteps, robotic heels. Things moved. Impatience. Something falls. The weeping doesn't cease. Now the tempo changes because vocal cords and throat are tired. Moans bounce up like tiny meatballs between pauses. Silence, meatball moan, silence, meatball moan. Felix's tears rummage around in Felix's body. Scours through the caverns seeking agreement: *am I right to weep and despair?* And finding agreement emerges, weeping more.

Weeping, the tears make sense. Anyone listening will understand why he's weeping. But what do his tears say? Do you hear? The message? Signs don't emit sounds. There's a soldier on a shingle of blood, body mangled, leg uprooted; first he shouts, now he's breathless, soon he'll be gasping. The tears protest. The footsteps are a galloping pack, and now they stop. The pack is here. Three more robots join the first. Two grab Felix's right hoof. Two, his left hoof. They drag him. A pig rug. Felix thinks only of weeping. He refuses to stand. He goes limp, won't walk. The robots hoist him up by his spine and lift him high. Plastic hands like spring and mattress; now Felix is on his back near the ceiling. In the light, the white, the weeping.

The move begins. Toward the exit. Felix alive and howling but holed up behind his eyes and in tears. Transferred in silence. The only sound his weeping. Felix lifeless if not for the tears that seep into the pores of his skin, soaking it, enter through his lips into his breathing, moaning mouth, and drip down even onto the robots. They graze past the merchandise. In the long aisle. His (absent) gaze is overwhelmed by salami and beef steaks. Felix on his back. His legs slip, hang down, brush the robot shoulders. His inert hooves signify surrender. The hooves confess the strength he lacks. Not even hooves. Call them hands. Red cheeks. Sweat. A grin deforms him until it becomes a sneer, and joins the wail, which, in a singsong rendition sounds like mockery, like hysteria, like laughter mixed with tears. But he's not laughing at all. He's weeping.

His whole body is palpitating. Not just the heart. The stomach, the chest, the lungs. The carotid artery. The jawbone. Going forward like a slow backstroke down the aisle. If there were water to carry him and a light current instead of the robots, the water carrying him would weep too. Tears would be his river. Not that it's so different now, the way the tears are coming. Snout pointed ceilingwards, bald pink hatless head, jaws drooling, claws limp, the pig focuses on what's crushing him (reservedly and wordlessly, apart from the weeping): *I'm all alone, and who wouldn't be on finding he'd been put on this earth to work and then one day, to be eaten?*

Here was the exit. Natural light. The fuzziness of the outskirts. They go down a flight of stairs. Felix stiffens, he's like a cadaver. He opens his eyes. Sees the spires of SkyTown. The robots put him in a MightyJet. Two robots get in. The MightyJet disappears. Inside, Felix switches off the damaged memory channel, the memories of today and yesterday, removes the recollections and the traumas that are now orphans of his mind (foster mother) and of reality (natural mother). Felix is now excused. Will he speak, will he weep again, will he blow the whistle on them?

Quiet now, the pig is resting.

TRANSLATED FROM THE ITALIAN BY FREDERIKA RANDALL

KATHERINE DUFFY

The Frankenstein Tree

I FIRST GOT wind of Éamon's news from the front page of the news-paper. I was mooching about in a souvenir shop in a resort town abroad. There was a motley collection of holiday stuff on display—snorkels, T-shirts, cigarette lighters, ceramic vases. I was handling a nice little wooden chess set, wondering if Oisín would like it, if he would say it was "cool," when the words on the newsstand caught my eye.

It wasn't a headline but one of those teasers they run in a side-bar, letting you know what stories are inside. The accompanying photo was small and blurry, but I recognized him straight away. I put down the chess set and went to buy a copy.

On the terrace of the café next door, I took a seat in the muggy shade of a large parasol, a view of the placid, yacht-cluttered har-bour spread out before me like the wares of summer. Éamon had won a big international prize. Honour, glory, a jackpot sum of money—the works! From now on everything he did would bear a seal of approval. His name would have a ring of greatness. He could go where he liked and do as he pleased.

"Where the hell were you?" Jo wanted to know, when I got back to the apartment. "I was afraid you'd been knocked down by a car! Did you get the bread?"

"Sorry, love." The original purpose of my walk had slipped my mind completely. "I was looking around the shops, thinking about what to get for Oisín . . . "

This was our first time away without our son since he'd been born. Nothing would do him this year but to make the break with us and attend an outrageously expensive basketball camp on the outskirts of Dublin. Neither of us was keen on the idea but he pestered so long and hard that we caved in.

I don't know why I didn't tell Jo Éamon's news there and then. Because she'd spoken so abruptly when I'd walked in, maybe. But even that wouldn't explain why I had left the newspaper behind me on the table in the café.

*

The evening sun has painted a bright path for me, out over the water. I make my breathing strong and steady, and put my heart into every stroke. From time to time I raise my head out of the water and clamp my gaze onto the little island, as if it might otherwise get away from me. How far out is it? A mile? A couple of kilometers? A good bit, anyway.

It's really nothing but a big cluster of rocks. I don't know why I'm so cracked on reaching it. I kept looking at it from the beach, during the first week we spent here. The thought that I should swim out to it popped into my head and, although I knew it was a silly idea, I just couldn't let go of it.

My crawl has improved a lot since we got here, and I've been working hard on my breathing pattern. I wouldn't dream of using fins or a wetsuit or any other props. All I need to travel through the water are my own limbs and heart and lungs. But towards the end of our second week here, as the time to go home drew nearer, I knew I wasn't ready to attempt it yet. I'd need to practise longer and harder if I was to get to the island safe and sound. By then, the notion had really taken hold of me.

I suppose Jo must have known there was something odd going on. Even so, she was gobsmacked when I told her I was going to stay on for a bit, a week or a fortnight more, however long it took. She froze, her eyes searching my face. Words usually flock to my wife on any given occasion but right then they seemed to have deserted her.

I could see her weighing up what I had just said, sifting for the sense of it. I'm the sort who enjoys going on holiday but who, by the end of it, is generally looking forward to getting back. Nobody knows that better than Jo. Her expression was a jumble of emotions:

worry, fear, but mainly sheer astonishment. I didn't mention the island or my swimming plans. I had no wish to add to her anxiety and anyway it would be too hard to explain. All I said was that I had enjoyed my time here immensely and that I wanted to extend it for a bit.

In the end, she accepted my decision quietly. I thanked her for that when we said goodbye at the airport a few days later. At the boarding gate she gave me another piercing look but still kissed me warmly when I hugged her close. I don't think there's any major damage done. I suppose she'll tell Oisín and her friends that the whims of middle age have descended on me. I don't mind what she says. I've no wish to hurt Jo. All I want at the moment is this freedom, the sea, the setting sun, the island in my sights.

I'm gliding through the water at a nice, steady pace but the island doesn't seem to be getting any nearer. The tangled cries of gulls streel across the sky, as if protesting the coming darkness. It's a lonely sound.

To look back at the kind of work Éamon used to produce when he, I and Jo were at art-college together years ago, you wouldn't think that he would ever come up with the stuff he's doing now. He was always very talented of course, a consummate draughtsman and a skilled painter. But he took a conservative approach, nothing like the great groundbreaking artists that I worshipped and tried to emulate at the time. At college, while the rest of us were flinging buckets of paint at canvases and straining to be innovative, Éamon laboured away quietly at his landscapes and portraits.

He would pitch in with his friends, though, helping out with whatever mad project we had lately dreamed up. I remember a piece of sculpture I made: a big travesty of a tree assembled from wood and papier mâché. I gathered fallen branches in the woods, driftwood from the shore, and pulled offcuts out of skips. Then I pasted and hammered and cobbled it all together. "The Frankenstein Tree," I called it. From its branches lemons, mirrors, bicycle wheels and I forget what else dangled. I was sure it was a work of genius.

Éamon would join us and the three of us would make raids on various parts of the city, trawling for materials. Jo had the wildest imagination of all of us. She liked to mould and weld metal to make large-scale, twisted, fearless pieces. She was always inveigling us into dragging lumps of iron and steel around for her. It's a wonder none of us was killed the night she persuaded us to break into an old factory to steal sheets of tin she'd spotted through the windows. I thought my heart would stop when a security guard we hadn't realised was in the building let two vicious-looking dogs loose on us. The three of us made a run for the wall and scrambled up over it in a blind panic. I still have a scar on my shin from the jagged glass embedded along the top. Needless to say, the sheets of tin were abandoned. Once we recovered, we had weeks of fun recounting our exploits in various hostelries around the city.

The surface of the water is still alight with the sun's rays but a small circle of darkness surrounds me, moving with me like a cloak. My left shoulder is aching a bit—I've noticed a weakness there before. I'll have to slow down. At least the distance between me and that damned rock has finally begun to shorten. I must be over half-way there. Nice and easy now. On we go.

It's odd, considering how close the three of us were, that Jo and I have just the one painting by Éamon in the house. Even that wasn't bestowed upon us, friend to friend. I bought it at an art auction, a couple of years ago.

Attending art auctions is a big part of my work. I buy paintings and sculptures for banks and other big companies, and for individuals who want to invest in art or simply to collect some beautiful pieces. It's an enjoyable job and I greatly prefer it to working in advertising as I did before. But it's a job that sprang from the jaws of that famous tiger which has now breathed its last. The client list has dwindled sharply in recent times and those who remain are buying less and less. Who knows how things will go.

If my memory serves me right, it was around the time Jo and I bought the house and settled down together that Éamon took off on his travels. We got postcards—from Europe at first, then from farther afield—India, Fidji, Bali. His travels left their mark on his work and it began to turn adventurous and strange.

Gradually the postcards stopped coming. I read somewhere

that Éamon was living in New York. But Oisín had arrived on the scene and we could barely tell night from day. We were busy with the house and the garden, with getting and spending. The years whizzed by and we hadn't a thought to spare for an old friend far from home.

The evening is my favourite time to swim. By the time I'm breasting the water, everyone else is straggling inland. Thinking of dinner, perhaps, or a nap, or seeking refuge from the sharpening breeze. I revel in the calm after they've gone, swimming in water that's free of all their stupid flotsam—beach balls and surfboards and lilos. Not to mention the jetskis and sailboards that sully the stretches of water further out.

Ouch! Oww! A cramp in my right calf sears through the muscle down towards my foot. Nothing to worry about, nothing at all, I mutter to myself, soothing panic before it has a chance to rise. I know how to deal with this. I stop pulling strongly and paddle lightly about. I turn on my back and float, stretching and twirling my feet.

I wonder how far down all that darkness below me goes. Miles between me and the seabed, maybe. Who knows what strange creatures are going about their business down there, scuttling and flitting and haunting the depths. There's a wide, indigo band of water now between me and the homely gold of the beach.

Inland, the first lights are beginning to twinkle. Back in their apartments and hotels people are singing in the shower, or opening the wardrobe, asking themselves and each other what they'll wear tonight, where they'll go to eat. Or maybe they're in bed together, or grappling on the floor (they're on holidays after all), yielding to the lust that's built up after a long, hot, half-naked day at the beach.

At home, Jo and Oisín are probably eating dinner right now. She was due to pick him up from basketball camp yesterday. She'll be doing her damnedest to get out of him exactly what went on, what his life was like during the time he spent apart from us. She hasn't a hope, of course. He'll skillfully ward off her every attempt at eliciting information. It's an old game with the two of them and they're both adept at it. Later, she'll check her e-mails to see if any orders have come in for pieces of jewellery. Or she'll go out to the garden to try to repair the damage her enemies, the slugs, snails, and greenfly, have wreaked while she was away.

She must have heard Éamon's news by now. She'll be thrilled for him, and will be trying to contact me to pass it on. Maybe right this minute onshore my mobile phone is ringing out. Jo won't be worried when I don't reply. She knows I go swimming in the evenings.

I'd love to be able to reach out and rest my hand on something solid for just a minute or two. The branch of a tree, say, or a friend's shoulder. At least the pain in my leg has faded, and I'm ploughing on again. The water is starting to feel a bit warmer. I think I'm getting close to the island.

To get out of the sea, I have to crawl on my hands and knees. Then I clamber up the tiny, pebbly shore, my legs buckling and a terrible heaviness clawing at my body. Oh, but it's nice to sit down! I've never before been so grateful for such a hard, rocky seat. Of course, I'll have to do it all over again shortly. But I'd rather not think about that right now.

The little town across the water is ablaze with lights now. I imagine that they're winking and flashing congratulations at me. A giddy little laugh burbles up from deep in my rib-cage. But I'd better not rest here too long. After its big show of radiance, the sun is down to its last rays.

Jo wanted to hang Éamon's painting over the mantel in the sitting-room but I wanted to keep it in my study. We argued about it and she gave in when I said I'd buy another piece for the sitting-room. It's unlikely I'll be able to do that now though. The price of his work will rocket now that he's won the big prize.

So I got my way and the painting hangs above my desk. It's an abstract piece, but naturalistic images bump and swirl within it. A woman's face. A tree. A deer. They seem to float to the surface then fade back, or morph into something else. That's the magic of it.

The painting is full of light but has veins of darkness running through it, like a chunk of marble. I'm so used to looking at it that I can close my eyes and call it to mind at will. Tonight, I glimpse new things in it, details I didn't notice before. Waves and clouds. Shades of a summer twilight. A mysterious, black mark on an indigo sea. A small, shadowy form approaching it, closing eagerly on it.

TRANSLATED FROM THE IRISH BY THE AUTHOR

HUGH FULHAM-MCQUILLAN

Winter Guests

A MAN IS staying in the hotel during the winter months for an indefinite time. He is working on an academic article. Or I think he should be, mostly he can be seen sitting on the larger balcony, beneath a blanket, with his back turned to the hotel, or he is walking the corridors at night. It is a given, I suppose, that he finds it difficult to sleep. That he insists on keeping his balcony door open to the frankly unnerving perpetuity that is the sea suggests he does not fit beneath the noun of insomniac, but rather the adjective obstinate. I do not especially enjoy watching him, but he is alive, and that is always interesting.

There are floods nearby, and the sea's cold lips foam all day at large rocks that must have fallen from the cliff upon which our hotel so carefully sits. For a while he has been the only guest, but two more have arrived this morning. He does not yet know this; there is no reason for him to be informed of this: just because he was the only guest means nothing to the staff, of whom there are few. It is winter, remember.

He wears a bathrobe (one of his own) when he walks at night. He knocks on the doors, an insouciant rap of the knuckles, as he passes each one. It is difficult to know really how loud he knocks, or what he expects to be inside those empty rooms, whether he is hoping someone might finally wake, and open the door, and welcome him inside. I wonder now, is this his first visit? How might he have stayed here before? So many people have briefly spread out their lives in these rooms only to pack them up again and return to what they call real life. They say this to us. They say this is not real life, and grin or laugh as they say so, as if we were not really working but only pretending and really just trying to reduce our living like them: eating and bathing and sleeping and eating and drinking and bathing and reading and sleeping: trying desperately to relax, to reduce their consciousness until they lie at the level of the animal lazing in the sun; all this in the attempt to reduce the friction inherent in living. Nobody ever achieves this on their hotel break, and nobody wants to admit it because that would be an admittal of a truism few want to accept, especially on holiday. So they find they must still shift their bodies every now and then so as to avoid discomfort in bed at night, and as they lie on the sunbed, they must apply oil to their limbs and torso if they do not want to burn; they must remove their clothes when it is late, and adjust the temperature of the room so that they do not sweat or shiver, and must shower, brush their teeth, perform ablutions, eat enough fibre, enough carbohydrates, and so on; they must, in essence, continue to live, and living as anyone recently deceased will agree, is tiresome. Yes, they assume we are not working, and I suspect we are not even living things to them, we do not even struggle to relax like them, there is no friction for us, because we are a part of the hotel for the guests, interchangeable as those bricks which must lie on top of each other smothered in plaster and paint to make these walls. I know this because I too have stayed in hotels.

He spots the new guests in the dining room while he fills a glass with orange juice. He is calm or pretending it, but when he returns to his table, he frequently looks away from the book he has propped against the vase, turning quickly, as if reviewing the empty room, to glance at the others at a table on the far side. One is attractive (our clientele often are—naturally, or they can afford the imitation of beauty), the other is unknown. This one sits in a wheelchair in a full-body cast with a small opening for the face. From where I sit, that face is hidden in shadow. The woman appears to speak tenderly to the other. Too tender to be a relative, a daughter or sibling, and I dearly wish she is not the mother, but no, as I have said the way her fingers roam that plaster speaks of the sensuous—as only fingers can; she must be a lover to that unfortunate being. What misfortune could be the cause of that total encasement? I do not know. She is not so young, not so young that I would immediately suspect that unknown individual to have wooed her with riches. They must once have been equals, and now she is the carer. The man continues to glance across the room, though she does not appear to notice, and the other—only they know what they see. They: inside that cast their gender is unknown, I could say "it" but I would be speaking only of that (possibly) temporary skin. They are hidden, they might even be true to the plural: there may be two or more persons trapped inside, small captive children perhaps. I wonder does she stroke that hidden face at night, in empty rooms, in silent corridors, how receptive that skin must have become to air, to touch. Whether the man is entranced by her beauty or intrigued by the unknown is, to me, a mystery. His table faces the sea and, if it were warm and lit by sun without, he would see in the reflection of the window those two guests among the bare tables. In the dull light all that can be seen is grey water flecked with white. He wears a soft oxford, dark chinos, worn leather moccasins.

A few years ago the tidal wave washed so much of this coastline. It decimated so many lives as if they were germs inhabiting an otherwise clean surface: the palm of a hand, for instance. At this height, our hotel was safe, along with the staff, the guests, the travertine tiles, the vintage liqueurs, the glass walls from where those waves could be seen rearing and rearing as if they would never stop growing (growling). The dead came back to us that day, carried by the sea into our lives. A local man, who would often drink in the hotel bar along with his associates (who still do in the summer season), woke in his bed to find the most recent of his victims floating against the wardrobe. The unfortunate soul had been killed over a drug deal, so I heard, and was buried somewhere between the town and the sea. He had been missing for a few weeks before the arrival of the waves. Finding his dead victim returned and lying floating by his bed was enough reality for that local man. It was as if he had said, I am finished with the things of this world, and being unable to leave out of some impulse, or lack thereof, he escaped inside the multifold cities of the mind where he must have lost himself, because I have not seen him around here since, and have heard he is now cared for by his old mother. Poor woman. The waves must have lifted the earth and, seeing the dead man, carried him back to his last contact with life.

It would have been better if the uprooted man had been washed into an armchair, so that when the woken man, the local assassin, groggily entered his sitting room in the morning, he would see the top of a stranger's head, resting, as it were. Carefully taking his gun from his waistband (he is the sort who must always carry a hidden, unlicensed weapon) he decides to surprise this rude intruder and see what it is he wants before shooting him. He jumps in front of the chair, gun raised, and sees the grinning (they always grin) face of his last victim. I would have preferred if the story had unravelled like that, but no, it wasn't half as interesting. The teller finished her telling with a joke about sleeping with the fishes, so perhaps she herself had twisted the story to suit her quip, and so really I should have told my more intriguing, and yes, classic version of the story, as I am sure now it would have been truer than her version. He found the dead man sitting in the armchair, with a book which had fallen onto the lap, no, a newspaper, opened to the report of the victim's disappearance—that's what happened.

The woman dresses as if she were at a garden party in the grounds of some large villa. The man's eyelids flicker when she walks behind his table in the evening—I am certain I hear those heels against that marble—and he turns the page of his book then, before turning it back some seconds later, and remains on that initial page for another few minutes. I suspect this turning of the page before he has finished is the result of an urge to do something, an impulse to assert his being at that moment, to wake himself from the dream of another so that he may enter into the dream of someone still living, someone who might be a product of his own dreams, someone he hopes to translate from those dreams to his memories. Yes, I believe he is no longer working on his academic article. I have seen him with pages and his laptop just the once, now he only carries a book with him as he moves through the hotel. I have been told it is an Agatha Christie: *At Bertram's Hotel*, which is fitting considering his surroundings. Often he walks and reads and trips on the rugs, throwing his arms holding the book out in front of him as if he were trying to dive through the floor, the book somehow providing an opening, a sinkhole through which he might disappear. He is never injured. I cannot speak for his feelings, his thoughts; these are much easier to hide.

The lobby is four stories high; many visitors have said it is cavernous, some have even referred to it as cadaverous—which is fair. It is the heart of this hotel, and that metaphor is not a careless one because the plans, which are encased in a glass case by the lifts, reveal its shape to be vaguely that of a heart; this similarity is underlined and elaborated upon in the bronze sign fixed below the casing. Corridors leave and enter the lobby in a manner deliberately reminiscent of the circulatory system, with more corridors opening on the third floor onto the upper balcony which overlooks the lobby on all sides: these, I am guessing, are the arteries—my knowledge of the inner body may be wanting, but I know my hotel.

A reclusive, but celebrated, artist was commissioned a number of years ago to paint a canvas to match the scale of our lobby. She painted a veritable *Guernica*: it is immense, four panels of thickened paint coloured, shaped and styled to represent this hotel, and this cliff, and the sea, and the sky which had been hiding in the background all that time. In the first of the panels the hotel is much as it is now, though changed slightly: it appears to teeter on this cliff more than is possible. Its age is more pronounced, as if she were finding its true character: the one beneath the tan and the sunglasses, the dyed hair. The second panel depicts this hotel ravaged by some unseen force. The north wall is collapsed, opening its emptied rooms to the wind and a furious spitting rain. It is distressing to see the many curtains so useless. In the third panel the hotel has vanished, revealing the bare and surprisingly smooth surface of the cliff: this panel resembles historical images, captured when we were not yet here. In the fourth panel the sea and the sky are left alone to battle for the horizon. Looking closely, as I often do, in some parts the sky can be seen to push onward down against the sea, and in others, the sea can be seen roaring up into the grey, its waves flashing white like the smoke of great guns. In all, as seen from a slight distance, the story of this panel can be discerned at once; there can be no winner, and no loser, the sky and the sea will fight each other until some greater calamity finishes them both. They are like paintings seen in a dream, brought over into waking life. There was supposed to be a fifth panel which would complete the sequence, however it was absent when the trucks transporting the other four arrived. The artist did not return our calls or answer our correspondence, and so we were forced to make do not knowing who would win that battle, or what terrible occurrence might defeat both the sky and the sea. Did that painting not survive the journey from dream to life? perhaps the dream itself consisted of five stages, and as they progressed it became a nightmare and at the end, just before waking, was where the artist discovered the final panel.

The man passes through there on his nightly walks. He glares at the paintings. How? His manner I can only compare to that of a man in a nightclub who sees a more attractive, more successful, younger man, standing close to a woman he still loves (so close their torsos touch), holding her hair in his hand as he whispers in her ear. It is as if he is envious of those panels. His posture stiffens, his arms swing heavier, his chin rises millimetres lifting lidded eyes that pretend that those panels are not so big, that they are not even worth pausing to admire, and he disappears once again into the long and twisting arteries of my hotel.

On the day the panels were revealed, local newspapers complained. Those at the opening had not stayed long. The artists had sent a letter, apologising, saying there had been a bereavement in the family and so they could not make it. Ever since the paintings went up, there have been complaints from the guests that these images frighten their children. Those who complained were informed that we, the hotel, do not assent to the fears of children or adults. And when they continue, whining and threatening to leave us, we ask whether they really believe a series of paintings are powerful enough to exert a force such that something dreadful will happen to this hotel and its occupants. Nobody has provided a satisfactory answer. Nobody wants to display their superstitions in the light for fear of what they might see.

The woman appears from a corridor slowly pushing the wheelchair and its stiff occupant into the lobby. I imagine the slow squeak of those wheels. She positions the person in the wheelchair in the middle of the room, facing the four panels. She caresses those plaster-of-paris shoulders and whispers something into that opening before strolling away down another corridor. It would be easy now to suggest a connection between this mystery in white and the pursuit of ultimate relaxation. It might even be a service available only for the very wealthy, which would make that woman an assistant to the customer encased inside that stiff outer skin. I can only imagine the pure ease the muscles might achieve with no other option but to lie arrested in position. I do not think I have ever allowed myself to fall fully limp, life has denied me that, but this person, this mysterious customer is free to slacken every inch of their body. Something that occurs only beneath the influence of the strongest drugs, or in the sleep of the innocent (and what adult is innocent? *chuh!*), or moments after death. That is luxury. Perfect luxury. Envy luridly paints me. The woman must have been chosen for her beauty, in fact now I think of it, the picture of her face is twinned in my mind with an Italian fashion house—she must be a model of some sort. She must care for the customer's every need. Whoever it is inside that cast I envy them. I wonder what the thoughts of someone so relaxed must be, I imagine them soft and malleable like their muscles, ponderous, rolling things: only someone who can think like that could leave themselves to the mercy of those four panels when the wind throws the rain against the windows of the lobby so angrily. (It is that peculiar species of rain so often found on the coast: shoals of it rush against the glass.) What if the power of the panels suddenly arrested that person's every thought? Because they can do that. The awful suggestion created by those panels often dawns on our customers days after their arrival. I cannot remember it ever being an immediate understanding, they are too large, and the eyes too small, for that.

The man enters the lobby wearing a red blazer over a white linen shirt, and white chinos. He pauses by the reception, turning the pages of a leaflet describing an attraction open only in the summer season, glancing now and then at the figure in the centre of the lobby. He strides toward it, bends over the person in the wheelchair who now looks very small. The man is shouting into the small opening to the face, his hands grabbing at those stiff shoulders. He really looks inside now, and pauses. He appears to be listening to something the obscured person is saying, then, as if overwhelmed, he reaches an arm across the back of the figure and wrenches the person toward him so that this mockery of a relaxed, reclined posture falls off their chair to sit squarely on their side on the floor. The man spits at this poor rich person, and walks back in the direction he came from. The person in the plaster cast appears unperturbed. Where the face should be it is still dark, and I wonder if they are so relaxed that they have accepted this violence, perhaps they are even sleeping. It is so difficult to know when they are so still and covered over.

The woman arrives and seeing her customer sitting sideways on the floor, arms and legs pathetically imitating comfort, runs and quickly rights the mystery into their chair and begins to wheel them away down another corridor. They don't speak, at least not that I can see. Just before they leave, she turns abruptly and stares at the panels, the way one would stare at an enemy when anger has moved all possible words out of reach.

In the morning, a member of staff notices that wheelchair-bound mystery sitting at the bottom of the outdoor pool, sans wheelchair. After calling for help, possibly fearing the person inside could not still be breathing, but possibly optimistic considering the calm seated posture of the cast, he dives in and drifts the white body to the surface where he edges it onto the poolside. There appears to be no face inside the small opening at the top through which to breathe life giving air. The staff member feverishly rolls the cast on its side and it gives way more easily than he seems to expect, though it is heavy, due to the water, and the dead, it seems. He turns it upside down, and on to its other side, running his hands over the plaster, searching for an opening, panic speeding his movements. His hands return to that palm-sized opening where the face should be. They reach in past his wrists. A sealed tomb, someone later said. More staff members arrive, and one carefully cuts the cast in half. Most of the staff, it seems, are now standing around the shape where a body should be. In its place is a congealed mass of paint differing in texture, colour, and density, covering the whole of the inside—some of it has run with water from the pool. As the staff watch, wondering, I imagine, what to do or say, the cast flattens out, like a tired piece of origami, revealing the fifth, and clearly the final, painting of the series. The staff turn as one to glance back at the hotel. Two paramedics emerge, and jog toward them. The staff slowly, reluctantly it seems, make an opening in their circle for the two who step forward. Nobody speaks.

*

In the centre of the lobby the wheelchair lies on its side. In the dining room the man sits with a page taken from his room on the table before him. A few words lie at the top of that page, illegible. On the floor are two halves of a pencil. The woman cannot be seen.

[ICELAND]

EIRIKUR ÖRN NORÐDAHL

From *Evil*

The Patty Winters Show this morning was about Nazis and, inexplicably, I got a real charge out of watching it. Though I wasn't exactly charmed by their deeds, I didn't find them unsympathetic either, nor I might add did most of the members of the audience. One of the Nazis, in a rare display of humor, even juggled grapefruits and, delighted, I sat up in bed and clapped.

—Bret Easton Ellis, *American Psycho*

CHAPTER ONE

EASILY MORE THAN two thousand people died in the making of this book. Two hundred thousand people. Six million Jews. Seventeen million men, women and children. Nearly eighty million people. The world will never be the same.

Just joking!

*

You must've heard of World War II. It's all over the history books. On the front cover of most of them. Photos of tanks, Adolf Hitler foaming at the mouth, emaciated Jews in mass graves. A mushroom-shaped atomic cloud. *Human history.* No one could have escaped it.

Ómar had no role in World War II. He wasn't even born until

after it was long over. But it was a persistent element in his life for almost four years—a little less time than the war itself lasted.

One day, Agnes threw herself into his arms. Agnes's arms were holding Adolf Hitler and all his goons, two thousand inhabitants of Jurbarkas, two hundred thousand Lithuanian Jews, six million European Jews, seventeen million Holocaust victims, eighty million war casualties over six years, 1939–1945.

And that's that.

*

Agnes didn't only have war in her arms: she had war on the brain and in the heart. And as tends to happen in successful relationships, Agnes's interests slowly became Ómar's: Agnes was on his hands and in his head and with her came all the "parties" of World War II: the victims, perpetrators, and innocent bystanders. A little later, he burned their home to the ground and fled the country. As improbable as it might sound, there's some strange causal link here.

At the risk of being redundant, we should make clear that Agnes didn't participate in World War II, either.

Her grandfathers did, though, Vilhelmas Lukauskas and Izsák Banai. They didn't fight in World War I; they were too young for that. They actually didn't "fight" in World War II, either; they were too old for that. But as the former war came to an end, the Lithuanian war of independence got going, and the two of them, Vilhelmas and Izsák, just happened to be adult enough to shoot people, according to the military recruiters. Later they would each in their own way fall prey to the Nazis. No one was especially happy about that, least of all the two of them.

Agnes was a Lukauskaite from the little town of Jurbarkas, Lithuania, which in 1940 boasted nearly 5,500 inhabitants. Of these, 2,300 were Jews. Today, 14,000 people live in Jurbarkas; not one is Jewish.

*

Scratch that. I take it back. Agnes was a Lukauskaite from Kópavogur, in Iceland. Her parents were from Jurbarkas.

Dalia and Kestutis Lukauskas fled Communism via a stopover

in Israel and came to Iceland in the summer of 1978, slap bang in the middle of *Grease* fever, six months before Agnes was born at the nursing home on Eiríksgata in Reykjavík. They weren't Jews—not in so many words—but during that icy winter they nonetheless managed to take offense at the initials of South-Icelandic Slaughterhouses (SS), at the Eimskip organization's swastika-shaped logo, at the newspaper's humorous articles on the "extermination issue" (not in fact a reference to the Holocaust but to an import ban on brewer's yeast).

Their hearts skipped a beat when overly dramatic Icelanders would pipe up about this or that "catastrophe"—the Lithuanian term for the Holocaust. Such and such art exhibition was a total catastrophe; the public transit system was an utter catastrophe; damned if the produce section of the KEA grocery store was not a prime example of an honest-to-God catastrophe.

When Agnes was beginning to "bloom," the euphemism for when a girl starts wanting to fuck, Nazism caught up with her and sunk its claws in. While her peers were going out to clubs and sneaking swigs of liquor, feeling up boys, trying out smoking, Agnes stuck her head into the mass graves her ancestors had dug and then been buried in.

*

Everyone knows everything about everything, of course, but's let's go over it again anyway. World War II began on September 1, 1939, according to the sources, when the Germans invaded Poland. In fact, the Third Reich had already annexed Austria and Czechoslovakia, the civil war in Spain had started and ended, Italians were occupying Abyssinia and Albania, and Japan had invaded China and the Soviet Union. War was long underway on three continents by the time World War II "began." It's not until the British get all het up that it's called a world war, in civilized parlance.

An estimated twelve to seventeen million people were killed in the Holocaust, including six million Jews. The plan was to exterminate two groups entirely, Jews and Gypsies, but on top of this all kinds of rabble-rousers and oddballs were sent to the concentration camps: communists, democrats, anarchists, socialists, Jehovah's

Witnesses, and Slavs who ran their mouths.

Slavs, while we're on the subject, ran their mouths a lot.

First up were the disabled. The retarded. The imbeciles. Or whatever they were called in Nazi execution papers. That was another time, with different standards. Not that we're going to adopt them now.

About 208,000 Jews lived in Lithuanian prior to World War II. After it: 8–9,000.

This, not least, piqued Agnes's interest.

CHAPTER TWO

Hi!

Hello there!

R-E-A-D!

Hello! Are you still following this?

This is the text. We are the text. I'm going to tell you all about the Third Reich. Do not turn off the book!

*

Here's one attempt to provide some context.

Seventeen million people is equivalent to the entire population of Chile. If everybody in Chile chipped in a nickel, we could buy one hundred Mitsubishi Pajero SUVs. Seventeen million people weigh roughly 1,300 million kilos; if they all jumped at once (and landed on the same spot) the Earth would be knocked out of orbit. By comparison, those 100 Mitsubishi Pajero SUVs weigh about 200,000 kilograms. Seventeen million people hold nearly100 million liters of blood and seventeen million hearts beat 595,000,000,000,000 times a year. One hundred seventy million fingers, thirty-four million ears, seventeen million noses, an estimated eight and a half million penises and as many vaginas. Eight and a half million average-size penises fully erect would measure 1,360 kilometers. Practically the length of Ireland's coastline.

If seventeen million people were arranged all in a line, it would belt the moon.

If they hadn't been slaughtered, of course.

*

But we were discussing Agnes Lukauskaite. Like most people, Agnes had four great-grandfathers and four great-grandmothers—all splendid folk, gray-haired and old and wise and disarmingly mischievous, as is often the case. Agnes's paternal great-grandfather, Vilhelmas Lukauskas, and the great-grandmother to whom he was married, Saule Lukauskiene, were Catholic Lithuanians. Her maternal great-grandmother, Masza Banai, and the great-grandfather to whom she was married, Izsak Banai, were Ashkenazi Jews.

The other four great-grandfathers and grandmothers barely enter the story because, although they were spectators during the part of this story which concerns great-grandmothers and great-grandfathers, they weren't involved, except insofar as spectators are involved by dint of their power to witness. Their spectating, it must be said, was very different from yours, since you have to make do with reading about these events some seventy years after they occurred. Your picture of events is more complete than what got whispered at the kitchen tables in Jurbarkas, but your part in the atrocities about to be outlined is also correspondingly smaller. Fortunately.

*

This might sound comical, but that can't be helped. Context depends on the story being told, and here we're telling a story about the story being told. Perhaps these strange comparisons have some value. Hopefully they shed light on the peculiar light that can be shed on things. On what makes a story a story. You might feel that I'm chasing my own tail here, but I assure you I'm not. History doesn't refer to itself but to other stories, our own and those of others.

*

Reykjavík, 2009. It was on the way to five a.m., the early hours of Sunday, January 11. Agnes Lukauskaite was still twenty-nine when she met Ómar. She was two days shy of her thirtieth birthday, but she'd celebrated it early that night—trying to stretch the festivities of Christmas and New Year's Eve a little further into the new year, trying to prolong the happiness, intensity. Trying to stave off the need to rest, draw breath.

The line of people waiting for a cab in the ice-cold wind writhed like an earthworm as it stretched past the hot dog cart on Lækjargata. Last year's Pots and Pans Revolution was tapering off, but it still had a few good squalls left in it—the most significant squalls.

Out beyond the light pollution was starlight, but it might as well have been overcast. The people in line were drunk and cold. Boys shoved one another in frustration. Girls chattered their teeth. Cabs arrived one by one. The line plodded slowly forward.

*

Here's a second attempt at context:

Poor Swedish Neo-Nazis. Poor xenophobes in Lund. Poor, poor them.

How persecuted they are, fired from their jobs.

Jeered at in the streets.

Their ideas are ridiculed. People say: "You're just a bunch of fools. Go back to Nazistan, you and your steel toes!"

*

Agnes tucked her chin down into the collar of her pale red down coat, stuck her bare hands under her armpits, and tried to shake off the shivering cold. Under her long coat she had on only a short party dress, underwear, nylon stockings, and high heels. She wore a black and gray wool hat on her head. She was freezing to death. Every time, she felt ashamed at wanting to look nice in winter. Out at the bar. Ashamed at being under-dressed in the cold, made up like she feared she would die alone. In high heels, as if she had no respect for herself. Her toes ached.

Still, the heels weren't all that high, not so high she couldn't dance in them. Not so high she couldn't shake her stuff. They were black and wide and gave Agnes a few extra centimeters of height, curving her body, making her look twice as alluring in the mirror as she was without them. But when the freezing cold bit into her toes, there were no shoes in the western hemisphere more despised.

Behind her in line stood Ómar, grinning. They did not know one another. Each awaited their cab as if the future held nothing in store for them, as if they needn't acknowledge in any way the journey they were about to share.

*

The poor little xenophobes in Lund want, more than anything, to live in Denmark. If only Denmark were just like Sweden, the Three Crown nation—if Denmark were yellow and blue like their own dear Swedish *folkhemmet*. Because to be a Nazi in Denmark is no problem. Even the ladies there are Nazis—Chief Pía Kjærsgaard herself is an Oberste SA-Führer—and the liberal newspapers can think of nothing better than baiting foreigners. Intolerant foreigners who circumcise little girls and hide women in burkas while burning the Danish flag.

Because Denmark is founded on tolerance.

But Sweden is founded on solidarity.

Iceland is founded on isolation and self-inflicted ignorance.

Perhaps that's just my bad temper talking.

Our bad temper.

Your bad temper.

*

Ómar was glassy-eyed and wobbly from drinking. He stared into the distance, slightly chubby in his heavy, secondhand seaman's coat with its double row of silver buttons up to the collar. His head was bare but he didn't seem to be cold at all.

Sorry, said Agnes, who had turned round and was looking into Ómar's eyes, but I can't help it. And, reaching out with frozen hands, she unbuttoned his coat. She ran her hands round to his back, past the white shirt and blue vest; she snuck her cold palms under his shoulder blades and rested her face on his shoulder. This bloody cold, she added, looking up. This is okay, isn't it? I'm so damn cold.

Ómar said nothing but he began to sniff her hair. She had long dark hair that smelled like Head & Shoulders.

*

A third attempt at context.

We're interested in knowing what you think of the Holocaust. Do you know anyone who "got caught up" in it? Do you know anyone involved? Anyone who knows the concentration camp prisoner Leif Müller, the Holocaust police chief Evald Mikson, or former Prime Minister Geir H. Haarde's big brother the Nazi officer (what's his name again)? Do you know the "refutations" of the neo-Nazis? What's your take on them? Does the Holocaust need a radical "revision"? Has the time come for a reappraisal? Will the time ever come? Is the Holocaust ever "over"?

*

The next morning, when Agnes woke, Ómar was brushing his teeth with her toothbrush. She thought it a bit cheeky, but didn't say so. Everything was as it should be. Routine, beautiful and good, nothing new, except this man standing in his boxers in her bathroom doorway, brushing his teeth with her toothbrush. Like they were an old married couple. In fact, he seemed like an eligible candidate for a husband, fresh out the shower, clean, spruced up, clear-eyed.

Thanks for last night, said Ómar, once he'd spit out the toothpaste.

Thanks yourself, said Agnes.

Where did we meet?

Yesterday, you mean?

If it wasn't yesterday, I was drunker than I thought.

Agnes considered this. I picked you up in line for a cab.

Picked me up?

In line for a cab.

What was I doing there?

Waiting for a cab, most likely. She raised herself up on her elbows.

I live right by there, on Þingholt, said Ómar.

It would have been a short ride, then.

*

Fourth attempt at context.

The significance of a momentous event like the Holocaust extends far beyond "what really happened," reaching first into "how could this happen?" and from there to "how can we make this work for us?"

The neo-Nazis play a double game. On the one hand, the Holocaust never happened—Rudolf Hess called it a Zionist plot to slander national socialism—while, on the other, the Jews "had it coming" ("We didn't kill you lot, but we had every right to").

All opposition to Israeli aggression in Palestine is seen as a continuation of the Holocaust (Europeans no longer have any outlet for their innate Jew-hating and so dress it up in humanitarian garb, the way right-wingers suddenly become feminists in the debate on Islam).

The Holocaust has become a common experience for everyone; everyone remembers it in their own way, in order to serve their own interests. Let's not fool ourselves any longer: the Holocaust is only being mentioned here to sell books.

*

Agnes crawled out from under the sheets. She turned her back to Ómar as she put on panties and a T-shirt. The winter sun, exaggerated by the snow outside, flooded the cramped basement apartment. Ómar squinted at Agnes as she retrieved the condom from the floor, tied the end, and turned back to him, this boy.

Aren't you hungover? she said.

Yes, a bit.

You don't look it.

What's your name? Ómar asked.

You don't remember?

No.

I'm Agnes, Agnes said.

Agnes, said Ómar.

Agnes.

I used your toothbrush.

I saw. Agnes walked briskly across the room and threw the condom in the trash - like she was resentful.

Is something wrong? said Ómar. She had green eyes, pale skin,
and he could make out her pubic hair through her white underwear.

I almost came, she said distractedly after a little silence.

Ómar fidgeted and moved over to the bed. What? Last night,
you mean?

I hope it was last night. I sure didn't come the night before or
the night before that.

The night before that?

None of your business.

Sorry. He shuffled about in the doorway.

Sorry that I didn't come or sorry that you're such a joker?

Both.

She smiled. Don't be. I just feel silly standing here practically
naked when you don't remember a thing. Not even my name.

Ómar hiked the waistband of his boxers up to his belly button
and scratched his head. I remember some stuff.

Like what?

Like you didn't come.

I just told you that.

But I remember it anyway. I remember it too.

*

A fifth attempt at context:

The Nazis didn't win World War II. But the Holocaust succeeded. They were victorious in the Holocaust. There are no Jews
left in Europe. To speak of.

*

Agnes sat on the unmade bed and Ómar edged closer. He sat next
to her, picked his pants up off the floor and put them in his lap.

I remember everything in the cab and once we got here.

Congratulations. They fell silent.

Who are you exactly? asked Ómar as he put his feet into the pant legs.

What do you mean?

I just mean . . . I don't remember, or maybe I don't know if I know anything about you.

Want to know what I "do"?

Something like that.

You first.

I asked first.

Doesn't matter. You first. Agnes smiled. Ómar smiled back. They weren't squabbling any longer. They were bantering.

You don't know? Ómar asked. I thought you knew everything.

I never asked, said Agnes. You never said. We didn't exactly talk on the way home.

Jack shit.

What do you mean? We talked a little.

No, I mean I don't do jack shit. I'm unemployed. "On benefits."

How old are you? Agnes got to her feet and put a bra on under her T-shirt.

I'm not allowed to see your boobs? I saw them last night. I remember them.

I was drunk. How old are you? She fastened the clasp and reached across Ómar for her pants, which lay on the floor by his feet.

Why do you ask?

Because. How old are you?

Boobs?

No. It doesn't work like that.

*

Sixth attempt at context.

Anders Breivik killed seventy-seven people in two attacks in Norway. In the Holocaust, seventeen million people were killed. But you have to start somewhere, of course. Rome wasn't slaughtered in a day.

*

Does a guy have to be a certain age to see your boobs? Is there an age restriction? You shouldn't be ashamed of your breasts.

I'm not ashamed. How old are you?

I'm twenty-eight.

Why are you unemployed?

Because I can't find work.

Yes, obviously, Agnes sighed. Don't be an idiot. Why can't you find a job? She put a shirt on over her T.

I finished my degree in Icelandic at the end of the year and only just started looking.

B.A. or Master's?

Master's.

What did you write about?

Are you going to tell me anything about yourself?

Sure, soon. What did you write about?

The new passive voice in Icelandic.

"It was forced on me"?

Exactly.

Isn't that a little 1998?

If you say so.

*

Seventh attempt at context:

Stalin killed more people than Hitler. In the sense that Hitler did not kill as many, but perhaps also the sense that Stalin (as good as) killed Hitler (and a few others). I don't remember how many, it's actually not easy to keep track of all this. You could just look it up. What else is Wikipedia for, anyway?

*

Agnes went into the kitchen, leaving Ómar alone in the bedroom. He put on his shirt and looked around. On the wall over the bed was a clumsily painted picture of a mother with a child in her lap. Or a reproduction, perhaps. The two were enveloped in dark red curls, broad brushstrokes. It was as if they had no noses, just two holes in their heads, two gaping nostrils. The mother had a serious expression but the child smiled like a retard. Ómar wondered whether the child was meant to look retarded or whether this was just the style. The work was evidently not a representation of any actual reality. It aroused feelings of disgust in him. There was something twisted about it. A mother in that situation wouldn't hesitate to smother her child in its sleep. He was certain.

Want coffee? Agnes called from the kitchen.

Yes, thanks, said Ómar. He buttoned his vest and made the bed.

*

An eighth attempt at context.

We talk of *Helför Gyðinga* in Icelandic, the Jewish journey into Hell, the state of the dead.

"Others" talk of *holokaust*, whole sacrifice—from the Greek word *holókauston*, Icelandic *heilförn*, referring to a Biblical ritual where the sacrificial victim is burned completely, so that nothing is left, all for the glory of the Lord. *Heilförn*: the most powerful and precious sacrifices you can make to God. Jews naturally dislike the name and instead speak of the Shoah, what Icelandic calls *hörmungina*, "the disaster." In Lithuania, they talk of *holokaustas* and *katastrofa*—catastrophe—which originally meant a "reversal of what was expected," and did not come to mean "a major calamity" until much later.

*

It was a double bed. He hadn't noticed before now. Not exactly. Ómar had a double bed himself, but he typically slept there alone. He wanted to be able to invite girls up for the night. Probably Agnes had thought along similar lines. When he bought the double bed, Ómar hadn't counted on the empty half making his loneliness all the more evident. But that was how it was. The bed was generally half-empty despite Ómar's own desires. The double bed was a clear statement of intent. You couldn't misunderstand a half-empty double bed.

When he had finished making up this double-sized symbol of loneliness, he headed into the kitchen. This was a poky U-shaped nook by a shoulder-height window which looked straight into grass. Agnes lived in a basement. Cupboards on either side, above and

179

below, and a sink at the end. It was full of dirty dishes. The table beyond the kitchen fitting was marked by rings past coffee cups had left behind; on it sat an old laptop, an ancient brick hooked up to two small travel speakers, wrapped in their cables and place on its lid. Agnes opened and closed cupboards, scowled and rummaged.

I'm out of coffee, she said.

*

A ninth attempt at context.

The key word in the phrase *Jewish Holocaust* is *Jewish*. Shoah, *helför*, catastrophe, the holocaust usually refers to Jews. Of course, it would be faintly ridiculous if Icelanders discussed the Nazi *helför*— because *they* did not go to Hell during the holocaust (only later). The focus, therefore, is on the Jews, as if the massacre was primarily committed *against* the Jews rather than *by* the Nazis. The Holocaust becomes passive, not active. The focus is not on the Nazis doing the killing, but the Jews being killed.

*

Agnes stroked her left palm firmly down her face and sucked her upper lip thoughtfully.

Should I go and buy coffee? said Ómar.

Why don't we just go to a café? Make a day of it?

What have we done to deserve such a luxury?

You need a reason to deserve a cup of coffee?

You made it sound that way, not me.

My achievement was giving you an orgasm. We can celebrate that.

So I don't get coffee?

Sure, I'll buy you coffee. Winner's treat. The loser gets the crumbs which fall from the table. Isn't that the way it works? Agnes took two swift steps up to Ómar, grabbed his hips, and kissed him on the mouth. You're cuter fully dressed, did you know that?

*

A tenth attempt at context.

And somewhere in that choice of words, we lose two million Catholic Poles, one and a half million Gypsies, we lose prisoners of war, political prisoners, missionaries, priests, homosexuals, mental patients, the handicapped, transvestites—all in all we lose eleven million victims of the Holocaust. We forget about them.

But we dare not say so out loud because then someone might imagine we are trying to *belittle the Holocaust*. On the contrary, we want to *make more of the Holocaust*, to say, No, you didn't die alone. We died with you. And we'll keep on dying with you.

*

Less than an hour later, they were sitting in a café in Hamraborg, taking turns looking out the window. They had skated right over all the obvious stuff, age, family, past pursuits. Agnes had earned a B.A. in history and was working on her Master's; Ómar was unemployed. Agnes was born and raised in the Hjallar area of Kópavogur, but her parents were from Jurbarkas in Lithuania. Ómar was born in Akranes and raised alternately by his divorced parents, who had variously lived in Selfoss, Egilsstaðir, Akureyri, Keflavík, Patreksfirð, Látrabjarg, Reykjavík, and Thisted, in Denmark. Two years after he left home, his parents got back together. Now they were married again. Agnes wasn't a real brunette but a dirty blonde, and Ómar admitted he'd seen her before.

You saw to me at a bookstore in the mall, Kringlán, a month back. You wrapped a copy of Dostoyevsky's *The Gambler* for me.

You aren't a total amnesiac, she said.

No, he replied, and they returned to staring out the window. The morning had noticeably warmed and the ice on the streets was now a brown sludge. Cars hustled back and forth along the highway to Kringlán, snow melted down the hills of Fossvogur, and Ómar and Agnes stared variously out the window and into their coffee cups.

I worked in a bookstore, too, said Ómar, eventually.

Agnes didn't answer.

*

An eleventh attempt at context.

It doesn't matter what you compare to the Holocaust: everything seems insignificant alongside it, if not actually just and beautiful. Pedophiles have never killed millions of people solely for being of a certain tribe. Nor have necrophiliacs. The banking crisis, that was bad, but it was hardly like the hyperinflation in Germany that cost tens of millions of lives. That artist who starved a dog to death in his gallery, he was an utter jerk—but have you seen Adolf Hitler's watercolors? The worst thing about getting testicular cancer is becoming like him. Not that he even got cancer; his ball was shot off. Or so the story goes (I don't know if it's true).

*

What do you mean you tried not to take it personally? Agnes asked as the silence began to get awkward.

Take what personally?

That your parents are back together. You said you tried not to take it personally.

Yes, he replied.

Shouldn't you be happy your parents found each other again?

Ómar rotated his empty coffee cup in its saucer. Sure. Certainly. And I am, absolutely. It was just strange. They divorced when I was four years old and got back together seventeen years later. I barely remember them together. Right after they divorced they hammered it incessantly into my head that it had nothing to do with me. I wasn't the reason they divorced. That's what everyone's divorced parents do, I suppose. I went around with this refrain in my head for two decades. *Not my fault, not my fault, not my fault.* It turns out, when it comes down to it, that it was my fault, most definitely.

That's not certain, said Agnes, grabbing Ómar's wrist to stop him turning the coffee cup around and around. That's driving me crazy.

Ómar looked up. No, it's not certain. But it sounds very likely, doesn't it? They couldn't be together, couldn't be in love, while having to raise me. Once I was out of the picture, they fell head over heels for each other again.

Three's a crowd, said Agnes. You're much more honest than I thought you would be.

Ómar sat up straight in his chair. Suddenly he felt on guard. Liquor leaves me dull, feeling naked, he said. My hangover has taken the little self-respect that otherwise keeps my whining at bay, seeing to it that nothing idiotic slips out.

You're cute when you're dull and naked.

Earlier you said that I was cuter fully clothed.

That was just to mess with you, Agnes said.

*

A twelfth attempt at context.

We're talking about the Holocaust. No one could have foreseen the Holocaust. No one realized Nazi racism could have consequences. Modern man's chief achievement is modernity and things like this don't happen in modernity. Not now, and not back then.

When Adorno said that no poetry could be written after Auschwitz, he meant this: From now on, we will not speak out loud. We'll see nothing, hear nothing, know nothing and understand nothing. This is all too painful. We cannot go on like this. Now we will fall silent.

*

Agnes tried to get a feel for Ómar. He seemed terribly sensitive. Maybe it was that seaman's coat—and the vest. They gave him a dramatic air. And his thick brown eyebrows were a sign of his introspection. On the other hand, he fiddled constantly. With everything. When Agnes got him to stop rotating the coffee cup, he started stroking his fingers rhythmically on the table. Like he was trying to lull it to sleep.

I didn't plan, said Ómar, to spill my guts like that.

You slept with me, said Agnes. I've earned a little gut-spilling.

You want me to pour out the bowl of my soul?

Maybe when we're engaged.

Should we get engaged?

Is that a proposal?

Hardly.

You could end up with a less awesome chick than me.

Chick?

Girl. Woman. Spouse. Ms.

I'm just not used to girls calling themselves "chicks" nowadays.

Girls "nowadays" call themselves whatever they want, I'll tell you that for nothing.

And the conversation stalled again. Ómar fell silent and fiddled with his jacket. Agnes silently stared out the window. It was as if they were afraid to say something unremarkable. Something everyday.

After they'd sat in silence for a while, stalling, Agnes offered to give Ómar a ride home.

Yes, I think that's for the best, said Ómar.

TRANSLATED FROM THE ICELANDIC BY LYTTON SMITH

GYÖRGY SPÍRÓ

The Problem

EVERYONE—INCLUDING THEY themselves—marveled at how well they were suited.

They had known each other since secondary school and at the age of sixteen they successfully relieved each other of their respective virginities. Although it was their first time it was very good and so they continued. They worked their way through Indian, Chinese, European, and other miscellaneous positions, and they all proved good. In the penultimate year of school this caused them a few problems, and they failed almost all their subjects, but then they learned to divide their time properly and somehow or other managed to pass their exams.

No one—including they themselves—was in the least surprised when, at some time in their twenties, they decided to get married. They worked, saved up for a small flat, and loved each other. Two children were born, the flat grew too small for them, they saved some more for a bigger one, and continued loving each other.

One day the boy, now a father of two, noticed a wart near the root of his penis. He didn't like warts, especially since his elder brother had been killed by a cancer that developed from one. He asked his wife what he should do. His wife examined the wart but it was small, and after an opportune bout of lovemaking they forgot all about it.

The problem was that the wart grew and grew and talcum powder did nothing to remove it, so he was forced to consult a doctor. The doctor prescribed an ointment. He applied it time and again but the wart kept growing. He went to the doctor once more, and the doctor prescribed another lotion, from somewhere far away this time and certainly more expensive. He applied it conscientiously but the wart still grew. He then visited a surgeon to see whether it could be cut out, but the surgeon was reluctant to do so in case removing it should result in cancer.

They might have got used to the wart but their lovemaking was becoming less satisfactory. It felt as though he was flopping about inside her. They couldn't understand this: it had never happened before. Suffice it to say that the boy's organ had begun to shrink as fast as the wart was growing.

It was a strange wart, and one day the girl—a mother of two let us not forget—remarked that it looked just like another peepee, only in miniature. Would you believe it! It was quite true: that is what it looked like.

Before long the boy had two peepees, one exactly like the other; furthermore, the original one (insofar as they could decide which was the original) returned to its rightful size, and that would have been fine, for he no longer flopped about inside her, or, more correctly, neither of his members did, but the boy could no longer come to a climax. They were too embarrassed to go to a doctor. The trouble was that one of the peepees always had to be left out of things and the other always regretted this and responded accordingly, or that at least was what they thought. Perhaps the two peepees felt a common bond of sympathy.

They were constantly worried and frustrated as to what they should do. The girl tried to conciliate the new peepee and to arouse the old one, insofar as she could tell which was which, but it was no use.

Then it occurred to them that maybe they should try to occupy both peepees at once in some fashion.

But the two peepees would not fit in together. The girl did her best to contort herself by stroking one peepee while admitting the other, though heaven knows which peepee was which, and that seemed to do some good but the position was so difficult that she strained her back doing it and had to spend weeks in bed afterward with acute lumbago. The endeavor had failed. Once she recovered they tried a new position: the girl stood with her legs open, bent right over and stuck her head between her legs so as to accommodate both members, but she strained her back again, which was a pity because the position seemed promising. She spent another fortnight laid up with lumbago.

They had to find some other way.

So the girl went to a gynecologist and asked him to fashion a second vagina out of her lower colon. The gynecologist didn't quite understand what was wanted but the girl offered him so much money (they had taken out a personal loan) that he finally agreed. Unfortunately the operation wasn't as successful as they'd hoped, for while the second peepee—but it might have been the first—fitted all right, the surgeon wasn't able to make the converted colon as sensitive as the vagina, so the second peepee remained unsatisfied, and, as a result, so did the first, however comfortably it personally was situated.

They worried and fretted once more. The children grew in the meantime, but being wholly and quite understandably preoccupied by the frustrating nature of their problem they neglected them.

Not being able to think of anything else they placed an advertisement in the paper saying, "Young professional couple seek free-spirited girl for fun and games," and waited. They had a couple of responses, met the people involved, wined and dined them and talked things through. After a few prostitutes there appeared an innocent, blonde, blue-eyed girl, as sweet as you like, about seventeen years old, who claimed to be a virgin and had, she said, to support her unemployed mother and father as well as her two five- or six-year-old little unemployed brothers all by herself. They couldn't, of course, pay her as much money as she needed for this purpose, but they decided to give her a try all the same. Once the girl had gone to think the offer over, the boy blushed and confessed that he found the sweet blue-eyed blonde very attractive indeed, and apologized for this, excusing himself by pleading that in many long years he had had no contact with any woman but his wife. His wife proved perfectly understanding and said she found the girl attractive too.

There was great excitement as they prepared themselves for the first appointment, and they planned it very carefully, sending the children to spend the night with their grandparents who, of course, were not party to the full arrangement. The young girl arrived, shyly removed her clothes, and asked what she should do. Then the wife took off her clothes and lay down on the girl and the husband in his turn quickly undressed and entered both women and pretty soon climaxed in both. Afterwards, all three laughed happily together and repeated the act as often as the peepees could manage, heaven knows how often.

And so it continued, though they had to take out another personal loan so the girl's family shouldn't starve to death, and everything would have been fine had not the boy, on one occasion, found that one of his peepees was prevented from entering. He took a close look and found that while he could enter his wife, he was unable to penetrate the girl because there was something blocking his path. He took another close look to see what the obstacle was and to his utter mortification found that it was his wife's peepee. What! But how?! cried the poor boy.

The blonde hadn't even noticed, a peepee is a peepee after all, but his wife blushed a deep red and confessed that ever since she first met the girl she had been dreaming of her and had even prayed that she herself might become a man. Now, it seemed, she had.

They were downcast, all three of them, then the boy generously declared that the girl should belong to his wife and watched as the wife took possession of her, at least eight times in a row. The boy stared amazed at the two women, one of whom had become a man, and he gazed at his two swollen unemployed peepees, and shed a tear or two thinking of it.

Once the girl had gone, miracle of miracles, his wife's peepee shrank back into a harmless clitoris as if it had never been anything else. Then his wife desired him in the normal way a woman desires a man but it was no use.

It would be nice to find a happy ending to this story but life is hard and the story has no ending of either a sad or happy sort.

In my view, the best thing would have been if everyone involved had entered a religious order and taken a vow of chastity.

TRANSLATED FROM THE HUNGARIAN BY GEORGE SZIRTES

AMANDA MICHALOPOULOU

Mesopotamia

EMI SAW HIM again on the last news bulletin of the night. She sat down with a glass of wine in front of the television, put her feet up on the coffee table, and there he was right smack in her face. Man of the day. It had been less than an hour since they ran the interview with him on *Friday Profile*. Now here he was again, approaching the cameras set up in the hall of the Parliament building. His green eyes squinted behind his glasses. It was his tic.

"The administration will demand that full light be shed on the situation," he told the reporters who had gathered in hopes of a statement. He stood there in the colonnade, waving his hands as if a fly were buzzing somewhere nearby. "As always, the opposition is simply wasting its time creating baseless accusations of scandal. Our primary concern is the well-being and interest of the Greek people."

His favorite phrases: "transparency," "curbing corruption," "making an example of the guilty parties." They made him seem shallow and incapable of thought. Emi had a hard time admitting to herself that she had ever been in love with him.

She listened to his entire statement. As if he were sitting there in her living room and it would have been rude for her to stand up and leave while he was still talking. She turned down the volume with the remote control and went to check on the kids. She could hardly believe that she'd had children with that man spouting bullshit on the television. Not that long ago he'd stood there beside her, in that very same doorway, and they had listened together to the boys' rhythmic breathing.

In summer his shirts wrinkled easily. He would come home from the firm, remove his cufflinks, roll his sleeves up to his elbows.

Emi would gaze longingly at those slender wrists. She'd be dying to tell him all about her day. Should she show him how their older son had learned to write his last name in trembling capital letters? Or should she relay the phone messages first, to get it out of the way so they'd have the whole evening to themselves? They would sit there on the sofa, slowly sipping their wine and saying, "You won't believe it," or "Did you hear what happened at the ministry?" In those days Emi was still working at the ministry. She would share information with him, important things he made the most of as soon as he became minister, before the scandals broke.

They were methodical in their habits. They watched the news at eight, then turned off the television and went in to admire their sleeping sons. Then wine, conversation, more wine. They drank a lot and made fun of people they didn't like. They were often invited to dinner by more powerful colleagues, people with connections, and made sure to return the invitations. Emi would serve champagne and cook stuffed pork and roasted potatoes, which were in fashion then. As soon as the guests were gone, they would snicker about the cheap wine someone had brought, or how someone else ate with his mouth open. Then, pleased with themselves, they would go into the kitchen and load the dishwasher together.

In the early years they undressed one another. Later on they undressed on their own; they were no longer so entranced by the ritual. During the final phase they skipped straight from wine to bed, where they dropped like logs off to sleep. Emi didn't remember exactly how that phase had begun: the first nights when he started coming home at all hours, the municipal council, the late-night meetings with Deli—and, shortly before the divorce, his assumption of the ministry. They distanced themselves from one another simultaneously and decisively, with the pragmatism of people who realize love doesn't last forever.

She had watched *Friday Profile* with the boys. She smiled when necessary and managed not to say even a single time, "Your father is a fool." They ordered pizza. They got up every so often to get paper napkins, or water, or to throw something in the trash, but they never left the living room for long. They didn't want to miss a word.

The host, sitting there with his legs spread as if he were in a coffee house, was known for asking very personal questions.

For an hour and a half they heard his praises sung on that set with its leather armchairs. Alkis wasn't wearing a single article of clothing Emi recognized, or at least none she'd ever ironed. His shoes were patent leather, and since he was sitting with one leg resting on the other knee, Emi noticed that the sole facing outward was barely scuffed. From the ministry to his car, she concluded. He no longer walked down the street like normal people. A little further up, beneath the buttons of his shirt, his belly formed a pillow. Under his blazer he was wearing pink, a pink button-down and a tie—good Lord—with flamingos on it.

Emi sighed. If she'd had daughters, they would all have been able to make catty remarks about his new wife who bought him those ties. With boys it was different.

On the show they were now asking him about the ministry, about the scandals that kept breaking and the first subpoenas of witnesses. And Alkis, spreading his legs like the host, as if he were in a coffee house, too, as if he felt utterly at home, used his favorite phrases about full light, polarization, and the government of the just. "It's in our hands," he said, "to strengthen our coalition with our citizens and with society."

"Mom, do you think he stole lots of money?" her older son asked, his mouth full of pizza.

Emi shrugged. "We'll never know."

"Konstantinos at school says everyone in the government stole lots of money," her younger boy said, scratching his head. "That's what his father says."

The roots of his hair formed a centrifugal shrub high on his head. Emi looked at him with a kind of tenderness that was coming to seem more and more like despair as the boys grew older. They were already ten and twelve.

The interview turned to personal matters. Alkis talked about the baby, who was eleven months old and had "stolen his heart." Emi turned discretely to see if there were any traces of jealousy on her sons' faces. Just then Alkis started talking about his boys, whom he called his "buddies"—a word that made Emi shudder. Since when did he use words whose sole purpose was to awake that vulgar kind of sentiment? Was it Deli's influence or his own aesthetic, which had been ripening within him all these years?

When they were younger they used to lie under the eucalyptus or walnut trees in the parks at Oxford, analyzing their personalities ad nauseam. Alkis told her about his father who was a minister of Parliament and used to take him on campaign tours. He was a tall man, and a bit the worse for wear when Emi finally met him toward the end of his life. He would look her in the eye and squeeze her hand when she bent over him to ask how he was. Did he actually like her or was it just a habit? After all, her former father-in-law had squeezed countless hands, sung pop songs into the microphones of packed tavernas, and often, after his speeches, had danced a zei-beikiko in the middle of some improvised stage. When he was little, Alkis thought his father was a singer. It wasn't until first grade that he discovered that his father's profession was in fact "political chicanery," as he called it one day, bitterly.

It was spring and they were walking down Thorn Walk.

"Why chicanery?" Emi had asked.

"He was a professional con artist," Alkis answered, looking away. "He lied all the time, about everything, you know? And he barely ever got through an entire conversation with me. Every time we went to the kiosk for newspapers he had to stop and shake everyone's hand. He couldn't ever finish a sentence. He ran around greeting every stranger on the street as if they'd been in the army together."

Emi had laughed. She always laughed when Alkis turned his childhood into high drama.

The only thing that bothered her about him in those days was his girlish whining, his sense that life had been tragic because his father was just another father like all the rest. Her father hadn't taken her to the park, either, like in American movies, nor had any of the fathers she knew. They didn't play Frisbee, they didn't wear loafers or checked shirts, they didn't have dogs. They worked all day and at night came home to eat whatever was waiting for them in the kitchen and go to bed.

"What's so funny?" he'd said, annoyed.

Emi found everything funny or exaggerated back then. No one she loved had died, even her grandmother was still alive, crocheting doilies for Emi's dowry. Everything flowed pleasantly and self-evidently like water over the riverbed.

She remembered that day quite well. They turned left on South Round and walked in silence toward Parson's Pleasure. It was a part of the park with weeping willows and walnut trees that led straight to Mesopotamia.

Mesopotamia means a region between two rivers—and at that spot the Cherwell in fact split into two. To all appearances they were a happy couple, forming a solid piece of land between two streams. Mesopotamia was a perfect image of their relationship back then.

They'd reached the point in the show when one of the reporters goes to the interviewee's home to show that he, too, is a normal person like everyone else, just with a bigger house. They'd filmed before the scandal broke, and there had been no attempt to cover up the extravagance of the place. Deli—Emi refused to call her by her first name—welcomed the crew at the front door of the house in Ekali with a surprised smile, as if she hadn't been expecting them. She was wearing a deep fuchsia caftan with a revealing neckline. Her hair was blonder than ever and her fingers tapered to squared-off nails, painted to match her dress. A dog wiggled beside her on the couch. It kept batting its tail on an enormous Chinese vase and Emi caught herself wishing, *Yeah, go on, break it.*

Alkis appeared at the top of a spiral staircase freshly shaven, wearing a track suit. He descended the stairs proud as punch, bouncing on each stair. The boys jumped up to show her on the screen how the staircase led up to a loft where the two of them slept every other weekend.

"You're blocking my view!" Emi shouted and the boys looked at one another and sat back down.

Alkis and Deli, arm in arm under an arch in the living room, were talking about how they'd fallen in love with the house at first sight. Emi greedily devoured every detail of their bad taste: the thick metal feet on the coffee table in the living room, the gilded candlesticks, the puffy curtains and behind them a glimpse of the yard. Then, as if the television crew shared her desire, they all trooped outside. The hedges had been shaped into cones. A significant chunk of the money embezzled from the ministry must have gone to pay the villa's gardener: the yard was enormous, dotted with guest houses and ornamental trees. Her sons were right. Only they hadn't told her everything. They'd gone on and on about the basketball court and the Ping-Pong table. But what caught her eye right away was the little bridge and the artificial stream that divided around a miniature island. She leapt from her seat and ran over to the screen.

"What's this?" she shouted.

"Mesopotamia," her younger son replied. "It's where dad goes when he wants to think."

Emi threw her head back and laughed a deep, satisfying laugh. When her sons asked what was wrong, she said, "Nothing, I just remembered something funny."

Her sister called later that night.

"Did you see him? My lord, what a charlatan!"

She was in the mood for one of their rambling, late-night conversations—two divorced sisters and the men who had ruined their lives. Emi realized that her friends and relatives insisted on her feeling abandoned and alone, but she was unable to exhibit the grief and heartache they expected.

Her sister talked on and on. Emi closed her eyes and effortlessly imagined herself back in Mesopotamia. The sun made her knees weak. Crocuses bloomed all around. She wanted to lay down on the grass, and to pull him down, too, to tell him, "Shut up already! Look at the squirrels, the mulberry trees, the sun peeking out from behind the clouds. Live a little."

On the other end of the line her sister was speaking in the same irritable tone as before. Emi asked, "Is it raining?"

"Not over here," her sister said.

It was a sudden summer storm. The rain fell suddenly and impatiently, as if telling her, "Speak up. Louder."

"I'm going to hang up now, I need to close the balcony doors."

Instead of closing them, she opened them all the way and inhaled the scent of rain. She ran out toward the front gate, splashing in the water. The yard had once been pretty, with trimmed grass and ornamental shrubs. In the past few years she'd left it to its fate. It was all dry leaves and mud.

She went as far as the gate and flung it open without knowing why. Water gushed in the gutter beside the sidewalk. The cheap asphalt the municipality had paved the street with had cracked. There were little streams everywhere, and a lake in the middle.

She kneeled down over the brown water. Its surface reflected a quivering moon.

"Shitty rain."

She went back inside, locked the door. She chewed an aspirin and lay down under the sheets.

She was woken by honking. The minister's driver had come to pick up her sons. Their bags were packed and when they heard the horn they ran into her room, shouting, "Mom, we're leaving!"

"You're not going anywhere yet," Emi said, sitting up in bed.

She put on her robe and dragged herself to the kitchen to make coffee.

"It's not the end of the world," she said. "He can wait. Saturday is the only day when we have any chance to talk."

"Yeah, but you were sleeping," her older son said.

"And we talked yesterday," said the younger.

"We didn't talk yesterday, your father did. We just listened."

"But that's what people on TV do, they talk."

She poured her coffee silently. "How did he seem to you guys?"

"He was okay," said the younger.

"Everyone's going to ask us about the money again," said the older.

Emi nodded. "It's natural. We live in the world. And the world gossips."

"What should we tell them?" her younger son asked.

She sipped her coffee. "That you're just kids and you don't know anything about it."

"Get real, mom, we can't tell them that," the older said. "They'll think we're total idiots."

"Don't you 'get real' me," she said, frowning.

"Dad doesn't care if we say stuff like that."

"Of course he doesn't. He has a huge house, sons every two weeks, a yard full of bridges. I got to keep the problems."

Her older son sighed and started tapping the toe of his sneaker against the kitchen closet. Emi covered her ears with her hands.

"OK, I got it. You can go now."

The boys hoisted their bags onto their shoulders and ran for the door.

"Wait a minute," she said. "Where's my kiss goodbye?"

He was young, around twenty-five, with harsh features. Maybe it was his deep tan. He was wearing gray sweatpants and a white T-shirt and was leaning against the hood of the car with his hands in his pockets. As soon as he saw them coming, he started cracking his knuckles.

"Who is this guy?" Emi asked.

He stood at attention before her, but kept cracking his knuckles. His fingernails were caked with dirt. "I'm Sotiris's son, I mean Mr. Sotiris's, the driver's. My father broke his hand."

"And now you're trying to break yours?"

He was handsome and very fit. He looked at her, puzzled.

"What you're doing with your fingers, I mean."

"Oh, that? I do it all the time."

The kids had made themselves comfortable in the back seat.

"Do you know how to drive?" Emi asked.

He started to crack his knuckles again, then stopped. He got into the driver's seat and reached over to fish his license out of the glove compartment. Then he came back and showed it to her.

"I was kidding," she said, glancing sideways at the license. "It's just, they're my kids, you understand."

"Mom, we know him," her older son said impatiently, sticking his head out the window. "He's the gardener."

Emi felt sick to her stomach and leaned against the hood of the car.

"The gardener?"

"Not exactly. I'm an agronomist, but I want to specialize in land-scape architecture. I do what I can. There's a whole team of us."

Emi looked at him. "Who built the bridge by the river?"

"Oh, I designed that."

"What's your name?"

"Michalis," he said, meeting her eye for the first time.

His eyelashes are very long, Emi thought.

"And you're Emi. My father told me."

"What exactly did your father tell you?" she asked, holding her breath.

"I know you're the minister's ex-wife."

She imagined them around the dinner table, eating and gossiping. They certainly wouldn't call him the minister, or her the ex-wife. They'd just say "him" and "his ex."

Michalis paused, as if awaiting instructions.

"Could you do anything with our garden?" she asked suddenly and a bit urgently. "It's drowning in weeds."

"I could come by this evening. Would after seven be okay?"

"Sure," Emi said. "I won't keep you any longer. And get well soon."

"Excuse me?"

"For your father, I mean. I hope he gets well soon."

In the back seat, the boys were already playing with their video games.

In Mesopotamia night was slowly falling—the sky was the color of lavender. Alkis and Emi were stretched out on the shore, facing one another. They were showing one another their precious stones. They each had a collection, and were exchanging the ones they had doubles of. She wanted the dark stones, he the pink ones. Emi thought: I'd rather no one have them than him. She swept the stones up in her arms and threw them into the river. Alkis grabbed her by the hair, almost pulling it out. Then Michalis appeared and started fishing the stones out of the river with a net. Only they weren't stones anymore, but tiny speckled quail eggs.

The doorbell woke her. Her mouth was dry from her afternoon glass of wine and she wondered what would have happened next, in the dream. She splashed some water on her face. The pillow from the sofa in the living room had left a crease on her cheek. She loosened her bun and let her hair fall in front of her face to hide the mark.

Michalis had changed. He was wearing jeans and a blue shirt with white stripes. He had cleaned his nails, too, and combed his hair back with hair gel, like a boy in a school parade. Touching, Emi thought. She opened the gate to let him in.

They stood in the middle of the garden and Michalis stroked the sad-looking leaves of the lemon tree. He shook his head.

"First of all, you need a good pruning."

"You're telling me . . . " She threw her head back and laughed hoarsely.

"After that you'll have to decide."

"What?"

"What kind of yard you want."

She looked at him thoughtfully. "What kinds of yards are there?"

"There are yards you take care of yourself, yards you have other people take care of, and yards you mostly take care of but need some help with."

"I think I'd be good at it. I just need some advice."

"That's what I thought," Michalis said, looking at her seriously. "And believe me, it's better that way. All those people who spend money on spas should just get their hands in the soil instead."

He made some proposals and explained how much each would cost. Then they sat on the veranda and she brought him a beer and a bowl of nuts. She poured herself another glass of the wine she had opened. They drank and looked at the trees in the garden.

"I want to ask you something," she suddenly said. "How did you make that river? Did he give you plans?"

"The minister?" He set down his beer and cracked his knuckles. "He showed me a photograph."

"What photograph?"

"From England, I think. A river."

He hesitated for a minute and then continued:

"I didn't know anything about rivers. I always swam in the sea. We never went on family trips inland, because, well, my father spent his whole life behind the wheel, so the last thing he wanted on his days off was another drive. You know, I don't think I ever even saw a lake when I was a kid. The minister asked, 'Can you do it, yes or no?' That's what he said, 'I don't have time to waste.' And I told him yes. I downloaded photographs off the Internet. But I'm not sure if I made a real river."

"It's a fake river, regardless."

"No, I mean if it's a river. If it's river-like."

They didn't speak. Emi scraped at a dried-up splotch of something on the table.

"I guess we all need to keep our hands busy somehow," Michalis said, smiling. One of his teeth was slightly crooked, which made his image a little less perfect.

"How do you mean?"

"There's no need to feel bad."

Emi stopped scraping at the stain.

"That's what you mean? I'm not doing it because I feel bad. I'm doing it because it's stained."

Michalis looked off into the depths of the garden.

"Your yard will be nicer, you'll see. More real. Building a fake river doesn't mean much."

Emi stood up.

"I'll go bring some more nuts."

"No, there's no need. I'm leaving anyhow."

"You're leaving?"

"I don't want to keep you."

Emi thought it was nice, sitting there on the veranda, listening to someone's rhythmic breath beside her. Almost as nice as life in Mesopotamia.

"I've got nowhere to be," she said.

It was getting dark. The leaves were starting to cast shadows on the wall.

TRANSLATED FROM THE GREEK BY KAREN EMMERICH

BRUCE BÉGOUT

Watching My Best Fiend

BACK THEN, I'D reached a certain refinement in the art of wasting time. I wasn't satisfied to just do nothing, which I wouldn't do, instead I would do nothing with style. I would sculpt the formless days I was spending, I would put the poems I wasn't writing into verse. Often, in the afternoon, I'd drop by Ernst's place for a beer; he, like me, sought to free himself of all commitments. I'd typically find him curled up on his sofa bed, reading a comic book or watching a film. He rarely left his apartment and in general cultivated a vision of the world worthy of Des Esseintes, but a somewhat peculiar Des Esseintes, who'd traded in the decadent style for the nonchalant attitude of a slacker. He spent most of his time in a tracksuit and wore sneakers without laces night and day. He was forever in the same white tee-shirt. But if his style of dress was to say the least sloppy, Ernst kept his apartment pristine. I never knew anyone so anal, so literally obsessed with cleanliness. He could run the vacuum three times in the same afternoon, and he always had a cloth or sponge within reach. He overlooked nothing. The toilet sparkled to the point it was blinding, the floor was polished, gleaming, without so much as a scuff or speck of dust. Like a spinster, he knew all the tricks for cleaning a pot, or for washing windows, baked enamel surfaces, glass-ceramic cooktops. He even invented his own potions for scrubbing the sink and shining his old furniture. But outside of these periods of frenetic housework, he wouldn't do anything, or more precisely he sought, as I did, to do strictly nothing. He'd surf the internet, watch DVDs, read magazines, contemplate the sky out the window. This lack of practical ambition didn't stem from an attitude of rebellion, nor from any philosophical position. It was simply laziness that characterized us, the exhaustion that comes before you exert yourself. Ours was not a deliberate opposition to the world of achievement, the triumphal posture of those who pride themselves on *not being useful*—the kind of crap the partisans of inaction readily dole out to a credulous public. It was more modestly a natural fatigue, which rendered any expenditure of energy thoroughly chimerical. And then it seemed our talent would disappear if we tried to exploit it. We were saving that thankless task for later. For a day when we'd regained our strength. Before he whiled away the days in his polished pad, Ernst had been a tattoo artist. We'd met at a Melvins show and got along immediately, knocking back beers till way too late in the night. And from then on we hung out every day, talking for hours on end—the only activity our weariness would tolerate—about any and everything, like two typical Tarantino characters, but we'd never plunge into these long rambling conversations without maintaining a certain rigor. In short, we spent the better part of our time jabbering and daydreaming. On the day in question, he happened to be watching a documentary by Werner Herzog. I knew he liked this German filmmaker, among whose admirers I counted myself as well. I appreciated his work for its baroque universe, at once violent and excessive, in which savage nature reveals the mental pathologies of a hero bent on taming it. In his films, one saw the anachronistic survival of a warrior ethic, which was almost touching in an age of the G4 and predator drones. But I'd never seen *My Best Fiend*. The film had already started; Herzog was recounting his longstanding conflicts with Klaus Kinski, his fetish actor (as underpaid French journalists like to say). I took a beer from the fridge and flopped down beside him.

No sooner was I settled than the doorbell rang. Four short, deafening bursts. Ernst paid no attention and didn't get up. But the person was insistent, like they knew we were there, the noise of the television probably giving us away. Grudgingly, Ernst finally got up. It was Julia, his upstairs neighbor. She had a favor to ask, she made clear it was urgent. Ernst called me over. Which wasn't like him. The situation was as follows: there was an animal loose in her apartment, and she wanted our help getting rid of it. Unfortunately, she couldn't say exactly what it was. While ironing her laundry, she said incredibly fast, accompanied by theatrical gestures, she'd seen *a big, black, hairy ball* run under the dresser. She'd screamed and run out. Ernst seemed like the obvious choice, the only solution. She appeared terrified, staring at us apologetically, her eyes mutely imploring. Ernst looked at me too, as though to read on my face how to proceed, and then, without waiting for my response, verbal or facial, he let out an "okay!" He grabbed his keys and phone, and we went upstairs. At no time (we were able to compare notes later when the subject came up) did we suspect a hysteric's fabrication, a nymphomaniac's trap.

When she opened the door, we were immediately struck by the apartment. As much as Ernst's place was straightened, and sparkled like a royal gem, Julia's languished in a state of utter shambles. Clothes, books, old newspapers, moving boxes, pizza boxes, discarded cups—they were all piled willy-nilly wherever you looked. It wasn't going to be easy to find the dreaded beast in this mess. On the furniture, reliefs of desiccated meals sat in disposable containers, alongside brimming ashtrays, half-emptied bottles, envelopes, and ripped-up letters. Starting from the entry hall, you had to weave your way through a dark narrow canyon whose walls were made of unsteady things. There wasn't a square meter free; everything was covered in things that didn't belong there. But it wasn't so much this chaos that impressed us as the moldy smell. It was like the sharp, stubborn odor of a dank, fungus-filled cave. Ernst made a face. He already regretted leaving Herzog behind to fend for himself with his interpersonal problems. Julia led us toward the dresser, under which the supposed beast had gone to ground before she came down to get us. Ernst again tried to draw out some useful information regarding the animal, its species, size, the dangers it might pose, but all Julia could say was *big, black, hairy ball*. Perhaps it was a cat. They like to patrol the roofs, entering *incognito* into strange apartments to expand their territory. Ernst asked for a flashlight and began looking under the dresser. Meanwhile, I positioned myself behind him with a sack in case the animal decided to make a run for it. The light's round halo plumbed the dusty dark, but revealed no presence. There was nothing of note other than an old athletic sock and a crushed packet of cigarettes. And these in no way resembled an animal presence. So we started moving boxes, stacks of books, unidentified heaps, on our hands and knees, coughing and inspecting the hard-to-reach, ordinarily overlooked places, as well as underneath, which wasn't much fun. After twenty minutes of intense, meticulous looking, we still hadn't found anything, except of course the residue left by neglect in the darkest recesses of the apartment.

We were beginning to have our doubts. But just then, a dull sound like a thud attracted our attention. It came from the kitchen, where we hadn't looked yet. Julia stared at us as though to prove telepathically she hadn't been dreaming, something bizarre really *had* taken over her apartment, something that shouldn't be there, something that should leave immediately. Ernst went in first. In the kitchen, which was just as much of a wreck as the rest of the place, the contents of a cereal box had been strewn across the floor, arrayed on the grimy tile like a wreath of puffed rice petals. The beast must have been hungry. We were beginning to put stock in Julia's fears, and what had once seemed a game now turned into a hunt. The potentially dangerous character of the prey was not without its allure; it added spice to the stalk. More and more, Ernst was getting into his role as bloodhound on the scent. But we didn't have to look long for the intruder. It was Julia who spotted him first, and she didn't seem startled at all, as though she expected him to be there.

Perched on cookbooks precariously piled atop the fridge, was a chameleon.

He didn't seem particularly bothered or shocked by our presence, but all the same, he was completely frozen.

Only his bulging eyes scanned the room in every direction.

His apple green body, striped with yellow bands, was quivering slightly, micro-trembles that traveled his entire length, forming muscular ripples.

His long tail was curled in a spiral.

He was as big around as a pencil case and seemed completely harmless.

Admittedly, we were a long way from the big, black, hairy ball that had terrorized Julia. We wondered if this was really the animal we were looking for, or was there yet another, more frightening and less comical than this one, as though the apartment had somehow become a refuge for exotic species. Ernst surmised—and he wasn't kidding, judging by his tone—that the chameleon had escaped from the Herzog film, which took place for the most part in the sweltering heat of the Amazon jungle. He approached, trying not to startle it. He wanted to examine the strange creature up close, to behold with his very eyes its mythic skin, replete with stunning subtleties The chameleon didn't budge. Now and again, it would stick out the tip of its long, flexible tongue, "which was capable of catching insects more than a meter away"—it was Ernst who furnished this detail. And while he squinted at the specimen, I asked Julia if she had any idea how the lizard might've gotten in. Could it belong to a neighbor? Might it have escaped from its apartment? She couldn't say. Had no idea. She knew no one in the building except Ernst (she insisted on the no one). And she had trouble imagining how this chameleon had so easily entered her apartment. She never left the windows open (which, by the way, might have aired the place out a bit) and never had guests over. In any event, something had to be done. We couldn't just leave the chameleon to wander in this chaos, which might pose who knows what dangers to it. So we all agreed to put him in a box with several holes poked in it. I suggested as well we give him some water in a bowl. Julia wrote a note, which she immediately took downstairs to post in the lobby, in hopes his owner would soon turn up. Ernst remained a few centimeters from the chameleon all the while waiting quietly for him to change colors. I on the other hand wasn't holding my breath; he seemed to me too bewildered by these non-indigenous surroundings to attempt a mutation. Julia's apartment was such a shambles, the poor guy didn't know how to imitate it on his skin. He was at a loss to reflect the mosaic of disparate objects around him. If he'd tried, it might have resulted in a tragic disturbance of his mimetic system. I for one was relieved he remained green and yellow. Julia wanted to offer us a drink *to thank us*. Without consulting each other, we refused in unison. The smell of the place didn't incline us to stay. The satisfaction we'd felt upon finding the animal had slowly given way to annoyance at having our daily routine interrupted. It was time to go.

When we got back to Ernst's apartment Herzog was describing in his mocking tone (he was forever taking jabs at his best fiend, for example: "I think in many ways Kinski possessed a healthy dose of natural stupidity") the tumultuous circumstances surrounding the filming of *Fitzcarraldo*. We both took our places on the sofa bed as if we'd only briefly paused to take a piss. As best I could tell, we'd missed more than a half hour. And yet we had no trouble figuring out that Herzog's relationship with Kinski was as fraught as ever. Screams, insults, fights filled the screen. The native Amazonians, dressed in costume as savages, incredulously watched as these tirades played out. They didn't find them funny in the least. On the contrary, you sensed at any moment they might decide they'd had enough, and start beating the two hysterics senseless. Ernst rolled a joint. And while a young boy, striking a pose both serious and proud, held out a dead parrot by the tips of its wings, the bird displayed in a spectacular fan of color, Herzog's voiceover spoke with detachment of "vile and viscous" virgin forests, of "putrid" nature struggling obscenely for its survival, a nature that was nothing more than "will and suffering," in short, his standard Darwinian drivel. I went to the bar to mix myself a vodka tonic in an immaculate glass. When I returned, an old man with flaccid tanned skin was calmly describing the innumerable and Dantesque difficulties the crew had encountered while trying to pull an enormous boat over the Andes with just wire and wooden logs. And then there was Herzog again, seated in the shade of an Amazonian hut, telling the story, still in that newscaster's neutral, detached tone, of a crew member who suddenly started screaming while out clearing brush with a chainsaw. He'd been bitten twice below the right ankle by a *chuchupe*, a deadly snake whose venom takes only minutes to reach the heart, paralyzing it forever in a black coagulation. This time, the reptile hadn't been frightened by the rustling and noise, nor by the gasoline smell. Herzog runs immediately with the rest of the crew (Kinski stays behind, Herzog makes sure to tell us) when suddenly they hear the chainsaw's motor start up again "like an outboard engine."

When they reach the spot, they discover the crew member has cut off his own foot, thus saving his life. The tragicomic sequences follow one after the other, from Germany to Peru, all of it captured by a shoulder-mounted camera. I was having trouble concentrating on the documentary. I found Herzog disingenuous and manipulative. As a sort of reflex, I reached my hand under the sofa and to my surprise found something lying there. It was a rock-music fanzine. The table of contents intrigued me, as did the layout and illustrations. There were monthly columns as well as feature articles, all elegantly done. I instinctively gravitated towards the last article, devoted to Jackson C. Franck. I'd heard a couple of songs by this American folk singer who'd influenced Nick Drake, and I wanted to know more. The article, entitled "The Tragic Story of Jackson C. Franck," recounted in an almost erudite manner—as though it were about an important historical figure—the key moments in his life. The author, who was none other than the editor of the fanzine, assigned enormous significance to the fire at Cheektowaga High—*a beautiful red-brick building*—near Buffalo, from which Jackson, then a teenager, miraculously escaped, while a hundred of his classmates perished in the flames. Following the tragedy, he spent months in the hospital to tend his burns. It was during this long stay that he started playing folk music on the guitar given to him by his music teacher. When he was released, Jackson put together a small band (guitar, bass and drums) that made the rounds of the local bars and venues, while Jackson dreamed of becoming the next Dylan; for a few dollars, they cut sad songs onto vinyl, which told of the broken destinies of soldiers in the war of succession, of hicks headlong in love, of stupid rednecks who were still somehow endearing. And then something unexpected happened, a real "event, the likes of which happen once in a lifetime." Almost ten years after the fire, Jackson received the incredible sum of 110,550 dollars, which the lawyers had finally gotten the insurance company to cough up. Since he was one of the few survivors, he made out like a bandit. But this unhoped-for manna from heaven wasn't exactly a gift; it marked instead the beginning of a long road of blood and tears, not unlike the tales told in his first songs. At the age of twenty-one, Jackson left college; he moved to England, bought a Jag, and led the high life. He had fun, got drunk, took drugs, went to bed late and got up even later, spent recklessly, composed music, ran into Paul Simon and Art Garfunkel then in exile in London, wrote sublime songs, developed some psychiatric problems, recorded, got married, separated, got back together, then separated again, traveled and came back, had himself committed, sent word to his parents, said everything was fine. But as the nest egg dwindled (and it dwindled quickly), there came in its place the slow, inexorable descent into mediocrity, the classic maelstrom for fragile rockers: heroine, helplessness, indigence, forgetting, a dearth of desire, a few flashes of brilliance here and there, dozens of vague attempts to get back on top, interior collapse, periodic support from friends, desperate and inauthentic cries for help, bad recordings, social-aid forms, dirty fingernails, chimerical dreams, barroom enthusiasm, and the long repetition of uninteresting days dedicated to your basic survival. After 1969, he disappeared entirely from the music scene. He succumbed to pneumonia on the third of March, 1999; he was fifty-six years old.

Just as I was finishing the article on Jackson C. Franck, Ernst went off on a long rant that had nothing to do with the Herzog film, nor with what I was reading (he was known to do this); it concerned what he called *listmania*. The contemporary passion for lists knows no bounds, he said. Everything is liable to be classified in order of preference: tastes, fears, passions, your most cherished memories, beloved landscapes, emotional experiences, successes, flops, accidents, injuries, kisses, bicycle crashes, favorite margaritas, floating floors, vacation rental sites, break-up texts. You can make a list of your favorite foods, films, or songs, but also your childhood traumas, your romantic failures, your political beliefs, your emotions, your hopes and fears. From the veal dish you ate last week to the memory of the birth of your child, it all finds its place on a list that reveals various parts of your personality. Someone's life could be completely summarized by going through his personal lists, ranking his joys and sorrows. Since what matters most in a list, he added, isn't the choice of the elements but their order of appearance. It's not enough to remember this or that, you have to say which one is better. And like that, you apply the rational methods of work to your spiritual life, you set up a strict order of feelings, just as though they were household chores. People today, he continued, are so used to living in an objective world of constant ranking, not only of their productivity, sexual performance, and artistic preferences, but also of the stock market, box-office receipts, real-estate prices and sports statistics—it's like they live in a world where everything is liable to be calculated and compared—and by contamination they start applying the same rules of incessant classification to life at its most intimate. On a Post-It note stuck to the fridge, they list their friends like cleaning products. They entrust the important moments of their life to mechanical recording, as though they were afraid otherwise they'd forget them, as though they no longer trusted their living memory and instead had to get their evanescent thoughts in order by ranking them. And just like that, he concluded, lived reality runs into the objective world of filing and classification. And to that, I had nothing to add.

TRANSLATED FROM THE FRENCH BY ANDREW WILSON

TAINA LATVALA

My Life as a Dog

IN THE TRAM, I wondered how I'd start the conversation. I even muttered some lines out loud: *Hi! Hey. Hi there.* My hands were sweating as I walked over to the terrace at the Fairytale. I could already see them from some way off, sitting opposite each other, laughing and listening to jazz. They looked as if they'd known each other forever, though there was no way they could have.

"Hi."

I gave them a warm smile. Bea didn't hug me, but touched my shoulder. Rabbe offered a handshake and half-rose from his chair. I saw from his face that he'd never heard of me.

"Nice to meet you at last," he said and introduced himself. I knew who he was of course; everyone did. He'd played Hannu the Puppy in one of my favorite childhood TV shows.

I sat down with the dignity of a princess, aware of my every movement. I felt I looked quite pretty, my hair was wavy—that was enough. Rabbe was looking admiringly at me—he liked me already.

"You've got something black on your cheek," whispered Bea.

I dug a hand mirror out of my bag. On my right cheek was a dark stain like a sticky piece of soot. I wet my finger and wiped it away. It was humiliating to have to lick my thumb in front of Rabbe Brander.

Bea said she'd read my column today; it had made her laugh.

"It was really good," said Rabbe, uncertainly. I said thanks and changed the subject, complimenting him on the drama series for which he'd been awarded a Venla statue. It felt safe to have someone else doing all the talking.

Rabbe said he'd been shooting a new film in Kilpisjärvi in June.

I imagined him crawling through the woods looking for just the right birch trunk, closely followed by the assistant producer and production secretary in their green cargo pants. In my imagination, film directors always wore trousers like that.

They'd filmed the love scene—the movie's climax—after Midsummer. He'd wanted to do it in a completely different way from anyone else ever and had shot close-ups of the actors' faces, recorded every quiver in the facial muscles, every tremble of the lip and flicker of the tongue. The orgasm had been filmed from five centimeters away; they'd practiced it over and over again to make it look and sound like the real thing—the *petit mort* itself.

"André Breton said: 'Beauty will be *convulsive* or will not be at all.'"

I watched the movements of his mouth: he was turning into Hannu the puppy again, panting in the July sun and wagging his tail on the way to school. 987,549 people had watched those clips on YouTube.

"What's the film about?" I asked. All artists get enthusiastic if pressed about a work's deeper significance.

"You've got cat's eyes."

Rabbe gave me a searching look, as if there were some kind of danger in me. I didn't know what I was supposed to say.

He stared into emptiness; his mind was on something far away. He said that when he was twenty-four, he used to work at the airport; he was already a father then and never stopped changing nappies and dreams. Every day he saw airplanes lifting into the sky, light as paper planes. He'd thought then that the people traveling in them were free.

"It was only later that I realized they had their own duties, too, their own crosses to bear."

He lit a cigarette and turned toward me, furrowing his brow as if he wanted to get to know me.

"What's your cross?"

A blush spread over my face. People generally only asked me what year I was born or where I'd bought my sequined jacket.

"Maybe this thing, "I said, pointing to the parting in my hair.

Rabbe and Bea quickly glanced at each other. It was all right for them: their mother and father were alive, they were recognized everywhere, every door opened to them. They had their own baggage, of course, but it wasn't visible to me.

"Well, we seem to be getting into deep water here," said Bea with a short laugh. She sipped her red wine; her teeth were already violet.

"It's our duty to," said Rabbe. "Life is short. Why waste precious time talking crap?"

He'd said something like that at the 2009 Jussi Gala; I remembered his red cheeks and the sheet of paper from which he'd read a long thank-you speech.

Some guy who'd had too much to drink lurched up to us, an ominous smile on his lips. I thought he would bum a smoke or a light off us, or ask for Rabbe's autograph. Slowly, as in a dream, he leaned down toward Rabbe.

"Woof."

He said nothing else. Rabbe's face fell; he took a long slug of beer. I looked at the ashtray; Bea fiddled with her wristband. The silence seemed to go on for a whole minute.

"If I ever publish my memoirs, its title will have to be *My Life as a Dog*," said Rabbe. He tried to smile.

"Good title." I raised my glass but Rabbe didn't want to drink to it with me. I knew then that the evening would either draw to a close or go on forever.

He sang like a drunken sailor the whole way, jumping over puddles and shouting for joy. He was so cheerful that I started to doubt whether it was really genuine. I felt like chatting to him, finding out where he got the strength to create new things, how carefully he planned the structure of his films, how he got himself out of bed in the mornings. I was curious about practical matters too. I assumed that a thirty-nine-year old would know more than I did about things.

"Have you got PP insurance?"

"A what?"

"PP. A pension policy."

Rabbe started to laugh. Bea smiled (she never took a position on anything involving numbers or percentages).

"I'm a film director, not a managing director."

"Rock stars think like that too," I said. "And then at fifty-five, they get slapped with a bill for 280,000 euro."

"You some sort of insurance auditor?"

"No."

Rabbe stepped back from me a couple of meters, as if I had some sort of disease.

"Let's not talk about miserable things," said Bea, twirling round. The wide hem of her skirt made her look as if she'd stepped straight out of the 1960s – all she needed was a Coke bottle in her hand. Rabbe swept her toward him and danced with her for a moment, swinging her around dreamily like they do in old musicals. The dark blue sea shimmered in the background, the same moon glimmered in the water and the sky.

"*Fly me to the moon, let me play among the stars*," Rabbe sang, bending Bea backwards in the way the old people do at their dances. I'd hoped he wouldn't choose that song—it brought back memories of my ex-boyfriend. I'd always imagined that song would be played at our wedding. I watched them dumbly with the same feeling I'd had at the junior disco when Harry Fossi had asked Laura for the slow dance. I had stood next to them all through "Forever Young."

Rabbe let Bea go and stumbled past me, marveling at the sky's purple glow. It was no use hoping for anything, I scolded myself; I was never going to get anything from anyone. They'd never give me what I longed for anyhow.

We walked along silently for a minute underneath invisible stars. The sea looked like a black beast that could swallow us all up in one second. I hoped I wouldn't see anything in the water to make me anxious: a shred of a coat, a plastic bag, a rock that looked like a back. They had no idea what was going on in my head. They knew nothing about me.

Rabbe linked arms with us, leaning against us like an old man of seventy-seven.

"You're wonderful."

He brushed my cheek lightly as if in some sort of compensation. "Wonderful girls."

*

She was floating lazily by the shore and on her side was written *Linda*. Rabbe had married a woman called Linda last winter—I remembered seeing them in the newspaper in snow-white wedding outfits.

He'd bought the boat on the spur of the moment. He went sailing with his friends, they fished for perch, went skinny-dipping, talked about women, mermaids, and the wonders of the world.

"This is completely silly," he said, leaping onto the boat. Bea jumped after him, agile as a gazelle. They looked at me: I only saw the black water beneath me.

"How do I get over there?"

"You just jump."

Rabbe stretched out his hand to me. It was a long way off, like another island. A single thought filled my head: Rabbe Brander wanted me to be in the same boat as him. I would have liked to tell Mom and Laura and all the people who'd grown up with me. They wouldn't have believed me.

"Trust me."

I grabbed his hand and jumped. My leg slipped over the last bit, but Rabbe grabbed hold of me. We followed him into the boat's cabin: it had leather benches, an old-fashioned feeling, a pile of faded *Film Buff* magazines on a shelf.

Rabbe opened a small brown cupboard full of frightening bottles. He selected one, twisted the cork out, and poured the red drink into some plastic mugs. I didn't dare say that I didn't like wine. I kept wondering if it would be bad manners to ask for a glass of milk.

"Welcome to the adventure."

Rabbe drank with his eyes closed, sighing with pleasure. In the oval window a strip of sea was visible; terrible things were hidden in its gloomy waves. I turned my gaze away.

"Sometimes I write here," said Rabbe. "And sleep, if I'm not needed at home."

He gave a cold laugh, and a sadness shone in his eyes. I'd read in the paper that Rabbe's wife was a personal trainer and Miss Aerobic 2003. In a short story, it would have been hard to believe—Rabbe had a comfortable little tummy you felt like patting.

He put his feet up on the table.

"Shall we play something?"

What did he mean? Not strip poker, surely? Under my skirt I was wearing faded beige briefs.

"Shall we play spin-the-bottle?" asked Bea. I wondered how she had the guts to suggest something so bold. She didn't like revealing her secrets to other people and even when she did, a lot remained beneath the surface. No one could know Bea any better than she allowed.

Rabbe pulled an empty bottle of cognac out of the cupboard. I began to sweat under my arms, my ears were ringing: I didn't want to confess anything. The bottle spun around several times, then slowed down and pointed at Rabbe's ribs.

"Truth," he said, looking into my eyes expectantly. My heart skipped a beat. I knew that my question would reveal something about me, almost as much as if I took off all my clothes.

"What do you fear most?"

"Death," he answered immediately.

It had started in childhood, when he'd seen a cat run over by a car. He'd prodded it with a stick; the cat was stone dead, a crow had been pecking at its blood-covered throat. He'd realized then it would never wake up again, would never leap up into a tree again.

"Do you believe in heaven?" he asked, staring at me. I wasn't good at deep conversations. I was afraid I might say something that would pigeonhole me forever, in his eyes, the whole world's and God's.

"Yes, I think so."

Saying "I think so" sounded wrong, but I didn't dare say anything further. Had I denied the existence of Jesus now?

Suddenly I remembered father, his windbreaker, his hand on the wheel of the motorboat. I realized that I hadn't thought about him yet today, maybe not even yesterday either. Or he'd been in my mind, but I hadn't noticed. Sometimes I feared that the image I had of him would gradually fade, the way he ate porridge, the sound of his voice.

Rabbe ran his fingers through his hair: he didn't give up.

"What happens up there in heaven?"

"I don't know. You meet good people."

Rabbe began to smile, as if slowly becoming aware of something. There'd been a slight change in atmosphere when I spoke: unlike the others, I couldn't make small talk. Bea span the bottle to save me. It pointed at her like an arrow.

"Recite a poem you've made up yourself," said Rabbe and poured more wine for us all. Why did Bea get such easy things to do while I got dragged straightaway into the essence of Christianity?

Bea said she couldn't write poems. I looked at her in surprise, I thought she could do anything. Rabbe gave a fifteen-second summary of the secrets of improvisation, describing the exercises they'd done at Theater Academy, how they'd darted around the classroom like rats. He then leaned back, closed his eyes, and recited a poem. It was surprisingly good—something about thighs, flames, and trembling flesh. He was probably one of Turkka's disciples, or one of his disciple's disciples. It was only a matter of time before snot would begin running from his nose.

We clapped and he tapped Bea on the shoulder.

"Just one poem."

"No."

So easy for some—Bea set the limit with one word, as if drawing on tarmac with chalk.

We sat silently for a moment. Sometimes the bottle chose Bea, sometimes Rabbe: it forgot about me altogether. The last time Bea had cried was yesterday, Rabbe on International Women's Day. Bea had to imitate a belly dancer, Rabbe a peacock. We laughed and were as riotous as three people over twenty-five could be. And then I said something without thinking: I asked Rabbe to say a couple of things in the Hannu puppy voice, to remind me of the old days.

"It would make me so happy."

Rabbe shuffled backwards on the bench, downed the wine as if it were water; his eyes darted here and there. He glanced at Bea's breasts, then my thigh, smiled to himself and laughed at a joke no one heard. Then he stared at me dumbfounded, as if he were seeing double.

He turned the bottle to point straight at my heart.

"Dare," he said on my behalf, and I was almost grateful. I would even have given him a passionate kiss—just as long as I didn't have to say anything about myself.

"Go and get a few things from outside, squat on the grass for at least half and hour, and then come back and build an installation with the objects."

"What objects?"

"Anything."

He couldn't mean it. Surely he didn't think that I was going to obey his commands, fetch him a stick, run panting back to heel. Surely he didn't mean me to sniff the tarmac, gather up pinecones, gnaw bones, and mark my territory with my own urine. He was a nice person; he liked me. He just didn't know me.

I stood up.

"Thanks for this evening. I had a great time. Good night."

They sat there, mouths open, eyes full of questions. I'd already turned away when Rabbe charged over to me. His breath reeked of stomach fluid.

"You cross?"

"No."

I kept my nails under control: he had such smooth cheeks. Pale, Bea looked at me, her bag in her lap, ready to leave. Rabbe grabbed my shoulder, his hand was heavy, like an oar.

"Sit down, my friend. Have a bit more wine."

"I don't like wine."

Rabbe took a bottle of Jaffa from the fridge, Madonna was singing "Vogue" on the record player, now my whole childhood was floating in the boat. Rabbe imitated gestures fluently, made a square with his hands, and smiled at me as if in a music video. Suddenly he pulled me over to him, drew me close like a daughter and put his cheek against mine. His skin was sweaty, though it wasn't warm in the boat.

When the song finished, he threw himself on the bench and lay down. His voice sounded sleepy.

"I'm going to have a little rest, dear friends. Just chat amongst yourselves."

We mumbled about this and that, listened to a couple of sad songs, talked of summers past. Rabbe started to snore, his tummy moved slowly up and down. This man, too, was able to get up in the morning and comb his hair, eat toast for breakfast, drown his sorrows in wine. This man, too, had been given a chance.

"What do we do now?"

Bea got up and poked Rabbe's shoulder.

"Time to wake up."

Rabbe did not react, if you don't count a fart. Bea sucked in a breath through her mouth and raised her voice. I tickled his feet, sniffed his cheeks, licked his ear lobe. The snores grew deeper. We wondered if a woman's scent would make him wake up and Bea half-lay on top of him. Rabbe stroked her hair and barely audibly murmured: "I don't want to go jogging."

We looked at each other.

"Let's leave him a note," said Bea. She found a pencil on the table and wrote thanking him for the evening, signing it with a flourish. I didn't want to write my name: I had a vague fear that the police would follow us. Heads down, we slipped out; the cabin door slammed shut after us and, in some way, it felt final. The sky was gradually brightening and a summer smell of hot dogs drifted from a snack stand. Bea bought one, her lips reddening from the ketchup as if she'd been sucking blood from someone's neck.

*

We walked the shortest way into the center of town, chatting, laughing at everything. Slim young sailors walked by; we felt like picking one up. Near the cathedral I saw an ambulance with its emergency lights on. I stopped all of a sudden and touched Bea's arm. It felt as if a holy spirit had spoken to me.

"We left him alone, dead drunk."

Bea gulped down the last bit of hot dog.

"He was just having a nap."

She didn't believe her words herself; she was just trying to make me feel better. I asked if we should go back, but Bea reckoned it wasn't worth it. "Let's send a message to his wife."

We got her contact details from the directory. Bea quickly and fluently tapped out a text message—she was a writer after all. Sometimes, it was an advantage.

"Hi Linda," she began, "Sorry to disturb you at this hour. We had a fun evening and night with Rabbe, but he conked out in the middle of it all in his boat. Hope he's ok. All the best, two girls."

We waited a moment for an answer—none came. We walked through the town center without speaking. The trams were already on the move, opening their doors to tired people, some of them on the way to work, others coming home from late-night parties, all hungry animals in the night. Bea hugged me before she got in, promising to ring as soon as she'd heard anything about Rabbe.

"Sleep well," she said patting me on the back. I knew I wouldn't sleep a wink.

"You too."

As I walked home, the sun was rising. It wasn't shining yet, it didn't have the strength, and I didn't wonder why. Not everything always turned out for the best: not everything ended happily. With a heavy heart I looked for my key, my comfort one sole thought: if anything bad had happened and it was my fault, one fine day I would surely get my punishment.

TRANSLATED FROM THE FINNISH BY SARAH WADE

MAARJA KANGRO

Fireworks

AND THERE HE was, damn him. The little man in the neon gilet stepped into the middle of the highway, inexorable as fate. Braking with courteous smoothness, Fox pulled up at the side of the road. He wound down the window, and the neon gilet came and introduced himself. Constable Peterson of the district prefecture patrol. With a surprisingly high tenor, which left you wondering if he might have trouble asserting his authority.

"Driver's license, please."

"Hello. Yes, right away." Fox found his wallet and fished out a pink piece of plastic from among the bank cards and store cards. He'd always liked the photo on his license. "There you are. I'll find you the MOT certificate right away."

"Where were we off to in such a hurry," Constable Peterson asked.

"I don't think I was speeding . . . "

The constable turned the display of the speed detector toward Fox. He could make out the black figures against the light grey screen: 118.

"The speed limit here is ninety," the constable said.

"Oh, really. Well, I was in a bit of a hurry actually. I have to be at N. County Library by five-thirty." In fact he had to be there by six.

"Do you normally drive that fast to get to the library?"

Fox shrugged.

"Well, yes, but I've got an important meeting there."

"So you should have set out in good time and kept to the speed limit. Now come and have a sit down in our van."

The back door of the police van was already open. Some character who was a deep shade of brown from head to toe was sitting in the front seat—a young man with a brown face and a scuffed leather jacket, writing his statement in slow concentration. Fox sat down next to him, glancing distractedly at his handwriting: it was rounded and unpolished, free of any pretension.

Peterson sat down in the front of the van, gave Fox's driving license to the policeman sitting at the wheel, and said: "One hundred and eighteen kilometers per hour."

"I see you've already caught some prey," Fox said.

"Sure have. You got any unexpired violations?" asked the one sitting at the wheel, who had a face like a fat pony.

"Yes, this June, for speeding," Fox answered.

"That's right, honesty is the best policy. Now then, have a look at this film. Watch the red dot." Fox saw his car getting closer and closer, a red dot on its snout like a sniper target.

"Do you agree with the decision?"

"Yes."

"Let's call it one hundred and twenty euros then. The maximum for this category is four hundred. Here: you need to write a statement explaining why you were speeding, and you should put that you're sorry too," Pony said, passing Fox an all-too familiar-looking form. "Music?" he asked.

"Okay," Fox replied.

Pony turned up the radio.

Oh, think twice, it's another day for you and me in paradise, it's just another day for you, you and me in paradise. Radio Three. Only the very best music!

Fox tried to remember exactly what this stretch of road was called.

The patrol's intercom started sputtering.

"Ssss . . . village . . . call-out to Härjapea farm, a woman's reported her ex-husband circling the house with an axe, threatening to break in. He's been walking around there for fifteen minutes already."

Peterson started humming to himself. "Right then. Once we've finished here let's go and see what we can do."

Fox looked up from his statement and snorted reproachfully, or as firmly and reproachfully as he knew how.

"Come on, peoples' lives are in danger, and you're tormenting a couple of petty offenders."

The man in the brown jacket mumbled something under his breath and half-raised his gaze. Fox examined his face. A lad like that might struggle with his math homework, but he was probably a dab hand at ball games and shotput. Or something like that.

"It's a life and death situation, you've got to go and help, isn't that your obligation?" Fox asked. The words accidentally came out sounding like a silly rap song he'd once heard. But no one else seemed to have noticed.

"We know all about that kind of danger," Pony said.

"He gets up to the same tricks at least once a week," Peterson added.

"And you don't go to investigate?"

Pony sighed wearily. "Nope. Can't see the point." He turned up the radio again. "Is that okay?"

"Sure," said Fox. "Walk Like An Egyptian." The brown guy said nothing, but just carried on writing, silently and diligently.

Pony completed the paperwork, asked Fox for his address and place of work, and passed him the form.

"Sign here, if you agree. Here. And here. That's your copy. The bank details are here, Swedbank, Cooperative bank," Gripping the pen, Pony's fat fingers marked crosses in a couple of places.

"Do you agree?" Pony asked.

"Do I have a choice?" Fox said. "Someone's about to be killed over at Härjapea farm, but at least the exchequer will get another hundred and twenty euros in its bank account. So justice will prevail."

"You've got fifteen days to pay the fine or dispute the decision."

"Yeah, yeah," Fox said, taking the pad and signing the fine in the required places. He wanted to say something in defiance at the unjustness of his lot. "I'll definitely post about this on Facebook tonight," he said, lamely.

"Ha ha," was Pony's reaction to that.

Peterson had already got out of the van, and Fox watched as he waved down the next victim with the nonchalance of a licensed huntsmen. A white Chrysler Sebring.

"The Estonian police aren't on Facebook yet are they?" Fox asked.
"No, not yet."

"You should join," Fox said. "See how many 'likes' you get."

"You could set up a fan page for us, there's no law against that,'
said Pony.

By now the character in the brown jacket was painstakingly eras-
ing a mistake he had made in his statement.

The intercom started crackling again.

"They just called from Härjapea farm . . . that maniac left of his
own accord . . . "

Pony smirked at Fox and the brown young man. "What'd we tell
you? It's the same every week. Here, take your driving license. And
your MOT certificate. Try to drive a little more carefully from now
on."

"All right. Good evening," Fox said. The hapless brown character was still sitting in the van writing, and Constable Peterson had
meanwhile brought in a lanky lad in a red jacket to replace Fox.

Fox walked back through the soft mud to his car. But what kind
of shoes did policemen usually wear? Certainly not rubber boots,
in any case. Some variety of boots, all year round? Strange that he'd
never given any thought to policemen's feet before. Or had he? He
shoved the yellow speeding ticket into the bag of books on the pas-
senger seat and started the engine. Before driving off, he glanced at
the spines of the books poking out of the bag. They were handsome
specimens, you had to give them that. With the refined intellectual
tones of their dust jackets, they somehow radiated lucidity and erotic
sadness. But the books now seemed strange, almost incomprehensi-
ble to Fox, like other people's lovers—you were sure there must be
something to say for them, even if you weren't sure exactly what. Fox
had another quick look in the direction of the van and waited for a
few seconds, but the character in the brown jacket didn't get out. His
worse-for-wear Berlingo was still waiting resignedly by the side of the
road like a loyal pet. Fox drove off.

It looked like Word was going to leave him. She just wasn't in love
with Fox any more, damn it. She couldn't be bothered to seduce
him, to flirt with him. Word wouldn't fake it—if the thrill was gone,

it was truly gone. Word was his beloved no more, no longer would she surrender herself delectably to him. Now she just performed a service, fulfilled her duties, slickly, coolly, quite efficiently sometimes. Who could reproach a servant for not showing much genuine interest, for not wanting to coquettishly expose all her psychosomatic illnesses, the knotty past conflicts, childhood traumas and perversions she'd inherited from her forebears.

Fox remembered a poem. "Word's Song for Rimbaud" by Mart Kangur. In it, Word asked Arthur imploringly why he'd deserted her. He was a cunning fellow, that Rimbaud—young, cocky, and flashy, like a performance artist. It was far more common for things to end the other way, as in Fox's case. And as is well known, in the game of breaking up things always go badly for the one who fails to make the first move. Like Fox. He'd been hanging on to Word out of sheer inertia, trying to pretend their relationship was still intact, that there was still something between them worth pursuing. Over the course of the last half year, he'd tried to keep writing, tried to tempt Word with crime and splatter fiction, and stories about downtrodden minorities with a moralistic bent. The stories got published, and Fox got his fee, but Word didn't change her position, she showed no signs of coming back. Silly Word. But maybe Fox didn't love her anymore anyway, maybe Word no longer knew how to keep his passions alight. Maybe he was badgering Word out of some obsessive yearning to bring back the past. But their relationship had once been so good, like carnal love.

Oh, even that passage which he'd just mentally drafted wasn't up to much, didn't exactly glitter with originality. Damn.

Fox drove through the foggy October evening trying to decide whether he had time to rouse his spirits with pork schnitzel and fries in a local café, somewhere on the way or in N. village, where he was headed. One of those eateries where the fries would come on a white plate with crimped edges, two glass pots beside them containing different-colored sauces, normally red and white, but sometimes pink and white, or pink and red. Pink mayonnaise or Georgian relish from a jar, for example. But no, thanks to Constable Peterson and Pony, he no longer had the time to perk himself up in the local pub.

Fox turned up the radio. Someone was talking in the gushing tones of the 1990s about evolution and semiotics, as if he'd just discovered those wonderful phenomena and was trying to inculcate them upon a backward country, like some sort of missionary. His zeal was enough to make you envious. If only you could buy it and install it into yourself, reinstall it. If only you could buy a battery charged full with the desire to discover, to disclose, to proclaim. If only you could somehow get the damned inspiration back.

A while ago, he'd read that David Foster Wallace once told an interviewer that all the reasons to live, all the things he'd thought important, no longer worked for him. "Just truly at a gut level weren't working any more." Well put, thought Fox. *At a gut level.* That's exactly how it felt.

When Helen Voronin, a young librarian who'd recently started working in N. village, wrote to Fox and invited him to give a reading at this place, about a hundred kilometers from Tallinn, he agreed pretty much right away. Of course he had. He normally went where he was invited. If he just loafed around at home never meeting the public, if he turned his back on vanity, love's hardier sibling, then very soon there'd be no way back. But then, he didn't get invited to give readings at libraries very often.

By now, Fox was already pretty close to the village of N. Judging by the road signs, he had to turn left off the main road at the next junction. And then he was already on the village access road, which was lit with streetlights; by the side of the road, he could see two long double-story brick buildings. Some of the windows had been replaced, and the white PVC window frames glinted back at him through the October gloom. Fox sighed. But what was there to sigh about? Only a narrow-minded person would sigh at seeing the PVC windows recently fitted to an ugly rural block of flats, as if it were a more wretched sight than any other.

And then, up ahead of him, probably somewhere outside N. village, he saw a green-plumed rocket shoot into the sky. The rocket exploded in a radiant, vivid green garland, followed by several white garlands bursting simultaneously into the night sky. Wow, they're welcoming me with fireworks, Fox thought. What message do I bring? Several more rockets of different colors flew up into the sky one after the other, prompting Fox to get out of his car, out into the cold damp air, to watch his firework display. *Greetings, oh great writer, he who has come to us in N. village to declaim on hopelessness, lofty sentiment, freedom, equality, and solidarity!—Oh, please, don't, I'm not sure about that, but thank you anyway for your kind words.* Standing in the street he could hear the cracking of the fireworks, too. Watching his welcoming ceremony through to the end, Fox got back behind the wheel of his car and set off again. He followed Helen's instructions and, getting lost only once, arrived in the backyard of the N. village library.

The floor tiles in the entrance hall dated from Soviet times, but the walls had been painted bright orange. On the right-hand side was a door with a sign which read: *Dentist, Wed 14-18, Fri 13-18,* and *Massage.* To the left was the library. Fox knocked and opened the door.

"Hello."

"Oh, hi."

Helen had dark-blond hair, and white butterflies in her ears. She was dressed in a light gray suit, consisting of a high-collared jacket with two rows of buttons down the front, and a spherical dress. Her attractive appearance immediately aroused tender feelings in Fox which almost resembled guilt. Fresh blood could sometimes still seep from his shriveled heart, even if it had been deserted by Word. Or something like that.

"Did you find the place okay, you didn't get lost?"

"The instructions were very clear. Someone even put on a firework show in my honor."

"Fireworks? Where was that?"

"Somewhere nearby, they must have been celebrating an anniversary or something."

"Most probably. I haven't been here long, about half a year. I don't know everyone yet. We actually live a little way from here, I come here four times a week."

"How far away?"

"Twelve kilometers. I have to go to Tallinn once a week as well."

"Oh, really?"

"I've just started doing an M.A. in andragogy."

"Good for you."

"It's actually pretty tough, all that driving back and forth, with work as well."

"It must be."

Helen led him between the rows of white laminate shelving. The signs and letters glued to the shelves—dark blue against a white background—looked brand new.

"I thought we could do the reading in this corner," said Helen.

Helen pointed at a red sofa behind a round table. She'd positioned fifteen to sixteen chairs and stools on the other side of the table. On the table itself was a large round tray with biscuits and sweets in colorful wrappers, an open wooden box containing Tetley teabags, a metal tin full of brown sugar, a tower of white paper cups and two large thermos flasks.

"How about if you—or the two of us—sit on the sofa and talk, and . . . "

"How about we use the informal 'you'. We're pretty much the same age."

"Yes, you're right," Helen said with an apologetic smile. "Are you happy to sit here? I can always bring some more stools, I'm not sure how many people are going to come."

"Yes, it's hard to say, it's still ten to six."

"That's one of those things about country life, people have a long way to come," Helen said, still smiling.

"Yes, I'm sure they do."

"I did a lot of promotion for it. I even made some posters."

"That's great," Fox said.

"I should say that two of the ladies informed me right away that they had no intention of coming to listen to such a foul-mouthed speaker. But then, they're not the only literature fans here."

"There you go then," Fox said and laughed. "I didn't know I was so famous."

"Teehee."

"Hmm . . . "

"I reckon there's actually quite a bit of interest, especially if one can find the right way of introducing them to writers who are a bit . . . alternative. Anyway, I'm opening this series of talks with you."

The clock above the door showed one minute past six.

"I wonder where they can all be. It really must take a long time to get here. But have a seat, please."

Helen sat down too, straightening her rounded skirt a little uneasily.

"Well, let's see if anyone shows up," Fox said, forcing a grin.

"I made sure to organize it so it wasn't on Friday evening. Oh, God, maybe there's some soap on TV tonight?"

Going by first impressions, Helen seemed a serious sort, the kind who didn't watch soap operas. If she did watch television or download films, it would be mainly arthouse stuff, adaptations of literary classics or films about writers' lives, for example. She would definitely have seen more than Fox, and he would eventually have to admit his ignorance. In all likelihood she read a lot of contemporary fiction, too, but with a critical eye, or maybe she had a weakness for magic realism, or a particular interest in postcolonial literature. Maybe she had a hard time working in this library, but somehow she braved it out.

"Maybe they all went to see the fireworks?" Fox suggested.

"I really don't know. I think that must have been some private party." Helen took another look at the clock. "Please, help yourself to tea or coffee."

"Aha, thank you."

Five past six, six past six . . .

The library door opened and an old man in a light-brown jacket entered. He took off his cap, nodded, and said "evening."

"Hello. Looks like the audience is slowly starting to arrive," Helen said, smiling at Fox a little more assuredly.

"I saw the poster at the shop this morning, and decided right away to come. As soon as I saw the name," the old man said, screwing up his eyes and looking straight at Fox. Fox sensed that the man's gaze was supposed to convey something, but he couldn't work out what exactly. He had round red cheeks, with a thin nose positioned between them. A bird's face—like an Estonian tit. Or maybe more of an owl. No, more like a plump tit. Under his light-blue blazer the old man was wearing a dark green jumper, and Fox got the impression he'd dressed up as for a special occasion. But who could say, maybe that was just wishful thinking on Fox's part, maybe the old man wore that jacket every day.

"Oho, I thought the room would be full already," the old man said.

"You're the first," said Helen.

"Do you live here in N.?" Fox asked.

"I certainly do. Last winter I spent three months at my daughter's place in Tartu, but otherwise I've been here since I was a little lad."

"You must have been to the library before, I seem to remember seeing you," Helen said.

"Yes. My name's Lembit. Mine's that yellow house over towards the river, you probably know it."

"Aha," Helen said. "Take a seat, there's tea and coffee right here."

The old man sat down on the chair closest to the red sofa. He nodded to himself as he poured hot water into a plastic cup, his hands shaking slightly. Helen helped him choose a tea bag, and the old man nodded again, turning his plump tit-face in Fox's direction. "Now I'll ask you right away, don't you know who I am?"

Fox took another look at the old man. A rounded head topped with a crest of receding gray hair, tiny blue eyes. His face wasn't at all familiar to Fox, he couldn't link it to a single name.

"I'm sorry, I have to confess I don't."

"Well, well. Then it seems I've got a little surprise for you."

"Oh really?"

"A little surprise."

"You're making me curious," Fox said politely.

"Well, well. And there'll be a little reward at the end of the evening too. When you're finished reading through all the poems. Then they'll be a little reward."

Fox smiled diplomatically, fearing the worst. The man probably wrote poetry and wanted to hear what Fox thought of it, and advice on getting published. Or he'd already self-published a small collection and wanted to get a review in the *Eesti Ekspress* paper or the *Looming* literary journal.

The old man stooped over the table and said: "You've got some fine books here—are they for sale?"

"Oh, I don't know," said Fox. "I thought I'd read something from them to start with. I brought them with me in case the library didn't have them."

"We've got two of them in stock," Helen said triumphantly.

"I'd buy one of them," said the old man. "I'd like to take a look at what you've written." The old man picked up a book. It contained some manipulated photographs of Fox's friends. "What about this one here, how much does this one cost?" His trembling fingers lingered over the book, and Fox started to feel awkward.

"Hey, why don't you take it for free," Fox said.

"Oho, I could never. I couldn't accept it. You're serious are you, huh?" The old man opened the book again with trembling hands. His skin was like liver-spotted crepe paper.

"Well, yes." Reckoning up how many copies of the book he had, Fox immediately regretted his generosity, but it wouldn't have been right to go back on it now. Giving away books always stirred up cautious, covetous feelings, as if it were some kind of portentous act. Of course, the decision as to who received the very first copy of a book had a major impact on a book's fate. Fox would sometimes bitterly regret giving it to the wrong person, either accidentally or by force of circumstances. Clearly a book wasn't like a pet, a mongrel puppy, whose well-being worried him as soon as he handed it over to a new owner. But still. Maybe giving the old man the book was some sort of magic rite which augured well for the future. Maybe Fox would now enjoy good fortune for the rest of his days, maybe Word would return, together with the Muses. It might even be that the old man in the blue blazer was some kind of raggedy underworld being, a mythical entity which fate had guilefully sent his way. Fox grinned.

"Can you write something inside too, be a good sport. I'd like it if you could put a dedication in there."

"Very well. I'll write something—to Lembit?"

"Well, yes, write that. Write 'To Lembit,'" the old man said with a wink.

Fox took a black marker and started writing.

Lembit examined what Fox had written, leafed through the book for a while, then put it down on the table and said: "Wait, I should ask you right away. Did your mother . . . "

Fox smiled in surprise. "Yes?"

"Did your mother ever tell you stories from her youth?"

"Well, yes, she did."

"Well, what did she tell you?"

"Hmm."

"Did she tell you about a fellow called Lille-Lemps?"

"I don't remember."

"Did she tell you about him?"

"I don't think so."

"About when she was a student at the Conservatory, and visited the collective farm here? She was studying singing. Well, I'm that very same Lemps, Lille-Lemps."

"Oh, really. But unfortunately my mother never studied at the Conservatory."

"What are you talking about?"

"I'm just telling you what I know. She never did."

"How can that be?"

"I've even met her classmates. I don't think she would have lied to me."

"Your mother's name is Black-Fox isn't it? Listen, I recently heard you on the radio saying that you have your mother's surname?"

"Yes, that's right."

"So how is it that your mother never told you?"

"I don't know. She just didn't."

"What's her first name?"

"Helle."

"That's it, Helle, that's the name I was thinking of. She was a Tartu girl."

"No, she wasn't, I'm afraid."

"She studied singing."

"Again, I'm afraid not."

"What are you saying?"

"There must be some mix-up."

"Well, well."

Lembit looked at the book, which was his now.

"Well, I never," he repeated.

Helen smiled politely. "Looks like Estonia isn't such a small place after all."

"I haven't got my photographs any more either, my late wife threw them all out one day," Lembit said. "But I started to write down what I remember, I'd like to show you. I'll show you what I've got written down, maybe you'll recognize something."

"Okay . . . "

"I'm living alone now as well, my dog died last year."

"Sorry to hear that. What kind of dog was it?"

"A cocker spaniel, my daughter gave it to me, it lived to fifteen."

"They're really great dogs," said the andragogy master's student, Helen Voronin.

"That's for sure."

The three of them sat behind the table with the biscuits on it, the old man looking straight ahead at the table, shaking his head and occasionally glancing expectantly at Fox and Helen.

Helen shrugged, and with a vexed smile said: "I'm not sure. It's now twenty past six."

"Looks like that's that then," Fox quipped.

Helen looked at the clock. "I'm not sure."

"I really don't know then," said the old man, shaking his big tit's head. "It's already dark this time of year, and it's started raining now too." He looked at Fox, then at Helen, and suggested: "I could still tell you about when the students came to visit the collective farm. Maybe you'll put it into one of your poems—use it as material, as they say."

Helen glanced at Fox with an anguished look and said to Lembit: "I think that right now it would be best if Fox were to read his poetry. He's our guest speaker today, after all."

"Doesn't seem to be much point now," said Fox

"The audience may be small, but it's the best we could possibly hope for," said Helen with touching cheeriness.

"That's true," said Fox.

"Do read something, I'd really like to hear it," Helen said.

Lembit nodded resignedly. "All right then, best that you read, I'll listen, we can have a talk after." He nodded his head again, and mumbled: "Well I never."

The prospect of reading his poetry to an audience of two seemed a pretty empty undertaking, and Fox found that even his vanity didn't want to get properly into gear.

But Helen smiled so cheerily that Fox said: "Very well, I'll . . . "

He looked at the books left on the table and picked one of them up.

"I'll read something from here then. I got the idea for this poem on a trip to Russia. During the train journey, I was trying to picture exactly where we were on the map, and so I thought up a character who had such a vivid imagination that he came close to having a stroke when a pencil was poked into certain points on the atlas. And then, taking that idea further, there's a character who's so connected to his native land that you could perform voodoo on him with nothing more than a map."

Fox read the poem, Lembit nodded in what looked like a state of rapture, Helen laughed; Fox liked to think that she wasn't just being polite.

"Now this next poem takes a small image and an everyday situation, and attempts to develop them into a catastrophe which was impossible to predict. So it starts with the image of a stain on some clothing, and then descends into turmoil. A bit like chaos theory, when a slight variation in the initial conditions can produce entirely unexpected outcomes . . . although there is a character in it who claims to have foreseen everything from that first blotch . . . but, it's best I read it."

Fox read. Helen listened attentively and Lembit carried on nodding.

"*It smells quite strange and, behold, has it not now grown larger?*" Fox read, and Lembit made an "uh" sound.

Then he made the "uh" sound again, jerked up in his plywood chair, and flopped sideways onto the linoleum floor.

Fox had always thought he would make a good doctor.

And now, right there in front of him, was the old man's face, skin covered in capillary-purple whorls. His old mouth with its old mucous membrane, wide open. As Fox clumsily attempted mouth-to-mouth resuscitation, he knocked up against the teeth. Or were they—they must've been—dentures?

When Fox got his driver's license, he hadn't needed to take any kind of first-aid course. So he knew pretty much nothing. One-two-three-four and blow twice, or that's what he thought. One time at the dentist, the Bee Gees' "Stayin' Alive" had come on the radio and the dentist had said: "If you ever need to—and hopefully you won't—CPR should be performed to exactly this rhythm. One-two-three-four." *Ah, ah, ah, ah—stayin' alive, stayin' alive!* Those Bee Gees boys with their bright white teeth and high-pitched voices weren't so far from this linoleum floor and Lembit's resistant body now. In fact they were all very close.

But his body kept up the resistance. It somehow didn't want to become whole again, it was in a state of revolt, the flesh and the limbs declaring independence. His tough parchment neck turned purple.

"You must be pressing too hard," said Helen quietly. She was still on the phone, answering the emergency services' questions and try-ing to explain how to get to the library.

The library's linoleum floor was imitating marble.

"Is the operator some kind of idiot? He must be a total idiot!"

Maybe a bit more zeal was needed, that was supposed to be a quality doctors had, wasn't it? A little bit faster, easy there. *Ah, ah, ah, ah—staying alive!*

"Try to be strong," the older paramedic told Helen. "You just need to get through the funeral, and then . . . "

"Me? Heaven forbid," Helen said, looking straight at the paramedic.

"So you're not . . . I thought you were his daughter."

"No. I'm the head librarian."

"He was visiting, they told us that," said the chief paramedic. He had long gray hair.

Helen leaned against the white laminate shelving, shaking her head.

"Neither of us knew him," said Fox.

Helen looked down at the floor, continuing to shake her head. The ambulance team packed up their equipment. Fox gawped at their bright red and yellow outfits. The whole scene looked like a genre painting which someone must have painted once. Rucked-up imitation marble, laminate white, neon yellow and tumescent red flashing in all their robustness. The doctor filled in the paperwork.

"What's his name? The man's name?" he asked

Helen shook her head.

"He said it was Lembit," said Fox. "Yes, Lembit."

"And his surname?"

"He said it was Lille-Lemps. But he had a wallet with him. Maybe there are some documents in there."

From his ID card, they established that Lembit Lille would have been seventy-six in two weeks' time.

"Was he a local?" the paramedic asked.

Helen sighed. "Yes. Or that's what he said. He's been to the library before."

"Does he have any relatives here?"

"He said that he lives alone," said Helen.

"His daughter's in Tartu," said Fox, sounding proud to have remembered.

Among other things, Lembit had a mobile phone in his jacket pocket, a decent-sized one with big keys, and the last number he'd called belonged to KADI, and this KADI turned out to be his granddaughter, her young voice clearly audible from the telephone receiver; maybe KADI was a student, but in any case she was shocked, and she wondered if there was some way she could get to N. Library, because she didn't drive, and Mom was on her shift, so she clearly worked at the kind of place where people did shifts; Mom could definitely get off work, but she didn't drive either, maybe they could ask someone to help, but then it turned out the ambulance crew was going to call out the hearse in any case, and Lembit would be sent for an autopsy, and the two of them, KADI and her mom, who was Lembit's daughter, the one who'd bought him the cocker spaniel that lived to fifteen, should go to the

* From St. John Chrysostom's (Russian: Ivan Zlatoust) Paschal Sermon: "The Lord accepteth the deed and welcometh the intention."

mortuary instead, where they'd be able to see Lembit with his body chilled, and by then his abject cavities and rigid arteries would have been severed and reassembled at least once.

Fox looked at Helen, who'd collapsed on the sofa like a rain-sodden paper doll. He sat down beside her, reached mechanically for a paper cup, poured some hot water, and submerged an Earl Grey teabag in it. He added three teaspoons of brown sugar. Helen looked at him with her large, dark, frightened eyes, and Fox immediately felt ashamed for thinking of drinking tea in the presence of the dead. He looked at the only attendee of the evening's reading, lying on the floor with his mouth drooping open. Fox noticed he'd already taken a couple of swigs out of the paper cup, and he set it back down on the table. He tried to smile reassuringly at Helen, which must have also seemed a little inappropriate.

Helen raised her eyebrows with a pained expression, but she didn't return the smile, instead she just wiped her pale forehead with the edge of her hand. "I was going to say . . . " She looked straight at Fox, sighed, and said gently: "I was going to say that you should make out that bill, as we discussed. One hundred euros. To N. district government. Together with the receipt for the petrol."

Fox looked at his books lying on the coffee table. One of them had a dedication to Lembit inside it. Maybe the library had something . . . maybe they had something to stick over it. They could use the books for prizes or something.

They sat for a while in silence. Fox reached out mechanically for a biscuit.

"Maybe I should go and get some wine?" he suggested.

"Wine?" Helen raised her eyebrows.

"Well, yes, I thought we could drink to Lembit's memory. While we wait. Is there somewhere nearby I could still get something to drink?"

"I don't want to be left on my own with him."

"Ah. Well, I don't know then. Maybe you could fetch something."

"What if someone comes while I'm gone. I'm not sure it's a good idea. We're both driving anyway."

"That's true. I was already stopped once on the way here."

"Oh, God. For speeding?"

"Yes, damn it."

Fox poured some more hot water into his plastic cup, in memory of Lembit.

When the ambulance arrived, Helen had switched on all the lights in the library, and they had stayed on. Fox thought she wouldn't dare switch them off now. Changing the lighting while keeping vigil over a corpse would seem like an act of high drama, inevitably imbued with some kind of significance.

They spoke. Quietly at first, as if still taking into account the presence, or half-presence, of another person. But then gradually louder. They dreamed up a past for Lembit, and Helen went to boil more water for tea. She moved very cautiously, trying not to look in Lembit's direction, but at one point she came to a standstill and then stood for a while, looking at the body lying on the floor. She told Fox she'd recently heard a radio program in which people were asked their views on euthanasia.

"The majority were in favor, which I found surprising. But the reason was that no one could be bothered with keeping those terminally ill people alive and caring for them. That's the kind of people we Estonians are." She stood next to Lembit, holding the teapot. "I reckon he couldn't have known he was dying."

Fox thought about warning Helen that one should never say "see you" to stretcher-bearers. But when they carried out the zipped-up green bag she just said "goodbye" of her own accord, quietly and composedly.

They stood in the middle of the muddied linoleum marble.

"I don't know. Are you sure that you don't want to go for a quick drink somewhere?" Fox asked.

Helen shook her head. "I can't. Really. My husband's in Sweden at the moment, and I was actually supposed to go to a friend's place tonight."

"What does your husband do in Sweden?"

"He's a door fitter."

"Aha."

It was already past nine when Fox started to drive home. The weather was milder and even damper than before.

When he got back to town, at first he didn't go home, instead he went to a hotel bar, the most unpretentious place possible. He ordered a chai latte in memory of his only audience member and sent text messages to a few friends. Maybe one of them would want to come out. No one was free, of course.

He had to completely change his life.

Maybe he could spend the rest of his days just shifting dead bodies around. Become a hearse driver. Oversee one of life's final stages, always present when it was all over, when wearisome hope had completely gone, do the kind of work which was free from any burden of hope. Be the largest, outermost *Matryoshka*, which held all the others. At parties, people would find excuses to sit at another table, neighbors would tinkle Tibetan bowls, or even try to sell up their apartments. Maybe the arrogance of Job would guarantee him an interview or a feature in some newspaper. Of course, the downside was that to economize, the hearse driver doubled up as stretcher bearer, and sometimes a corpse might weigh up to three-hundred-and-fifty pounds.

He got back behind the wheel, drove through downtown Tallinn, stopped to fill up on gas (he had to submit the receipt to N. district government), and then drove out of town again, this time in the opposite direction. He whizzed through some of the nearby villages, then back onto the main road, sped down some side roads, then back onto the main road again, driving further down it, not spotting any police this time. By one in the morning he realized he couldn't carry on this way much longer. At the Loksa junction with the Petersburg motorway, he did a U-turn and headed down the tiresomely familiar roads back home. There, feeling totally numb, he collapsed into bed.

TRANSLATED FROM THE ESTONIAN BY MATTHEW HYDE

LOTTE KIRKEBY

Violet Lane

WE HAD RUNG Lise to see if she wanted to come up to us. It doesn't hurt to be nice to her you know girls, my mother said, and I nodded even though I could see my sister's scowl.

And it was me that had to be goody-two-shoes now when we went shopping. Holding the car door open for Mom and all that. My sister had begun to sit in the front. So she had her own door. But I had to wait till Mom flipped the driver's seat forward to let me out on her side. And 'cuz I'm standing there anyway, she says, I may as well hold the door open while she gets the shopping bags out. The bags were next to me, in the place where my sister used to sit.

Lise had moved in with her family that spring. Nobody had a clue where they'd come from or why they had to move here. Maybe they needed more room, Mom said, 'cuz they had four kids and that was a load more than most families.

We were actually sitting on the low wall with the others when their moving van came around the corner. I had plucked a bunch of forget-me-nots from the common near us, but threw them away when my sister asked what I was doing with them. Mom had baked a cake in the big baking tray. WELCOME TO VIOLET LANE, it said on top in thick brown chocolate icing, but TO and LANE were in yellow. The yellow looked mad against the brown, and we followed them out to their garden and sat on the grass all full of daisies, after Lise's mom asked us if we wanted to. Then she went and got some rugs and blankets and lemonade.

Before we headed off on our summer holidays, we let Lise in on our secret games and, probably, we should never have done that. That's what Carsten said anyway. Afterwards. We never played them in or near front gardens, or out on the street. Only on the common, where the grass grew to our knees. All the parents and adults told us to keep away from there, 'cuz it was somebody's property or something, though there's never been a building there.

But we went anyway. As soon as we could after school. Sometimes we'd take turns squatting down, closing our eyes, then seriously breathing in and out through our mouths. First twenty times really deep and slowly, then twenty really-really quick. Then jumping up fast and seriously holding our breath. You fell backwards then, into the arms of the one standing ready behind you who squeezed you really tight with their arms around you and then put their fists hard into your breast cage. Just there where your ribs meet. The place that's hard to find in girls that have started to get breasts. But it was usually the boys who stood behind them. Then you were let slump to the ground very carefully and slowly.

If you were lucky, you disappeared for a minute. It was a bit like dying, said Carsten, who stole smokes and sweets over at the little shop. Porno mags as well. None of us asked him how he knew.

Sometimes nothing happened. So we just lay there looking up at the sky and cracking up laughing at the weight in our chests. Like when you've run too fast or for too long. But without a stitch in your side or anything, and loads better.

When our parents got home we were back in the street. Mostly, the adults were in the backyards looking after the youngest kids. If we were playing tennis, we tied a rope to the handlebars of two standing bicycles on either side of the road to make a net. If a car came, one of the kids from the classes below us at school had to run and put the bicycles down, so the car could pass.

Last year it was me that had to put the cycles down. And it was me that had to go home earlier in the evenings as well. But when I had my pajamas on, I was allowed to nip out again for a bit. So I'd slip through the gap in the hedge, so the others wouldn't see me, and down to Helle's to get a goodnight story at her place. Even though Helle was a bit too young to be my friend, and I was too big. Because I can read myself, no problem.

In Helle's house they got coffee in the morning, plus toast and jam. Then coffee again in the evenings with cupcakes and biscuits.

Her mom stayed at home all day, and if she'd known what we got up to on the common she would have said something. Definitely.

I didn't know what she did during the winter. But in summer she'd lie on a sunbed in the garden. It had big orange and white flowers on it. Just sunbathing. She was brown by the time we got to May and black by August. And every morning she'd listen to Elvis while she made lunches and got everyone packed off good and early.

But one morning there was no music. Elvis was dead. He was only forty-two and it was terrible. A tragedy, Helle's mom said, and she pulled me into a hug. She whispered that Elvis had the same birthday as me and that was how she could always remember it. And then she cried.

She cried in the afternoon, too, when we got home from school. And then Helle ran down to the back garden shed for her dad. He was always in there fixing something or other. But we knew very well he wouldn't do much, 'cuz he just sat in there on an upturned bucket drinking beer.

It was us that found the bottles and got money back on the empties. Helle's dad never said a thing. We got sweets on the money from them. Down at the newspaper shop where the owner was missing two fingers. His sweets were the cheapest. They were sort of stale and hard and sat in your teeth and Mom said it was because they were ancient. Like those chocolate-covered marshmallows she'd bought once, which had stood on display somewhere for years. She told us not to buy sweets there anymore, but even though it was yukky to think the shop owner had touched all the sweets with the fingers he had left, we still went there.

That day, when Elvis died, Helle's dad went up into the house to comfort her Mom. But the next time she cried, he couldn't do that, 'cuz he was dead as well. He'd hung himself in the shed. I wanted to ask if he'd stood on that upturned bucket to reach the loop. Carsten said they found him hanging from a noose. And also. How could you manage to kick it away yourself and you hanging there?

But we didn't talk about things like that. I was waiting for my mom to ask me if I missed Helle's dad, seeing as it was him that read bedtime stories to us. But she never did. Then they flitted,

Helle and her mom and her little brother who was called Peter. And that's when Lise and her family moved in. No one was sure if they really knew about the shed.

It was me that rang Lise. She answered right away. She was really happy and said she'd love to come over, but she couldn't budge until tomorrow.

I put the receiver down and looked over at my sister. She turned away from me and went out into the garden and I followed her. Down behind the rabbit hutch there was a load of wooden pins. They weren't sharp, but were quite long and had rubber foam at the end, held on by tape. I couldn't remember what we'd used them for, but my sister lifted them and said she was going down to Carsten.

When she came back for her tea, she told me the plan. I said I wasn't sure if I wanted in on it, but she said not to be a total dunce. All I had to do was go down to number sixteen and she would bring the pins. The boys would do the rest. It was Carsten's idea and he'd decided that if she started blubbering she was out.

I didn't like it but I knew it was just the way things were. I'd been the permanent server in rounders for the whole of last summer, while the others switched between batting and fielding. So I was always left out. 'cuz I wasn't on a team. And if you're not on a team, you can't win. You can't even die when you're a permanent server. At least if you die, something's happened.

This year it was Lone that was the permanent server and I got on a team, even though I was the last to be picked. My hair had grown so long that it blew across my face when I ran, but it was still too short for putting up properly. And my sister was still mad that she'd been grounded and that Mom had freaked so much after I'd agreed to let Big Sis fix it.

The day after, I went down to number sixteen and stood there. Then Lise appeared. Running down the road with her two long thick braids banging at her back. She had two packages in her hands. She handed them over to me. She had brought presents for us back from her holidays. They'd been camping near Lake Garda. Even though I hadn't realized we'd become such good friends before the holidays, I was very pleased. I could see she was dying to show us what she'd got for us and I was dying to see them, but then my sister jumped in and started hitting Lise with those long pins, like we'd agreed. We didn't hit hard. And not in the face. She just needed to get that this was serious and she went with us with no fuss down to the common where the worms had eaten almost all the raspberries. But the elderberries were fully ripe and hung in big clusters.

The boys had got everything together and Carsten was already there, waiting. He didn't normally let his little brother tag along, but he was here today. He'd been given a fiver to take part and keep his mouth shut, my sister said afterwards. They'd tied him to a chair and blindfolded him. He was sat like a statue. Everyone was in on what was going to happen. But not him. And Lise didn't have a clue either. Needless to say.

Carsten had a knife in his hand. He'd stolen it off his dad who was in the civil defense forces. He'd also stolen some of those small ration packs they got for going on maneuvers—or if it got really serious and the Russians came. He only ever shared these with the really big kids. My sister knew what they tasted like. But she wasn't sure if Carsten's dad had a pistol as well, like some people said.

We handed Lise over to the boys, and they tied her to a tree so that she was directly facing Carsten's little brother. She dropped the holiday presents when they bound her hands behind her back. Carsten's little brother had a pair of long trousers on. They were far too big for him. They had taped big tight bags of crushed berries and cordial in the inside legs with sheets of polystyrene against the skin to protect him.

Carsten lifted the knife and looked at Lise. The only thing you could hear was the wind in the leaves of the weeping willow. Then a berry that fell down and hit the grass. She didn't look like Lise anymore. She had shut her eyes, but he told her to keep them open and she'd get ten times worse if she blabbed.

She did as he said. Both then and afterwards. And that's the way it was for all of us. Then he turned and stuck the knife into his little brother's leg. Rammed it into first one leg then the other, and a deep red liquid spurted out in a thick jet that could easily have been blood if you didn't know better.

Lise screamed and screamed and she closed her eyes again and maybe she fainted as well. She went white as a milk bottle anyway. But my sister said afterwards that you can't faint if you're still stood up. If you faint properly, you collapse and she was still standing against the tree trunk when we ran off from the common. I knew this 'cuz I turned a bit and looked over my shoulder before I got round the corner.

Before they ran off, the boys had untied the cord around Carsten's brother's hands and removed the blindfold. Carsten was whispering to him about what had happened, but his brother just laughed and said he would set her free when we were all gone.

My sister went with Carsten, and I went home. I didn't know what they did when they were alone. I was dying to find out. So I asked her. But she wouldn't tell me and Mom said it was just what happened when children got older. They stopped telling their parents everything. And their brothers and sisters too, by the way, she added.

My mom was sitting in the living room, knitting. I could see this as I opened the garden gate. The bottom of the apple tree was surrounded by rotten apples and most of them were half-eaten by wasps. Nobody ever gathered them up, even though our granny said you could use fallen apples for stewed-fruit desserts and jams. But now here they were in a heap and stinking like those beer bottles we'd found in Helle's garden. So then I began to think of her dad and then Lise, who couldn't be in our gang. Not a chance. And I started to cry.

I found an apple that wasn't rotten and went to the hutch and took the rabbit out. I buried my head in its fur as it ate the apple. And I told it everything we'd done. Then I thought of the holiday presents and started wondering what they were. I got an urge to run back and get them.

But I just put the rabbit back in its hutch and went over to the wasp-trap my mom had set up over the weekend. She'd taken a used pot of homemade raspberry and elderberry jam, that still had some jam in in it, half filled it with water, then put the pot on a low bench near the apple tree. Most of the water had evaporated, and the jam had gone to gunge. The stiff dead wasps looked like they'd been molded into the red goo of jam. Stuck in the remnants of fruit I'd plucked on the common. Where the elderberries were hanging over Lise's head right now, like tiny dead eyes.

One of the wasps was still alive. Buzzing like mad. I lifted it out with one of our pins and set it carefully down on the chair. Its legs were totally stiff with sugar. I knew Mom was going to ask how we'd got on with Lise and that I couldn't tell her a thing. The wasp tried its best to crawl off along the bench. Just before it reached the edge, I lifted my foot and trod down.

TRANSLATED FROM THE DANISH BY PAUL LARKIN

IGOR MALIJEVSKÝ

Multicultural Center

YOU OPEN THE iron door and grope your way through some kind of dark-colored blanket and then a swinging gate. It takes a few seconds. Meanwhile, inside, they tune their antennae and put on indifferent expressions, and the expectation of new information is ratcheted up to the maximum. It's as if you're entering someone's living room. Just to be sure, you say hello a few times and bow uncertainly in all directions. You don't know all of them by name, and you don't really want to. There's the carpenter who owes you a set of shelves; ever since his wife died, he's been diagnosing himself with one fatal disease after another. Last fall he had leukemia, but they chased it off with vitamins and Xanax. Denis, the eternal class president, is also sitting here today with his little contingent. In the corner, a few twenty-year-olds are flirting with each other, Standa is getting change at the bar, and the cat Macíček is watching it all.

The last bench on the right is for strangers; that's where I usually sit. The other benches are arranged by generation: old, middle-aged, young. Elena brings me a beer and asks how things are looking in the great wide world. Worse there than here, I say. She laughs and walks over to the bar to take care of Macíček, a valued customer with lifetime credit. He sits next to the beer taps and occasionally strolls possessively across the counter, where the slips of paper with drink tallies are laid out in rows next to the chocolate bars and candy. He rarely starts anything with the customers. He eats his fill and then, with evident reserve, spends a long time observing the goings-on. In a certain sense, we are intimates. That's why we respectfully ignore each other.

I drink without talking. Slowly, I enter that rare, quiet mood where things appear as a single whole, where everything is comprehensible, at least for a moment, and worldly canons disappear along with the exhausting, endless game of lustration: like/dislike, good/evil, beautiful/ugly, right/wrong. Where the world mysteriously and quietly purrs. I watch Standa playing the electronic slot machines; he only has one-and-a-half fingers on his right hand after this year's cruel winter. Standa had made it, somehow, from the pub to his house; he'd taken hold of the door handle, grasped it firmly, and then fallen asleep. "I'm going to have to start making the rounds in my car," laughed Elena, "to see if anyone's still lying around out there, or else all my drunks will drop off one by one. Then I'd have no choice but to shut this place down."

In the long run, though, only God can keep sitting, listening, and nodding his head—no one can sit down next to him, and ultimately the looking game is his alone; no living creature can play it for long. Not even Macíček, who's jumped down from among the slips of paper and walked over, with open scorn, to the middle-aged table, to cadge a bit of pork. Sooner or later, you'll start to care about something. Pork, people, whatever. Sooner or later, everyone can be wounded, there's something you can't handle, something forces you to show your true colors and surrender your impartiality. Like when the guys tried to pour a shot of Fernet Stock into Macíček and Elena hurled a pint-glass at them.

Denis suddenly turned on me. "What's your liquor?"

"I don't drink much liquor," I lied.

"Elena, bring us some plum brandy! Listen, we live right near each other and we still don't know each other properly. Strange, isn't it. You'll be coming to the maypole celebration, right?"

I kept on lying. "I'm not sure yet."

"People have to stick together, don't they? At least for the maypole. Look here, we're each bringing something to the table . . . You bring your camera, you'll do a great story . . . " Denis was hallucinating. They say he semi-publicly chooses his lovers at the maypole celebrations and then has sex with them in the multicultural center.

While I've been keeping to one side, staying at the strangers' table and refusing to join the middle-aged, Standa has lost the rest of his money and is now sitting down in the corner with the old men, where Bohouš used to sit. Bohouš used to sit there both before and after they made a hole in his neck, beautiful singing voice or no. He used a big plastic toy syringe, the kind children spray each other with, to squirt beer into the hole. Day after day he grew thinner and smaller, until he disappeared entirely.

"Black-and-white's fine! Definitely! Time for another!" bellowed Denis, and he stuck a second brandy in my hand. "And now, listen closely . . . " He lowered his voice so that the rest of the pub fell silent and the customers turned toward my table. "You'll get paid from our grant money. I'll arrange it with the association. Then we'll do an exhibition together—in the multicultural center, you and me, because I do some photography, too."

The carpenter broke in:

"And why not do it in the pub? At least they serve beer here."

"I'll tell you why . . . That's what the multicultural center is for—for things like this. It's new and the furniture is nice."

I sat there, listening and nodding. At one point Macíček jumped down from the beer taps, walked over to my table with conspicuous indifference, rubbed against my leg, and then went back.

In the bathroom, I saw that Elena had put up a new placard next to the existing ones, which strive, humorously, to keep customers from urinating on the floor. To read it, I had to do two quick side-steps over to a different urinal. Then I could make it out:

When you cry, everyone is indifferent to your tears.
When your heart aches, no one notices your pain.
When you're happy, no one notices your smile.
But just try farting . . .

As I finished reading, I felt a man's hand on my shoulder. It unnerved me. I wasn't quite finished, so I couldn't turn around, let alone defend myself. I pretended nothing was happening. Then a fine bass voice rang out.

"Mr. Malijevský, I've started work on it. The thing is—I don't want to scare you, but I've got some kind of lump here. I took it to the clinic in Rakovník, but they don't know shit about tumors. So I went straight to Homolka. They won't do much there unless you give them something extra, but in the end they admitted me. The first tests didn't turn up anything, which might mean it's pretty bad, so I'm conserving my strength now. But I've been working on it at home whenever I'm up and about. Will you be home on Thursday at 4:15? Or more like 4:20?"

"Probably. Why do you ask?"

"I'll be there with the shelves, and I'll also make you a little shoe rack, gratis."

"But that's what you said a month ago. I waited for you at 3:45 on a Sunday and no one came."

"I had the flu. Luckily, just the ordinary kind."

*

The middle-aged table called it a night around ten o'clock, because the middle-aged table does its real drinking on Fridays and Saturdays. As the pub grew quiet, I could again hear the cat purring. The feeling of safety returned. I ordered one last beer and waved my wallet in the cat's direction.

"You also had the two brandies, right?"

"What do you know. Add on the brandies."

Outside, the stars were shining and Standa was urinating. When he saw me, he shook himself off and staggered over in my direction. "Wait. Look." He stuffed his shirt into his pants and managed to find his way to me. "Look." There was a long, oppressive silence. His crumpled face was weakly illuminated by the orange streetlamp. Baseball cap, faded jeans jacket, deep wrinkles. Insistent gaze, restless, wandering eyes.

"Come home with me," he said, and it sounded shy, half-questioning. A few awkward seconds passed. Then I nodded uncertainly and right away began to reproach myself. Though Standa probably isn't into men; his wife had moved out just a few years ago. We made our way slowly, with uncertain steps, through half the village. Standa stopped twice to make sure no one was following us. "They wouldn't understand. No one here would understand." We stopped in front of his house while he hunted for his keys. Then he turned the key in the lock with his left hand, pressed down the handle with the finger on his right hand, and opened the door with his body.

"Miládka planted tulips there." He waved into the darkness,

stepped into the entryway, and turned on the lights. I followed cautiously. The house was uncared for—more of a workshop than a living space, everything soaked in the smell of diesel. "You can leave your shoes on," he said, unnecessarily. We continued through the entry, stepping around a jar of Vaseline on the floor, and we reached a door at the end of a narrow hall.

"Miládka and I had our bedroom here." Standa pointed at the door. "But you'll have to go in by yourself." I began to feel a bit nauseous. I felt like I'd been washed ashore; I didn't have enough information. Had anyone heard from Miládka, actually, after she moved out?

"Don't be afraid. The light switch is on your right."

There was no backing out. I took a deep breath and opened the door. The room stank of gasoline and there was an enormous piece of furniture in the middle of it. I groped along the wall and turned on the light. The only things left from the former bedroom were a picture on the wall and a filthy rug on the floor. The remaining space was taken up by a tractor. It looked much bigger inside than it would have, for example, out in the field. A monstrous, gigantic monument, a homemade Stonehenge.

"I moved it in here three years ago. Piece by piece. It works. You can start it up if you want. But keep it in neutral, so you don't drive into the living room."

"That's fine, Standa, thank you." It seemed to me I should say something more. Something to do justice to this exceptional moment. A person had put in an enormous amount of work, and for the rest of his life, probably, he wouldn't do anything so . . . Nothing occurred to me. When I drink too much, my memory goes. I walked around the tractor a few times, the least I could do, and twice kicked its enormous tires. Standa was leaning against the doorframe and watching me with poorly feigned indifference. I walked over to him and clumsily patted him on the shoulder. I must have been thinking of some movie. "Thank you, Standa. Beautiful work."

The starry sky shone over the village square. There was a muffled purring somewhere in the distance. The chill night air pushed into my face. I was slowly returning to that quiet mood, things were appearing as a single whole, for a moment you could understand everything. Cast off those war games, the informer's like/dislike, good/evil, beautiful/ugly, right/wrong. The world is fragile and purrs softly. Everyone can be wounded. Everyone's hiding something at home, something they care about.

I try to remember what I have at home. On the other side of the street, Macíček walks along in the same direction. We pretend not to see each other.

TRANSLATED FROM THE CZECH BY JONATHAN BOLTON

ZACHARY KARABASHLIEV

Metastases

THANK YOU, GOD, for sending him this disease!

My father made it through a single round of chemotherapy and categorically refused to do another. He also turned down radiation and every other form of treatment. He wanted to go to the village "for some fresh air" and to talk with my mother.

Sit down here and let's chat, he would tell her.

Why don't you go down to The Television and chat with the drunks there this time of day? my mother would answer. Then, with a half-smile, she would sit down next to the stove.

"I should warn you that sometimes something comes over him, he drifts off, starts rambling incoherently, maybe it's from the pills, who knows?. . . Last night, for example, if you can believe it, he was going on about some phone conversation he supposedly had with you, when a hawk swooped down and snatched up a rabbit. Come on now, I said, what's this about a hawk and a rabbit, honestly! I think . . . I think you've had a little too much morphine, to tell you the truth."

For the first and final year of their life together, my parents started talking. Did they say what needed to be said? I know that my father told her his dreams (when he managed to fall sleep at all) and that my sister and I played starring roles in many of them.

It's 1:43 in the morning in California. Where they've dug his grave, it's not even noon yet. I suspect that his coffin is the lightest that those men—used to carrying other peoples' coffins—have ever carried. In the last days of his life he was lighter than a child.

I have to retouch three hundred and sixty-two digital photographs and the deadline is tomorrow. Three hundred and sixty-two photos of successful silicon implants. My eyes sting from the colors.

My wife and daughter went to bed long ago. I haven't seen my little girl in four days—I get home after she's asleep, and in the morning when her mother sends her off to school, I'm sleeping.

I abandon the monitor and go to the fridge for more Coke to mix with my vodka. I push aside the watermelon and take out a plastic two-liter bottle. I bought him the watermelon today, after Mom called to tell me he'd finally passed away. He loved watermelon. He also loved vodka and coke. I go into the closet, turn on the light, shove aside cardboard boxes, sit on the floor and start digging through the shoeboxes stuffed with pictures, opening up the photo albums.

What I'm looking for is a small, old photograph with wavy edges, showing my mother and father dancing. From the way they're holding each other's hands I can tell it's a tango. He is wearing a jacket, a light, unbuttoned shirt, sweaty and smiling like in a black-and-white Italian film. My mother has thrown her head back and is laughing with her beautiful, even, healthy white teeth. At that moment my father is happy. My mother—even happier than he is. I haven't come across that picture in a long time; I'm not even sure it's here. Now, however, at 1:54 in the morning, in a quiet apartment at the other end of the world, far away from the place I spent my childhood and from the grave destined for my father, I see that picture more clearly than I ever did when I held it in my hands. I see them dancing, I hear the music in that workers' cantina (what ridiculous banquet were they at? whose shabby wedding?), I can smell the lilacs in the vases on the table and my father's sweat. I remember how he smelled. If I went into a room where my father had been for a long time, a soury-sweet tang hung in the air, as from a chunk of raw meat.

He's so handsome in that picture, which I can't find right now. It's from before my sister and I appeared. I think mom is pregnant with me there. So that means she was nineteen, and my father—twenty-six.

My mother graduated from the agricultural votech and was appointed head of the newly opened post office in a relatively bustling village not far from the sea. She found herself an admirer from the nearby army base. She'd talk to him endlessly on the phone, he'd sometimes play guitar for her into the receiver. She would sing for him. Perhaps they saw each other for a few hours when the soldier was granted leave. Maybe they drank lemonade, or maybe milkshakes. What did they talk about? Many years later, on a slushy winter day, she'd run into him at the courthouse as she filed for divorce from my father. They would recognize each other. They'd shake their heads and laugh as they took off gloves and hats and scarves and their eyes would ask what had happened to that time. What had happened to all that time, during which he'd transformed from an army recruit into a judge, while she—into a monument of a failed marriage. Where had all the time gone?

But let's not get ahead of ourselves. Let's go back to the time when my mother coped with the boredom and the sweltering village heat by listening to her admirer strumming his guitar over the phone and leafing through illustrated East German knitting magazines. It was nearing lunchtime when a motorcycle exhaust pipe roared from around the bend by the post office and the culprit responsible for these lines appeared. He stopped in a cloud of dust, leaned his motorcycle on its kickstand, and sank into the plastic streamers in front of the green door with "Horemag" written above it. A short while later, my mother crossed the street and also entered the cool restaurant, to buy a candy bar and make the biggest mistake of her life—smiling at that charming stranger.

"Even then it crossed my mind, but . . . When I saw him leaning against the bar at noon. He said he didn't drink. He said it was just a small one. Well now, talk about a stupid goose! Just listen to what people are telling you. But no, oh, no! Love. There's love for you now."

My mother's parents, of course, were against it. Everyone was against it. With the money from their wedding, the newlyweds bought pots and pans.

I don't know whether there was a specific incident, a decisive turning point when my father turned into that which I grew up with. He drank every day. He got drunk almost every day. No matter how hard I try, I can't remember a single day we ever spent happily together as a family which I could revisit in my thoughts.

Over time, my younger sister and I learned to imitate our class-mates' normal childhoods. I had friends I played with after school, I did my homework and was a good student, albeit somewhat absent-minded, according to my teachers. In reality, however, my days passed in an expertly disguised fear of what the evening would bring. If we were lucky, an invisible force would prevent our father from getting drunk. If we were less lucky, he would've had a few drinks, but would be in a relatively peaceful mood, so we'd get by with just run-of-the-mill arguments and insults. If he'd had a lot to drink, he'd be aggressive at the beginning and there would be fights, but he'd get tired quickly and fall asleep. The worst was when he had drunk just enough to aggravate him, but not quite enough to satisfy him. Then it didn't even show that he'd been drinking, but we could tell. He hated being accused of drinking.

"You've been drinking. Your eyes give it aw . . . "

A sudden swing, a smack, my mother's head jerks to the side, she lets out a sob, tears spring to her eyes. They enrage my father even more, my sister and I hurl ourselves between them. He looks through us, reaches through us, punches her through us, his eyes locked on hers . . .

My father never drank alone. Alcoholics drink alone, he liked to say. And he would never admit to being one. There was something totally unique about my father's alcoholism. Uncle Dobcho, for example, who lived on our street and who everybody knew was a drunk who beat his wife, Stefka, at least once a week, was a real alcoholic. But Dobcho was also an incredible carpenter, a true master. Yet another true master was Grandpa Stefan, the other alcoholic in the neighborhood, a mechanic. There was no car that could stump him. Most of the alcoholics I would meet later in life were blue-eyed and very good at what they did—housepainters, brick-layers, artists, machinists, or poets. My father didn't have any talents. If he had to pound a nail into a board, he would inevitably bloody up his finger. And he'd bend the nail. If he had to put on a spare tire, he'd break the jack. If he changed a blown-out fuse, he'd get a shock. In every case, the first thing he'd do would be to glance around for my mother with that enraged look and yell at her. My father wasn't good at anything.

A year and a half ago, I woke up from an exceptionally vivid dream. The dream was so strange and striking that I immediately turned on my computer and wrote it down, trying to preserve what I could of it before the world barged back into my head to chase away the details and turn it into average, run-of-the-mill gibberish. I saved it on my computer as "Dream about My Father," together with other dreams of mine in a special folder called "Dreams."

That same day Mom called to tell me about his illness.

Carcinoma recti etani.

"Dream about My Father" is on Local Disc (C:). When I tried to "import" it into this story, here's what I got:

⬛◀▲✕✕ ▦▦▶ ▨⬛▶▸◣▸ ▲▲✕ ▦▶ ▦▧ ▦✕✕8◀ ▦◉▲▲✕▦◉▲▶ ▦▦▶ ▨⬛▶▸◣▸ ▸
▦✕ ▨ ▦▶✕✕✕ ▦✕▨▲▦▦▶▸ ▱▲◉▦◉▶ ▦✕8▦▸ ▱▸ ▦▦▸ ▀◀ ▶▶◀▦▦▶
8 ▦▦—▀▸▶▲▲▦▦▪▪▪

When the operating system was reinstalled and the formats and folder names changed, something happened to this document. The strange thing is that the other files in the folder are legible, only this one needs to be decoded. What I remember about the dream is the end. It's New Year's, I'm at some party here in America, everyone around me is having fun, but I'm talking to my father on the phone. I'm trying to hear what he's saying, but it's really noisy and I can't quite catch it. The only thing I get is that he needs help. And I sense that for the first time in his life he's being absolutely sincere with me. I start crying. From the other end of the line I can hear that he's crying, too. I remember the taste of my tears—warm, salty, tasty tears—the tears of a child. And as only happens in dreams, I know that they are actually *his* tears running down my face on the other side of the globe.

But in reality I cannot cry. I have a form of xerophthalmia ("dry eye")— something tied to a deficit of Vitamin A and characterized by an atypical dryness of the cornea of the eye. It's really nothing to lose sleep over, so I've never done anything about it.

Carcinoma recti etani.

My father loved watermelon. Sometimes my mother would buy a watermelon, and my sister and I would find it cut in half, the middle eaten out of both halves. What parent would eat up the best part of the fruit?

My father couldn't keep a job. Something always happened and they either laid him off or fired him. Over time, it became ever harder not only to live with his drunkenness, but also to support it financially. And although during those years life was somehow more tolerable outside our home and all the dads had work and all the moms had girlfriends, at a certain point things began to change.

The bar my father went to was known as "The Television" because it was up on a hill and from there you could see the whole street, the bus stop, who was getting on and off the bus, who was going up and down and what they were carrying home from work.

My father loved The Television. I loved "The Pink Panther," which came on only once a week on a show called *Every Sunday*. The most unbearable days of my childhood were Sunday afternoons. Ball games on the radio, the brown radiator, boring shows on TV, the yellow light bulb in the middle of the room. My father would get restless in the late afternoon. He'd start fidgeting, wondering what to do with himself, he'd get irritated by my mother who, without raising her head from her knitting, was giving him the silent treatment because of the argument the evening before. Which in its turn had been a result of her silence because of the argument the evening before that. This would inevitably lead to:

I'm out of cigarettes.

Didn't you buy some?

Well, I smoked 'em.

Yeah right, you smoked them. You think I don't know what you're up to?

Now listen here . . .

Why listen? I know where you're going.

I'm not going anywhere. I'm going to get cigarettes.

Suit yourself.

Why do I even waste my breath on you . . .

The door slams. Mother rolls her eyes in that helpless way, purses her lips and bends over her knitting more intently than ever. From time to time she shakes her head, raises her eyebrows, sighs, and sinks into her dark mute dialogues with our invisible father. It gets dark. My mother puts supper on. She sets the table under the hoarse yellow light bulb in the middle of the room and glances toward the door with that "when-will-he-finally-get-back" face. She violently cuts thick slices of bread with our eternally dull knife and tosses them between the plates. Our father does not return, of course. We sit down. We watch *Every Sunday*. "The Pink Panther" will start any second now. I've been waiting all day for that "Pink Panther." My mother can't take it anymore.

Go on, go tell him to come home.

But . . .

No "buts" about it. Get a move on.

Can't I . . . ?

What, are you giving me grief now, too?
Just let me watch "Pink Panther."
The Pink Panther isn't going anywhere.

I hated going to The Television. It was a grimy, smoky place and my dad was always annoyed to see me, he'd make fun of me, saying I was a "momma's boy," calling me names. When I'd get there, he'd already have had a lot to drink. But if I didn't go, he would get even drunker and that would be worse. I often missed "The Pink Panther." And even if I didn't miss it, the inevitable fight put a damper on my enjoyment of it.

Over the years, the sheet metal The Television was made of started rusting from the rain, while the people creeping up the hill grew ever more stooped and came back down with less and less in their striped plastic bags. Then, suddenly, bars cropped up in every garage and my father quit going to The Television.

When he got drunk, sometimes he'd clench his teeth so hard they would squeak. Especially when he started *raging* and attacking my mother. Sometimes he hit her, sometimes he choked her. As time passed, my sister and I discovered a sort of logic and rhythm to the repetition of these episodes, which did not, however, help us head them off. In general, our father would *rage* around all the best holidays—New Year's, our birthdays, Easter, important anniversaries . . . The creative reasons he came up with for slipping out of the house are a whole story to themselves.

At eighteen I was drafted into the army. My mother's letters didn't paint a clear picture of how things were at home, but my sister's tone gave me a good idea. I didn't have anything to say to him. From time to time I heard about some of the absurd extremes his alcoholism had driven him to—how he had found and drunk up the plum brandy my Uncle Angel had set aside to bring me during visiting hours, how my sister's money for a class field trip to a monastery had disappeared, how he'd drunk up my grandma's monthly pension in a single afternoon.

After two years I was discharged. I met the girl I would go on to live my life with. My father somehow began to fade within me and his transgressions started to seem unreal. The image of my mother, however, kept growing richer and more nuanced. She gradually started changing from the beautiful martyr of my childhood into the weak-willed victim of an oppressor. Why didn't the woman just get a divorce? Why did she keep living that nightmare? The old argument—for the kids' sake—didn't hold up anymore. I was no longer a child, and I didn't live there, besides. Why didn't she think about my sister, who was still in high school and living under the same roof as him? I started becoming ever more aggressive and judgmental in my conversations with my mother. I'd stopped talking to him long ago. I didn't want anything to do with him. I didn't allow him to see my newborn daughter. I changed my family name.

Then we left for America. Not long after that my sister got married in Sweden. My mother, finally faced with the reality of being left all alone with him, decided to take the bravest step of her life.

She divorced him.

For the first time in decades, my father was left to cope with his days without any outside help. During that period in my life, I didn't have the time or inclination to think about him, I was busy enough with myself.

Carcinoma recti etani.

There's no trace of the photo I'm looking for. I've dug through half of the boxes and albums. I've found lots of others, which hit me as only old photographs can. Take this one, for example—I spend a long time studying a small color photo taken by my wife by a lake in Ohio. My three-year-old daughter is on my shoulders, laughing in that way of hers that she hasn't laughed in for years. I notice there's a scab on one of her knees, miraculously unpicked.

I was surprised to find out that instead of hitting existential rock bottom quickly, as I'd expected, my father had found a job as a night watchman at my old high school. My father with a job? Like never before, I wanted to talk to him. I called up the school and got the phone number for the booth he spent his nights in.

"Hello? Dad, it's me." Silence. "Hello?"

"Hello-o-o . . . " A slightly softer voice than I had expected. Must be the connection.

"Hi, Dad."

"Hey, Mr. American! Where are you calling from?"

"America."

"You sound like you're in the room next door. What time is it there?"

I looked at the palm trees outside.

"It's noon where we are."

"Well, how about that. Here it's night-time already."

"What are you doing?"

"Well, you know. Watching TV."

"How is the job?"

"Well, what can I say… it's a job. I just loaf around here."

"Dad, I'm coming to Bulgaria next week. I want to see you."

We met in the Alba Beer Garden at 11 a.m. We sat outside at the green wooden tables, still damp from the previous night's rain, the June sun peeking through the leaves of the huge lindens.

My father had no teeth.

He'd dolled himself up in one of my Hawaiian shirts that stayed behind in the closet after we'd left for America. On his feet he wore those pitiful tan mesh shoes, soggy from the puddles he hadn't managed to jump. And he had no teeth. He looked like a benign version of the man I remembered. I drank a beer with French fries and ordered him vodka with Coke and a salad. What happened then? What was I so hoping would happen? Was I expecting to find all the answers? Just like that—because I'd flown in from America, dragged him out of his fly-spattered booth and treated him to vodka, Coke, and salad? We chatted a bit about the weather in California, how nice it was, how there was no winter, how stupid the American president was, and how the kids at my old school all do drugs.

Carcinoma recti etani.

Then suddenly a group of old acquaintances appeared out of nowhere and let out a whoop when they saw me and we started hugging and . . . that was it. My father excused himself, saying he had to be at work in two hours and left. I promised to call him so we could really see each other, not like this—just in passing. I didn't do it.

I found a dentist, paid her in advance, and sent my dad to her for dentures. I couldn't leave my father toothless.

Years later, during a very muffled, final telephone call, he would confide to me that that was the greatest gift anyone had ever given him. Such words, coming from him?

"Hello?"

"Hi, Mom. How are you?"

"Your father is really sick."

"What's wrong with him?"

"Cancer."

"Cancer?"

"He's having surgery today."

"How bad is it?"

"Really bad."

"I'm coming home."

"Wait. Don't be too hasty now. You know how much I want to see you, but if it's only for that, don't . . . "

"I'm coming home."

It takes me precisely twenty-four hours to reach my father's bedside from California. It's cold. The streets of my childhood are piled with snow, the mayor has declared a snow emergency. I barely manage to find a cab. It takes a terribly long time to reach the hospital. The driver has turned on the radio and is sunk in his own thoughts. Off to the side, I see a passerby slip on the sidewalk and wave his arms to regain his balance. We stop at the barrier in front of the hospital. I pay without a word.

"You won't recognize him," my mother warns me. It's not visiting day, but one of the cleaning ladies, a Gypsy, lets us in—she had been a janitor at mom's post office back in the day.

"Come on, quick!" The Gypsy-janitor leads us down the deserted hallway and looks around. "Come on quick-like, 'cuz if that doctor see us, he gonna yell like crazy. He real mean. If it somebody else, no problem, but this guy—whooo-eee!"

We go into the ICU. My father is sleeping. That which resembles my father is sleeping. His face is brownish-yellow, thin and peaceful. Tubes full of liquids reach out from his body, like thin, pale tentacles grasping at life. He had the operation yesterday, while I was in the air. I take out my old Nikon and snap a close-up of his fingers. I notice black stuff under his fingernails—don't they wash his hands here? Then I open the shutter as wide as possible, leaving the unnecessary details out of focus and shoot his arm, lying limp on the brown hospital blanket. I change the angle a few times, gradually letting the lens creep upwards. When I reach his face, I'm jolted by two blue eyes, still hazy from the anesthesia, fixed on me.

"Hey . . . Mr. American." He tries to smile. Something yellowish has coated his dry lips. "Snapping shots for my obituary?" Flustered, I set the camera down on top of the day-old newspapers on the nightstand, next to the cup holding his dentures, and hug him.

Carcinoma recti etani.

"We had to cut a lot out." The surgeon who operated on him gives me his soft cold hand and for some reason won't meet my eyes. "I understand from your mother that they don't live together and that he keeps in touch with you. His cancer is very advanced . . . Why did he let it go this long?" There's something slimy in this doctor's voice, I don't like him. "We'll keep him here a while longer to let the incision heal and do some irrigation. Then he'll continue with the chemotherapy and so on . . . "

I leave his office, find one of the nurses, slip her some cash, and ask her to bathe my father and take care of him. And get rid of the dirt under his fingernails. As I leave the hospital I mentally recalculate, wondering whether I've paid her enough. How much is enough? As a photographer, I earn more in a single day than my father makes from his pension in a year, plus the extra he earns from sitting in his fly-spattered guard booth in front of my old high school. I've never sent him a single dollar—I knew he would drink it up.

"All the more room to put my head up my ass," my father, his face now a more normal color, tries to joke a few days after surgery.

Carcinoma recti etani.

They've cut out his rectum. They've put some tubes in there and stuck a bag out front on his stomach to collect the waste.

"Do I really need to be looking at my own shit all day?" he asks indignantly.

"Well, at least this way you don't have to wipe your ass." I try to joke in turn.

"But they're gonna fix me up again later, right? They'll replace my intestines . . . back there, won't they?" he says, hesitantly.

"Relax, of course they will. It needs to heal over first and then they'll sew the intestine back on where it belongs," I lie shamelessly. The doctor had explained that in order to "clean up" everything, they'd had to cut out quite a bit, so there was no way of reconstructing the rectum afterwards.

"That's how it is, he'll have to wear a bag. Lots of people wear them these days, it's not a problem," said Dr. Slime, as he tucked the folder with my father's name on it into his drawer.

All the more room for his head up his ass.

It's now way past midnight. I keep digging through the old photos, but still no luck. They've already buried him. My mother has made beans and meatballs. My father didn't like lamb, the usual fare at Bulgarian wakes. All our relatives and friends have gathered together. They'll eat, drink, tell stories about him, and toddle off home.

"This type of tumor metastasizes relatively late, so your father just might get lucky," Dr. Slime says in the hallway before we go our separate ways. "But he has to continue his treatment. Irrigation, chemo, the whole works. There are people who have lived for years after this."

Carcinoma recti etani.

"Your Uncle Gosho told me he'd seen him and that he'd lost a lot of weight. I dunno, he said, maybe he's sick or something. You better go check up on him. He didn't look well to me at all. So I went."

My mother found him in his studio apartment, alone and rail-thin, wrapped in an old woolen blanket in the middle of the afternoon, watching reruns on TV. She was horrified. She rounded up some friends to load him in a car and take him to the doctor. They ran some tests and it became clear that it was a tumor. Then came the operation, and after that I arrived.

Mom wouldn't hear of anyone else taking care of him. My sister and I tried to convince her that it would be best for us to pay for someone to look after him. In vain. Our mother calmly and firmly rejected any such suggestion.

After they released him from the hospital and he'd spent some time recuperating at Mom's apartment in the city, our father asked to go to the village, where we have a house. My mother prepared one room for him and one room for herself. The two of them spent the following year there. How did they pass the time together; what did they do, left alone with the demons of their past?

I started calling him on the phone all the time. We talked about completely insignificant things, and sometimes more serious things, too. International affairs was a mandatory topic, although we also delegated time to the European Union and Bulgaria's membership therein, to our neighbor Stoyan and his nasty dog, to the dew in the garden, to the roof of the house, which looks like it might need some fixing come springtime. I usually called from my cell phone while driving. I often had jobs in Los Angeles, so I spent hours stuck in traffic on the way there and back, I went home only to finish my latest project and sleep a little, if I was lucky.

I never spent more time with Dad than I did that last year on the telephone.

Once, while driving on the freeway above Solana Beach and talking to him, I notice how to my right, in Laguna Del Mar, a small hawk dives down into the grass, sinks his talons into something and quickly swoops back upward. He flies over a few yards away from me, and I see that he has seized a small rabbit in his talons. Right away, I interrupt whatever we were talking about and tell him what I've just seen. He whistles: "Wow, what are all these hawks and rabbits!? You mean there's still some wildlife left there? I always thought that America was just skyscrapers, concrete, glass . . ."

In time, I began to feverishly anticipate the moment he'd pick up on the other end of the line.

"Hel-lo-o-o?"

"Dad, how's it going?" I'd say cheerfully.

"Watching TV."

"Oh, great! So what's on?"

"Same crap."

"So why are you watching it, then?"

"I ain't really watching. I'm waiting for your call."

Dad spent the last year of his life unable to walk. The last six months—unable to sit, or to lie down. He'd sleep half-standing or half-propped-up, my mother explained. The last few months—not sleeping. The last few weeks—not eating. The last few days—not drinking water.

Carcinoma recti etani.

I had one more extremely lucid dream in which dad was an actor in a theater. He was very good in his role, very natural, he moved and spoke with lightness and ease. I called my mother in the morning to tell her about it.

"Well, he used to be an actor. They had a group and put on plays."

"Really?"

"Come on, why would I lie to you now? He was an actor when I met him."

"How come no one ever told me until now?"

"Well, I guess it never came up, that's all. They put on a play called *Every Autumn Evening.*"

"*Every Autumn Evening?*"

"Yes."

"Was he good?"

"Oh, he was very good."

The next day, my father died.

I finish off my vodka and get up. I never managed to find that damn black-and-white picture. Without turning on the light in the kitchen, I toss the empty bottle into the trash and put my glass in the dishwasher. I remember that there's watermelon. I take it out, leaving the fridge open for light. I set it in the sink and stick a knife into it. Its freshness bursts into the room with a crackle. I cut the watermelon in half. I cut out the middle of one piece and bite into it greedily. My teeth hurt from the cold, the sweet juice is dribbling down my chin. I eat up one half and stick the knife into the other. I stop and take it out. I slowly wipe the blade and lay it aside. I put what's left of the watermelon back in the refrigerator. Then I tiptoe into my daughter's room, feel for her face in the dark, stroke her. I slump down on the floor, my back against her bed, and plant my head between my knees.

At some point I get up again and close the door behind me. I turn off the light in the stuffy closet where I've spent the last few hours and suddenly catch a barely noticeable scent. Soury-sweet, like a chunk of raw meat.

A droplet runs down my cheek. I'm not sure it's a tear—I can't remember ever crying before, but I don't feel like wiping it away. I go out on the terrace and stand by the windows, inhaling the fresh humid air. The silhouettes of the palm trees sway, an ambulance siren wails somewhere in the distance. I open up a lawn chair, sit down, hug my knees and look east until the stripe of horizon above the desert starts growing light.

TRANSLATED FROM THE BULGARIAN BY ANGELA RODEL

CAROLINE LAMARCHE

Léo and Me

FOR A LONG time we're silent, Léo and I. Léo sleeping and me reading. Maybe the cat has stretched out in a corner, maybe the pendulum clock has chimed, I don't know. I was aware only of the silence. Then I looked at Léo. A quick glance. Léo's beauty is piercing, a real dagger. Some days it's diminished, and it stings even more keenly. When that happens, I hardly look at him. Because I'm afraid.

Suddenly, a dog barks. My blood starts coursing again, as intense as the times we live in. Nowadays, everything happens fast. Love. Death. Even the visits to Léo. To get to his place, I take the Ardennes Autoroute. Recently, several well-maintained tunnels have been constructed under it—passageways for wild animals. The deer understood, but the rabbits and hares are still getting themselves squashed on the surface. The age is rife with similar concessions to safety that will be ignored for at least ten years. The time it takes for people to change their ways. It's the same with safe sex. Or safer sex. I believe either term is acceptable.

It's been raining almost all the time. This morning, during a sunny interval, I went for a walk. I broke Léo's umbrella using it as a cane. I thought of burying it under the leaves so I wouldn't have to carry it around mud-stained and broken in two, but in the end I decided to take it back and explain to Léo, with the evidence in hand, that his umbrella was beyond repair.

He was waiting for me on the doorstep. He laughed. He said: "I'm going to fix it. Like before. You remember the last time?" Of course, I remember: Léo, the cleverest of my cousins. The one who used to make everything out of nothing. Model cars made of wire. Fortresses fashioned from rolled-up rags. Functioning bicycles reclaimed from mangled ones. I can't say how. Do-it-yourself projects were annoying to me. He'd say: "You're a real girl." I'd say thank you. Thank you for the playhouse. Thank you for the bike. And for giving the doll those new eyes. Thank you, Léo.

One day, I thought that things would be different. That he, the boy, would say thank you to me, the girl. I was going on sixteen. We bumped into each other in the city one evening in May. A coincidence. "Come with me," Léo proposed. "A girl like you, you're stronger than the city. You're always laughing. You walk straight ahead, and you stay out of trouble."

We did walk straight ahead. On our right, building façades. On our left, building façades. Women in the windows, like giant fish. Men leaning against the walls, barely more than children. I didn't laugh for a long time. Because I said. Because I did. Something. That required no effort on my part—I'd carried it inside me for ages.

Squeezing his arm, I said: "Léo, I love you." Then I died. Just like that. Like a rabbit daring to cross the autoroute. Because Léo had tensed up. He pulled his arm away. He picked up his pace. He walked ahead of me.

It's crazy what animals do. Darting across without a care. Ending up totally destroyed. A flattened pelt, a blackened clot. There was no telling what it had been before. Rabbit or hare? Girlish cousin? Young hussy?

I fix different things than he does. I'm repairing that thing that happened in the city, one evening in May, during my sixteenth year: Léo wanted no part of me. Me like an orange dancing on the point of a knife.

That same year, he restored the cemetery gate. I remember that very well, because we talked about it a lot at home. Léo reinforced the gate by hammering sheets of lead all around the posts so that they conformed snugly to the angles of the wood. The parish priest will be happy, my mother said. The work of a professional, said my father. Of an artist, I said. The artist is inhabited by a calling he can't shake off, my high school philosophy teacher used to say during that same year. I wondered what it was like for someone who was born an artist and who's obligated to make the best of his calling every day of his life. I wondered what it was like for someone who was a boy who only liked boys and who had to pull his arm away from a girl's touch, obeying a calling, or rather an obligation, or a *categorical imperative*, as Kant described it. That's something I still retain from philosophy class, that clear-cut and practical expression, which can be applied to art as well as love. Or to sex. To safer sex.

At home, Léo still does a bit of repair work. Defective locks. The toilet's flushing mechanism. The rotted window frames. And the old-fashioned beehives. Last year, he grew honeysuckle vines on the shelter enclosing the hives, a tar-roofed overhang set at the bottom of a ravine—a ridiculous location considering how he had to climb back up the slope with heavy frames laden with honey and a swarm of bees in close pursuit. A lovely spot nonetheless. Protected. I haven't been down there today because of the bad weather. But from the facing slope, I smelled the fragrance of the honeysuckle, and I said to myself: "It's there."

Léo will never carry up the honey again. For ten years the warm poison has been lurking in his blood. Now the illness is asserting itself. It's exploding, galloping, spreading out, finally doing its work. How do I know? From the smell of the honeysuckle. From Léo's light daytime slumber by my side. From this sudden silence, as piercing as his beauty.

I'd like him to leave quickly, without any of the symptoms whose painstaking progress will devastate his face and his laugh. I'd like him to leave just as I'm looking at him—furtively, with half-closed eyes. I don't imagine his death any other way than this—something that will come like lightning, with the same inevitability as the movement of his arm pulling away from my grasp one evening in the city.

TRANSLATED FROM THE FRENCH BY PAUL CURTIS DAW

ANDREI DICHENKO

The Poet Execution Committee

THE COMMITTEE'S FINAL DECISION

DECEMBER 21, 2021

The Department of Culture and Propaganda has received poems by Dimitri I. Filippov in the quantity of four (4) units. Written in iambic tetrameter, these works are a proletarian critique of bourgeois society, the significance of which is reduced to a gross distortion of contemporary reality. During an interrogation by members of the committee, D.I. Filippov (referred to hereafter as "Poet") testified that he wrote these lines of poetry with a sound mind and clarity of thought. In summary, after our initial familiarization with the work of citizen Poet, several of his works were submitted to the special committee. The committee, which is comprised of citizens E.A. Elatomtseva and E.B. Furtsman, has declared these texts to be works of poetry, and considering the author's mental competency, has rejected the option of punitive psychiatry in reference to his case. Therefore, an adequate reaction to further creations of these "artistic products" shall be a sentence of execution for citizen Poet in a government basement in Building No. 24 on Slobodskaya Street, performed by members of the committee.

The poetic compositions shall be transferred to a special archive. These findings shall be published in the central organs of the press.

Chairman of the Committee,
Citizen V. M. Yerofeyev

*

"Did they shoot this kid already?" a man in a black leather jacket asked the young woman sitting across from him at the table.

The young woman was lost in thought and writing something on a piece of paper. She looked up. "Huh? What? Who?" The man showed her a yellowed form, the heading of which specified a sentenced surname. "Filippov? What's the date on it?" she asked.

"Report's dated 21 December," said the man, opening the drawer under the table and putting the piece of paper all marked up with black ink in a stack of other such procedural documents.

"The execution takes up to three days, Mikhail," the young woman said in a monotone as she started up on whatever she was writing again. The smooth skin of her face was reflected in the blue glow of the monitor. "What's today's date?"

"It's 25 December, if I'm not mistaken," Mikhail answered, glancing tentatively at his watch. Then he got up and began to pack up the notebooks on the table in his black leather attaché case.

An attaché with a white handle was the hallmark of members from a special committee on culture and the arts; the sight of it caused men and women to give nods of respect when they crossed paths with the employees of this esteemed government department amid the vast expanse of this desolate Siberian city.

Mikhail bid his colleague farewell. Completely absorbed in her paperwork, she responded with a mechanical nod and Mikhail made a point of slamming the door, exiting into a tract of dark corridor. The walls in the corridor, once upon a time painted white, were cracked and yellowed in spots. He walked past propaganda posters hung several meters apart. Colorful pictures and slogans set forth in large letters caught the eye and ushered in a dissonance among the dozens of doors that comprised this dismal panorama.

Mikhail stepped out onto the quiet street and headed for his car. He unlocked the door, arranged his briefcase neatly on the back seat, and sat down behind the wheel. Before long, he'd be on his way home to explain to his wife and children that his workload would be rather heavy now, with the approach of the New Year.

*

A man entered the room and sat down at the round table. Several more people in black suits took their seats beside him. The man clicked his pen and, after some initial jotting in his notebook, inscribed on a white piece of paper in calligraphic handwriting:

The committee's final decision:
February 25, 2021 . . .

"Is the time significant or shall I omit that part?" he said to the group. He had perturbing cheekbones, which were so shiny they looked as if they'd been oiled. His Adam's apple was twitching—perhaps from annoyance, or perhaps from the pleasure of completing his assignment.

"Skip it," said the man with the shaved head, shaking his head for emphasis.

The young woman was sitting beside him, perusing some scraps of notebook paper, faded and covered in writing, her black pen in hand. With a deep sigh, she handed the papers to the elderly lady sitting next to her. She, upon receipt of the much-anticipated poetic composition, removed her glasses elegantly from their gilded case and ran her eyes over the rhyming lines.

"Why, this is pornography, not poetry!" the older woman said with emotion, crumpled the papers into a ball, then made a big show of throwing them under the table. Her boiling rage wrinkled into a scowl so ugly her cosmetic powder looked as if it wanted to flee her face.

With the older woman's comments, the reviewers had completed their proceedings. Its four members regarded each other. Then their eyes shifted to a young man in a chair in the corner. The man's hands were bound in such a way that he couldn't move very much. His eyes darted back and forth. In all the excitement, the poet kept licking his chapped lips, swallowing his saliva with difficulty, unable to diffuse the moisture to his parched throat.

"Pardon my language, but I would wipe my ass with these. What a disgrace!" the bald man said, laughing. The rest kept tensely quiet until the young woman broke the awkward silence. She rose from the table, presenting her audience with a full view of her beauty, walked elegantly over to the the young man, and punched him in the face. His head bopped to the right like a balloon. As she rubbed her fist, the young man licked at a fresh clot of blood, lifted his head, and looked her straight in the eye. His face lit up with a bloody smile.

"I don't see any cause for laughter, young man!" With these words, she sat back down at the table and, pretending only the committee members could hear her, said: "What are we supposed to do with this piece of shit?"

The bald man, who was clearly the more sympathetic of the younger participants in these secret proceedings, spoke up first:

"Our committee was established for an important reason. We grant each deserving author of great poetic works the honor of a basement execution. But this one . . . I mean, this poem is simply an insult to the greatness of our civil society, the greatness of our freedom of thought . . . "

The bald man's speech was interrupted by the final report of the committee's secretary:

"In conclusion, I am entering into the record that we are denying citizenship to Ivanov Sergei Stepanovich, as well as the right of residence in this nation."

After he made a few small notes to complete the report, the four heard a wretched sob from the bound young man.

"It takes real audacity to submit something like this to our committee," the older woman said indignantly. She got up and threw on her black leather coat, hiding her overweight figure, then tucked in her chair under the table.

"These are the times we live in, as you know. We have had the honor of sentencing many deserving poets. But this one . . . " the younger woman nodded at the young man. "This one is just a degenerate."

In a short time, all four participants left the committee meeting. A brawny hulk of a soldier took their place, who, looking contemptuously at Ivanov, freed him from his handcuffs. Without warning, Ivanov jumped up, clenched his hands into fists, and began to howl like a preschooler resentful of his elders. The soldier knocked him into silence with a rifle butt to the chest. Ivanov fell with a crash, leaving several pale drops of blood on the floor.

"Rope and soap would be your best bet. Or maybe knife. You

can get what you need at the checkpoint." To conclude, the soldiers kicked the disgraced poet in the ribs. Before he left the room, the soldier looked at the portrait of the Patriarch and crossed himself. "Just don't go too far out in the forest, it would suck to have to drag you back in, asshole."

The soldier slammed the door. Ivanov just lay there until the end, unaware of his dishonorable fate.

*

January 12, 2021. "It's been six years since I got sent to Biysk . . . "

Kirill had been taking notes in his journal every day since he arrived in this Siberian city with his beloved. It was morning. Kirill had been writing nonstop for two hours since she left for work at the factory.

"My involuntary tenure in this artistic black hole shall finally arrive at its finale . . . "

He made his final elliptic dots, slammed the notebook shut, and lit up. Flicking his ashes in a coffee can, Kirill debated which of his works he should present before the stern examination committee and what would be better for him to do after that: hang himself or slit his wrists out in the forest. Or just freeze to death.

"This is the Altai, my dear. Some nights get down to -52," Snezhana told him when they first moved into their mold-covered Khrushchev-era apartment and were warming themselves in front of the tepid radiator.

Biysk had at one time been a tech city, and behind the walls of its secret laboratories the leading minds of a long-forgotten country had designed rockets as gifts for a distant and terrible enemy. Then it turned out that the country was teeming with enemies of the internal rather than external variety, so they made Biysk a city for people whose words might carry a note of protest to the amorphous masses.

Just a few days were left before the deadline. If Kirill did not submit to The Committee, he could be written off as "unnecessary human material" with the infamous stamp: "suspected of poetic deeds."

Being a complete outcast wasn't something he wanted, but he was still hesitant to submit his poetic creations to this court, whose members functioned as knights of public morality.

"You should just not go. Let's run away," said Snezhana, as they lay in bed looking at the ceiling and listening to the wind raging beyond the window, shifting tons of snow per second across the mountainous terrain of southern Siberia. But they couldn't hide from the impartial cameras and the omnipresent satellites. Everything lay within the system's field of view.

Kirill felt as though this was his destiny. He gathered up all the pages of lined notebook paper covered in writing and put them carefully in an envelope.

In a few hours Snezana would be home for lunch. It was possible that by that time Kirill would no longer be alive.

He took a thick, dusty book off the shelf and opened it. A thin knife was hidden between its pages. It glistened seductively in the rays of the miserly morning sun. Kirill held the blade carefully and scratched his beloved's name in the table. Then he cut his palm and traced a little heart of blood on the wood with his finger. His hand was still bleeding, but Kirill blew on the image. The blood on the table was almost dry.

After hastily bandaging his hand, the poet put a cap on his head and threw on his coat. It was about two-hundred meters to the nearest Bureau of Culture and Propaganda. Kirill had often walked briskly past the building with the red door, locking gazes awkwardly with other citizen-exiles like himself. Everybody walked past, but nobody ever went inside. He could easily determine from their harried eyes which ones were like him and which ones were respected officials and brave soldiers.

He walked down the street, squeezing his eyes shut when the harsh, dry wind blew in his face._Pedestrians flashed past him, but they didn't seem to notice anything going on around them as they tried to evade the bone-chilling cold.

Kirill passed a large shield with a single line of white lettering on a red background: "The Patriarch will forge your prosperous future." He approached the five-story building made of prefab concrete panels and stopped. There was a massive door in front of him. There was absolutely nobody around—only from the windows behind him could his activity perhaps be observed by some sick child, staying home from school.

The poet opened the door and went inside. After heading up the stairs to the second floor, Kirill encountered the soldier on duty. He was watching ballet on television when Kirill offered a businesslike "hello."

"What do you want?" asked the lazy soldier, and picked up a remote wrapped in cellophane with his left hand to lower the sound. With his right hand, he stirred sugar in his tin mug of tea.

"I need to turn in my rhymes," Kirill said. He could hear footsteps at the other end of the corridor.

"Understood." The soldier picked up his machine gun and stood up. Kirill wondered if the rules had perhaps changed and he would be shot on the spot. "Close your eyes and don't move!"

The poet gripped the bag holding his treasured manuscripts with both hands and squeezed his eyes shut.

The blow was both anticipated and a shock, all at once. In that single moment, it felt as though several thermonuclear weapons were exploding inside his brain. As he fell to the floor, Kirill instinctively hugged his portfolio close, as if it were his sole surviving child.

After he knocked Kirill down, the soldier inspected the polished butt of his rifle, then the incapacitated poet. After spitting on Kirill's coat and kicking his fallen hat, he put the rifle on the table and pressed a red button, which was artfully recessed in the wall. Soon two men in camouflage appeared from somewhere down the long corridor. One of them had a thoroughly battered face, and the other looked puffy, as though he'd recently downed a hearty dose of alcoholic beverage.

"Awaiting orders, Comrade Sergeant, sir!" one of them said. The two soldiers stood at attention.

"Carry the body to the dispatcher who deals with . . . " the sergeant scratched his head and yawned. " . . . these fucking poets."

The private nodded in silence, then lifted the unconscious Kirill under his arms. They followed him off into the distance down the corridor.

Several hours later, Kirill awoke. He tried to get up, shivering and gritting his teeth from the piercing pain in his neck. He felt sick.

He found himself lying on a metal bunk consisting of two iron bars on legs with a rusty metal grate stretched between them. An unshaven man with drooping eyes was sitting on the floor in front of him. The man was wrapped in a blanket and staring at the ground, completely oblivious to his new neighbor. Kirill didn't remember how he'd been brought here. But it appeared to him that this character had been in the place far longer than he had.

When he turned around, Kirill saw a sink, a window with bars on it, and a portrait of the Patriarch hanging above it. He walked over to the sink and puked. Then he turned the handle and murky, icy water flowed from the tap. He washed his face and looked out the window as he waited for the vomitous fluid to embark on its journey down the rusty pipes. His neighbor looked as though he had something to say, but all that came out was a hacking cough. Pulling a plastic bucket from somewhere in the bowels of his pile of baby blankets, he spat up a wad of phlegm and mucus. The man appeared to be suffering from tuberculosis.

"I've got my eye on you, there. Maintain fucking order!" he said, gruff and angry, to which Kirill nodded in response.

After washing himself, he went back to his hard bed and stared at the ceiling, which was decorated with black mold in the corners, and thick streaks of the stuff all across. He closed his eyes and tried to imagine what Snezhana was doing at that moment.

"Tell me about Vitebsk. What's there?" she asked, sitting naked before him. Her figure was also reflected in the dusty mirror. It seemed perfect to him in the moonlight.

"Vitebsk? It's just an average city. In the eastern part of Belarus. Lots of prefab apartment buildings and spotless squares. The people there . . . " Whenever she asked him about his past, he always clammed up and didn't know what to say.

His memories were interrupted by the creak of the massive cast-metal door.

A soldier appeared in the doorway, pointed a finger at Kirill, and made a beckoning gesture.___

Kirill got up, and as he was walking past the soldier took a rifle butt to the back. He lurched forward abruptly and nearly fell, then turned around and glared at the soldier's smirk. When he closed the door, the soldier looked back at Kirill as if to interrogate him.

"What'd you get up for? Go that way! Your judgment is coming!" It was clear the soldier wanted to spit in the poet's face, but instead he turned and briskly followed him down the corridor. The soldier spat on the floor instead. "Do anything stupid, kid, and I'll end you! Go to the door!" he shouted after him.

Kirill walked to the lone green wooden door, behind which he would have his much-anticipated meeting with the committee, with its severe outlook on the writing of poetry._

He opened the door and saw a group of four. The man was completely bald, with a high, wrinkled forehead. He was dressed in a black jacket and was looking sternly at Kirill. A woman was sitting near the bald man. She was crying and wiping the tears from her drenched cheeks with a handkerchief. Behind her were two youth members of the committee. Twins, probably. Both had buzz cuts and were wearing black coats. They looked angry.

When Kirill walked in, all four of them stood up and bowed to him.

"We decided not to handcuff you," said the man, and pointed to a chair. Kirill greeted them with a shy nod and sat down. There was a blackboard behind him, and slightly above it was the ever-present portrait of the Patriarch. The woman looked at the portrait, then at Kirill, then crossed herself and started crying even harder.

"What's the matter, Tamara Vasilievna?" said the bald man, hugging the tear-stained lady. One of the brothers was drawing something in a notebook, while the other looked contemptuously at Kirill. He smiled for some reason.

"You . . " the woman said to Kirill through her sobs. "You're so wonderful!" She finished her thought, and covered her face with her hands.

One of the twins, who'd been drawing in his notebook, took a deep breath and stood up. He looked at Kirill, then at his notes, and began giving his speech while the sounds of female weeping went on in the background.

"Esteemed Kirill O. Nikodimov! We have considered your poetic compositions and recognize them, in accordance with the Codex, as works of art in the highest category. In addition, we are prepared to inform you that, for the first time in the history of our renowned committee, these poetic works, in this instance the ones written under your authorship, have been assigned the highest degree of significance. In accordance with lawful statutes, you are hereby sentenced to capital punishment, in view of the public, by hanging. Your punishment will be memorialized in the Biysk annals as a noteworthy day, and will commence in half an hour on the city's main square during a ceremonial worker's meeting."

When he finished, the twin closed his notebook. The woman settled down as he announced the poet's sentence, and the bald chairman of the committee rubbed his temples, as if he were pondering something important.

After the official sentencing announcement, the now familiar soldiers entered the room. One of them hit Kirill in the head with the butt of his rifle again. This time it was only symbolic. Kirill didn't even lose consciousness, just fell to the floor. The soldiers grabbed him under the arms and dragged him down the corridor.

Kirill found himself in the fresh frosty air long enough to take a deep breath, then immediately landed inside a police van, on a metal floor smeared with blood stains. Inside this holding area there was a stifling stench. It made him nauseous.

After throwing the poet inside, the soldiers brushed off their hands and slammed the door behind him.

As Kirill rode to the city square on the ninth of January, he could hear megaphones through the holding area's metal walls broadcasting his impending execution. He would be alive for about fifteen more minutes. During that time he thought about Snezhana and remembered Vitebsk. A few days ago, he'd imagined that they might go back there together, maybe even be happy. But he'd decided to take a different path. To fulfill his predestined covenant of duty to the Patriarch.

They hauled him out of the police van and instantly the crowd of drunk, barely upright workers filling the square fell silent. They all followed the poet to the scaffold, which had been empty until now, with their dull, utterly vacant stares. The hangman was urgently summoned. As soon as Kirill began to climb the creaky wooden steps, the first questioning whisper emerged from the crowd. Each face from the multitude of human bodies watched him, then whispered in a comrade's ear: "That's a real Poet!"

Kirill didn't give a damn about the crowd of spectators who'd been forcibly driven out of the factory to watch. His eyes were searching for Snezhana. She was sure to be here somewhere, lying low and keeping quiet.

Next to him on the scaffold was one of Biysk's finest—a burly bearded man uniformed in a winter tunic. His chest was decorated with innumerable insignia. While they prepared Kirill for his lynching, Biysk's finest launched a diatribe into his megaphone that the poet realized was addressed to him. Behind them, a priest was shifting his weight from one foot to the other. He was the only one bored with the whole display. He was merely waiting for it all to be over so that he could get back to work.

Biysk's finest came to the end of his shrill speech. In conclusion, he said something about the Patriarch, poetry, and duty and sacrifice. None of it made any difference to Kirill. Most of the crowd kept an eye on every movement of the poet's face and turned a deaf ear to the public servant's grandiloquent speech.

When the noose was placed around the neck of the condemned and Biysk's finest offered him an opportunity to speak his last words, Kirill frantically scanned the throng of faces awaiting his execution.

All of a sudden, a second before his death, his eyes found the blue eyes of Snezhana. She looked frightened and lost, and her face was wrapped in a shawl. There were only her eyes. They were troubled, like thunderclouds in nasty weather.

Kirill smiled, and the board underneath him fell through. The last thing he heard was loud applause from the crowd. The fire of death crept from his feet to his head. With it came the lull of darkness.

TRANSLATED FROM THE RUSSIAN BY ANDREA GREGOVICH

SUSANNA HARUTYUNYAN

God Has Passed Through Here

WHEN THE EUROPEANS came to see the girl, they were still naïve because the driver hadn't told them yet: "When we get there, we'll be offered strained yogurt. Folks in these parts eat strained yogurt with rose-petal preserve and that's the best. When'll we get there? In about twenty minutes, when the highway ends and we turn right. Then we'll take the first side road, it's about fifteen minutes long, after which . . . No, we won't come to the village yet . . . but it will be closer. When we get off the first side road, we'll turn left and get on the second side road, which is twice as long as the first one, so we'll be on it for about half an hour. And then the village . . . will be even closer. Once we get off the second road and keep going straight, we'll get to an incline, after which . . . Yes, we will be closer to the village. But not quite there . . . We'll have to go up the incline . . . If we make it . . . we'll reach the top of the mountain. You'd think the village would finally appear because it has nowhere else to go. And it will, of course, but not right away. If we make it up the incline, we'll reach the path that'll take us—it's three kilometers on foot—to the cliff, which we'll have to climb . . . It's worth the suffering . . . Strained yogurt with rose-petal preserve . . . "

When the Europeans came to see the girl, they were still naïve. The driver hadn't told them any of this yet and he wasn't really inclined to. For the moment, he was just mumbling a song: *There's no one else with me in this place but God.* The car was dancing over the stones. Sometimes, when the driver suddenly braked, the passengers in the back would be thrust forcefully forward, banging their stomachs against the backs of the front seats which would bring up the food they had eaten seven days ago. The driver warned them in between singing his song: "Tell me if you're getting sick, don't vomit on my neck." The visitors took it as a joke, laughed heartily, and thought that they'd arrived as soon as the car turned off the highway. One of them kept steadying the camera hanging on his chest, with which he hoped to photograph weeping rocks and mountains cracked by the sun—to impress his technocratic countrymen with nature's ways. But when the car with thick American tires turned off the highway, two kilometers in, after passing over rocks as sharp as Satan's nails, the tires were shredded and the passengers now had to carry the car instead of the car carrying them . . . And when, unwillingly, they got out of the car, and looked at the world of stones around them, the steep incline ahead of them, they whistled in surprise and fear. They began sweating in the sun and had no choice but to push the car, ripping their shoes and pants on the sharp rocks . . . They were still naïve, because they thought that the hardest part would be going up the incline and then they would reach the village, because it was impossible to imagine a higher and steeper place. But . . . there *was* a steeper place—it had simply been impossible to imagine. So when the Europeans came to see the girl, they were exhausted, beaten by the rocks, shoes and clothes torn; they were singing national anthems out of despair, encouraging each other and moaning, pushing the car, spitting dust and stone. They were still naïve . . . And when they saw, after reaching the top of the incline, that there was yet another unimaginable, rocky incline at the end of this one, with rocks blacker and sharper than Satan's nails between which one could see the glimmering, coiling vein of the gold mine, one of them cursed and wept, removing his hands from the car and beating his head. The car moved back, almost crushing everybody else. Panic-stricken and shouting, they drove their feet against the ground, ripping their soles and heels; red in the face from all the tension and howling foreign words, they somehow stopped the car . . . Even then, the terrified Europeans were still naïve. The driver kept looking at them with pity, he wanted to say something to comfort them and diminish the cruelty of the stones and the sun. "The sky is so close here," he said, "that it rains when angels weep. But that happens in October, when the mountains are already covered in snow and dreams can't find their way to the sky."

When the Europeans finally reached the village hidden in a cavity at the top of the mountain, having swallowed the sun and scorched air, bleeding and with clothes torn like the persecuted escaping from Hell . . . they were still naïve because they had already lost their hope that there was such a place where one could finally reach. And as they went—staggering, hungry,sweaty and cursing . . . they were still naïve because when they, dragging their bodies, passed by the first pile of stones, the old men weeding behind the stone fence straightened their backs, one of them wiping his soiled hands on his shirt and squinting his right eye, blinded by the sun, and examining the foreigners with the other eye, said:

"Who are the visitors this time?"

"Europeans," said the man next to him and smirked at their tattered clothes, the cameras hanging from their necks, their sweaty backs and legs weak with exhaustion.

"And where is Europe?"

"Oh, thousands of kilometers away!"

"U-u-uh," the first old man who was weeding the bean beds drawled indulgently.

When the Europeans came to buy the girl, they were naïve because everyone knew that she'd already sold her body once at sixteen.

It was her father who brought the buyers from Yerevan. Or, he brought the second buyers. The first ones came by helicopter . . . It was August when they came, the sun had scorched the mountains and the peaks looked like tortured souls. The small and large stones had covered themselves with moss so as not to crack and their singed skin smarted underneath the moist roots of moss. It was an ordinary summer, and the helicopter, together with the passengers, melted and dripped down on the cliffs. The father met the second group in Yerevan and brought them to the village on a lame donkey that had been attacked by a pack of wolves a few months ago and had lost its right hind hoof. The visitors took turns sitting on the lame donkey, respecting one another, granting the privilege to moan and groan to the elders, tormenting themselves, and admiring the height of the mountains, the and closeness to God. They suffered, but did not complain. They said: "At this height, entry is easier for creatures of heaven than for men of the earth." From that day on they'd boast that they'd taken part in the building of the Tower of Babel because they'd reached the knees of God and gotten tangled in his beard. Praising nature, getting sunburned, envying those who lived in this pristine place, they arrived in the village to buy the girl. These were polite Russian men who kept kissing the women's hands from the moment they arrived until their departure. In the village, they called such men *castrates*. Hiding behind trees and rocks, the village children followed the visitors and laughed at their hand-kissings, their "sorrys" and "thankyous."

The father slaughtered a lamb born in the fall (it had been coughing and might have been sick). They put the table outside, somewhat away from the scarecrow, where the sunflowers had thrust their heads so high up into the sky that the angels might have thought the birds flying around them were spies.

The guests ate the steaming lamb stew with great gusto, throwing the gnawed bones to the cats gathered under the tree.

"Which one of your daughters are you going to sell?" the Russian asked, taking a piece of *lavash* from the youngest girl's hand. The host pointed his index finger at Noem, who was washing greens in the spring to bring to the table.

"I like this one better," the Russian said, picking up some more *lavash* and eyeing up the youngest. "The one you're pointing to's a bit faded and pale."

"Nonsense," the father disagreed. "Wait till night falls . . . You haven't seen such a wonder. No one has ever seen such a wonder!"

Noem had known for a few months that they were coming to buy her and that she would have to get undressed. She even tried to get undressed in front of the mirror, and her mother made her do it twice in front of her brothers and sisters, so that she'd get used to the idea and not make a scene in front of the guests. But she felt nervous now that the buyers were here.

At around eleven at night, when the mountain exhaled the moon from its mouth, the mother came to fetch her.

"I don't want to," whimpered Noem.

"You have no conscience," the mother reproached her. "Your father nearly killed himself going back and forth to the post office and sending letters. He spent so much money, slaughtered a lamb . . . What are you ashamed of? You have undressed in front of your brothers so many times! What's to be ashamed of?"

"My brothers are ten years younger than me, I see their naked bodies too when I bathe them, but these . . . a bunch of old men," Noem sat huddled on the edge of the sofa, crying. "I don't need any money."

"I don't either," her mother said. "But we aren't talking about just *any* money—it's a *lot* of money . . . You can build a church with that kind of money. What's to be ashamed of? Imagine you have gone to the doctor, say, your chest hurts or you've broken your leg. Aren't you going to show it to him? Aren't you going to let him examine you? But it's all right if you don't want to," she said, sitting down on the edge of the sofa and sighing. "Your father's knee? Let it hurt. The bones get soft like chalk anyway. He has lived healthy for fifty years, he can live with a little pain now . . . There are people who are born sick, what about them? We aren't fascists after all! We don't want to torture you . . . if you don't want to . . . Although what's there to be ashamed of? Men become sexless with age like angels. And your father . . . Well, you're of his flesh. Are you ashamed of your hands, your legs, your eyes, your heart? You would've saved us if you agreed. We'd have gone to live in the city. Everything is made for people there—for their convenience. You call this life? But it's all right, you don't have to," she stammered tearfully. "We've lived on the edge of this mountain for a hundred years, and we'll live on it a hundred more . . ."

The Russians were standing by the door and listening to the sound of tumbling stones mixing with the breath of the mountain, greedily sniffing the air and the sky, waiting for the moment when Noem would come out from the back door of the house.

"My God," gasped one of them, seeing the girl running through the garden, "What a marvel!"

"A living moon," another said eagerly.

"Didn't I tell you?" the father boasted, "You didn't believe me. What's the moon compared to this? They say it's artificial, made by extraterrestrials to keep an eye on Earth, while this here is all natural, created by God."

Noem ran through the rows of sunflowers and stopped near the scarecrow. The scarecrow stood proud and tall with its straw hair piercing the sky's eye like a thorn. Its three-meter-long dress made of varicolored rags reached to the ground, hiding its body made of boards. It had no arms because it was only a scarecrow and its straw hair was enough to terrify the birds. A rusted iron pail hung from its neck, which was now just above Noem's head. The children believed that stars would fall into the pail at dawn, but her mother dutifully cleaned it once a month, emptying the bird droppings under the trees. The girl clutched with both hands onto the scarecrow's dress grown stiff with dirt.

"Come home, you'll catch cold," her father shouted in the direction of the scarecrow.

Noem pulled the scarecrow's dress. It slipped down. The girl took it from the ground, wrapped it around her naked body, and walked home through the rows.

The charmed men were sitting inside and their eyes burned when Noem entered. The oldest, with blue eyes and a beard, resembling a kindly sorcerer from a fairy tale, approached Noem.

"Can you lie down somewhere, say, on the couch or the table . . ? Wherever you like."

"Of course she can," Noem's father responded instead of her.

"Please, go outside," said the other man, "We don't need you anymore, we'll take it from here."

The father left the room and one of the men locked the door after him in order not to be disturbed.

Shivering, Noem laid on the couch. The men encircled her. One of them turned off the light.

"Forgive us," said the old man, bowing over Noem. "Due to the specificities of your body, we have to carry on in the dark," and he carefully pulled down the dress from her chest. One man carefully moved her toes, another man started examining her chest, leg, and then her arm, with a microscope . . . Yet another pinched her thigh, and another made a scratch near her elbow with a needle.

"Can you please bend your knees . . . the position you're in isn't convenient for us . . . we have to see everything and ascertain everything . . . You see, my girl, it's sacrilege for a man of my age to touch a woman of your age, but I must examine you, that's my profession. We can produce any effect now with the help of medicine and chemistry. We're going to spend a large amount of money to acquire you, so we must examine everything," the old man turned on his small flashlight, shining it in the girl's face, brushed her hair to the side, felt a spot on her neck and rubbed it with a wet cotton ball. Leaning down, he breathed on her face for a few minutes without removing his gaze from her neck, then he rubbed her with the wet cotton again, breathed on her face some more, and finally, satisfied and victorious, mewed under his nose: "Wonderful! Excellent!"

They each approached, looked curiously at her neck, breathed anxiously on her face, not believing, each in his own turn rubbed her neck again, slightly right or left of the original spot . . . they waited, took the microscope and examined her cell by cell and they all came to the same conclusion: "Wonderful! Excellent!"

Then they turned on the light. Two of the scientists approached Noem, one held her arm while the other said: "Don't be afraid, it won't hurt," and pushed the needle into her vein.

"There is no deception," said the blue-eyed old man, coming out of the room, "Everything is all right, everything is perfectly natural . . ."

"I know," replied the father smoking by the window, "the local doctor says that seventy percent of her body is phosphorus. That's why she glows at night like that."

"It's possible," said the old man, "But it's a fact that she's a wonder."

They drank wild apple wine sitting in the garden, beneath the heads of the sunflowers. The lawyer, papers and stamp tucked under his arm, kept tapping the glass to get rid of the bubbles in the young wine.

"My girl," he said, taking Noem's hand, "regardless of what your parents think, you must know everything before signing the papers. I'd like to tell you the most important details you need to know before selling yourself . . . We are Christian Armenians, after death we have to be buried in the ground and go either to heaven or to hell, there are no other options. You must know that after this transaction you'll lose all of that. You won't have a grave or a gravestone in the form of the ancient Armenian cradle, your parents won't come to your grave to burn incense for you, after death all of your relatives and neighbors will be buried in the village cemetery, but you won't be there. After death, your body will belong to science. Scientists will study you, in order to understand why some people, like you, can emanate light like the moon does, while others can't. By study, we mean that after death you won't be buried, that they'll break your body, cut it into pieces, dissolve, decompose, boil, treat it chemically and with high temperatures . . . They must mutilate you, my girl, to understand why you aren't like everyone else. Do you consent to this?" he asked. "If we sign the contract now, the government will immediately pay half of the sum, while the rest will be paid to your parents after your death, after handing over the raw material, so to speak. Think about it, my girl, do you consent to this?" Everyone was anxious with expectation. Her brothers, sisters, and neighbors had gathered near the scarecrow, and even the cats had left the bones under the tree and joined them.

"A psychological study could also produce some excellent results. It wouldn't be a bad idea to discuss that as well," one of the members of the group suggested to the blue-eyed old man, while Noem was thinking.

"I wouldn't advise it," said the lawyer, who'd been invited from Yerevan, leaning in toward the speaker, "Armenian women don't open their souls completely even to God . . . That's going to be an unnecessary expense . . . a loss of time and money."

"I wouldn't have agreed anyway," said the father, taking the plate with sliced fruits from his wife's hand and setting it on the table. "Despite everything, only God may touch my daughter's soul. Humans are unworthy of that."

The group of scientists left early in the morning. It was so early that the rooster hadn't called yet, but the stars in the cool mist around the mountains had already disappeared. The guests said thank you for everything—for the hospitality, for the generosity, and for signing the contract.

"We really enjoyed you, we're very interested in you," the old scientist said, shaking Noem's hand: "Until our next meeting! We'll be waiting . . . for your death," he joked.

"We will too," laughed the father.

They hadn't even spent half of that money when the Soviet Union collapsed and the ruble was devalued. Armenia declared its independence from the Soviet Union and entered into a new partnership with the European Union.

When the Europeans came, they were naïve because they didn't know that the Russians had been there before them. The Russians, who'd come before the Europeans, came after the Ottomans. The Persians, who'd come before the Ottomans, knew that before them and after the Seljuks came the Tatars and the Mongols, and even before that—the Arabs, who came, it seems, after the Greeks. They had come at the same time as the Egyptian pharaohs, before the Romans, who had come before the Byzantines, who came after the Assyrians, who came after the Khuris. But even before that—Noah had passed through here and he had stopped, because God himself had passed through this place. And Noah was the only one who'd left something instead of taking away, otherwise it would have been impossible to know that God had passed through here. And then the Europeans wouldn't have come.

TRANSLATED FROM THE ARMENIAN BY SHUSHAN AVAGYAN

ARDIAN VEHBIU

From *Bolero*

THE IDEA

"I HAVE A great idea for a novel," I said. "After buying a newspaper at the newsstand, a man enters a subway station in midtown New York. He goes down the stairs, passes through the turnstiles, down another set of stairs, and finally arrives at the uptown train platform. There he waits for the train. But, because of an accident in Brooklyn, uptown trains aren't running. And the man just waits."

"And then what happens?" she asks.

"That's it, nothing else."

"That's it? And this is your great idea for a novel?"

"In a nutshell, yes."

"What kind of idea is that? How can you hope to write a novel where nothing happens?"

"Why nothing? A lot can happen."

"Listen," she said, trying to sound calm and convincing. "With what you've told me, you don't have a novel. At most just the vague promise of a novel. No characters, no plot, no narrative complexity . . . "

"This novel's going to be about the narrativity," I explained. "Narrativity, the effort of narration, the possibilities presented to the narrator. Just look at all the avenues that open up: Who is this man? Why aren't the trains running? What could've happened in Brooklyn? Why does this guy decide to wait, instead of . . . "

"Still, all these things you're saying simply hint at the possibility of a novel."

"No," I said. "On the contrary, I have in mind a novel about the possibilities. Of course, for the novel to come to life, something has to happen. Consider for a moment, though—why must this be?"

"Hmm . . . because that's how novels are written nowadays?"

"Well, then, I want to take the plot and make it a protagonist in the novel."

"The plot?"

"Exactly. Things will happen *to* the plot. It will be attacked, thrown onto the tracks, tied to the rails, and run over by the train. It will be split in two, replicated with errors, rendered unrecognizable."

"Like a cockroach after an atomic catastrophe."

"Yes, like a cockroach after an atomic catastrophe. In short, my novel, instead of being a narrative about an adventure, will be a narrative adventure."

She hesitated for a moment, looking at me intently, maybe thinking of me as a character in a novel she herself should write, at least in her imagination.

INTRODUCTION

In which our protagonist, an incessantly nameless man in his thirties, goes down the stairs of the subway station at the intersection of Seventh Avenue and Fortieth Street in Manhattan, trying to scan the headlines of the newspaper that he's just bought, somewhat bewildered by the odor of the typographic ink. Hostage to his own unpunctuated and chaotic thoughts, he forgets to pay attention to an announcement about an accident somewhere in Brooklyn, which has stopped all the trains on the line; he forgets, or perhaps his subconscious deliberately filters out any information that would compromise his daily routine and propel him to the brink of an existential dilemma. Now, on the platform, he leans leisurely against one of the steel pillars painted the color of a gallbladder, focusing on the crossword puzzle on page sixteen. And so he doesn't notice that he's alone, absorbed in the porous space, while his profile appears and reappears, in multiple simultaneous versions, at different angles, on the temporarily unmonitored black-and-white screens inside the station's chilly security room.

OUR SOURCES INFORM US THAT . . .

The suspect, after buying a newspaper, entered the subway station and headed for the uptown platform, entirely disregarding the announcement about an accident in Brooklyn, which temporarily suspended all Bronx-bound traffic. We were able to identify him from the surveillance footage, and from a single hair stuck to a blotch of fresh paint on one of the steel pillars along the platform, which he had leaned against.

FUTILE OVERLAP

The man had been on the uptown subway platform for a long time, perhaps even a few hours. The security guard in charge of video surveillance was the first one to notice him; she radioed one of her colleagues to go and check it out. Check what out? Well, see what's happening I guess, why this fool's standing there; ask if he needs anything, what else can I say? He was reading the newspaper page by page, pausing every now and then to look at his watch, but otherwise oblivious to the boisterous comings and goings of trains on the other platform tracks, the screeching of the brakes, the tide of commuters swelling on the stairs, the recurring announcements on the station loudspeakers about other trains, other delays, other complications. Then, go ask if he's aware that uptown trains aren't running on that line because of the accident in Brooklyn. Who knows, maybe the man went to the platform to escape his enemies, or maybe he's waiting for someone, a familiar face, or someone following, or someone being followed, to appear in the crowd. Just like in the movies. What if he's armed and dangerous? No, thought the security guard, these things never happen to me. They always happen to others, always somewhere else, always in the past. He must be one of those psychos who photograph the track rats, like those *other* psychos, who photograph birds in Central Park. Or pigeons. If he's not hard of hearing, or dim of wit. Excuse me, sir, said the guard, now on the platform, while the other guard watched the whole scene unfold on a soundless monitor, can I help you with anything, you've been standing here for a long time. I'm waiting for the train, the man said. Didn't you hear the announcement about the accident in Brooklyn? The guard stepped a bit closer, mindful of the recommended distance. Trains aren't running on this side, you need to cross to the other platform and take the N train to 59th Street and from there change to the 4. What incident in Brooklyn? he asked. It was impossible to follow the conversation from the monitors. Not an incident, an accident, said the guard. What does it matter, incident, accident—same thing, he said, waving his hand in front of his face, for no reason, as if scaring off a harassing fly. Leave me alone, please; go back to your novel, so I can continue with mine.

DEAD END

A man stands on a platform, in the Seventh Avenue Fortieth Street subway station, waiting for the train. A broadcast repeatedly announces that uptown trains have been temporarily suspended because of an accident in Brooklyn, but having no other destination except uptown, he is determined to wait on the platform. Another fellow approaches him, looking to chat. "These interruptions are a drag, aren't they?" he says. "It's not the first time this has happened to me in this station, waiting for an uptown train delayed because of an accident in Brooklyn. Last time I waited for almost two hours." "Wait a second," the other replies. "Now that you mention it, I also remember waiting here for hours, just last week. Did we meet that day as well?" "Yes, of course, of course," says the first man, "how could I forget? We've met before, excuse me, it's the lights in here that go on and off at will. Of course I remember! What a day that was, we stood on the platform waiting for hours on end. At least we had each other. And the train came eventually, right?" "Forgive me," the other man says, "but I'm not so sure. I think it came. Logically, it must have come . . . " "Excuse me, guys," a third voice interrupts from behind, "I couldn't help but overhear part of your conversation—it's not like any of us have a choice here—and I think all three of us might be stuck in the same quicksand. I was here last time too and, as I recall, the train never came. Also, I remember, from that other day, there was a man bemoaning the fact that he'd been through this agony before, on this very same platform." The first two, who seem to have sprouted the same frozen smile on their lips, agree with him. "So," continues the third, "it's clear that the uptown train will never come; it's just that, once in a while, we forget, so that hope might endure."

CLAIRVOYANCE

I see an empty subway station. No, wait, it isn't empty. There's a lonely man on the platform, barely standing on his feet. Tired, weary, exhausted, possibly even wounded, if not in his body, at least in his heart. I can't make out his face, but he seems to be holding something in his hand . . . a newspaper, perhaps? Yes, definitely, a newspaper. Oh, God, he's reading, the poor thing. The station is soundless, a death trap patiently waiting. And then suddenly a voice shrieks from behind, from above, from everywhere around. A strong, piercing, metallic voice. Something tragic has happened, in some faraway black hole beyond the river. No, not here, not in the station; nothing has happened in the station, nothing can happen in the station. But this poor soul hears nothing; I can't say why he doesn't hear. I hear.

INSTRUCTIONS

At the corner newsstand buy the *Daily News*, and then enter the subway station on Seventh Avenue and Fortieth Street. No, don't take any notes; try to memorize what I'm saying. Take the stairs and go to the uptown platform and lean against the third pillar facing the station wall, counting from the start of the platform. There'll be no trains running on that track because of the accident in Brooklyn.

Pretend to be reading the newspaper and pay no attention to the announcements. Once in a while lift up your head, so the security cameras can capture your face.

THEY WERE ALL WATCHING HIM

He bought the newspaper at the last moment, just before entering the subway station on Seventh Avenue and Fortieth Street. Usually, he wouldn't buy the paper before taking the subway, but something on the front page had caught his attention, in spite of which he lost all interest the moment the newspaper vendor handed him his change, and then it was too late to return it. So here he was, going down the stairs; a useless rag in his hand that he'd never read, never even flip through, but he'd hang on to it, since he'd bought it with his hard-earned money. Berating himself for making such a stupid purchase, he nearly forgot he needed an uptown train. Crossing the overpass with chicken-like steps, he held the newspaper in his left hand and the briefcase in his right, but the newspaper seemed heavier, a punishment for innocence. How embarrassing! What if he ran into one of his friends, caught red-handed with this garbage? How would he justify it? Now he couldn't even hide it, even from casual onlookers, nor could he use the back page as a disguise; the ad on the last page was even more embarrassing than the headlines. He secretly scanned the other commuters holding newspapers but didn't see anyone with *his* newspaper, which apparently no one bought, unless they wanted to send a specific message. What kind of message would that be? Look at me, I'm a porn addict, a child molester, trashy, vulgar, a piece of hog waste! Or better yet: I'm a fascist animal, a white supremacist, a drug dealer! It was best that he throw his newspaper away in the first trashcan he came across, but, wait a minute: what would everyone think, if they saw him throwing away a newspaper he obviously hadn't read, or even flipped through? Logically they'd assume there was something suspicious going on, something illegal and threatening to public order. *If you see something, say something.* Mr. Policeman, arrest that man, he just threw a newspaper he didn't read in the trash. A booming announcement in the station snapped him out of his paranoia. Because of an accident in Brooklyn, trains were no longer running. Commuters, dragging their feet, began to leave the platform. As they passed, a couple of them took a cursory glance at the newspaper in his hand, and then up, at him. Damn newspaper! He'd bought it without thinking of the consequences, as if he didn't know the way of the world today, people instantly judging you, based on a single detail, even if totally marginal and insignificant, because no one had time anymore for careful assessments. Without a doubt, someone like him, holding that newspaper, was in itself an unusual subway event. The platform surveillance cameras had surely recorded everything, and now there was no way to undo this absurdity. After everyone left, and he remained alone on the platform, drowning in solitude and shame, he finally approached one of the trashcans, as big as a barrel, and tossed the newspaper in it, with lightning speed. "Excuse me, sir," he heard a voice, behind his back. He turned slowly, like someone expecting to be executed. A subway guard was walking toward him, staring at him with an impenetrable gaze. "Well, see for yourself," he said to the guard. "I bought it by mistake. I meant to buy another newspaper, but somehow I ended up with this one, which I have no need for." The guard didn't break his distrusting gaze. "Trash, isn't it? But I discovered it too late. Too late. And still, to think that people read it . . . this crap! What can anyone do? In fact, I never buy newspapers, especially in the subway. The risk of selecting the wrong one is big, too big; and the vendor won't let you return it. It's not like it's his fault, right? Just doing his job, he has kids to feed . . ." The guard didn't let him continue. "Sir, you can't throw newspapers in this trashcan," he said. "There's another trashcan, over there, just for newspapers." Oh, God, how embarrassing, how embarrassing. He put his hand into the trashcan like a veterinarian reaching into a cow, and pulled his newspaper from a labyrinth of cold, wet, sticky stuff. This would be his last time in New York. What a pity!

FROM AN MTA PRESS RELEASE

The Daily News had again come out with an exposé on the inadequate security standards of our subway system, to which we responded this afternoon by sending one of our workers, in plain clothes, to the uptown platform of the station at Seventh Avenue and Fortieth Street, during the temporary interruption of traffic because of an accident in Brooklyn. In this way, we were able to check the entire video surveillance network without compromising, in the meantime, the security of commuters.

URBAN NEUROSIS

My problem—because that's what I would call it, and not a disease—with a little care and advance planning, can be kept under control. As Dr. Kiddalla has explained, I simply must regularly take the necessary medication and allow fifteen or twenty minutes for it to take effect.

Today, for example, since I have to take the subway uptown—let's not go into too much detail why—I need to predict the critical situations I'll have to face, so I can plan ahead and not be caught unprepared.

And so a short list forms in my mind:

1.   Leaving the house: 100 mg Zumor® (macrolizam), against *agoraphobia*, or fear of open spaces.

2.   Crossing the street to the subway station: 5 mg Imidax® (imidazolam), against *bathmophobia*, or fear of stairs and steep slopes.

3.   Entering the underground platform: 30 mg Pabix® (diazolam), against *claustrophobia*, or fear of closed spaces.

4.   Waiting on the platform for the train: 12.5 mg Citrex® (amazolizab) against *siderodromophobia*, or fear of trains and rail lines.

5.   Entering the train car and riding: another 30 mg pill of Pabix, in case the claustrophobia reappears.

I call Dr. Kiddalla before leaving the house and together we agree on the five steps of the plan. If you sense an impending *acoustico-phobia*, or fear of loud noises, you can take another 5 mg of Calmia® (chlorpazolimab), he advises me, adding that everything will be fine, that after all it's not my first time taking the subway uptown.

On the way to the station everything does go fine: I successfully cross Sixth Avenue and Broadway with no symptoms of *scopophobia*, or fear of being seen by others. What's to see, anyway? A person like me is nondescript, quiet, minds his own business, is well adjusted to the metropolitan way of life.

Before entering the station on Seventh Avenue and Fortieth Street, I buy one of those dailies at the newsstand and—I almost forgot—a bottle of mineral water, which I might need for swallowing the obligatory pills, one at a time, as needed.

Breathing abdominally, I go down the station stairs, bothered only by a single skipped heartbeat—but there's no risk that it'll ava-lanche into tachycardia: *Imidax* has it all under control. I go through the turnstiles and head for the uptown platform. A drove of com-muters charges up the stairs toward me and nearly takes me with it. A train on my platform must have just ejaculated its load.

I don't know if I've already mentioned that *Zumor* helps fight even against social phobia, defending me from crowds and their often irra-tional reactions toward a particular individual—an individual like me.

Relaxed and even placid, I go downstairs to the uptown subway platform, which is now ready for me. My mouth feels dry from the cocktail of medications I've just taken: but I'm calm and relaxed, as I should be. I continue breathing abdominally. I approach a steel pil-lar, lean against it, and open the paper to read, aware, although not yet scopophobic, of the surveillance camera fixed on me.

I read for a while. My pulse is stable. Seventy-seven beats per min-ute. My armpits are starting to sweat, and more and more there's a feeling of creeping dampness, signaled by a humid whiff coming from my masculine Gasp deodorant: a side effect of the Imidax that no one will notice. (I sense the warning signs of a slight sociophobia, but Dr. Kiddalla says that, given the circumstances, this should be considered normal).

An announcement spews out boisterously from the platform loudspeakers: *Because of an accident in Brooklyn, uptown trains on this line are temporarily suspended.*

What does this mean? What does this mean for *me*? (He breathes abdominally.)

I cautiously cast about me and find other than me, there's no one on the platform, no one waiting for the train. Out of the corner of my eye, somewhere in the periphery of my view between the tracks, I make out a moving shadow: I don't even want to confirm it, because of my *murophobia*, or fear of mice, which might take advantage of this shitty situation to parasitically feed on my other phobias, even the most subconscious, deeply buried ones.

By a stroke of good luck, a payphone on one of the pillars is working. I grab the greasy handle, insert a quarter in the coin receptor, dial Dr. Kiddalla's number, and in a few words explain to him what's happened.

I don't get it, the doctor says to me.

Before entering the subway—I say between two skipped heartbeats—I took 30mg *Pabix*, for the claustrophobia; which counteracts the effect of the *Zumor* that I took before leaving the house.

Wonderful, says Dr. Kiddalla. Just as we'd agreed.

Well, now that the uptown trains aren't running, I continue, there are no commuters waiting in the platform and I'm alone, in the middle of an empty space.

Agoraphobia again. Dr. Kiddalla reads my mind.

Exactly, I say. And it's getting worse and worse, what with the residual features of claustrophobia. I'm experiencing agoraphobia when, logically speaking, I should have expected claustrophobia to rear its head. My neurovegetative system doesn't know how to handle this.

You *must* go back above ground, Dr. Kiddalla instructs me, and wait there for Pabix's effect to pass. Pabix has a short half-life. Very short. Go drink a Papaya juice somewhere (he knows how dry my mouth tends to get) and refresh your gastric passageways. Then return to the station, but don't go to the platform unless you're sure the uptown trains are running again. And don't forget the breathing exercises. I repeat: do not forget the breathing exercises!

As always, Dr. Kiddalla is very reasonable. I hang up with the idiotic hope that perhaps I'll get my coin back, then I head towards the platform exit. I approach the stairs; they're not so much a threat to me as a problem that needs to be negotiated, a problem that forces me to interrupt my already pointless breathing exercises. There must be a gaping hole in my ribcage that doesn't let me inhale or exhale properly.

Bathmophobia, or the fear of stairs and steep slopes: 5 mg *Imidax* sublingually, so that it takes effect within five minutes. I fish in my messy bag for my pillbox: I look for the *Imidax*, but I do not see the small bicolored white-blue pill.

I try to be rational: (1) I must have forgotten to pack the *Imidax*; (2) I forgot to pack the *Imidax*.

I turn and face the platform, and unwittingly my eyes dart to the tracks where a rat is taking great delight in a handful of fries, irresponsibly discarded by a fast-food customer. As if the agoraphobia weren't enough! (Pulse: 104)

I take out another cool moist coin from my pocket and head for the public payphone to bother Dr. Kiddalla again.

In a few words I explain the problem.

I don't get it, my doctor says again.

To exit the platform, as you advised, I need to take the stairs; but to take the stairs I first need to take *Imidax*, but, damn it, I forgot to pack the *Imidax* capsules before I left.

I can call a pharmacy nearby, in midtown, and you can go there and pick it up immediately, says Dr. Kiddalla, afterwards adding: ah, but you still need the *Imidax* to tackle the stairs.

Reasonable as always.

Remind me again, what do you have on hand in the pillbox, Dr. Kiddalla persists.

I rattle them off: Zumor, Pabix, Citrex, Diabemol®, Empor®, and Calmia.

Okay, he instructs, then take 250 mg Empor (zadolol) and chew, swallow and then wash it down with a little water so it goes into effect as soon as possible.

This is the right decision: I usually take the Empor for the tachycardia and skipped heartbeats, which—as you might imagine—are caused by the bathmophobia.

I thank my doctor, friend, and savior, hang up and once more hope that the payphone will cough up my coin—but no, the coin's been swallowed like a pill following countless others swallowed in this underground hospital pavilion.

Chewed like candy, the *Empor* has the keratinous taste of a squashed fat beetle (*entomophobia*). I wash my mouth with a little water from the bottle, and wait for the pill to kick in, breathing through my mouth all the while.

Because of an accident in Brooklyn, uptown trains are not running, says a loud voice from the loudspeaker.

Suddenly, two steps away from me, the platform payphone urgently rings.

Hello? Who is this? It's Dr. Kiddalla, attentive as ever, empathetic and humane. Did you take the 250 mg *Empor*? Did you chew it well before swallowing it with water? Very good, I just called to be sure.

I wait a little longer in the platform, leaning against one of the pillars, trying not to see the shadows lurking between the tracks. Incidentally, the announcement that uptown trains are no longer running has completely freed me from suicidophobia, or the fear of impulsively committing suicide, by jumping in front of an oncoming train.

After the requisite five minutes pass (pulse: 98), I once again approach the mouth of the stairwell, planning to go from the platform to the mezzanine.

But I'm not ready. I can't go up. I can't. A hand is clutching my chest and my heart feels like it's no longer beating, only jumping in a wild *parcour* from one skipped heartbeat to the next. My feet are stuck in the glue trap of the platform, and my breathing is shallow, like the breathing of a paralyzed mouse, my sweat smelling like acetone, my mouth dry like sand, my knees shaking, and my bladder, even though it's practically empty, fluttering in agony. Pulse: 130.

I am not ready.

I approach the payphone, insert a coin, and dial Dr. Kiddalla's number to ask if maybe it's time to take the 5 mg Calmia, to calm me down.

Because of an accident in Brooklyn, uptown trains are not running until further notice, the voice from the loudspeakers screams, making my entire body quake.

My coins are gone, and with them Dr. Kiddalla's calming voice. The water bottle: it has less than 1/5 of the original amount. Pulse: 130. Nearing dehydration: symptoms of depersonalization.

Is it time to call an ambulance?

My problem—because again I wouldn't call it a disease—can be kept under control, with a little care and planning. What happened to day can be blamed on the MTA, which failed its function and mission, inventing all sorts of pretexts to justify the total chaos, the empty platforms, the noises, the rats binging on trash among the tracks, the payphones sequestering coins from taxpayers.

Time to call an ambulance then. Let the MTA foot the bill.

EVERYTHING WAS COMING TO A HALT

"Leave the TV on," the eldest daughter said, "let's watch this lonely guy standing on the subway platform." "There's nothing about him you don't know already," said the other daughter: "At least the scene of him buying the newspaper on Channel 12 had some action. It's been a week since we last watched that. He keeps going around, smiling. And they show real money. And I even like that newsstand vendor, he's totally right, with the goat teeth. So natural." Their mother, who was listening to her favorite radio show, interrupted from the other room: "Your buddy there's waiting for nothing, they just announced on the radio something happened on the subway, in Brooklyn, and it's stopped all the trains." Silence followed, only slightly spoiled by the occasional clicks of a surveillance camera in the ceiling. No trains are running at this hour, the mother thought.

WE CAN TALK, TOO

You bought me, but you are not reading me, said the newspaper.

Here, you can get on your train, said Seventh Avenue.

We know where you're going, but you don't know where you're going, said the base of the stairs of the subway station.

Welcome. my loyal friend. Keep me company, said the uptown platform.

Because of the accident in Brooklyn, uptown trains are temporarily suspended, said the loudspeakers.

I like the feel of your back, said the steel pillar.

You're handsome, but also a little shy, said the surveillance camera.

THE DARK SIDE OF ORDER

The corner newsstand was an open invitation to buy a newspaper, but she never did. Newspapers kept her from thinking and making sense of everything whirling in her mind. She entered the station, went down a set of stairs, and reached the uptown platform at precisely the moment a voice from the loudspeakers announced that all northbound trains were running on time. She sighed: she'd hoped, in fact, for the train to be delayed a little, giving her enough time to make peace with herself. An accident in Brooklyn would've been enough. She imagined how, in that case, everyone would have left the platform, and then she wondered if even a two-hour wait, just by herself in the station, would be enough? Two whole hours, without having to go anywhere—but maybe she was asking too much from life. Just then, the uptown train pulled in, she stepped through the car doors that opened in front of her, and the dreaded forgetfulness overtook her mind.

LITERATURE AND REALITY

In his book, *Winged Cockroaches: A Pocket Encyclopedia of the Everyday in New York City*, the late Pineas Sorian mentions a certain Moz Vodak, an aspiring writer who'd made it a habit to spend hours, or sometimes days, on the uptown platform of the subway station at Seventh Avenue and Fortieth Street. To those curious enough to ask, he would always patiently explain that he was preparing to write a novel about a man who waits, and waits, and always waits for an uptown train that never arrives because of an accident in Brooklyn which has suspended all train traffic to the station's uptown platform.

Apparently, Moz Vodak belonged to that school of thought that requires writers firsthand experience of everything about which they intend to write. And so he would appear on the platform almost every day, at noon, a newspaper in his hand, and he'd stay there until late in the evening, sometimes until dawn, waiting, as he would say, for *the* accident in Brooklyn to happen. Extraverted, easygoing, endearing, he very quickly befriended the station personnel and was soon able to call each station security guard by name. Occasionally, he would even offer treats, candy, and other symbolic gifts to commuters, sanitation workers, and police officers.

Then, one day, a tragic accident occurred in Brooklyn, when a rush-hour train derailed, hit the platform, and instantly killed two Mormon missionaries. Moz Vodak, hearing of the accident from the platform loudspeakers, felt, if not happy, at least vindicated, because *this* was what he'd been waiting for all these weeks. He remained on the platform till approximately midnight; considering the experience complete, he was about to exit the station, when two detectives in plain clothes stopped him and asked him to join them at the La Migra bar for a friendly chat.

After settling into their seats at the bar, the detectives asked Moz what he knew about the accident in Brooklyn, and Moz answered that he knew nothing more than what was announced in the station loudspeakers. They told him exactly what had taken place, and Moz was moved, his eyes tearing up with authentic grief. At this, the detectives asked why he'd been saying to everyone, day after day, for several weeks running, that he was "waiting for an accident in Brooklyn to happen." And Moz Vodak told them about the book he was planning to write and explained how it was necessary for him to experience firsthand everything that his fictional hero would experience.

The detectives, who didn't entirely dismiss him—perhaps because by now they were informed about this would-be book—added nevertheless that Moz's explanations weren't very convincing, and that this whole enigma begged for some further attention and scrutiny, so long as Vodak didn't pretend to predict the future. Once again, and with great patience, Moz explained that, according to the mathematical laws of probability, the subway accident in Brooklyn had to happen someday, and although, naturally, you couldn't know the *exact time* it would happen, you didn't have to be supernaturally gifted to predict it would happen.

Finally, before they left, the detectives asked Moz whether he felt any remorse, seeing that his idea for a book had already killed two innocent Mormons. Visibly shaken by this bitter and unwished-for incident, Moz Vodak walked back to his apartment in Chelsea, meditated for a couple of hours, then decided to abandon his idea for the book. In the days that followed, and even weeks, he could not use the subway, because most of the people working there—the security guards, the sanitation workers, the electricians, the information attendants, the track maintenance workers, the station managers, the train operators—would recognize him, even at a distance, and openly avoid him.

Word spread that he brought bad luck, that he was a blind instrument of Doom. It was at this point that he finally decided to leave New York for good, but before this could be accomplished, word spread that he'd started collecting experiences for a new book, about a cab driver who waited and waited for a client who never shows up. In response, the NYC cab drivers' union, though they categorically denied it, distributed an internal memo declaring Moz Vodak a *persona non grata* in all licensed cabs in the city. This anecdote—concludes Pineas Sorian—demonstrates how literature, itself an innocuous art, may become dangerous when it meddles with reality, just as, for the sake of symmetry, reality, when forced into art, may react and push back, compromising the artist's integrity and reputation.

TRANSLATED FROM THE ALBANIAN BY ELONA PIRA

AUTHOR BIOGRAPHIES

Izara Batres (b. 1982, Madrid) is a writer and poet who received her doctorate in literature from the Complutense University of Madrid. She is the author of six published books: the poetry collections *Avenidas del tiempo*, *El fuego hacia la luz*, and *Triptych* (Mundial Prize for Poetry, 2016); the multiple-award-winning collection of humorous stories *Confesiones al psicoanalista* (2012), which includes "Bureaucracy"; the novel *ENC o El sueño del pez luciérnaga* (2014); and the scholarly monograph *Cortázar y París: Último round* (2014). Also a screenwriter, a playwright, a comic writer, and a journalist, she teaches literature at the University Camilo José Cela and creative writing at various academies in Madrid.

Bruce Bégout was born in Talence in 1967. A philosopher specializing in Husserl, he has dedicated himself to exploring the urban environment and analyzing the everyday in such books as *Zéropolis* (2002), *Lieu commun* (2003), *La Découverte du quotidien* (2005), and *De la décence ordinaire* (2008). In 2010, he began writing fiction and has published several books, including *Le Park* (2010) and two collections of stories (2010) and *L'Accumulation primitive de la noirceur* (2014). *On ne dormira jamais* (2017) stands as a culmination of this work, at the crossroads of Gothic and science fiction. Bégout teaches at the University of Bordeaux and is the recipient of the 2016 Bourse Cioran.

Born in Kaliningrad in 1988, **Andrei Dichenko** is a Belarusian novelist, poet, and journalist. He has been editor-in-chief of the lifestyle magazine *Я* ("*I*") and several other magazines in Minsk. His books include *Minsk Sky*, *Slabs and Abysses*, *Sun Man*, and a collection of stories called *You and Me*. His short fiction has been published in Belarusian, Russian, Azerbaijani, Serbian, American, and Israeli literary journals. Dichenko characterizes his genre as metaphysical realism, and credits Yuri Mamleev as his literary mentor.

Katherine Duffy has published two collections of poetry in English: *The Erratic Behaviour of Tides* (1998) and *Sorrow's Egg* (2011), both with Dedalus Press. A selection of her work was translated into French by Anne Mounic and included in *Quatre poètes irlandais*, edited by Clíona Ní Ríordáin (2011). She writes fiction in both English and Irish. Her short story "Must-See" (*Sunday Tribune*, May 2006) won the prestigious Hennessy New Irish Writer of the Year award. Her work in Irish, including a novel for young adults and many short stories, has earned numerous Oireachtas na Gaeilge awards. She is also an accomplished translator and has translated leading Irish language writers into English. *Rambling Jack*, her translation of Micheál Ó Conghaile's novella *Seachrán Jeaic Sheáin Johnny*, was published in 2015 by Dalkey Archive Press and in January 2016 was featured as a Nota Benes on the website *World Literature Today*. Katherine Duffy's website is www.kateduv.com.

Julia Fiedorczuk is a Polish poet, prose writer, translator, and lecturer in American literature at the University of Warsaw. She has published five books of poetry, a collection of stories, and two novels (including the Nike-nominated *Nieważkość*). She is the author, with Gerardo Beltrán, of a trilingual essay on poetry and ecology: *Ekopoetyka / Ecopoética / Ecopoetics*, and a member of ASLE (Association for the Study of Language and the Environment). In her writings, she explores the relationships between human beings and non-human nature, as well as questions of identity, otherness and ethical responsibility. Her work has been translated into nineteen languages. Her website can be found at www.ekopoetyka.com.

Hugh Fulham-McQuillan is an Irish writer and Ph.D. in Psychology in Trinity College Dublin. His fiction, and essays, have been published in *Ambit, gorse, The Stinging Fly, The Irish Times*, and *The Lonely Crowd*, among others. His first collection of short stories will be published by Dalkey Archive Press.

Susanna Harutyunyan was born in 1963 in Karchaghbyur, Armenia. She graduated from the Faculty of Philology of Yerevan State Pedagogical Institute and has written for various literary periodicals published in Armenia and the Diaspora. She is the author of several short-story collections and novels that have been translated into German, Greek, Persian, Romanian, and other languages. In 2015 she received the Presidential Prize for Literature for her novel *Ravens Before Noah*.

Lídia Jorge was born in Boliqueime, southern Portugal, in 1946. She studied French Literature in Lisbon and spent some years teaching in Angola and Mozambique, during the independence struggle. She now lives in Lisbon. Her first two novels placed her in the avant-garde of contemporary Portuguese literature, and she has since received numerous prestigious awards for her work. In 2013, Lídia Jorge was honored as one of the 10 Greatest Literary Voices by the renowned French magazine *Littéraire*, and in 2014 she was awarded the Premio Luso-Español de Arte y Cultura. She was given the 2015 Vergílio Ferreira Award for her body of work.

Maarja Kangro (b. 1973) began her literary career as a translator of Zanzotto and Enzensberger, and as an author of libretti and lyrics for contemporary classical composers. She has published five books of poetry and four volumes of fiction. She has twice won the Estonian Cultural Endowment's Literary Award, the Tallinn University Literary Award, and the Friedebert Tuglas Short Story Award, among other honors. Her works have been translated into more than fifteen languages. She lives in Tallinn, but prefers to spend winters around the Mediterranean.

Zachary Karabashliev is a novelist, playwright, and a screenwriter. His debut novel, *18% Gray*, is a bestselling title in Bulgaria and was published in the United States, France, Poland, Croatia, and other countries. It won the prestigious Novel of the Year Award in Bulgaria and was chosen by anonymous vote to be among the 100 most loved books by Bulgarians in the BBC campaign "The Big Read." His short stories have been translated and published in many languages and made into short films. His award-winning stage plays (*Recoil, Lissabon*) have been produced in Wiesbaden and New York City. Karabashliev is now the editor-in-chief of the Bulgarian publishing house Ciela. He lives in Sofia. His forthcoming novel, *Freedom*, is scheduled for publication in 2017.

Lotte Kirkeby (b. 1970) holds a degree in literature and French language. She has worked as an editor at Gyldendal Publishers and is currently a literary critic and translator as well as a writer. After three non-fiction books, she made her fictional debut in 2016 with the highly acclaimed story collection *Jubilee*. In nineteen stories, she examines how we handle loss—of childhood innocence, as in "Violet Lane," of the ones we love, or of our conception of the perfect life. Kirkeby has contributed to several anthologies and magazines in Denmark and abroad, and is currently working on a novel, to be published in 2018.

Caroline Lamarche lives in Liège (Belgium). She received the Prix Rossel for her first novel, *Le jour du chien* (1996). Her second novel, *La nuit l'après-midi* (1998) was translated by Howard Curtis (*Night in the Afternoon*, Grove Press, 2000). The novels she has written since are all published by Gallimard: *L'ours* (2000), *Lettres du pays froid* (2003), *Carnets d'une soumise de province* (2004), *Karl et Lola* (2007), *La Chienne de Naha* (2012), *La mémoire de l'air* (2014), *Dans la maison un grand cerf* (2017). She also writes short stories, radio plays, texts for choreographers, photographers, plastic artists, and actors. Her address on the web is www.carolinelamarche.net.

Taina Latvala, born in 1982, is a Finnish author and playwright living in Helsinki. She holds an M.A. from the University of Helsinki and the University of Salford. She was awarded the Kalev Jäntti Prize in 2007 for her literary debut, *Arvostelukappale* (*Review Copy*), a collection of overlapping short stories. She has since had three more books published: *Paljastuskirja* (*Kiss-and-Tell*) in 2009, *Välimatka* (*Distance*) in 2012 and *Ennen kuin kaikki muuttuu* (*Before Everything Changes*) in 2015. Her first play, *Välimatka* (2014), dramatises her novel of the same name and tells the story of a mother and daughter who travel together to Tenerife. She has written three plays that have all been performed in Finland.

Kalina Maleska (b. 1975, Skopje) is a writer, essayist, scholar, translator, and editor. She has published three short-story collections, *Misunderstandings* (*Makedonska* Kniga, 1998), *The Naming of* *the Insect* (Slovo, 2008), and *Clever Pejo, My Enemy* (Ili-Ili, 2016); two novels, *Bruno and the Colors* (Slovo, 2006) and *Apparitions with Silver Threads* (Slovo, 2014); and one play, *An Event Among Many* (Slovo, 2010). Her stories and essays have been published in various periodicals in Macedonia and abroad. Maleska teaches English Literature in the Faculty of Philology, University of Skopje, where she earned her M.A. and Ph.D. Maleska also translates literary works from English into Macedonian and vice versa. Some of her translations into Macedonian include Sterne's *Tristram Shandy*, Ambrose Bierce's *Selected Stories*, and Twain's *Huckleberry Finn*. Maleska is the prose editor of *Blesok*, an online journal for literature and other arts.

Igor Malijevský was born in Prague in 1970. He studied theoretical physics and philosophy at Charles University, but since the mid-1990s has devoted himself primarily to photography and writing. He has published three books of poetry and two collections of short stories, including *Moon Above the Tagus River* (2014); he established and leads EKG, a well-known monthly literary cabaret in Prague. His stories and poems are based on a poetical understanding of our everyday reality, a style he describes as "photography in words." His works have been translated into Russian, English, Polish, German, and other languages, and he has exhibited his photographs in the U.S.A., China, South Korea, the Philippines, and Europe. His recent work includes *Znamení Lvova/Signs of Lvov/знаки львова* (2016), a book of photographs accompanied by poetic texts in Czech, English, and Ukrainian.

Miha Mazzini (b. 1961) is a best-selling Slovenian writer, screenwriter, and film director. He is the author of more than thirty books and one of the most widely translated Slovene writers, his work having appeared in nine languages. His much-acclaimed short stories have been included in many anthologies, and in 2011 he received the Pushcart Prize for short fiction. He has written screenplays for four award-winning films, as well as numerous television programs and documentaries. He holds an M.A. from the University of Sheffield in Creative Writing for Film and Television and a Ph.D. in the Anthropology of Everyday Life from the Institutum Studiorum Humanitatis in Slovenia.

Amanda Michalopoulou is the author of seven novels and three short-story collections. She has been a contributing editor at *Kathimerini* in Greece and *Taggespiegel* in Berlin. She is a winner of the Academy of Athens Prize for her story collection *Bright Day* (2013). The American translation of her book *I'd Like* (Dalkey Archive, 2008) won the NEA International Literature Prize. For the same book, she was awarded the Liberis Liber Prize of the Independent Catalan Publishers. Her stories and essays have been translated into fourteen languages. She lives in Athens, Greece.

Xabier Montoia was born in Vitoria-Gasteiz (Basque Country) in 1955. He began publishing in 1983 with a collection of poetry that he then followed with two others before moving to novels and short stories in the early 1990s. He has twice won awards from the Ministry of Culture of the Basque Government for his collections of short stories, first the Media Prize for *Gasteizko hondartzak* (*The Beaches of Gasteiz*) in 1998, and later the Basque Literature Prize for *Euskal Hiria Sutan* (*Basque City in Flames*) in 2007. To date, he has published some twenty works spanning three and a half decades. Mr. Montoia is also a musician and was the singer and songwriter for two different bands before embarking on his solo career.

Thomas Morris's debut story collection, *We Don't Know What We're Doing* (Faber and Faber) won the 2016 Wales Book of the Year, the Rhys Davies Fiction Trust Award and the Somerset Maugham Prize. He is a Contributing Editor at the Dublin-based magazine, *The Stinging Fly*, and in 2017-18 he will be Writer in Residence at University College Cork. He wishes to acknowledge the award of a Literature Wales Writer's Bursary supported by the National Lottery through Arts Council of Wales

Davide Orecchio (b. 1969) is the author of *Città distrutte. Sei biografie infedeli* (2012), a collection of imaginative biographies which won the SuperMondello Prize. He has also published the novel *Stati di grazia* (2014), a reflection on individual lives and the large historical tides they are part of, and *Mio padre la rivoluzione* 2017), a collection of short stories about the Russian Revolution. His work has been translated by Frederika Randall ("Diego Wilchen no more," *ZYZZYVA* 105, Winter 2015) and Allison Grimaldi Donahue ("The Revendication of Matilde Famularo," *The American Reader* 4, February-March 2013; "Éster Terracine," *Lunch Ticket*, Winter/Spring 2016).

Eirikur Örn Norðdahl (b. 1978) is an Icelandic poet and novelist. His novel *Evil* was awarded The Icelandic Literary Prize, The Icelandic Booksellers' Prize, nominated for the Nordic Council's Literary Prize, shortlisted for the Prix Médicis Étranger, the Prix Meilleur Livre Étranger, and received the Transfuge award for best Nordic fiction in France. Since his debut in 2002, he has published seven books of poems, five novels, and two collections of essays. Eiríkur is active in sound and performance poetry, visual poetry, poetry film, and various conceptual poetry projects, and he has translated over a dozen books into Icelandic, including a selection of Allen Ginsberg's poetry and Jonathan Lethem's *Motherless Brooklyn* (for which he received the Icelandic Translation Award).

Goran Petrovic was born in Kraljevo, Serbia, in 1961. He studied literature at the university in Belgrade, where he and his family live today. He has published numerous novels, stories, essays, and a drama. He has won almost a dozen major literary prizes, including Serbia's most prestigious, the NIN Award, for his novel *Sitničarnica "Kod srećne ruke."* His works have gone through many printings in Serbia and have been translated into sixteen foreign languages; his novel *An Atlas Traced by the Sky* (2012) is available in English. Petrović believes that literature is one of the few remaining disciplines of intimacy allowing us to glimpse the great in the small, and the small in the great, in our fast, short lives.

Ravshan Saleddin was born to a native Siberian family in Bekovo Village, Siberia, in 1989. He is a screenwriter and a columnist for a number of Russian publications, including *Snob* and *The Russian*

Muslim. His first collection, *Ravshan's Real Stories*, was shorlisted for the Russian Debut Prize in 2013 and described as a "pupa soon to produce a beautiful butterfly of a novel." His first novel, *Silence Full Blast* (2015), proved worthy of that description. Saleddin graduated from Ust-Abakan Professional College of Crafts as a Master Woodcarver. Since 2012, he has lived in Volzhsky, where he works as a forester and leads a small woodworking shop specializing in writer's furniture.

John Saul's short fiction has been published widely, appearing in several anthologies and in four collections in the U.K., three at Salt Publishing. The *Times* has described his writing as "witty and playful," proof that "the short story is not only alive but being reinvigorated in excitingly diverse ways." His novel *Heron and Quin* is published by Aidan Ellis, and his novel *Seventeen* is available digitally. He was shortlisted for the international 2015 Seán Ó Faoláin prize for fiction. In 2016, work of his was included in *Best British Stories* (Salt). He has a website at www.johnsaul.co.uk.

Born in Geneva in 1985, **Aude Seigne** studied French literature and Mesopotamian civilization at the University of Geneva. She has traveled to more than forty countries, worked as a web designer and editor for the city of Geneva, and as a cultural administrator for the choreographer Cindy Van Acker. She published *Chroniques de l'Occident nomade* (2011), which won the Prix Nicolas Bouvier and was one of the 2011 selections of Le Romans des Romands. In 2012, she received a cultural grant from Leenaards Foundation for her second book, *Les Neiges de Damas* (2015). In 2017, she was awarded a one-month writing residency at the Jan Michalski Foundation and published *Une toile large comme le monde*, a novel that conjures up the end of the Internet and whose protagonist is a submarine cable. Seigne is also a member of the Collectif AJAR and publishes regularly in magazines and anthologies.

Alvydas Šlepikas was born in1966 in Videniškiai, Lithuania. A year after graduating secondary school, he was recruited into the Soviet army and served for two years in Kazakhstan. In the 1990s he studied acting and directing, and since then has worked in numerous Lithuanian theaters. In 1997, his first book of poetry was published. Since then he has written a second book of poetry, two collections of stories, and the novel *Mano vardas Maryté* [*My Name Is Maryté*]. This novel was awarded Book of the Year in Lithuania, received the Lithuanian Writers Union award, and was translated into German, Estonian, Latvian, Ukrainian, Dutch, and Polish. Šlepikas is a member of the Lithuanian Writers Union and a Lithuanian PEN member. At the moment he is working on a novel to be published by the German publishing house Mitteldeutscher Verlag.

György Spiró was born in Budapest in 1946. He is a playwright and fiction writer, the author of a collection of short stories and five novels, including *Captivity* (2005), which won the Aegon Literary Award and was published in 2015. His writing has been translated into nine languages. He lives in Budapest.

Born in Albania, **Ardian Vehbiu** is a writer, translator, researcher, and the author of fourteen non-fiction and fiction books. Vehbiu was awarded the 2010 Gjergj Fishta Award for a study of patterns in public discourse under the totalitarian regime, as well as the 2014 Ardian Klosi Award for an essay dedicated to the image of the West in communist Albania. Since 2007, he has managed and been a regular contributor to *Peizazhe të fjalës*, one of the leading cultural and social online magazines in Albanian. He has also translated several works from Albanian into Italian, as well as from Italian, French, and English into Albanian. He has lived and worked in New York City since 1996.

Nora Wagener was born in Luxembourg in 1989. Educated multilingually, she chose German as her literary language and studied creative writing in Germany. In 2011, her first novel, *Menschenliebe und Vogel, schrei*, was published in Luxembourg, followed by the collection of novellas *E Galaxien*, which was published in Germany in 2015. That same year, her play *Visions* was staged. In 2016, *Larven*, a collection of short stories was published in Luxembourg, as was *d'Glühschwéngchen*, a children's book in her mother tongue, Luxembourgish. She has received several awards (Prix Arts et Lettres, Institut Grand-Ducal) and scholarships (Literarisches Colloquium Berlin) in her home country and abroad. She publishes regularly in anthologies and magazines across Europe.

Maartje Wortel (b. 1982) was expelled from the School of Journalism for making too much up. As a writer, she has become one of the most characteristic voices of her generation. She received the Anton Wachter Prize and the BNG Literary Prize. Wortel's latest short-story collection, *Something Has to Happen*, was nominated for the 2016 Fintro Literary Prize. Wortel was lauded as the "literary talent of the year" (*de Volkskrant*), "the best contemporary writer of short stories" (*Humo*), and "the figurehead of a whole generation of young Dutch writers" (*Psychologies*). The novella *Goldfish and Concrete* is Wortel's most recent publication. She is currently working on her next novel.

TRANSLATOR BIOGRAPHIES

Kristin Addis translates primarily between Spanish or Basque and English, and is one of few who translate directly from Basque into English. She specializes in literary translation (short stories, novels, poetry), and has also translated works about the Basque language and culture. Ms. Addis has spent many years in the Basque Country; she currently resides in Iowa.

Jesse Anderson is a writer and translator originally from Olympia, Washington. He's published several book-length translations of contemporary French literature, and his own writing has appeared in various literary journals and online.

Anna Aslanyan is a journalist and translator. She writes for the *London Review of Books* blog, the *Spectator*, the *Times Literary Supplement*, and other publications. Her translations from Russian include *Post-Post Soviet? Art, Politics and Society in Russia at the Turn of the Decade*, a collection of essays edited by Ekaterina Degot (University of Chicago Press, 2013).

Shushan Avagyan is the translator from Russian of *Energy of Delusion: A Book on Plot, Bowstring: On the Dissimilarity of the Similar, A Hunt for Optimism* and *The Hamburg Score* by Viktor Shklovsky (Dalkey Archive), *Art and Production* by Boris Arvatov (Pluto), and from Armenian of *I Want to Live: Poems of Shushanik Kurghinian* (AIWA). She currently teaches at the American University of Armenia.

Jonathan Bolton is Professor of Slavic Languages and Literatures at Harvard University. He has edited and translated *In the Puppet Gardens: Selected Poems, 1963-2005*, by Czech poet Ivan Wernisch; his translations of Wernisch, Petr Hruška, Radek Fridrich, and others have appeared in *Circumference, BODY: Poetry, Prose, Word*, and elsewhere. His studies of Czech culture include *Worlds of Dissent: Charter 77, The Plastic People of the Universe, and Czech Culture under Communism*.

Jeffrey D. Castle is a literary translator and Ph.D. candidate at the University of Illinois at Urbana-Champaign.

Gregor Timothy Čeh lives in Cyprus and regularly translates contemporary Slovene literature for authors and publishing houses in Slovenia. His translations have been published in both the U.K. and U.S. Brought up in a bilingual family in Slovenia, he studied at UCL in London, taught English in Greece, and holds a Master's degree from the University of Kent.

Margaret Jull Costa has been a literary translator for over thirty years and has translated such writers as Eça de Queiroz, Fernando Pessoa, José Saramago, Javier Marías, and Bernardo Atxaga. In 2013 she was invited to become a Fellow of the Royal Society of Literature and in 2014 was made an OBE for services to literature.

John K. Cox is a professor of East European history at North Dakota State University in Fargo. His translations include book-length works by Danilo Kiš, Ajla Terzić, Ivan Cankar, Vjenceslav Novak, Muharem Bazdulj, and Miklós Radnóti, Cox's historical works include *The History of Serbia* and *Slovenia: Evolving Loyalties.* He earned his Ph.D. at Indiana University (1995) and is currently translating all three novels by the late Biljana Jovanović.

Paul Curtis Daw practiced law before turning to translation. In 2015 the University of Virginia Press published his translation of Evelyne Trouillot's novel, *La Mémoire aux abois* (*Memory at Bay*). His translations of works from France, Haiti, Belgium, Quebec and Reunion have appeared in *Words Without Borders, Subtropics, Asymptote Blog, Indiana Review, Cimarron Review, carte blanche, K1N, nowhere, frankmatter,* and the 2016 and 2017 editions of *Best European Fiction.*

Karen Emmerich is an Assistant Professor of Comparative Literature at Princeton University, and a translator of modern Greek poetry and prose. Recent books include Sophia Nikolaidou's *The Scapegoat,* Amanda Michalopoulou's *Why I Killed My Best Friend,* and Yannis Ritson's *Diaries of Exile,* co-translated with Edmund Keeley and recipient of the PEN Poetry in Translation Award.

Paul Filev is a Melbourne-based literary translator and editor. He translates from Macedonian and Spanish. His translations from Macedonian include Vera Bužarovska's *The Last Summer in the Old Bazaar* (Saguaro Books, 2015) and Sasho Dimoski's *Alma Mahler* (Dalkey Archive Press, forthcoming). He recently completed the translation of a novel from Spanish, *Blue Label*, by Eduardo Sánchez Rugeles.

Andrea Gregovich's translations have appeared in a number of literary journals and anthologies, including *Best European Fiction 2014* and *2015*. She has published translations of two novels: *USSR* by Vladimir Kozlov and *Wake In Winter by* Nadezhda Belenkaya. She also writes about professional wrestling and other whimsical topics.

Matthew Hyde is a literary translator from Russian and Estonian to English. He has had translations published by Pushkin Press, Vagabond Voices, *Words Without Borders*, and *Asymptote*. This is his fourth contribution to the *Best European Fiction* series. Prior to becoming a translator, Matthew worked for ten years in the British Foreign Office as an analyst, policy office, and diplomat, serving at the British Embassies in Moscow as well as in Tallinn, where he was Deputy Head of Mission. After that last posting, Matthew chose to remain with his partner and baby son in Tallinn, where he translates and plays the double bass.

Paul Larkin worked for five years in the Danish Merchant Navy before taking a degree in Scandinavian and Celtic Studies. Larkin then went on to train as a film director with the BBC. He had a long career in journalism and in film- and documentary-making before going back to work with Scandinavian languages and fiction in general as a translator, literary critic, and author.

Elona Pira is an Albanian native who lives and works in New York. She translates between Albanian and English. She holds an M.A. in Humanities and Social Thought from New York University.

Born in Pittsburgh, writer and translator **Frederika Randall** has lived in Italy for thirty years. She has translated fiction by Helena Janeczek, Giacomo Sartori, Igiaba Scego, and Ottavio Cappellani, as well as Luigi Meneghello's *Deliver Us*, Guido Morselli's *The Communist*, Ippolito Nievo's *Confessions of an Italian*, and three books by historian Sergio Luzzatto.

Angela Rodel is a literary translator from Bulgarian. Her translations have appeared in *McSweeney's*, *Two Lines*, *Ploughshares*, and *Words Without Borders*, among other places. She has received NEA and PEN translation grants; seven novels in her translation have been published in the U.S. and U.K. Her translation of Georgi Gospodinov's *Physics of Sorrow* won the 2016 AATSEEL Prize for Literary Translation, and was shortlisted for the 2016 PEN Translation Prize and ALTA's 2016 National Translation Award.

Ursula Meany Scott is a literary translator based in Ireland. She translates fiction, literary criticism, and academic texts from French and Spanish to English. She holds a Master's in literary translation from Trinity College Dublin.

Born in the U.K., **Lytton Smith** lives in western upstate New York, where he teaches at SUNY Geneseo. He has translated eight novels and many poems from Icelandic and is the author of two collections of poetry published by Nightboat Books.

Jan Steyn is a scholar, translator, and critic of contemporary works in Afrikaans, Dutch, English, and French.

George Szirtes is a poet and translator. Born in Hungary in 1948, he has been awarded various prizes, including the Faber Memorial Prize and the T.S. Eliot Prize for his poetry, and the Best Translated Book Award and the Man Booker International translator's award for his translations. His latest book is *Mapping the Delta* (Bloodaxe, 2016).

Sarah Wade is a British translator living in Brussels. She graduated from Oxford University with a degree in French and German language and literature. After studying Finnish at the University of Helsinki for two years, she worked as a translator for the European Institutions before deciding to pursue a career in literary translation.

Jayde Will is a literary translator. His translations of Estonian, Latvian, and Lithuanian authors have been published in numerous periodicals and anthologies, including the *Dedalus Book of Lithuanian Literature* and several *Best European Fiction* anthologies. Forthcoming translations include Lithuanian writer Ričardas Gavelis's novel *Memoirs of a Life Cut Short* (Vagabond Voices) and a collection of short stories by Latvian author Daina Tabūna entitled *The First Time* (The Emma Press). He lives in Riga.

Andrew Wilson is a graduate of the Master of Philosophy Program in Literary Translation at Trinity College Dublin, where he is currently affiliated as a creative practitioner. He is the translator of Sébastien Brebel's novel *Villa Bunker*, published by Dalkey Archive Press in 2013.

Anna Zaranko translates from Polish and Russian and was an ALTA mentee from 2015–2016. She has translated several of Julia Fiedorczuk's stories and is currently at work on Fiedorczuk's novel, *Weightless*.

ACKNOWLEDGMENTS

PUBLICATION OF *BEST EUROPEAN FICTION 2018* was made possible by generous support from the following cultural agencies and embassies:

DGLB—The General Directorate for Books and Libraries / Portugal

Estonian Literature Centre

Extepare Basque Institute

Fédération Wallonie-Bruxelles

Illinois Arts Council

Kulturstyrelsen—Danish Agency for Culture

Luxembourg Ministry of Culture

Polish Cultural Institute

Pro Helvetia, Swiss Arts Council

Slovenian Book Agency

Welsh Books Council

RIGHTS AND PERMISSIONS